THE LAST WARRIOR

The Ninth Century Book II

M J Porter

Copyright © 2020 M J Porter

Copyright notice
Porter, M J The Last Warrior
Copyright ©2020, Porter, M J
All characters and events in this publication, other than those clearly in the public domain, are fictitious and any resemblance to actual persons, living or dead, is purely coincidental.
ALL RIGHTS RESERVED. No part of this publication may be reproduced, stored in a retrieval system or transmitted in any form or by any means without the prior written permission of the author, nor be otherwise circulated in any form of binding or cover other than that in which it is published and without a similar condition being imposed on the subsequent buyer.

Cover design and map by Flintlock Covers

ISBN 9781914332296 (ebook)
ISBN 9798649269735 (paperback)
ISBN 9781914332265 (hardback)

Also available in a Clean(er) version

CONTENTS

Title Page
Copyright
Map of England   1
Prologue   3
Chapter 1   9
Chapter 2   20
Chapter 3   41
Chapter 4   51
Chapter 5   62
Chapter 6   74
Chapter 7   94
Chapter 8   108
Chapter 9   123
Chapter 10   134
Chapter 11   156
Chapter 12   175
Chapter 13   189
Chapter 14   201
Chapter 15   217
Chapter 16   231
Chapter 17   257

Chapter 18	263
Chapter 19	276
Cast of Characters	280
Historical Notes	284
Meet the Author	287
Acknowledgement	291

MAP OF ENGLAND

M J PORTER

PROLOGUE

The River Trent, close to Torksey

"Will you shut the fuck up?"

Even the roar of warriors squaring off to face him can't drown out Edmund in full flow. He's astride a horse that tosses and dips its head, unhappy being in the water while war is waged all around.

Between one blink and the next, the grey light of dawn has lessened the gloom, and I can see so much fucking more than before. That includes both Edmund and the man who thinks to take my life by travelling beneath the level of the murky water and then erupting in front of me, weapon raised, ready to strike. Only Edmund's unexpected arrival and the breaking of daylight have undone my foe's plan.

Edmund continues to howl, his voice rising above the fiercest of bloody battles, the roar of iron on wood, the screams of those who fight for the right to breathe another day.

"A man of the Hwicce,
He gulped mead at midnight feasts.
Slew Raiders, night and day.
Brave Athelstan, long will his valour endure."

"I've heard that one before," I snarl at Edmund. My double-eagle headed blade is in my hand. Blood shimmers along its edge in the glowing light as though the silver sheen has been festooned in ruby dew throughout the long night.

I'm quickly assessing how best to take the life of my freshest opponent. Water pools down the man's white face, his teeth flashing against the growl of his lips. His eyes try to pierce me with the power behind his gaze. It's as though the sun pours through him only to condense into one single beam of light.

"Beornberht, son of the Magonsæte.
A proud man, a wise man, a strong man.
He fought and pierced with spears.
Above the blood, he slew with swords."

"And that one," I bellow, still reeling from this stunning turn of events. My seax is raised to ward off the reasoned blows from the man who thought to kill me by stealth. I can see how much he desires my death in the careful placement of his reaching blade. It only makes it more imperative that I'm the one to deal death.

I thought Edmund dead, but evidently, he isn't. Where the fuck has he been?

"A man fought for Mercia.
Against Raiders and foes.
Shield flashing red,
Brave Oslac, slew Raiders each seven-day."

"Will you shut the fuck up?" I'm all but screaming. Edmund is never one to be silent when words of battle are in his mind. But those words distract me, as does his sudden arrival.

I war against one of Halfdan's warrior, while Jarl Halfdan attempts to make his escape. I can glimpse Halfdan's ship over the shoulder of my enemy. I can see it begin to track upriver, my enemy on board. I can't allow Jarl Halfdan to escape. This man is an inconvenience, but a bloody good warrior all the same.

Edmund is not helping me, even if he thinks to excite me and my warriors to greater endeavours.

"Sturdy and strong, it would be wrong not to praise them.
Amid blood-red blades, in black sockets.
The war-hounds fought fiercely, tight formation.
Of the war band of Coelwulf, I would think it a burden,

To leave any in the shape of man alive."

The words elicit thunderous acclaim from the men who fight beside me, their positions revealed more through sound than sight. Edmund knows how to stir the blood of even the most exhausted man. And we are drained. This battle has waged all night.

I growl once more, using my seax to finally make a killing stroke against my opponent. I watch with satisfaction as the man slips back below the surface he tried to use against me, only to pivot into another opponent.

This warrior, beard filled with blood and spittle, dripping translucent water from the river, leers at me as well. I want to dismiss his well-aimed strikes with contempt, as they ricochet against my fast-moving blade, but I know it'll be my downfall. The wealth of scars on his exposed cheeks and lower arms, rippling with life as the water continues to slither from his body, testify to his skill. The fact he still stands, after all the battles I've fought since Repton, shows he's either a lucky fucker or a warrior of immense skill.

But, again, I focus on Edmund's roared words. This part is new to me. He must have composed it in the last few days, while we've been apart, and I thought him dead.

Damn the fucker.

What do the words mean? Every other verse he's ever composed has been for a bloody good reason. Why would this one be any different? He names none of my men, he mentions no one who has died. It's a strange departure for him. My mind considers its meaning, even while I fight.

I wish I could just ask him, but I can't. Not here, and not now. My breath heaves through my body, great gulps filling my chest, as my enemy tries to trick me with a weapon in each hand. I'm unsure where his real strength lies, is it his war axe, or his sword? Is it in both? I've faced such men before. They're fuckers to kill.

And of course, Edmund hasn't finished his performance.

"Bitter in battle, with blades set for war.

Attacking in an army, cruel in battle.
They slew with swords, without much sound.
Icel, pillar of battle, took pleasure in giving death."

These fresh words freeze me. My enemy lands a blow with his sword on my lower right arm, my grip instinctively failing on my seax. Although the blade is useless against my war gear, the weight and shock are immense.

I don't know these words. I've never heard them before. But more horrifying, they speak of Icel's death. Edmund has never given words in his scop's song unless a man was dead. I want to turn, face him, demand answers to his verse.

"What?" I howl, trying to catch my seax before it plummets into the icy depths, while at the same time avoiding the reach of my enemy. My opponent tries to dance forward, take a slice at my arm again, but the water is too deep. Instead, he flounders, his balance deserting him, giving me the time I need.

With my weapon under control and raised menacingly to my right, my teeth bared in a growl of fury, I hack the flailing man's left arm. The sudden well of blood stirs my warrior's heart. Another fucker, just waiting for me to find the right way to kill him.

The man snarls, momentarily shocked into rearing back from my reach. I finally pivot, and see Edmund in all his battle glory. He's dressed for war in his leather byrnie, with his shield, and his helm, although it seems somehow different to me. But I don't have the time to determine what it is.

My eyes flash downwards. The horse, the horse I recognise too well. Icel's mount.

"What the fuck?"

Edmund's bellowing voice, his staccato of words, lends a rhythm to every warrior's movements that I admire. Yet I wish he'd meet my gaze. He's said nothing since snarling my name in surprise and then beginning his recitation, as though he's the lord here and not me, overseeing everything from the back of that horse.

"Icel?" I call, disbelief colouring my voice and making it too small. "Icel is gone?" I force the words through my tight lips.

I need an answer. I need to know what's happened while my men have been divided.

I can't imagine fighting without Icel. I peer into the distance, beyond the straggling warriors engaged in battle in the shallow depths, wishing for more light to see by, desperate to catch sight of Icel's too familiar stance.

My seax is busy, even though I don't face my resurgent foe. When I don't see Icel where he should be, I focus only on Edmund. Fucking Edmund and his bastard words.

"Icel?" I plead once more, for while Edmund has finally become taciturn, his actions are far from still. He moves to batter aside the enemy who attempts to slice his mount's legs. The man is small and wiry and somehow manages to withstand the rushing water to remain upright.

"Icel?" I screech, hoping against hope that Edmund will answer me before I have to threaten him for a response.

His silence tells me too much, and also far too little.

The fact that none of my other, abruptly returned men, answers, makes my blood run with more than just the icy cold of the damn river.

"Fucker," I scream. Only then, with the Raider dismissed from my thoughts with a cut to his water-wrinkled neck, turning his chest pink, the water as well, can I take the place of the opponent that Edmund's just slain.

Edmund's low strike, from the back of Samson, found the artery high on the leg. Now blood rushes from the body, pooling faster than the river current, surrounding him in the fading warmth of his life. The man finally stumbles, his eyes already rolling in his head. He knows he's dead. His body just hasn't caught up yet.

Edmund pants, his chest rising and falling, his green eye busy around the scene, checking the state of the attack, until it finally settles on me. The contempt I see chills me, as does the realisation of his wound. I've been snarling for news of Icel, to know why he's now a part of Edmund's song, but I should have been asking more immediate questions.

"Your eye?" I probe, my gaze rushing over the other figures that fight from their mounts, desperate to know if others are missing. It's impossible to tell as broad backs greet my eyes. Neither can I see enough to recognise all of the horses encouraged into the fast-flowing water.

And it seems, I shouldn't make that assumption anyway.

Edmund's finally quiet lips twist in anger, his bloodied sword poised high, seemingly ready to attack me. His silence continues, as does his defiant stare.

"Icel?" I breathe the word, and the flicker of agony in Edmund's green eye tells me all I need to know.

"You fucking bastard," I rage, three quick steps bringing me within killing distance of him, my seax ready for the strike, even though the water tries to push me away from him.

Edmund doesn't even flinch, the over-confident fuck.

"I gave you one fucking job. To keep my men safe."

His lips warp once more, a slight tick of unease on his unshaven chin. Then he grins, the movement so quick I almost miss it.

With his own rumble of fury, Edmund encourages Icel's horse on in the frigid water. His iridescent sword is outstretched, his intent clear to see, his gaze never baulking, Samson unable to ignore the command to rush toward me.

I always knew he'd be the one to turn fucking traitor.

CHAPTER 1

One week earlier
Repton

"Here," I don't expect to hear the voice, and neither do I expect to have to duck when I'm barely beyond the barricade that surrounds the interior of Repton.

"What the fuck?" but the complaint dies on my lips as two pieces of leather hit my naked feet. His warning could have been a little more precise.

"For fuck's sake," and I'm hopping. My feet are white, beneath the blood and muck, but goddamn, my big toe hurts on my left foot and my smaller toes on my right.

"Sorry," Icel's voice is filled with both contrition and humour, and I swear I'd kill the daft fuck if it weren't for the fact that I really, really appreciate having my boots back.

I spring into them, trying not to think of my grimy feet and where they've been while Icel guards my front, and Edmund my back.

"How the fuck did you get all the way up here?" I ask Icel, but now that my feet are covered, and I can step without fearing the crap on the floor and the sharpened edge of unseen blades, I feel far less vulnerable. He's gone, almost as though he was never there at all.

"Daft bastard," Edmund mutters sourly, his hands flashing wetly, his sword in one, and a stolen shield in the other.

"Really? Do you want to fight with that?"

Edmund has the good grace to turn the shield and gaze at the sigil there. I don't expect his smirk and gleaming green eyes when he sees Jarl Halfdan's wolf on the shield.

"I don't give a shit what it has on it. I just don't want to die. Not now."

I shrug my shoulders, noting they still twinge from having my arms tied behind my back for so long. Edmund has a fair point.

"Well, get me one as well," I complain, turning to focus on the view before me.

Icel, with his vast height, is already scything his way through the campsite that once belonged to the jarls that claimed Repton. Men, and some women, rush from the slowly folding canvasses, more often than not as naked as my feet were only moments ago. Icel takes great pleasure in taking the lives of all of them when they cross his path.

"Here you go, you ungrateful bastard." Edmund thrusts a shield at me, and I only just get a hand on its edge before he drops it and steps away from me, licking his lips. I can see where he looks, and I imagine I know what he's thinking.

We've already killed a massive amount of men this day, but in all honesty, the work has only just begun. But, for this next part, we'll not be alone. That's important to remember. All of our allies, apart from Icel, might be at the furthest part of what will become a field of slaughter before the day is much older, but they are there. We are not alone.

"Watch my fucking feet," I grumble, but he's already racing to follow Icel. It seems I'm the only one concerned with my feet.

"Damn fuckers," I mutter to myself, working the shield in my hands so that I don't see the owl sigil emblazoned on the front. Typical of Edmund to go for the wolf and leave me with the owl. But they're both opportunistic hunters. I think he might have forgotten that.

The rest of my men, led by Pybba, puffed up on his one-handed kills so far, are quick to follow Icel and Edmund, but I stand back.

I'm not scared, far from it, but it feels good to know I have the time to consider what I should do next and to appreciate the skill of my fellow warriors.

I love all of the damn bloody gits. All of them. Not that I'm ever going to tell them that. And as the new day began, I did hate every damn last one of the fuckers with their ridiculous idea.

How I allowed myself to submit to Pybba and Rudolf's mad scheme, I'll never know. The fact that it's worked so well, so far, is neither here nor there.

With a sigh and a ripple of my shoulders, twisting my neck from side to side, I heft the weight of my seax. I secure the grip on the owl-painted shield and determine to follow the rest of my warriors into the bloody spray that's starting to water the parched ground.

"Fuck," I realise I have no helm. I really need one. Turning in a slow circle, mindful that I'm exposed without such protection, I spy one of the lifeless gate wardens. His helm is part off his head, his long hair falling down his shoulders, his mouth twisted in a grimace of pain. But, at least he's not breathing anymore.

I bend, and go to tug his useless helm from him, grimacing as part of his severed neck is abruptly exposed to me, the greys, whites and reds flashing in the bright sunlight. I turn aside and spit, warding off the spirit of the man who once inhabited the helm, and then I ram it on my head. It fits, in a fashion, and at least I can see clearly before me, the nose guard is a thin thing where it begins, more level with my eyes than my nose.

It's not my usual helm, but Icel brought me shoes, not a helm. What the fuck does that say about his priorities? And my own!

The ground beneath my feet is scorched and solid. The summer has been long and slow. I feared to fall from my horse and land on the hardened surface, but now it aids me.

With a start, I'm sprinting to follow my warriors, aware that the noise of the battlefield is just beginning to ramp up. I confess, a grin touches my cheeks when my eyes take in the view before me.

Our work is far from done. We might be outnumbered, heavily, but we still have the element of surprise. That can never be over-estimated. But neither will we have it for long.

In front of me, a path has been cleared through to the main body of the camp. Marble flesh flashes before me, from those who've already fallen, as I determine on my first target.

Icel and Edmund, with Wærwulf still dressed as though he's Jarl Sigurd, have already made any number of kills. But that doesn't assure our triumph. Not yet.

Somewhere out there a warrior of great renown could be about to surface, someone with the ability to lead these Raiders to safety and ensure they live to fight another day. Someone who will make his reputation this day, defeating Coelwulf and his warriors. I won't allow my men to be the broken and bleeding in another man's scop-tale.

'Watch out," Edmund's cry has me raising my seax and shield even before I hear the thunder of running hooves.

"Bastard thing," I flick the flat of my blade over the stray animal's hide, as it rushes passed me, encouraging the grey-flecked mare onwards and away from the battle.

"Keep your damn eyes open," once more, Edmund snarls at me, but I accept his complaint. I should be paying more attention than worrying about songs and poems that I'll never hear anyway.

My seax slices through the taut fabric of the tent in front of me. I step through the slit, my eyes seeking out any who might shelter within. The snores of a sleeping man fill my senses, and I confess, my mouth drops open in shock to realise that the man sleeps while outside all is chaos. Only then the stench hits me, the acrid smell of bad breath and too much mead.

Stupid fucker.

With my shield in front of me, unprepared to take any risks, I step to the man's side, and wince as the aroma of sweat and alcohol becomes ever greater. Even the gaping hole in the tent can't drive away the claustrophobic smell.

I stab down, aware I don't want to be left behind as my group of men work their way through the camp. I've never killed a sleeping man before. Still, blood flashes redly on his chest all the same, his breathing coming to a gurgling stop although his eyes never open.

Daft bastard. Died in his sleep, too fucking drunk to defend himself. He'll never have a scop sing about his great deeds.

I step back through the slit in the wall, unprepared to tangle with the toggles that keep the door of the canvas tightly closed. No man in battle-gloves can manipulate such things.

I squint, the bright sunlight causing objects to shimmer under the haze.

Edmund has moved forward, but Icel still lingers behind me, whereas Pybba and Rudolf are working as one unit to the left of me. Rudolf seems to take on the warrior, who thinks he's getting an easy kill because of Rudolf's slight build. In contrast, Pybba steps in to take them with a killing stroke from behind, and with his left hand. I smirk. Not a bad technique.

A woman runs screaming toward me, a fur draped over her naked body, a slash down her face dripping red down her breast, leaving a trail on the floor. I sigh as I meet Edmund's appraising eye.

It's no effort to intercept her, slice my seax through her side. As she crumbles to the floor, I'm not even sure she knew I was there through her terror-filled eyes.

I spit once more. Two such easy strikes against defenceless people are not my idea of true kills. I want a warrior worthy of my time and energy, not a sleeping prick and a naked woman.

"A pity," Edmund hollers, as I near him. "She had a lovely backside."

"She was a Raider whore," I complain.

"You could have just said she was a Raider. There was no need for the whore part," Edmund chastises, a grin on his face, white teeth showing above a bleeding lip. "Anyway, she had a mean head butt."

"For fuck's sake," I complain, rolling my eyes. Edmund's high chuckle does nothing to assure me that the daft sod is taking this at all seriously. It seems the battle rage has entirely claimed him. I just dare him to overstep his abilities and get wounded, or even killed, in the process.

The sound of footsteps beside me, and I'm staring up, and then even further up. The warrior who comes to face me is taller even than Icel.

"Fuck me," I huff. It seems I'm about to get my wish, as the blond-haired giant, with his fierce blue eyes, swings his massive war axe in his hand.

The length of the haft is almost my size, and I feel the whistle of admiration leave my lips before I can stop myself.

"You've got yourself a fair fight now," Edmund calls from where he stabs down to ensure his opponents are truly dead. My foe is already aiming at me, his intent clear as he sucks his boulder-sized teeth.

"Well, you're a big fucker," I offer, but it seems the man doesn't hear me or perhaps chooses not to as I thrust my shield in front of me. I don't think it'll do much to protect me, but I'm prepared to try all the same.

"Urgh," the force, when it hits me, is more than colossal, and the owl shield fractures, leaving me with nothing but the handle and a few stray pieces of wood inside its outer iron rim.

"Bastard," I complain, releasing my grip on it, and thrusting it to the floor. I have no time to see if anyone notices my peril.

"Fuck this," I state, dashing forward to attempt a slash on his upper thigh. It's not my preferred place to strike, but it's the natural place for my reach and height.

My seax thrums in my hand, reverberating its way up my arm, as the man's leather rebuffs the attack and I step back, my lips twisted as I consider what to do next.

"You need a hand with that troll?" Icel's rich boom assures me that I'm not alone.

"Maybe," I confess, my opponent only now realising that I've even struck him, no doubt because I caused him so little pain.

"Fucker's made of iron," I complain, stepping as far from the tall man as possible, rubbing my shoulder at the same time, and cracking my neck from side to side once more. This is just what I didn't need. I wanted an enemy to kill, not a bloody fortress all on its own.

"Big bastard, aren't you?" Icel darts forward, or as much as he can, and manages to land a blow on the giant's arm, just above his right hand. All the action seems to accomplish is to make the man grip his war axe ever tighter.

"Shit," Icel's complaint reaches my ears. I become aware that Icel isn't the only one to have spotted the massive warrior, encased almost entirely in battle gear somehow tinted with a bluish tinge. He truly is like something from the legends, but my eyes are on Rudolf. He better fucking not.

I open my mouth to shout a warning, but it's too late, and I watch, unable to glance away, as Rudolf braces himself and seems to run vertically up the giant's back.

"No," I shout, and I'm not alone, Pybba's echo joining mine. But Rudolf has laced his legs around the giant's neck, covering our foe's helm entirely with his body. The giant roars, only it's a muffled sound from beyond Rudolf's belly.

"Fuck this," Edmund hollers, and he dances inside the giant's reach, his sword busy trying to hack against the well-made byrnie, that encases the top of the blond opponent's legs.

"Bloody hell," I complain. I rush to follow, wondering if anyone else on the battlefield is facing any other opponent, or if all my warriors' efforts are being squandered on just one man.

My seax once more makes no impact, and, blinded, the giant has become a hazard himself. He steps forward and backwards, albeit slowly, as though his feet can dislodge Rudolf. I skip back, crash into Edmund, and catch a flicker of movement behind me as I try and stay upright, grabbing hold of Edmund in the process.

Pybba.

"Fuck no," I roar, but once more, my men are better at listening to, than actually following my orders.

Pybba, his eyes on the giant's feet, rushes close, his seax

glistening crimson with the life force of those he's already killed. I thought him mad earlier, when he faced the shield wall inside the complex, now it's as though rage pours from him. This is the man he always used to be, albeit, one-handed now.

"Work together," I scream at Edmund, hoping that four of us will be enough to fell our opponent. Why, I consider, was this enemy not inside the complex? Why didn't the jarls rate him enough to keep him close? Perhaps he was just too dangerous.

As one, Edmund and I turn to hack against the metalled coat with the handles of our blades. Slicing won't work, not on this equipment.

"It seems the dwarf craftsmen aren't a fucking story after all," Edmund huffs, his right arm rising and falling, opposite to my own. I wish we could slice the mail coat open, but that's just not going to work.

I can't see how Rudolf fares. I'm too close to the giant, and glancing up affords me nothing but the view of a bulging belly covered in leather and iron.

"Icel," I roar, hoping that he's still there if only to fight off any who might think to take advantage of our compromised situation.

"My Lord," Icel rumbles, closer than I would have expected. But I don't turn to look. He would have warned me if something were amiss. Surely?

"Will this stuff not break?" I huff, aware that sweat beads my face and drips down my chin. "What the fuck is Pybba doing?" I ask, not expecting an answer, surprised when I get one as I once more rush backwards to avoid the stumbling steps of the man we all fight. The sound of the giant's roaring complaints has faded into the background, but Rudolf still hinders him.

"The same as you," Pybba exclaims, "only from the rear."

"This isn't fucking working," I complain, and when Pybba and Edmund don't offer a denial, I know I'm right.

But Rudolf's cries from above assure me that he's doing all he can to prevent the giant from fighting us. I try not to listen to his words. They would make a nun blush, that's for sure.

Only then I hear the sound of a heavy object rushing through the air above my head, and I both duck and jump backwards, keen to avoid the floundering leg once more.

"Fuck," I complain through gritted teeth, dropping once more, as first a loud thud echoes above my head, only to be followed by another beside me.

"Move," Icel's bellow holds so much force that I'm obeying before my mind realises, only to turn and trip over a collection of legs and arms.

"Ow," Rudolf's squeal of pain has me dropping my seax before I can impale him with it, and moving to offer him my hand. All the time, I can feel that something is happening behind us.

"Hurry," I exhale, only then Rudolf is on his feet, and we're both running away, back to where Icel stands, a grinning Hereman at his side.

"Shitting bollocks," I exhale, breathing heavily, turning and finally focusing on the giant.

"Shitting bollocks!" I whistle this time, not quite believing my eyes.

"Where did you find that?" I demand to know.

"How did you lift that?" I ask awe in my voice, not giving Hereman the chance to reply.

Before us, Pybba has stepped away from the giant as well. The man is severely wounded, rage on his face, as he staggers, from one side to another, even more lethal than when we tried to work together to bring him down.

I'm pleased that no one else is close enough to be trampled, because beneath his feet first one canvas is destroyed, the crash of a heavy metal object assuring me that the previous occupier has lost his battle gear, and then another. The material tangles around those feet, adding to the confusion.

A roar of fury and a whimper of pain come from the gaping mouth where I can see blood gleaming on his lips.

But, protruding from his chest is a massive piece of metalwork. I don't even know what it could have been used for. Somehow, Hereman has managed to not only lift the shimmering object, he's also managed to aim, and fling it at the giant, just close to where his heart should beat.

"You could have missed?" I exclaim. Hereman grins widely, still not having answered any of my breathless questions.

"He never misses," Edmund exclaims hotly, the disbelief in his voice almost obscuring the fury.

"You could have hit any of us?"

"But I didn't," Hereman finally speaks. I can already tell that this matter, regardless of the positive outcome, is going to cause another of those arguments between the brothers that I'd sooner not take part in.

"But where did you get it from?" Rudolf pipes up, and I'm pleased. He might distract the two. For now.

"Over there." Hereman angles his head towards where the enclosure was protected by a gateway until we destroyed it. "Fuck knows what it's for, but it's going to do the trick."

A tremor runs through the ground as the giant falls to one knee, his gaze drawn to where a ripple of crimson has started to stain the blackened iron that pierces him.

Yet, the warrior grips his war axe, and even from where we stand, he tries, one final time to take us with him.

"Fuck this," I complain. Now that the man is closer to my height, I can take him. I'm sure of it.

"Leave him," Icel rumbles, but, no matter what else might be said about me, I'm not a man to revel in cruelty. Death, yes, but not prolonging it.

With the giant's war axe falling from his fingers, I rush forward, timing my steps so that I can swing my arm at the right moment for it to slide into the monstrous mouth. I can't take his neck, it's still covered by his battle gear, but as he silently agonises, his mouth wide open, I can end his suffering. And so, I do.

His blood blazes on my face, as with tight lips, I wrench back my seax. It comes loose slowly, and I fear it might never be released from the dead man. But then, just as he's about to fall forward, perhaps crushing me under his great weight, it finally relinquishes its hold, and I dance clear. My breath is ragged as dust blows into my eyes, while the man it's taken five of us to kill finally falls still and silent, face first.

"Bloody bollocks," Rudolf's voice is high with relief, and excitement both, and I want nothing more than to berate him for his reckless actions, but he's one of my men now. I must stop thinking of him as a child who doesn't know what he's doing.

"Thank you, Hereman," I exclaim, reaching out to grip his forearm. None of us misses Edmund stalking away, his anger evident in the line of his tight shoulders.

"Daft fucker," Icel shrugs before he too sights a target and moves away.

CHAPTER 2

For all that we've been focusing on this one enemy, around us events seem to move quickly. The line of men who fought with me inside the enclosure is at least three canvas rows away now. In the far distance, I can see where the rest of my allies are slowly beginning to make progress toward us.

The field is vast, the number of enemy tents almost impossible to count. Still, the line of my allies makes itself known in the continual tumbling of the temporary structures, as though the giant man we just felled yet lived and walked the camp as my ally, not my adversary.

But my eyes alight on something else, to the left of me.

"Fuck it," and I point. Hereman, a faint smirk on his face as he watches his brother's back, turns to follows my finger. So too does Pybba and Rudolf.

"Fuckers," Hereman growls, already striding left, making it clear he's going toward the river, rather than joining the remainder of our force.

"We can't do it on our own," I complain, wishing Edmund and Icel had stayed rather than rushing off to claim more kills.

"We can try," Hereman decides, already loping off to where some of the Raiders have realised that their leaders are abandoning them to the enemy.

"Right," I sigh, aware that Hereman certainly can't stop the flood of those trying to escape alone. "Let's cause them as many problems as we can."

Rudolf grins, his face bruised and bloodied, but clearly not felt, whereas Pybba's lips twist, before settling on a grimace. I'm not sure whether it's of pleasure or pain.

But then I realise that not all of my men are struggling amongst the forest of rapidly falling tents.

"Sæbald, can you fight?" I demand of him, and he nods, although through clenched teeth, the strain in his jaw evident because his face is clean-shaven.

"Always."

Goda is with him, and he nods his canted head as well. Pain shimmers in his eyes, but also a desire for revenge for the wounds he carries. I realise then that I can't protect them, not in this. If they think they can fight, then I have to let them.

"Good. We need to stop as many of them as possible from sailing off back to bloody Torksey."

"Agreed." Our small group of warriors, numbering only six, races, not toward the rest of the force, but rather, to the north, where we can all see the sails of the retreating ships along the River Trent. I confess I'd not realised that they'd be so visible, but the River Trent doesn't just go north from Repton. First, it goes east. Or so it appears from the sight of those brightly woven sails.

"Where are the Welsh Gwentmen?" I demand of no one, running, my feet, although covered by the new shoes, slick inside them. I know I'll never be able to wear these boots again without thinking of what I've dragged into them.

It seems, as we sprint, that more and more of the Raiders are realising that there's a chance to escape, if only they can make it to one of the ships suddenly visible on the river.

There are at least ten ships, whether *knarrs* or *langskips*, I don't yet know. The sails have been raised, but there's little enough wind. I imagine that the jarls will be pleased to allow more of their followers on board. It'll add to the number of rowers and speed the sluggish retreat.

The ships are making such slow progress, it's almost as

though they don't move. I appreciate that it's the effect of distance, but all the same, it gives me hope that we'll get there before the ships sail clear of Repton, and we have no means of capturing them.

I crave for the Raiders to be gone from Mercia, completely gone. I don't want them to be able to retreat to their winter camp at Torksey. If they settle there, we'll only have to do this all over again. Of course, they know who I am now. My ridiculous ploy will not work twice.

I wish we had horses. The weight of my battle gear saps at my strength, as the strength of the sun slickens my face. I'd gladly discard my byrnie, but that way lies madness and the promise of death.

"Bloody bollocks," Pybba exclaims when he's forced to pause his headlong dash and bend double, breathing heavily. I wish I could do the same. But more, I'm envious of Rudolf's stamina and light steps, as he seems to bounce along in front of me.

"Damn boy," Hereman huffs, and I grin, my face tight. I don't have the breath to agree.

A sudden gust of wind and I focus on the ships. Three of them seem to be pulling away from the others. They have sails of varying colours, but I can see the rippling wolf sigil on them, depicted in a shimmering thread. I know that Jarl Halfdan, the man who commanded the most warriors, is sure to make an escape.

"Where are the fucking Welsh Gwentmen?" I ask of no one once more. I wanted them to stop the Raiders from escaping, and I was sure they'd done a good job. Now I'm not so sure.

"'Ware," Pybba's warning forces me to a stop, although I can see, almost within fighting distance, where a mass of about twenty or so men and women are taking their chances to run from the riverside and try and land in the prow of one of the moving ships.

A few Raiders on each of the three ships are standing, braced and ready to pull them on board if they make it, but also seemingly prepared to abandon them if they fail.

I watch as a woman makes it to safety, pulled on board by a man with appreciation in his eyes, whereas as an older man flounders mid-air. The warrior on his ship of choice makes no effort to aid him, rather standing and watching.

The eyes of the men on the ships are wary as they rake the riverbank for any sign of Mercians. Although they wear leather byrnies, weapons belts glimmering with seaxs and war axes, they're uneasy, and I smile, just once. We did this. We made grown men fearful for their lives.

But there are more of the Raiders coming up behind us, as I turn to determine why Pybba warns me.

"Bastards," I huff. "To me," I holler next, turning to focus on the Raiders rushing toward us, and realising that I've been a damn fool. I only have five men. I need many more than that. Have I truly survived the audacious attack on Repton, only to fall here?

There's a small rise in front of me, a humped back of green rising from the slowly tapering land. It's not much, but it'll have to be enough.

"To me," I bellow once more, aware, although I don't look, that Rudolf is not yet at beside me. Damn the boy.

I risk a glance behind me and see that Rudolf is finally making his way to my side. Only the Raiders will reach us first. And perhaps worse, they might even reach Rudolf first.

Those who stream toward us do so with determination on their faces, eyes seemingly focused only on the leaving ships. Some are dressed, some even carry wooden chests in their hands, no doubt filled with their treasures, but others are all but naked. Exposed flesh flashes under the bright sunlight.

Some of them are armed, and others are not.

I know I said we wouldn't take prisoners, and not that we could, not here, and so heavily outnumbered. But can I allow defenceless men and women to be murdered? Wouldn't that make me no better than them?

But then I have no more time for thought. Rudolf lands with a thud beside me, and I turn and grimace at him. His wide eyes show his fright, and I know better than to berate someone who already realises he's been a stupid bastard.

I stand, stance wide, seax raised before me, just waiting for the first of the Raiders to attempt to attack us. And there my hand waivers, as does that of Pybba, Rudolf, Icel and Hereman.

"What the fuck?" I breathe, far from understanding what I'm seeing.

"It seems, My Lord, that killing you is less important to them than surviving." Hereman's words thrum with respect and derision combined.

"Cowards," Pybba all but shrieks, but I reach across Hereman and touch his arm, a caution there. This might save us from being wedged between Raiders in front and behind us.

"Stay alert," I warn, sure that at some point, at least one of those trying to flee will think better of it, and attack us.

Sæbald stands at our rear, Hereman turning to assist him, as I watch.

Are these people gutless or have they simply realised that living is more important than risking that to be forever associated with my death.

Rudolf growls whenever anyone looks our way, his seax high and menacing, if in completely the wrong position to make a kill. I grin. I admire his tenacity.

"They're all getting away," Hereman comments, his voice a growl, but not of complaint.

I can't go after them. I don't have enough men, and the rest of my warriors are far distant, where the heart of the fighting is taking place.

I can just pick out the rest of my allies on the far distant battlefield as they seem to make easy work of felling the enemy. Of those who don't fall, they merely turn and begin to race toward the river and the promise of survival.

I didn't foresee this problem. I thought that to have the Gwent Welshmen on the other side of the Trent, attacking from the west instead of the east, would be enough. I didn't realise that the river would curve around, as it does. I should have.

Yet, what could I have done? I have no ships to call my own, and I imagine, although I don't know, that the Raiders, while making a forward base in Repton, have maintained their position in Torksey as well. No doubt the now dead Ealdorman Wulfstan allowed them to stay on the land, without the threat of attack, as part of the peace accord made with King Burgred last year.

I really should have paid more attention to the politics of the court. But then, if I'd spent all my time bending the knee to King Burgred, I wouldn't have been able to protect the land I command near Gloucester and Worcester.

And it seems I've not been alone in being largely absent from King Burgred's court. Not if my conversations with Bishop Wærferth are anything to go on.

But, the problem is what to do now. Again, I wish I had Haden. I could have scythed through these fleeing men and women easily, just as I did when we attacked Jarl Sigurd.

And I wish I'd had warriors on the far side of the Trent. It would have made it much easier to attack the retreating enemy.

But I have neither of those options.

What then, do I do?

I can't win back Repton and lose this part of the battle.

It would not sit well with my allies. But in all honesty, I don't care what the bastards think. I want to win this for myself.

"Lord Coelwulf?" Rudolf's high cry has me turning to look at him. He stares, not at the Raiders rushing toward us, but to the west. I squint, unable to see what he does. All I know is that the enclosure of Repton lies there, nothing else.

But then I do see what he means.

"My thanks," I cry, and pause again, considering what to do.

My Gwent Welshmen haven't abandoned me. Not yet anyway, and they race toward me now. It seems they've crossed the River Trent at Repton itself, no doubt wondering why the fighting was on-going and yet they'd won their battle. Now they see a new threat, and they don't recoil from it.

I confess. I'm surprised by their loyalty to me.

"Right, when they arrive, we spread out, make a shield wall as best we can, and try to stop any others from escaping."

Grunts and groans reach my ears, but I have their attention, and seemingly they'll follow my instructions as well.

But we're not the only ones to realise that the useless defence is about to be reinforced. A ripple of shouting follows a murmur of unease. The speed of the Raiders fleeing towards the River Trent increases.

"Fuck it," I command. "We need to start now."

And without waiting to see what my other five warriors do, I slide down the small rise, seax raised, another stolen shield in one hand, and sight my first target. He runs at me, frantically trying to thread his arm through his byrnie that flaps behind him, as though a duck about to take flight. There's a gasp of surprise from his mouth when I stand before him. We both crash to the floor. And then we're grappling.

Of course, as I wear more clothes, there's more for my enemy to grab. But equally, I'm armed, and he's not. Only my shield works more to pin me down than keep me safe as he lies over me. I feel as though the giant from earlier tries to crush the breath from my body.

His face is too close to mine, and I can smell his sweat and fear. With my right arm held tightly against my body, I'm more in danger of slicing myself than him with my tightly held seax.

"Fuck," I complain, abandoning the seax, wedged as it is, working on getting my right arm free. He's made a fist with one hand and tries to batter my face, despite the helm there. His blows are powerful but edged with desperation. As the next punch finds its target, I thump upwards, my curved fist finding the exposed area beneath his shoulder.

His breath explodes into my face, and I seize my chance to thrust him aside and reach for my seax in one fluid movement before he can recover. He flounders on the floor, brown eyes wide with pain and understanding. Hastily, I make it to my knees, and then stab down, holding my seax with both hands, ensuring the blade travels deeply enough through his chest that he'll die.

"Fuck," I complain, trying to stand with the kill complete, only more and more people are running around me, even trying to get through me. I'm forced to stay low or risk standing only to be knocked over once more.

Not that I see it as a disadvantage. Instead, I shuffle around until I can grab my discarded shield, taking a few blows from running feet in the meantime. Then I position myself behind the body of the man I just killed, crouched as low as I can be.

His eyes watch me reproachfully, as I make him part of my defence against the flow of hurrying enemy. I would reach out and close his eyes, but I have other concerns.

I stab upwards, or slash sideways, grasping for as many of the fleeing as I can. Shrieks of pain reach my ears but from further away. It seems that in their desperation to be done, the warriors don't realise they've even been struck until a few moments have passed.

As low as I am, I can't decipher what the Gwent Welshmen are doing, and neither can I see my men, although I do hear Rudolf's high cry.

"Lord Coelwulf," increasingly frantic, echoes from where I assume he still stands on the small rise I found.

"Here," I bellow, filling my lungs as fully as I can, and allowing the sound to rumble away from me. Whether Rudolf hears or not, his cries cease, and I hope that's a good sign.

The whoosh of air as a body hits the ground just behind me has me turning to see the pain-glazed blue eyes of a man old enough to be my father. I can't see where he's injured, although it's evident that he is, because although he uses his arms to lever himself up, he doesn't stand.

At that moment, his entire body seems to judder, as his eyes bore into mine. His mouth contorted, and I can see his throat, not just his tongue. Nothing happens, only then I realise he's moving, coming toward me using his hands, rather than his legs. A foot kicks him in the face from a racing Raider, and somewhere beyond the advancing man, I hear yet another crash as that person goes down as well. But my scrutiny stays focused on the other man because although I thought he'd been taken down, he continues to come at me.

"Fucker," I complain. I need to keep my gaze on the man, and that means that above me, more of the Raiders are getting away.

"Bollocks," I continue to complain, wishing I could move my shield from where it's propped against the dead man, but it's been run into so many times, it's wedged half under the body, and I need all of my focus on the advancing man.

I lick my lips, tasting the salt there and wishing I had something to drink. It's been a long morning, and my work is far from done.

My seax is slippery in my hand, blood sheeting over my hands, and onto the handle, despite my leather gloves. In a flicker of daylight as fleeing feet and bodies seem to momentarily clear above me, I notice, with a wry smirk, that the double-headed eagle appears to be drinking its version of a fine Southern wine. It's my emblem, the sigil of my Mercian heritage, and I'm not about to let a man who can't even walk take my life.

With a heave of strength, I thrust my legs in front of me, kicking the man in the face as he edges closer. His eyes close from the impact, and not confined to the dusty earth as he is, I force my body upwards so that I stand once more. As part of the same movement, I vault over the approaching enemy, landing on his back, his sudden exhalation of air evident in the puff of dust from the ground. Then my seax is through his back, pinning him to the ground.

A spasm of his useless legs and a flail of his arms, and he's suddenly still.

I breathe deeply through my nose, trying not to taste the rankness of his sweating body.

"Lord Coelwulf," the cry restores me to the fact that while my battle is over, there are many more to fight. I stand, peering to where I left my five warriors, relieved to see that the Gwent Welshmen have reinforced them. They snake a much longer line along the earth now. They all stand, ready and poised to face the enemy.

I peer into the distance, shielding my eyes from the bright sunlight, and then I bend, wrench my shield free from my first kill, my seax from my last kill, and rush to stand beside my warriors.

I only have as long as it takes me to make the run to see what's happening on the river.

"Fuck," I complain, but then I'm turning, forcing myself between Rudolf and Hereman, preparing for the onslaught that speeds toward us. I saw, in my brief glance, that five of the ships making their escape are almost out of sight. How long, I consider, was I on the floor for? Long enough, it seems, for the area before the slight rise to have sprouted a field of the dead and dying, a distortion of its real purpose.

But the ships. With the five gone, it means that only five remain, and the warriors who were still fighting in Repton, have realised. Now, all those who had thought to fight for their jarls and lords, are dashing toward the river, desperate not to be left behind.

There are so many, I can't count them. Certainly, there are more than we can hope to overcome, with just over fifty warriors.

Only, that's not quite the end of it.

Even now, I can detect dark shapes in the sky circling over the field of slaughter just waiting to feast. The remainder of my allies follows the warriors who've fled. If we do this right, the Raiders will be wedged between the two forces, and unable to reach the river and the implied sanctuary of the ships. I will turn my earlier fears into a reality for the Raiders.

But it means we must hold firm against the assault, and I don't know if that's possible.

"Lord Cadell," I roar his name, hopeful of a response, and yet surprised when I get one.

"Lord Coelwulf?"

"Together, we'll defeat these Raiders," I bellow. "And then you'll all be rewarded."

This concession receives a muffled cheer, perhaps because not all of them can understand my English. A smattering of syllables rings through the air, I hope from Cadell, and this time there's greater acclaim.

I've just given them something to fight for. Before, it was to satisfy a debt obtained when the Gwent Welshmen were marooned in Gloucester. Now they'll earn a share of the battle spoils as well. Provided we win.

"Are you ready?" I ask, hoping Rudolf knows the words are for him, but it's Pybba who responds.

"Aye, lad, aye. I'm ready for more of the fuckers. Take a man's hand, and then he'll take your balls." I grimace at the leaden tone.

"Live through this, you damn bastards," I holler, and then the enemy is there.

The thud of so many hitting the wooden wall rocks us all backwards. Not everyone stands on the small rise. The Gwent Welshmen also stand on level ground, but our line holds firm, and that's all it needs to do.

A babble of confused conversation erupts from the enemy. How they didn't see us here, I don't know, but it's evident that they didn't. I'm pleased then that Hereman and Sæbald are at the end of our shield wall. Men such as them know how to fight, even if Hereman is reckless with it.

And then I grasp that the shields we hold are all Raider shields. No wonder there's confusion from our enemy. They took us to be allies.

We need to keep them from getting behind us. The shield wall is only one man deep. It would be more of an annoyance for Raiders in proper formation. But this onslaught is far from orderly. The fear and panic will see their lives end much more rapidly than if someone had decided to lead.

"Hold," I instruct, already feeling the strain in my back and down my thighs. It's been a rough day, on top of many other rough days. I'm feeling my age, and yet determined to ignore it.

My shoulder digs into my shield where I hold it high, and although I keep glancing at my feet, there are no probing weapons. The enemy is even more poorly armed than I realised.

Only then I feel a slither of something down my back, and turn, without thinking, to meet the crazed eyes of one of the Raiders. In the quick glance, I appreciate that we're being surrounded. This man is much better provisioned than many of the others.

I'm lucky that my thick byrnie kept his weapon from drawing blood.

"Form a shield," I cry, hoping that Lord Cadell will know what I mean, and instruct his men, but I have no time to ensure he does.

I turn, leaving my shield wedged between Rudolf and Hereman, in the hope that the enemy won't realise I'm missing. I reach for my weapons belt, but of course, it isn't there. I went into Repton as a prisoner. I'm lucky to have the seax that Edmund kept for me.

"Bollocks," I complain, but my opponent is already leering at me. I'll make do with what I have.

My opponent is of average size, his weapon, a seax, like my own, seems to flow from his arm with ease. I take that to mean that it's his weapon, and that he's well used to it. Perhaps a man with some skill. Certainly, I admire him for thinking to kill me from behind. I'll teach the bastard a thing or two about not ensuring the killing stroke was completed.

Without pausing, I move quickly toward him, mindful that with each step, he takes one rearward. That means he's now fighting me up the small incline, whereas I'm fighting him down it. It could be an advantage. It all depends on just how intelligent my opponent is at using his abilities.

I slash downwards with my seax, keen to know if he'll counter it, or simply spin away from me.

The man is dressed for war. Wherever he was, maybe out scouting, or keeping watch at the edge of the encampment, he's more prepared than everyone else I've met since winning free of Repton's enclosure. Well, apart from the giant. Why it's taken him so long to get here is beyond me.

My opponent's decision to counter the attack brings a grin to my tight face. A true warrior then, one who knows there's often little to be gained from sacrificing defence for offence. I think the same. On this occasion, I allow my seax to be entangled in his, the barbs of the handles seeming to hold them locked together in a deadly embrace. With my other hand, I bunch my fist and aim for his neck.

My blow is far from as brutal as I'd have liked it to be, but my adversary stumbles all the same. Unfortunately, his breath still flows evenly, and I know I should have hit him much harder if I wanted to drive the air from him.

Before he can recover, I've jabbed my fist into his face, aiming for his nose, and the satisfying crunch of bone reaches my ears. All the time, the warrior is trying to force his seax loose from mine. But with blood flowing freely from his nose, into his mouth and down his bearded chin, it's too much for him. His grip on the seax slackens, and I take advantage of that to pull my seax toward me, and then point it downwards.

His weapon falls heavily, forcing him to skip backwards to avoid impaling his foot. As he does so, he slips and then stumbles, before collapsing. I follow him down the slope, not realising how steep it is, and with his weapon in the ground behind us, he has nothing but his hands to shield him from my attack.

Quickly, I aim downwards before he can recover and stagger to his feet. Only my blade doesn't penetrate his leather byrnie, instead jarring against my hand because of the force I've tried to exert.

I grunt and offer another jab to his cheek. It slides almost harmlessly free because of the mass of blood. At the same time, I consider another target for my blade.

A collar of leather covers his neck, and while I approve of the addition to his battle gear, it leaves me with little alternative.

He holds his arms tightly to his side, his legs struggling to find purchase so that as I leer at him, I can do nothing else but once more slide my seax into another man's mouth.

I would sooner kill a man with any other blow, but this man needs to die.

His end is not calm, as he bucks against the point that temporarily pierces him and holds him locked to the ground. I sigh at the ruin of another, as I yank my blade back. My foe rears once more, his head coming so far off the ground that it almost knocks against mine. And then he deflates, returning to the ground with an unsatisfying squelch.

"Bastard," I complain, licking my lips, and turning quickly to see how the rest of the shield wall fares.

It doesn't. It's come apart into several blocks where the fighting is heavy. While some effort has been made to encircle the slight rise, I can see that it's faltered. No doubt a lack of understanding on the part of my Gwent Welshmen. I didn't think we'd be fighting together. I never considered that I might need to tell them how I fought.

Pybba and Rudolf are not, surprisingly, the hardest pressed. Indeed, they have a good system going, both working to shore up the other's shortcoming. Rudolf is fast, Pybba is faster. Rudolf lacks the strength for sustained fighting, whereas Pybba lacks only his missing hand. It's Sæbald and Hereman who fight the hardest of all.

"Shit," I complain. It's clear to me that my men's skills have highlighted them as the men who need to be killed first. They're only two, but I can see ten men trying to fight them, as they stand, back to back, fending off blades and shields.

"Bastards," I exhale deeply. I'd like a moment to catch my breath, to find something to drink, but the battle is far from won.

With quick steps, I begin the business of hacking the backs of the men who want to end their lives on Hereman and Sæbald's weapons.

The enemy is as oblivious, as I was earlier, that they expose their backs. That works in my favour. But still, there are many of them to kill.

The first man is short and squat, and my seax falls too high to have any significant impact on his back, alerting him that he's not alone.

He turns to face me, black eyes glinting from behind a silver helm. The nose piece no longer lies flat on the nose, making it appear as though his right eye is too close to his nose, while his left eye is too far away.

I blink, focus again, and lash out with my seax.

My enemy holds a war axe, but no other weapons. While he wears functional boots, the leather supple in the flickering sunlight, he only wears a tunic to cover his torso. How he's survived for so long, I'm unsure. Bruises are already forming there, and I can see a deep slice that's been exposed for so long, it's already beginning to crust over.

It must have been painful, and now I focus on it. If I can reopen the wound, it'll allow me to make a killing stroke elsewhere while he's distracted.

"Fucker," his fury assures me that I'm doing the right thing. My blade flashes once more, and hits the target, red welling immediately, even though a war axe is being held tightly. Why I consider, does he not hit me with it?

As his left hand unconsciously covers the fresh bleed, I aim for his shoulder, trying to stab, not slice. Still, he doesn't try to deflect my blow, and my weapon easily pierces his bruised skin.

His hiss of pain sees his left hand moving again, but still, his right is immobile, and I have no idea why. My attack is effective, but he yet stands, despite bleeding from two different places. I reverse the hold on my seax, direct the attack once more at his initial wound, and this time, the cut is much deeper. I step back, panting heavily, just watching him.

"*Skiderick*," he mouths once more, staggering forward. Blood gushes from his belly wound, covering his legs and forcing him to his knees. His axe continuing to hang uselessly, and I can't help it.

"Why not attack me with your axe?" I ask. A flicker of something in the man's eyes, and I think he'll answer me, only when his mouth opens, it's not words that pour forth, but rather a stream of gleaming ruby.

"Urgh," I jump clear of the mess, not wanting to wear more of his blood.

He tumbles to the floor, and despite everything that's going on around me, I bend and seek out the unused axe, sprawled, still in his hand, to the side of him. Only, his hand is not attached to his body, and I grimace as I touch the cold flesh.

How the fucker attached it to his stump, I don't know. I stand, kick the object aside, noting as I do that the hand still clenches the handle, and it turns with the weapon, the grey of the long-severed hand forcing bile to my throat.

"Bloody bollocks," I wheeze, keen to be distracted from such a grizzly scene. And I am, by the enemy who continues to attack Sæbald and Hereman.

A few men have fallen, their bodies tumbling down the incline to land in an assortment of twisted positions. I step over them carefully, a quick glance to ensure they are truly dead, and then I dash back up the slope.

The men still don't guard their backs, even though one of them has already died. I'm surprised by such an oversight, even if it makes my job easier to accomplish.

When my seax glances across the neck of one of the attackers, I'm staggered to see how dirty my glove is. For a moment too long, I fixate on my gloved-hand, and not the wrathful warrior turning to face me.

A stream of words erupts from his mouth, but I don't understand the gabbled nature of them. It might be Danish. Equally, it might not be.

"What you say?" I ask him, jutting my chin toward him, considering how best to disable the warrior.

This man is much taller than the previous one, with long, tightly braided hair, showing beneath his helm. It fits well, the cheek pieces closing neatly to cover his chin, the nose guard, straight and wide. I consider whether his nose is truly as full as the nose guard suggests. Maybe. Maybe not. Around his neck, a flash of silver informs me that the man wears some pagan symbol of his strange gods.

In his hand, he carries a heavy weapon. I wouldn't say it was a sword, but neither is it a seax. Perhaps it's a sword for a smaller man. Maybe he lost his own when he was roused from his bed by the fighting.

Or maybe not. He wears his byrnie, and all of his clothes, including well-worn boots. This man wasn't caught sleeping. Or, if he was, he slept in all of his clothes.

Just as I realise that the scent of him reaches my nostrils, and I appreciate that he's probably been sleeping in his clothes for many days, if not weeks.

"Lord Coelwulf," he knows my name as well.

"King Coelwulf," I retort, unsure why. I don't really want to be king, but if I must be, then I expect the Raider bastards to use it.

"You killed my brother," the man states, his English heavily accented.

"I kill a lot of people's brothers," I retort, pleased the man wants to talk, as I try and determine the best way to end his life.

"Who was it?" I ask, when the man's face, what little of it I can see, flashes red, his mouth grimacing at me. Two of his front teeth are missing, one from the top, and its twin from the bottom. It looks like a fall to me, or perhaps what happens when a man falls asleep while feasting and drinking and hits the table beneath him with his mouth open.

Not the wisest of men then.

"Sigurd."

"Jarl Sigurd?" I ask, feeling my forehead furrow in confusion. How has the man learned of that so quickly?

"He put up a good fight," I offer, not wishing to give my actual thoughts.

Behind me, I can see that Sæbald and Hereman finally face only two men each. This man is slowing me down, and I'd rather finish him as soon as possible.

My opponent growls, hefting his weapon. I see that the strange half-sword, half-seax belongs to him because it carries a depiction of a dragon on the pommel, just as Sigurd's did.

Perhaps the man will be a better warrior than I first thought. Add that to his desire to seek revenge, and we might have a decent fight brewing.

Only, and I try not to focus on this, Sæbald has fought free from the two men he was fighting. He now stands, breathing deeply, watching both Hereman and I. No doubt he waits to see who'll need some assistance first as his eyes flicker between us.

Hereman fights with his usual tenacity, using his strength to batter against his opponents. It lacks subtlety, but it's always successful.

I determine then that I won't be the one to need assistance, and at the same moment, Sæbald seems to decide on the same as he moves closer to Hereman.

So, I'm on my own.

Sigurd lost his life because I had a horse. I don't have a horse this time. But I have no problem taking the life of Sigurd's brother, none at all.

I rush at the man, deciding that we've talked more than enough.

My seax is to the right of me, the momentum of my arm moving forward, hopefully, more than enough to pierce the warrior's byrnie. The man's eyes open wide at my unexpected movement, and I almost grin. Only I don't.

His half-sword is abruptly where I'm running, and I almost trip over my feet trying to change direction. Instead, it's he who laughs, the sound burbling from his open mouth.

"Bastard," I complain, managing to redirect my body so that I aim squarely for his chest instead. My feet are quick, my mind already thinking a few strikes in front of me, but it seems I don't need to.

At that moment, my opponent seems sluggish. He's too slow to realise the new threat. Before I can actually process what's happening, my blade is slicing across yet another byrnie. The metal links pop open under the strange angle of my blade, and without thinking, I reverse the grip on my seax and drive it beneath the ruin of his protection.

A gasp of hot air in my face, assures me that I've hit my target and that the man has finally caught up with what's happening. My breath erupts from my mouth, as his half-sword clatters against my back, almost holding me in an embrace.

I want to step back, but he has me, and my blade is embedded so deep inside his chest, that I can't wrench it back in the confined space.

"Fuck," I huff, far from panicking, but aware that I thought I was winning, but the bout is far from decided.

Instead, I heft all of my weight onto the handle of my seax, driving it deeper and deeper as my opponent seems to hold me ever tighter with his half-sword. Does the fool not realise that he kills himself all the more quickly with his actions?

Clearly not, for he doesn't stop, and I can feel the wetness of his wound, turning my gloved hands slick, my grip slipping.

"Bastard," I complain, lifting my foot to stamp on his own, and at the same time, moving my head back and down so that I can heft it into his chin.

The chin guard digs into my forehead as much as it does his chin. Still, his distraction releases me from his clutch. I step backwards, dragging my seax with me, even though it's difficult to hold tight with the quantity of fluid pouring forth. I pant, pleased to be free from the man.

I eye him, but his gaze no longer focuses on me. Instead, he watches the blood all but erupting from the cavity in his chest. His hand clamps over the wound, but it does nothing to stop the flow, and I step aside, aware my job is done. Hereman and Sæbald both watch me, their eyes flickering from the man to the fighting taking place all around us, and I know it's time to move on.

"Sigurd's brother?" Sæbald asks, and I nod, wondering how he knew when he never met Sigurd. "I heard him say it," Sæbald explains, and I nod, words beyond me as I try to recover from the fighting that was almost too close for comfort.

"What's happening?" I ask, striding to their side, the thud of my fallen enemy almost making the ground reverberate behind me.

"Not much," Hereman chuckles, but the sound is forced, a little too breathy, and I glance at him, immediately concerned that he's been wounded.

"It's nothing. Just need a few moments," Hereman states when I attempt to turn him around, seek out any injury.

I grunt, unconvinced, but needing to see what's actually happening.

Pybba and Rudolf remain fighting together, although the pile of dead at their feet is already substantial.

My eyes flash to the riverside, and what I see there frustrates me.

"How many of them were there?" I complain. More and more are trying to jump on board the ships, and it's beginning to feel as though no matter what we do, and no matter how many we kill, there will always be a new force to come against us.

"Three thousand, you said," Hereman comments in his rumble.

"Yes, I fucking know that, but how many are there now?"

"Fuck knows," is Hereman's less than helpful response, as I growl with annoyance.

"Where the fuck's Edmund? And the rest of the men?" I ask, turning in a full circle. From this slight vantage point, I can see a great deal, and I need to, in order to determine my next move.

"With the rest of them, over there?" Hereman points to the north, and I see where another small battle is taking place, my men having formed a shield wall to try and stop the enemy from escaping. Behind them all, the rest of my allies are just about in shouting distance.

"This must be the last of them," Sæbald states, and I realise with a start that he's right. The whole of the battle is being played out close to the riverbank. I thought it would be outside Repton, but instead, the Raiders try to find the sanctuary of a ship to aid their escape, while we try and stop them.

More and more of the ships are making their way upstream, oars flashing wetly under the sun, as though they're sunbeams themselves. And a realisation dawns that when this battle is done, I will have to fight another one. And maybe another one after that. Will it never end?

CHAPTER 3

Not that I have the time to dwell on my realisation.

"If this is the last of them, then we need to kill as many of the fuckers as we can." I snarl, circling tightly and trying to decide the best place to lend my support. I decide, for no other reason than because I can, that the Raiders being followed by my allies are not where I can do the most damage.

There, the warriors provided by the ealdormen and bishops can have their fill of what it means to truly fight. I need to assist my warriors, first and foremost.

"I'm going to Edmund." Without pausing to see if Hereman and Sæbald join me, I rush down the incline, pulling my useless gloves from my hands before bending to try and wipe my gory hand clean on a single clump of long grasses. Rather than cleaning my hand, it merely seems to smear the gore all the more.

"Fuck," I'm aware that Hereman, Sæbald, Pybba, Rudolf and Goda have joined me. We lope in a long line, one next to another, next to another, and I hasten a glance at us all.

We look fearsome but determined.

Rudolf has lost the helm that protected him, and his hair is plastered to his head, glimpses of his scalp showing where the helm, before it was lost, pressed too tightly. His stride is almost as long as mine, and his exposed face is flecked with blood splatters.

"Find a sodding helm," I direct to him, indicating the dead all around us, but he shakes his head.

"Na, I've got a fucking great big lump on my head from where some bastard bashed me. I had to take my helm off because it was agony."

"You took it off?" I'm incredulous. No one ever willingly removes a helm in the heart of a battle.

"It bloody hurt," Rudolf tries to explain, but I'm shaking my head. He glances away from me, hungry eyes rushing over the scene of our next engagement.

I turn to Pybba, hoping he can make the young lad see sense.

"It hurt," Pybba echoes, a cackle in his voice, and the respect the older warrior has for my newest addition thrums in just those two words.

"Daft fuckers," I mutter, turning instead to take in Hereman and Sæbald.

Sæbald looks as though he's just been to the stream for a wash. Not a single speck of blood mars his byrnie or face, although he does grimace with every other step. I imagine the old wound in his leg pains him. Other than that, I envy the fucker, as my feet continue to slip and slide inside the boots because of my bloodied feet. I wish I could pull them off as easily as my gloves.

Goda puffs heavily through his cheeks. I wince every time I happen to glance at him. The fuckers beat him well, his eyes almost swollen shut, but he has a fierce expression on his face, and I realise that he wants to fight. He wants to kill. Such a quiet rage can make a man deadly on the field of slaughter.

Hereman, I imagine, looks how I feel. He has a slight cut down one side of his face, and it drips down his neck below his byrnie. I'm curious as to how he got it, but perhaps, the byrnie isn't his. In his hand, he hefts a shield, not his usual one brightly coloured one, but one of Jarl Sigurd's with a writhing dragon and it's bashed and broken. Yet he holds it tightly.

"Find another shield," I bellow at him, shocking him from his thoughts so that a shiver seems to run over his body.

"Nah. This is a good one. I like the weight."

I turn then, to meet Sæbald's eyes. He's not smiling, but

neither is he grim-faced.

"The men know their own minds, My Lord."

"Fuck off you cock-sucker," I complain, and now he does laugh, the sound nipped only by a sharp intake of breath as he steps too widely, no doubt aggravating his wound again.

I shake my head. Who are these men that I command and stride into battle beside? I hardly recognise them. Yet I know that these elements of their character have always been there, hidden, but there.

I blame myself for their stubbornness and refusal to take my instructions.

I've trained them far too well.

"Right, reinforce the shield wall, or kill them from behind?" I ask of no one, as we get closer and closer. The groans of the dead and dying fill my ears. So do the grunts of those who fight, shield to shield. I lick my lips, still tasting of salt, and again wish I could drink.

But the battle needs to be won first.

"The rest will take them from behind?" Hereman comments. I agree with him.

"Right lads, reinforce the shield wall. Let's keep the fuckers from reaching the ships."

And so spoken, I increase my speed and dash toward the shield wall my allies have formed. They've found a flat piece of land to stand their ground. Why the enemy doesn't just rush around the shield wall, I don't know, but they don't. Perhaps they're too well used to fighting an enemy in this way.

I don't much care as I seek out Edmund in the press of bodies.

"What kept you?" Edmund complains as I add my weight to his, forcing the shield upright, a wary eye on my feet to ensure no one nips my ankle or severs my foot.

"I had a few others to kill," I comment sardonically, aware that Edmund is breathing heavily.

"Take a breather. I'll take over," I offer, knowing full well that he'll refuse.

"Fine, be a stubborn wanker," I grumble. Hereman has found

Goda, and I can hear the two of them laughing, further away, as they greet each other.

"Hold," I bellow, my cry mirrored by whoever has taken command of the Raiders that we face. "Hold," I reiterate. I debate shouting that reinforcements are coming but decide it won't help in any way, other than to make the Raiders that little bit more desperate. I'd rather it was a pleasant surprise for them.

I'm sweating again as I shore up Edmund's flagging strength. I've no idea how long he's been holding the shield in place, but from the shaking of his arm, I decide it's too long. This needs to be done with.

"Fuck it," I complain, shoving my way into Edmund's place. Worn out, he can do little, but allow me to force him to relinquish the grip on the shield strap, and stagger to the floor beside me.

I have my seax ready, but what I could do with is a spear or something long enough to pierce our opponents despite the shields between us. My seax is far too short, and I've nothing else.

I lift my foot, stamp down, hard, on a snaking blade that the enemy tries to draw blood with, and I feel my temper begin to build.

This has been going on for too damn fucking long, and I want it done with.

I don't like to feel helpless, and right now, I do. Not as powerless as when I pretended to be a prisoner to trick the four jarls, but any sort of exposed right now is too damn much.

My heart beats too loudly in my ears. The cries of my warriors, and those who fought with me inside Repton itself, fill my hearing. The exhaustion is apparent, as is the fear that they won't beat this.

And there's nothing that I can do. Nothing. But hold up the shield, and hope that the rest of my allies arrive far more quickly than I anticipate they will.

"Hold," I cry, hoping that the sound of my voice will bolster the resolve of those as exhausted as Edmund. "Hold," the call resonates up and down the line. But still, it doesn't feel as though the men I fight with have obtained a fresh desire to win.

"For Mercia," I holler instead, and this does the trick. Almost one by one, I hear the men echoing the cry. I can even pick out individual voices, those of Sæbald and Wærwulf the final two, and then the entire shield wall seems to stand taller, push harder. I know that we can keep it together for long enough to overcome the enemy.

Only then, we don't. With no warning, the force pressing on my shield disappears, and I'm falling forward, unable to stop myself until I land on my shield. My knees hit the raised iron edge, my elbow impacting the leather strap ends, and somehow, I've lost hold of my seax.

Hastily, I scrabble around amongst the dead and dying, aware I almost lie on someone, and yet there's no sign of my seax. I nearly fear to look up. I've nothing. Not even my shield to protect me, because it's wedged beneath my body.

"Fuckers," I huff.

"Need a hand," the voice is that of Ealdorman Ælhun. I look up, meet his eyes, feeling my forehead wrinkle with consternation. I notice his frost-rimmed beard is now stained with pink, his metal coat somehow obscuring the fact his body has gone to fat.

"What happened?" I ask, finally managing to disentangle my legs and arms, accepting his bloodied hand as I rise to survey the battle site.

"You didn't have to kill them all yourself," Ealdorman Ælhun huffs, bracing himself on the slimy ground as I haul myself upwards and stand before him.

"Well, I've got a reputation to maintain," I exhale, almost bending double again so that I can catch my breath.

"I assure you. You've maintained your reputation. Men and women will sing of this great victory for centuries."

Finally, the pieces of the puzzle begin to fall into place, and my jaw drops open, as I appreciate the scale of destruction that has been wrought, almost with one blow.

"All of them, just like that?"

"All of them, just like that." Ealdorman Ælhun confirms as I see where each and every Raider has been stabbed fatally in the back. Every single one.

"Why didn't they fall forward?" I ask, my insatiable curiosity overcoming all else. But Ealdorman Ælhun has moved on, and my words hang uselessly in the heated air. I can see him, hastening toward the riverbank with as much speed as he can muster, surrounded by twenty of his warriors and that reminds me of the biggest problem.

More ships have escaped than I would have liked. Even now, the odd remaining Raider staggers to the river and attempts to throw themselves onto the ships as they glide passed.

I watch one woman, dress ripped and all but naked, stagger, her back a mass of blood where a long slicing cut has severed her dress. She calls, feebly, to someone on one of the ships, and I watch as the man beckons her onwards, his face a mask of fear, because we all know she's not going to make it.

Rather than run to propel herself from land to ship, she limps, and I wince when I hear a splash rather than the thud of a body hitting the wood.

"Good, another one dead," I mutter, my eyes on the man being restrained from diving in after his lost lover by men on board the ship who know there's no hope of survival.

"Poor bitch," Edmund calls, and I reach out to lever him up from the ground. His face is a welter of bruises, as he pulls his helm free, and I shudder, as his tongue probes a ragged cut on his bottom lip.

"Bastard, that stings," Edmund complains, accepting my hand. "Fuck, I'm thirsty," he continues. I say nothing. Agreeing with him won't make a beaker of water materialise before me.

His breathing is as laboured as my own. I stay standing, calling greetings to my equally spent warriors. I want to know that all of my men live. But realise that it's impossible to say when the battle has raged so far from where it began.

"What now?" Edmund asks, and I could cuff him around the head for his insistent questions. Only I'm thinking the same.

"We go after them," I complain, wishing Haden was here to take my weight. My legs won't last much longer.

"Where, along the River Trent?" Incredulity thrums through Edmund's words.

"Yes, along the Trent. Otherwise, they'll hole up in Torksey again, and we'll have to do all this again."

"Fuck," Edmund winces, his hands feeling inside his byrnie for some suspected hurt.

"We don't have ships?" Edmund states, as though this makes the suggestion impossible.

"True, but we have horses. Somewhere?" I turn and peer toward the three smoky fires that show me where Repton is. Another four have joined those three. I can't imagine anyone needs a fire on such a hot day and that means that somewhere amid the campsite, someone is probably burning. The stench will be disgusting.

"You want to ride to Torksey?" Icel has joined our small party by now. His voice shows less incredulity than Edmund's, and for that, I'm grateful.

Hereman is also there, staying far from Edmund, and Goda pants roughly, a small smirk just visible amongst the welter of bruises.

"Fucking bollocks, look at you all." My hand indicates their bodies, and all of them look down and then across, small smiles beginning to appear on sweaty, weary faces.

"We look like we were in a small fight," Icel rumbles, his being the only face not to be grinning in amusement.

"A small fight?"

"Tiny," Icel booms again, seeming not to detect the sarcasm thrumming through Edmund's voice.

"Well, I suppose you weren't there for all of it," Edmund continues, and I can already feel the edges of an argument beginning.

Surprised, Icel turns to the other man. Whatever rivalry has been growing between them seems to both reach its peak and subside in just one look. I watch, unsure what will happen next.

"When King Wiglaf reigned, I was involved in a huge fight," Icel begins, prepared to prove his point, his arms held to either side, to show how massive the battle was. Rudolf hangs on every word, as he sprints to join our grouping, while Edmund huffs in annoyance.

"How many warriors?" the youth asks, spitting blood clear from his mouth so that it almost lands on his boot.

"More than this," Icel continues, his large hand indicating the mass of dead before us.

"So, just a small fight," I comment, determined to get more out of Icel than this. If Edmund isn't going to be the one to do it, I'll take his place.

Icel inclines his head from one side to another, his expression pensive.

"Not the biggest, not the smallest," he eventually concedes, and I can't stop the laughter from bubbling forth.

"You fucking bastard," I exclaim, for once actually thinking that I might agree with Edmund's opinion of Icel.

"Look how many dead there are," Hereman offers, his own voice flecked with suppressed outrage.

"I've killed more," Icel states flatly.

"I've killed more," I find myself mimicking Icel, making my voice as loud as his. Icel watches me, and in that look, I understand far more of what he's doing. I subside, but only because Icel isn't actually trying to be condescending, but rather drive the edge and heat from what we've just done.

"How many more?" Of course, young ears, and Rudolf wants to know. With a quirk of his heavy eyebrow, Icel flings his arm around Rudolf's slim shoulders, noting, as I do, how the boy grimaces. Icel's touch is much lighter than it might have been.

"How many did you kill?" Icel asks.

"I don't know. Pybba. Pybba," Pybba isn't paying a great deal of attention, as he too joins us in surveying the battle site. "Pybba," Rudolf demands, and the older man jumps and then looks at him.

"What?"

"How many did I kill?"

"Why would I keep count of your kills? I was too busy keeping track of my own."

Rudolf's face deflates, and then he seems to realise what Icel is doing as well.

"How many did you kill?" Rudolf demands, his eyes squeezed tight in thought.

"Many," Icel detracts, and I laugh once more, the sound more natural.

"He killed a small amount," Edmund comments, his mouth downcast, his disgust with the other man still evident.

"And how many did you kill?" Icel asks.

"Fuck knows, I was too busy killing the bastards."

"So no one actually knows?" I ask, trying to remember how many men met the edge of my blade that day.

"Does it matter?" Hereman asks. He's attempting to wipe his blade clean on his byrnie, and it's not really working. Not as far as I can tell.

"It never matters as long as they're all dead," I interject.

"But they're not, are they?" Icel comments, and I grunt.

"No, but they will be when we finish this." Now I have the attention of everyone, as more and more of my men gather together. Some have taken the time to end the lives of any wounded they've come across. In contrast, others have left them to the other warriors who owe their allegiance to one of the ealdormen or bishops.

I try and keep track of everyone who drifts toward us, but I know Edmund is keeping a closer count. He'll bring me the numbers when he has them.

"What are we going to do?" It's Wærwulf who asks. His purloined battle gear that used to belong to Jarl Sigurd marks him as a Raider, and I confess, I'm overjoyed to see he's uninjured. It's not always easy, in the heat of battle, to determine an ally from an enemy.

"We're going to follow them," I announce, but actually, I'm not sure if we will. I'm trying to decide. I look at my warriors, at all of them, even Rudolf, who has certainly earned that name today.

"We're going to make sure they don't settle elsewhere in Mercia," I begin, only to be interrupted by the return of Ealdorman Ælhun from the riverbank. I would have thought him employed on the river for some time, but it seems he has other matters on his mind. I also realise that the sails are no longer in sight. All of them have gone. I can't even see them, but no doubt, that's because of the snaking nature of the river. I'm sure we can catch them, and soon. If only everyone would hurry up.

"You must have your coronation first. The people must see you as the rightful king of Mercia."

"The bishop has declared me as king. Having a ceremonial helm wedged onto my head isn't going to assure the Mercians of their freedom in the future." I speak with some heat.

Ealdorman Ælhun looks as though he wants to argue, and I'm surprised when he merely bows his head, showing his baldness, his helm finally removed.

"My Lord King, you know the best actions to take. My men and I will do whatever it is you require of us."

His words, more than anything else I've endured that day, stun me.

I am the king. I'd almost forgotten what that actually meant.

"Excellent," I expel, trying to decide how to phrase what I want to do next. I feel all of those eyes watching me, the surviving Gwent Welshmen amongst them. I hold my tongue, giving myself an extra few moments to consider whether what I suggest is actually possible.

Fuck it, I decide. The attack on Repton worked. There's no reason while the next offensive won't as well.

CHAPTER 4

Not that it's as decided quite as easily as I hope. I want to be gone. I want to be on my mount, and I want to be making my way from Repton before the sun sets.

"For fuck's sake," my temper is high as I turn to face all the questioning faces. Despite the bruises, missing teeth, broken noses, and other cuts and abrasions, I do feel as though my men have survived with few injuries. Edmund has brought me no news of deaths, and that cheers me. I'm sure my allies haven't fared quite as well.

I'm aware of those injured in the battle, from the shrieks that fill the air, the calls for water and aid never seeming to cease.

The representatives of Bishop Wærferth, Eadberht and Deorlaf as well as Ealdorman Beorhtnoth and Ælhferht quickly join me. Æthelwold doesn't appear, but I hold my question. I don't to distract the men who are keen to speak about what's been accomplished, by asking after someone who is missing from our party.

Ealdorman Beorhtnoth has barely a flicker of blood on him, and I want to be derisive about his involvement in the battle. However, I still need the men he brings to our alliance. He might not have fought, but his men have, and I'm prepared to overlook his gleaming mail coat in light of that.

Ealdorman Ælhferht, in stark contrast, seems to be as bloodied and beaten as I am, even though he was not with me in Repton. He greets me with a smirk on his young face.

"It worked," Ælhferht crows, and I allow myself to smile as well, as I reach out to grip his left arm in the warriors embrace.

"It fucking did," I roar, aware that men must be praised for what has been done before what needs to be done can be spoken about. His right arm is bound in a grubby sling, and I'm careful not to touch it. His breath hisses between clenched teeth, all the same, his black hair and face showing the starkness of his pale skin. The injury must pain him. I admire him for trying not to show it.

"Broken it, I think," Ealdorman Ælhferht explains. "The crush of the shield wall," he goes on to explain, and I nod. I've not heard of such wounds before, but I'm not about to admit that. Again, I need to be grateful for the sacrifices, not scornful. I might have joked had the same happened to one of my men, maybe even roasted them for allowing such to happen. It's different with one of my new ealdormen, and I'm aware that Edmund and Icel watch me carefully to ensure I don't piss 'em off.

The discussion between my warriors, the Gwent Welshmen, and ealdormen Ælhferht, Beorhtnoth, Ælhun and the representatives of the bishops takes so long, that Rudolf saunters passed me, the ghost of a grin on his face. It seems the little shit enjoys seeing me so hampered by new responsibilities.

"Two hundred and sixty-four," Rudolf announces. I turn to glare at him, annoyed he's interrupted the useless arguments raging amongst men who should simply follow my directions. I'm almost at the point of announcing that I'm the bastard king and they must do what they've been commanded to do. Rudolf's declaration forces all eyes to gaze at him, and he doesn't even flinch under the gaze of so many.

Has Icel put him up to this? Or even Edmund? I wouldn't be surprised.

Rudolf looks no worse than when I saw him earlier, and if anything, somehow looks even fresher. Damn, I remember being so young and undaunted by battle and the stinking remains left behind. Seeing him like that reminds me of how uncomfortable my feet are. They might be booted, but they're still damn cold, and I can feel the layer of blood and guts that covers them, and it itches at me. No doubt that doesn't help my rising temper.

"Two hundred and sixty-four what?" I demand to know in the sudden silence.

"Dead bodies. Sorry, dead Raiders."

"Where, on the field of slaughter or inside Repton?"

"Combined," Rudolf shrugs, perhaps not realising why I make the distinction. Equally, I can't believe the debate has gone on for so long that Rudolf has had time to get back to Repton, count the dead and return to where I still stand close to the riverbank.

"Fuck," I spit, only now realising that Rudolf has done me a favour.

"Are you sure?" It's Edmund who asks, and I bite back a derisive comment. Icel is less restrained.

"We can all count, you daft sod. It's not a skill only you've bothered to acquire."

My eyebrows furrowed, I meet Rudolf's eyes.

"How many wounded?"

"None," and then he pauses before continuing. "Now."

"So over one thousand five hundred men escaped, in fact, closer to two thousand!" I almost can't quite believe that. I killed at least seven men, maybe more. What were the rest of the fuckers doing?

"Potentially," Rudolf nods, his young eyes alight. "Not that we could count those who drowned. The river has them now."

That might not be quite right. I'm sure the bodies will float to the surface in good time, or even get wedged on the riverbanks further downstream. But the immediate count of the dead is both good, and also not so good, not at all.

Near enough five hundred and fifty men to kill less than half that number. And I've killed at least seven.

"Well, even accounting for some of them drowning, that's a fucking lot of Raiders that escaped on foot, or on a ship, and now move northwards."

Ealdorman Ælhun is nodding at my words, his face stiff as he runs his hand through his beard. He knows as well as I do that the battle might be over, but the war is not yet won. Maybe now he'll stop arguing with me. The other ealdormen look somehow dejected, and any moment now, I expect someone to ask where Ealdorman Æthelwold is.

"So we pursue them then?" Ealdorman Ælhun asks, nodding as he does so, turning to meet the eyes of the other men who've become part of the unofficial witan. I can hardly believe that I preside over my kingdom from the slight rise we sought an advantage from earlier. Most kings would demand a wooden hall, not an outdoor conversation. But, in all honesty, they're lucky I stand, and I'm not mounted. If someone would hurry and bring Haden to me, I'd be long gone from here.

"My Lord King." I recognise the lilt of the voice, even before I meet the eyes of Cadell ap Merfyn. He still lives, although he'll have some scars to show for it. I believe many of his men do as well. That means he commands nearly fifty warriors.

"My Lord Cadell," I incline my head toward him. The unease in his eyes alerts me that he's about to bow out of our arrangement. I can hardly blame him.

"We'll take the northern bank," he surprises me by saying, and I'm nodding before I've genuinely considered whether it's a good idea or not.

"You'll be far from home," I comment.

"We made an agreement, My Lord King. The men are keen to fulfil their end of the arrangement and count the debt as settled."

"Then you have my thanks. Do you have horses?" I rub my face, aware I don't know how they made it to Repton from the borders, and that I should.

"Yes, My Lord King. Small beasts, but sturdy. We'll make good time."

"You'll need a guide?" I ask. I can sense some unease amongst the other Mercians at letting the Gwent Welshmen roam so far into Mercia, armed, and at my command, but it's not as though they've offered.

"If it would please you, My Lord King." His tone oozes with respect, but I've no stomach for it."

"My Lord King," it's the commander of Bishop Deorlaf of Hereford who demands my attention. I search for his name and settle on Osferth. I can see that he's had a hard fight of it. Blood gleams on his exposed left arm, and below his right eye, a small drop of blood forms on a ragged piece of skin, as though he weeps blood and not water. He's lucky the blow just missed his eye.

"Yes?"

"We'll travel with Lord Cadell's men. We know them of old, and would be pleased to accompany them." I like the idea, and yet apprehension still prickles along my skin, and not least because of the flickering relief I've seen on Osferth's face. I'm not used to having too many men to command. Normally, I'm there, able to make snap decisions if the situation dictates a rapid reassessment.

I catch sight of Edmund's face and know he's thinking the same.

"Good. Do you have a full quota of men?"

I can't remember how many men Bishop Deorlaf sent. I look at Edmund, but he seems reticent to help me. Damn stubborn fucker. It was Icel who took the piss out of him for questioning whether Rudolf could bloody count. Not me. Only then he seems to relent.

"Fifty-four, My Lord King," Edmund's voice oozes with insolence, but I've got more important things to think about right now.

"No, My Lord King. We have forty-one men now."

I lower my head, considering those lives lost for the cause of Mercia.

"My sympathies," I offer.

The man nods, although it seems he sways as he absorbs the words. The loss of so many men will be a big blow. For all of them. I refrain from saying what everyone is thinking – that the Raiders lost far more than the Mercians did.

Only then Rudolf pipes up. I could curse the lad for his quick wit and eager eyes, and for not speaking more quietly.

"My Lord King," the words slide from his glib tongue easily, and yet they startle both of us. "A ship, maybe two, travelling south, not north." Rudolf stands just above us all, higher up the small rise, and no doubt able to see much further than all of us. It probably helps that he looks inland, and not toward the northern flowing river.

"What?" I turn to peer where I imagine the ship has gone, but there's nothing to see, other than the tendrils of flame that slip into the sky from the burning crafts left behind at Repton. I look to Edmund for confirmation. He has the best eyesight of everyone.

"Are you sure?" I demand to know, and now Bishop Deorlaf's man looks uncomfortable, as does another warrior who's joined our grouping, Heahstan. I know he leads Bishop Eadberht of Lichfield's men. I understand his unease. The Trent flows through lands that look to Eadberht.

"My Lord King," he steps forward to speak to me, but I'm sucking my briny lips and considering what should be done.

"Lord Cadell, will you join Heahstan and the rest of Bishop Eadberht's men and travel along the Trent in the opposite direction to the one I'll be taking?"

I sense unhappiness from both men, and I'm unsurprised. The borderlands lie ever westwards. But Lord Cadell quickly nods his acceptance.

"Closer to our kingdom," Cadell grunts. In those words, we all hear what's unsaid, closer for the Gwent Welshmen to retreat to if they need to.

"Heahstan?" I ask, turning to watch him. He's a broad man, the years of his training evident in his stance and physique, his lack of hair attesting to his skilfulness and longevity to date.

"My Lord. As you command," the reply is far from grudging, but it lacks the resolve I would have preferred to hear. Abruptly, I wish I'd instructed Edmund or Icel to go with Cadell, but I can't retract my decision, not without sowing more unease between the groups of men.

"So who goes north then?"

Edmund's tone is waspish, and I wish he'd thought before he'd spoken. He's as bloody bad as Rudolf. I can't help thinking he expects too much of me, and yet I know I'd not have it any other way.

"I'll travel with Bishop Deorlaf's men and half of my force on the northern bank of the Trent. I want Edmund and Icel, with Ealdorman Ælhun's men to head north on the south of the river. Ealdorman Alhferht will hold Repton until we're sure all the Raiders who went the wrong way along the Trent are dead. Lord Cadell and Heahstan, send word to Repton when the enemy is slain." I realise I'm snapping out instructions, but no one seems to want to argue with me. Not now.

"Unfortunately, holding Repton will also include burying the dead. The Raiders must have separate burials to the Mercians."

This announcement causes a ripple of consternation, but we can't leave the dead to grow over-ripe in the fields. That's too gruesome.

I'm trying to decide what to do with the force still left to me. Bishop Wærferth won't thank me for sidelining his fighting men, and neither will he appreciate it if I send them into battle to be slaughtered. And where the fuck is Ealdorman Æthelwold? Time has moved on, and he's still not appeared.

Bishop Wærferth's man is keen as he looks at me. Pybba's words, back in Worcester, haunt me a little. He spoke of treachery he overheard, and although I'd sooner not consider it after we've all fought together, I do need to consider it.

"Kyred, will you take your men and ride south? We need to know that we've not missed any warbands sent to hunt me down?" There, a reasoned request and one that will keep the bishop of Worcester's men in an area that's always been loyal to me.

Kyred inclines his head, making it impossible to tell whether he approves of my words or not.

"The Severn and Stour, as well as the Avon, might provide an incentive for the Raiders to try again."

Now Kyred stands a little taller. I haven't given him a thankless task after all.

"Visit Kingsholm. Inform my Aunt of my intentions, and have her swell your ranks with six of my remaining men." There, I've both given him some freedom and neatly curtailed it in one move. Kyred tries to keep his facial expression mutual, as I keep my eyes on him. We war without speaking, and when he looks away, Kyred is aware than I am the king of Mercia and will be obeyed.

"Where the fuck is Ealdorman Æthelwold?" I can't put off the inevitable any longer.

Rudolf, of course, has a reply for me.

"He's in St Wystan's."

"He's what?"

Rudolf sighs.

"He says the church must be resanctified. He's having the bodies pulled clear from it. That's how I know the number of men who died there."

For a moment, I'm speechless. I've not considered the need for such action, but Mercia's bishops support me.

"Then Ealdorman Æthelwold will remain in Repton to finish his task," I announce flatly. And then I realise my mistake.

"I'll assist him," Ealdorman Beorhtnoth is too keen to make the suggestion, and I only just stop my eyes from rolling in exasperation. One battle and Ealdorman Beorhtnoth is out, or so it seems.

"Keep your men with you as well," I order then, and Edmund seems to let out a long held-in breath. Ealdorman Beorhtnoth looks as though he might argue, but then clamps his mouth shut.

"And Ealdorman Ælhun," the ealdorman fixes me with his bulging eyes. He was the first to denounce Bishop Wærferth's suggestion that I become king, but he's proven his loyalty since. "You will have overall command of Mercia in my absence. Remain at Repton, or wherever you need to go. Keep a contingent of your men with you."

There, I've made a fuck load of decisions, and now my head pounds with more than just the need to drink a bucket-load of water.

I eyeball every man there, daring them to argue with me, relieved when my ealdormen hold their tongues.

"Will we stay in sight of each other?" Edmund's question is snapped and ends the prolonged silence. I shake my head slightly.

"If possible, but I doubt it will be."

No one says anything to dispute my decisions. However, I can already see that Edmund and Icel are uneasy at being thrown together without me to referee.

"What of your coronation?" Ealdorman Ælhun is like a dog with a bone.

"Such ceremony will have to wait for Mercia to be truly free. I am accepted as king, by everyone here?" I pause, a question, but also not a question. Silence once more.

"Then I make the decisions, and when there's time for more pomp, there'll be more. But for now, the infestation needs to be removed from Mercia, the peace accord that King Burgred agreed with them must be reversed."

Fuck, I hate making speeches. As I finish speaking, Rudolf presses a beaker of water into my mouth. I swill it gratefully, as my stomach growls so loudly he hears it and grins.

"I plan on leaving immediately." The smirk leaves his face.

"Is there a ford close by?" Blank expressions meet my question.

"I'll think of something else," I explain, my gaze once more struck by the burning ships. Perhaps enough remain, maybe not! A new thought consumes me.

"Those in Repton, block the river in both directions with whatever of the ships remains. We don't want those who went west escaping, and we don't want any other ships coming along the Trent from the Humber." I add a final thought. "Remember, stay alive. There are only so many Mercians. The Raiders constantly seem to reinforce their ranks. We don't have the same options."

With that, I turn away, prepared to find Haden. I need to make the decisions as to which men are coming with me, and which are staying with Edmund and Icel. If I let my men make the decision, it'll lead to arguments, and I can't be fucked to deal with that. Not at the moment.

I've dealt with enough prickly arseholes for one day.

Rudolf refills my beaker, and I swig it thirstily, keen to drive the salt from my lips. My body thrums with all that's been accomplished that day. At the same time, my mind is busy with the decisions needed to make our victory overwhelming and decisive.

Too many times the Mercians, working with Wessex, have defeated the Raiders in battle only to fall victim to them once more when they've decided the Raiders won't dare return. I won't allow that to happen under my watchful eye.

"Lord Coelwulf," Icel is at my side. I'd not expect him to be the first to complain. "We need someone who knows the area well to escort us." I quirk an eyebrow, shaking my head at the folly that Icel would complain, rather than plan.

"Find someone. Have them sent to me. It's an excellent suggestion." I can't deny that I don't know the north of Mercia well. My hunting grounds have always been the southwest, close to Gloucester, Worcester and almost to the Thames.

As I talk, I'm striding back toward Repton, minding where I step so that I don't slip on the blood, gore and piss that litters the ground. I can't help but see the clumps of the dead, perhaps the result of a combined attack against them by a handful of Mercians. Only then I'm forced to pause, staring down and gazing at the ruin of Oswald, Ealdorman Ælhun's man. I'd not realised he'd even arrived in time to join the battle. I bow my head, clear my thoughts, and allow a flicker of grief into my heart. But no more.

The mourning must be done when Mercia is safe.

The fact that time might never come only doubles my resolve

to ensure it does.

I'll fight for Mercia all of my life. If it brings my death, then that's as it must be.

CHAPTER 5

Striding through the destroyed barricade forces me to confront just what's been accomplished in my name.

Rudolf may have counted the dead, but it seems that some of the heaviest fighting must have been within Repton. Wherever I look I'm greeted by the ruin of someone who woke that morning expecting little more than to eat, train and maybe fuck a little. There'll be none of that now.

Edmund accompanies me, strangely silent at my side.

His words don't surprise me.

"You can go home now if you want to. You've scattered the Raiders."

I suppose he thinks the offer must be made, but I shake my head, not even bothering to give a vocal response.

The door to St Wystan's, now standing wide open, is no longer the dark chasm it was this morning. Despite the mass of destruction that greets me, it feels as though it might be a place of God again, one day.

Ealdorman Æthelwold's men have been busy, hauling out the dead, and I greet them as they rest, cheeks red from the exertion. I even hail Ealdorman Æthelwold from his conversation with a man wearing the garb of a monk, although his hands are as bloody as everyone else's.

"My Lord King," Æthelwold bows to me, although he tries not to peer too closely at my clothes, his throat moving as though he swallows bile.

"Ealdorman Æthelwold. You do good work here. You'll remain in Repton with the other ealdormen while I hunt down the Raiders. The dead must be buried, the church made holy again."

The words are a barked order, and I almost take them back, only they seem to stiffen his resolve. Both he and the bloodied monk stand taller, and I grunt at them.

"When I return, I'll expect Repton, and St Wystan's to be as they were before the desecration. Any problems, speak to Ealdorman Ælhun, he'll deputise for me." Even this knowledge seems to please the pair.

I don't linger, my concern is with what will greet me on the river bank. I need to know how many ships remain and how many yet burn, sending plumes of smoke high into the air and signalling to all what's happened here today.

The enclosure is almost silent as I erupt into it. Here nothing moves but the settling corpses of the dead. Even the men left to guard the gateway that leads to the riverbank, prefer to stand close to the river, rather than amongst the detritus of the disbanded warriors.

"A fine victory," I call, sweeping beyond them before coming to an abrupt stop.

A low whistle emits from Edmund.

"Bloody bollocks," I exclaim. Despite the bodies I've seen, it's the devastation of so many ships that reveals to me, for the first time, just how vast the number of Raiders was.

There are smoking ruins, half-sunken ships valiantly trying to stay afloat, while in other places, nothing remains to be seen but the very tip of a sunken mast. A whole selection of debris mingles in the water, anything from an oar to a balled-up piece of cloth, no doubt forgotten about when the Raiders scrambled to escape, leaving all these ships behind.

But as overwhelming as that is, it's not what I came here to see.

The steeped bank of the defences that towers above my head is almost flush with the equally steep riverbank.

"A clever device," I commend, mouth downturned, as I

indicate where I'm looking with my outstretched arm.

"Easy to limit those gaining admittance."

It seems that the Raiders knew only too well that they were an enemy in a kingdom that hated them. Why else would they have invested so much time and effort into building such a fortification? I'm pleased to see it. The Raiders might have banished King Burgred, but they knew they weren't safe, even before I came to kill them all.

"I need to get across the river," I state, striding to the closest buoyant ship, and jumping down into its hill to test its suitability having decided it will have to do.

"Be careful," Edmund all but yells, as my weight brings forth a worrying creak and crack of straining wood and the entire vessel seems to sink. Only then it stabilises, and I nod. But I don't weigh as much as a horse, or even a few warriors.

"Get down here," I shout to Edmund, turning aside so that I don't have to witness the indecision warring on his perplexed face.

The creaking of the struggling wood only intensifies as his weight forces the vessel down once more, as the river starts to infiltrate the craft.

"Fuck," Edmund complains, his lips a tight line of unease, as I face him, daring him to speak. Of course, the fucker does.

"Are you really thinking what I think you're thinking?" I nod, trying to sight the next suitable place to lead a horse.

"Just go around, or even swim across. The horses could do with a wash," Edmund suggests, and while it has merit, I've not just witnessed enemy men and women drown in the River Trent to attempt the same feat myself.

Somehow, one of the other stricken vessels has managed to settle, almost on top of the sinking ship I'm standing on. I walk to it, striding confidently, and then pause, reaching with my foot to test the suitability of traversing that way.

A whoosh of hot air reaches me as I do so, and I stagger back.

"Bastard," I complain. The Gwent Welshmen have fired many of the ships, I knew that. This particular one seems to burn almost below the waterline. I'd not thought it on fire at all.

Edmund helpfully pats my back, as though I'm burn as well, and then he glares at me.

"This is fucking stupid. There must be a bridge somewhere, go and find it." But I'm shaking my head.

"It's been burnt. Look." I point to the remains of the bridge. It's not been scorched recently, but quite recently. Just another sign of how insecure the Raiders were in Repton.

"No, this will work, and it'll be quicker." As though to prove my words, I spy another ship, wallowing in the water close to the one that burns beneath the water. I eye it critically but decide, with all my ship skills, that it's at about the same level as the ship I'm on. I step onto it, with only a slight grunt of effort. Unlike the first wreck, there's no creaking or groaning, or cloud of heat, and it doesn't even rock with my added presence.

Edmund follows me, his silence filled with fury.

I ignore him. It's often the best way.

The River Trent is wide behind Repton and fast flowing. I can hear the water sucking at the beleaguered ships, trying to wrench them away and rip them apart with the next rainstorm. I almost think it'll be too easy to block the river. The problem, I realise, will be in unblocking it at a later date.

More ships stretch before me, and I imagine it'll take another four stable surfaces to make it to the far side, where I can see brown grass waiting to greet me. The sun has parched Repton. If I was holier, I might think it the wrath of God, but I know it's just the damn hot weather.

I jump my way across, being careful to only trust ships that are entirely upright. I don't touch those with one end or other slowly being covered by the voracious river. A fish flops in one such pool, and I spare a thought for it. Will it live, will it die, will the water covering it grow, or will it abruptly disappear? The choice of life or death is not for the fish to make unless of course, it flops back into the river.

Turning away, I focus on the next ship, a wry smirk on my face when I hear the slap of the fish being returned to the water.

Edmund. For all his bluff, he's soft as shit at heart.

I step onto the next ship, bracing myself as it seems to sink beneath my weight, only to even out. From there it's easy to walk the length of the abandoned *langskip* and finally stand on the far side of the River Trent.

Between the discarded *langskips* and *knarrs*, the Raiders have all but replaced the bridge they destroyed. I find I approve even though it was done by chance.

On the riverbank, I'm surprised to see a small herd of ponies. They're not alone but rather shelter under an expanse of woodland stretching away from the river. A good hiding place, but now the youths who watch the animals creep free, no doubt desperate to know whether Lord Cadell yet lives.

"All is well," I bellow, waving at them, but not one of them makes to move, instead trying to sink back into the welcome shade and cover, as though I've not even hailed them.

"Suit your fucking self then," I complain, turning back, to watch Edmund unhappily follow in my footsteps.

"Alright, enough is enough. Yes, we made you do something fucking crazy to get inside Repton. But this is way beyond crazy. Ludicrous perhaps, or just fucking ridiculous. I don't even think a word exists to adequately explain what you want to do."

I grin.

This is how it should be. I should be the one being reckless, not everyone else.

"It'll work," I reassure him, clasping his shoulder as he stands before me, breathing heavily. I shake him when he refuses to meet my eyes.

"It'll bloody work," I reiterate, and he nods his head slowly.

"Perhaps for everyone but fucking Haden. He's a shit."

"He'll do what I ask him to do," I retort, refusing to admit that Edmund is more than likely correct. Haden was a git on the River Severn. But, well, he's a contrary bastard, he might just like the half-formed bridge. It wouldn't surprise me.

"You'll take Icel, Goda, Wærwulf, Ingwald, Eadberht, Beornstan, Eahric, Osbert and Eadulf. You'll have overall command, but Icel will be your second like you are to me."

Edmund opens his mouth to protest, but I shake my head.

"I'm your king, and you'll follow my orders."

"I wondered how long it'd take you to start with all that 'king' crap," Edmund all but explodes. He steps away from me to skip agilely back the way we've come, going from ship to ship without any concern. His ability to remember the way frustrates me. I know I won't be so damn lucky.

"Bastard," I mutter beneath my breath, starting out to follow him. He makes it look simple. He doesn't wobble or totter, as I do, every time the wood lurches or groans. Am I really going to take my men and Bishop Deorlaf's men across the wooden structures? I am, I resolve, unless whomever Icel finds to act as a guide can show me somewhere better to cross.

As I step back onto dry land, Edmund offering me a hand, I can't help but force the issue.

"The bastard Gwent Welshmen did it," I all but spit, pleased when fury clouds Edmund's bright green eyes.

"And they're all fucking mad, as I've heard you say on innumerable occasions in the past. But, yeah, the Gwent Welshmen did it, so the bloody King of Mercia can." Edmund stalks away from me then, back through the gateway, curious eyes watching us, and I shrug. I can't deny his logic. But I refuse to defer to him.

I'll get my damn horse across the twisted wreckage, and I'll do it in fucking style.

I don't.

Haden is a temperamental shit. Of course, fucking idiot that I am, I try and lead him across first. It doesn't go well. Not at all. Despite the small space to manoeuvre outside the earthworks, it feels as though everyone stands to watch my failure, Edmund the smuggest of them all.

"You go first," I eventually force Rudolf. He's done nothing but laugh as Haden has refused my commands. I don't even ride him, but rather try and lead him, and still, the damn horse won't put his hoof on the first ship. Not even when I jump into the boat and try and tempt him down.

"Come on, you daft shit," I state, although my cajoling tone belies the words I use.

"Come on. You're making me look like a fucking idiot." For this statement, Haden's head comes right up, almost toppling me onto my backside because I grip his halter so tightly.

Of course, Rudolf's animal, an older horse named Dever, happily saunters beyond the Haden. He steps delicately as the first boat bucks beneath his weight and then recovers under his weight. Rudolf leads him without any problems to the far side. Rudolf and Dever make it look as easy as Edmund did when I showed him my plans.

"See how easy it is," I chastise Haden, but still he refuses to move, his fierce eyes glowering at me. If I didn't know better, I'd think that Edmund had bribed him to defy me.

"Fine. You'll go last then," I exhale with a huff of annoyance. I force him aside as I jump back up from the ship, and then along the narrow ledge that's all the space there is between the riverbank and the start of the Raiders defences.

"You can watch all the other, more amenable horses, do as their bid, and feel like a total arse." My voice is rich with derision, and I should like nothing more than to prove Edmund wrong, but right now, Haden may as well be holding his own halter, for all the good it's doing me.

Instead, I stand and watch as twenty-five other horses all make it safely to the other side. The twenty-sixth has a slight problem when his hind leg is bashed by one of the boats shifting with the tide, and then the remaining men all struggle along easily.

And then there's only Haden and me.

I've been aware for some time that he's keen to make the trip now. He's been tugging and pulling on his halter, perhaps realising that he, who is allegedly the leader of all the horses, has been left on the side of the river. In contrast, those he rules over have made the journey with no fuss. I've been holding him back, and only now take him once more to the disembarkation point.

"Come on then," I command, infuriated when he stops again.

"For fuck's sake," I huff. "I'll just leave you here, with Edmund and Icel, and take another horse."

Whether Haden understands or not, he's suddenly stepping onto the first ship, his front two hooves steady as the wooden structure bobs and then holds steady. Edmund is watching with amusement dancing in his green eyes, and I turn aside, focus on my footing instead. I'll not have him laughing at me. Or rather, I'll not see the fucker laughing at me.

As I step onto the next ship, Haden hesitates once more, confusion in his eyes.

"We've got to go the whole way," I explain, my voice filled with exasperation, as I point at our destination, "on these sinking ships." Why the fuck I'm explaining to a horse, I don't know!

It seems Haden's not much interested either.

Abruptly, he begins to progress forward once more, and it's all I can do to keep up with his increasingly quick movements.

"First you don't want to go, and then you don't want to stop," I complain, far enough away that I can't hear whatever it is that makes Edmund and Icel chuckle so much.

It's a relief to reach the other side, as Haden all but drags me up the riverbank, and then turns, head high, to survey the rest of the riders who accompany us.

"Daft bastard," I slap his shoulder, aware that his antics might well have damaged the way these men view me. They think I'm a fearless warrior, prepared to face any foe. Little did they know that my horse could make me appear like an ale-sodden fool.

"Right, are we all here?" I call. Behind me, the Gwent Welshmen are following in our tracks to be reunited with their ponies. They skip as lightly as Edmund did from one creaking piece of wood to another.

Heahstan and his men are still debating whether to follow my example or not. Icel has found several local men to act as guides, one of them the blacksmith's son. He's an ugly brute of a boy. His nose continually drips, and his face is a welter of bruises where the Raiders have seemingly tortured him to make his father work the forge harder.

The lad, Wærstan, has assured Heahstan that there's a shallow crossing to the south. I think that they'll take that. But for my men and I, it would have been counterproductive, taking time to ride there and then back again. No, now I've got Haden across the mass of wood and broken ships, I'm pleased to turn him to follow the path of the River Trent that will lead me to Torksey

"Get on with it," I bellow at Edmund and Icel, still laughing together. Slowly they raise their arms in greeting, their mouths moving at the same time, although thankfully I don't hear their mocking conversation.

"Lead on," I instruct Pybba and Rudolf. The pair of them are inseparable. They may as well ride together. The rest of the men quickly fall into place as Lord Osferth brings his horse close to Haden.

Lord Osferth rides a dun-coloured animal with deep brown eyes. The horse is a good hand smaller than Haden, and I feel as though I tower over him as we begin to track the river.

I can see the ruin of Repton clearly from here. The fortress that the Raiders built was no small thing, but rather well constructed. It still stands, almost mocking the bodies that lie outside its extent. Warriors are busy pillaging the corpses and moving them for burial. It won't be a quick task, and it'll be gruesome as well, but it must be done, especially in this relentless heat. I don't want to return to Repton and find it fly-infested. I've made that clear.

Lord Osferth is silent at my side. We're all exhausted and yet alert as well. My hand is never far from my seax, once more nestled on my weapon's belt, returned to me along with Haden. I also now have a war axe, sword, and my shield, as well as my helm.

I feel like a warrior again, although I still need to wash my feet. No doubt, when we stop for the night, there'll be time. They've been cold, covered in shit, and then sweating. I nearly don't want to remove my boots.

I almost can't believe it's still the same day, but it is, and it won't be dark for some time yet. Time remains to kill more men if the need arises.

I pass the remains of the burned bridge, pulling Haden close enough that I can see clearly how much damage has been caused, and just what's needed to repair it. Beneath Haden's hooves, the ground is well worn. It seems that many have tried to use the crossing, only to be thwarted by the Raiders. On the far side, I can see no trace of the trackway. It's a clear sign of just how long the Raiders held Repton, and it boils me.

Eventually, I catch sight of Edmund and Icel, leading their force of warriors on the far side of the river, as the expanse of the Raiders fortress finally ends.

"Took their sweet fucking time," I complain while lifting my hand in greeting.

They ride as alert as I hope the warriors and I do. Who knows where a Raider might have gone to ground. Any moment, one of them might jump up and menace a horse. I hope they don't. But then, I reconsider. In their dying moments, it would be good if they realised how skilled a true horseman was.

Icel has found a local man to lead them as well, whereas we have a young lad, who reminds me too much of Rudolf. Indeed, along with Pybba, the three of them talk as if they're out for a jaunt on a summer's day, and not as though they ride to the next battle.

Youth. Clueless.

And then I groan. Ahead I can see, now that we're entirely clear of the extended slaughter-field on the far side of the river bank and my focus has moved away from it, that there's a point ahead where the river meets another watercourse. I hadn't realised. Someone could have bloody mentioned it.

"Bastard thing," I mutter, Lord Osferth immediately alert to what worries me, only then he settles, at realising what it is.

"Did we cross the river for no reason?" His voice holds the hint of rebuke, but I ignore it.

"I fucking hope not," I mutter, encouraging Haden to the front where Pybba and Rudolf speak to our guide.

"What?" Rudolf demands, surprised to see me. I point toward the river, looming large before us, and he nods as though it's not a problem.

"There's a ford. Don't worry," Pybba offers before Rudolf can say anything.

"Well you could have told me?" The words whip through the air, the ill temper too easy to hear.

"You didn't ask," Rudolf responds, and I almost reach out to cuff him around the head, forgetting for the moment that he's now one of my warriors, and I can't do so anymore.

"Where is the ford?" I snap, instead of apologising, and a wary look enters my newest warrior's eyes.

"Not far. At all. Scef mentioned it as soon as he realised your intentions. That's right, isn't it Scef?"

The young lad nods, words seemingly beyond him as he faces me. I bite back any angry comment I want to make and instead try and find a hint of a smile from deep inside my reserves.

I know it's a poor thing, and the fact that Rudolf notices the weak attempt with the hint of amusement playing around his lips does nothing to ease my fury.

"Then, please, lead on. I'll be relying on you to let me know of such problems in the future. Inform Rudolf and Pybba as soon as you realise we're close to one."

Scef nods, still not speaking, his face pale beneath the healthy shade of summer sun, and I turn Haden with barely disguised ill grace.

We're barely out of sight of Repton, and already the prickle of not knowing the land as intimately as I usually do is plaguing me. Close to Gloucester and Worcester, I'm the lord of a landscape and people that I know intimately. Here there could be people watching me, laying down an ambush, and I'd have no clue, not until it was almost too late.

I rub my neck, trying to dispel the unease that lingers there, disgusted when I feel the mass of dried blood clinging to it.

I shouldn't have sent Edmund and Icel together. I should have kept one of them close to me. I barely know Lord Osferth, and he's no substitute for either of them.

"Fuck," I complain to myself.

"My Lord?" It's Hereman who speaks, but I shake my head. I'll have to make do with him and Sæbald as my closest advisors now, Lord Osferth as well, all be it grudgingly.

I swivel my head to see Edmund and Icel on their reciprocal journey opposite me. I ensure they are where they should be before I follow the line of horses being led away from the River Trent by Scef. Despite the distance, I can see that Edmund's face is pensive, as I raise my arm in a gesture of farewell.

I hope the damn ford is close.

CHAPTER 6

The ford proves to be too far away from the main flow of the river for my liking, and yet, also close enough. The haze of the fires that continues to burn at Repton are still visible when the line of men turns to lead the horses down a steep incline.

I peer back the way we've come, considering why the water is so low at this point, but before I can decide, I hear my name being called.

"Lord Coelwulf?" I hasten forward, the question in Rudolf's usually exuberant voice warning me that all is not well.

Lord Osferth hurries to join me, and together our horses take careful steps down the bank, only to come to an abrupt stop, high above the low water mark.

I now see what the problem is.

The ford is an area that's been raised above the rush of the water, by the careful placement of long, grey flagstones. Still, to either side deep pools of water are visible. When one pool reaches a certain level, it overspills into the other. And on both sides, there are dead bodies. Five of them in total.

"Fuck," I complain, already sliding from Haden's back to take a closer look.

"Beware," Hereman cautions from just behind me, and I appreciate then that it might be a Raider trick. My naivety of the situation surprises me.

"Weapons ready," I bellow to cover up my oversight. I'm too

close to Haden, for he whinnies in response, as though warning his horses, as I do my men. I thump his shoulder in apology.

Only when I've heard the rattle of seaxs and swords being drawn do I continue my exploration into the water, hand on my seax. The sound of another sliding from their horse reaches my ears, but I don't look to see who it is. I know it'll be Hereman.

The water covers my feet and while I'd sooner not be there, I welcome the coolness.

The first carcass is almost entirely submerged in the gentle flow of the river from the upper pool to the lower one. The head seems to rest on folded arms, legs extended behind so that the body rises and falls as the river dictates. With the flat of my seax, I prod the body in the armpit, eager to know that the warrior is indeed dead.

When there's no movement, I bow and angle my boot beneath the arms and head, keen to kick the body over. Of course, it's too heavy, and I'm forced to hand Hereman my seax so that I can bend and finally turn the body.

Pale marble greets me, more shocking because of the jagged cut that runs from forehead to chin, clearly long bled out.

One eye is open, the other closed, and the smell of over-ripeness is already prevalent.

"This isn't fresh," I announce loudly, dragging the body clear so that it rests half on the ford and half on the riverbank. It's impossible for a body that lived that morning to have collapsed so much in on itself.

"Check the others," I instruct, turning to reclaim my seax, aware that Rudolf, Wulfstan and Ordlaf are quick to follow my orders.

"Dead, three days at least," Hereman confirms when the body he lugs has been pulled up onto the flat of the raised riverbed and turned over. I glance at the dead man. Young, but not as young as Rudolf, and with a fuzzy auburn beard.

"Armed?" I ask.

"No, a farmer, I would say."

I turn, peering all around me, the sense of unease returned to me.

I'd been assuming that all three thousand Raiders, or rather those that yet lived after trying to capture me, had been inside Repton at the time of our attack. Is it possible that they weren't? Is it possible that even now more Raiders ride the countryside, no doubt seeking out food and easy kills? On poorly cared for horses, with little or no skill involved?

"We need lookouts, in front and behind, until we can determine what's happened here." Lord Osferth is quick to instruct his men, but mine know what to do without further words.

Rudolf struggles with the body that lies tangled in riverweeds, almost, but not quite, floating freely downstream.

"I'll help you," I shout to him, wincing as I see him labouring without any results. The lad is already a welter of bruises. I imagine that, as his body cools, the aching pains are making themselves known as well.

Rudolf says nothing as I wade deeper into the water than he was prepared to go, and hook my hands around the shoulders of the deceased. I try and stand upright, but the weight of the body is monstrous, and I can see that Rudolf doesn't struggle without good cause.

I try again, bending down, ensuring my grip is as good as it can be on the sodden fabric of the tunic that covers the dead person. Then I stand upright, while Rudolf tries to tug on the feet. They're bootless, the white flesh of the ankles a strange sight amongst the green lushness of the riverweeds.

With a disturbing squelching noise, the body comes free all at once.

I stagger, trying to keep my balance, but knowing all the same that I'm about to get a dunking of cold water as thanks for my curiosity.

"Lord Coelwulf." I hear my name as the rush of water covers my head. My legs falter, and my arms instinctively go to either side of me, as though to counter the pull of the water. The body slumps down on top of me.

I push upwards, my knees straining, and then I'm free albeit spluttering and gasping for air, shoving the body aside.

"Fuck," I complain, flicking my sleeves as though that'll force all the water to drain away.

"Well, let's have a look at the poor bastard," I complain, wading through the shallow water to join Rudolf.

Rudolf is torn between watching me and determining the identity of the dead.

I make hurry up gestures with my hands, and he bends to the task, rolling the body with little effort now, only for a cry to rip from his mouth.

"Bastards," I complain as the sightless face is revealed to us, the eyes either eaten by the fish or picked clear by whoever killed this woman, for scars show around the eyes. I've no way of knowing whether the woman was blind or not before she met her killers.

Around her white neck, the skin beginning to slough away, I can finally see why the body was so heavy.

"A holy woman?" Rudolf exclaims, and I nod.

Where she must once have worn a holy cross, perhaps made from gold or silver, a grinding stone has been threaded through the leather strap. It both weights her down and makes a mockery of her missing religious symbol.

"Fuckers," I can hear unease from the watching men, and all of the horses are growing restless, regardless of which side of the ford they're on.

"Pull her clear," I command, aware that we've not managed to entirely escape the need to bury the dead by leaving Repton.

Hereman, Wulfstan and Ordlaf have also snagged their dead, and now all five bodies lie on the ford. All are white. All show signs of having been made a feast for the denizens of the river.

The first man might well have been a farmer, but more probably a monk, maybe a lay monk. Two of the other bodies are women, about the same age as the first, while the remaining one is that of an old man. The women's eyes have all been taken from them, and I consider the possibility that they might have been poorly used by whoever killed them. Perhaps the sick fuck prized their eyes out so that they couldn't witness what was happening to them.

All the same, the deaths have been cruel, their abandonment in the river, more barbarous still.

"But where did they come from?"

I gaze all around me, aware that water is still dripping down my legs, desperate to return to the river. If it weren't for the residual warmth of the day, I'd be a shivering wreck. I bend, release my feet from my boots, and allow the water to rush over them. I might as well have clean feet inside my clean boots, even if the water is bloody cold.

"Upstream, My Lord King," Scef states. "There's a small religious house." He points as he speaks, almost desperate not to view the bodies, his eyes focused only on where he knows the religious house lies.

I sigh then. Knowing that I have no choice but to see if the rest of the inhabitants are well even while wishing to make it back to the side of the River Trent so that Edmund and Icel don't fear the worse.

I don't want to split the force, but it seems I'm left with little choice. Not if I wish to accomplish everything and quickly.

"Right," I state, striding to Haden where he waits for me, the water flowing over his front hooves. He's half in the water, and half-out and I can already tell that he doesn't fancy stepping fully into the water.

I reach for my saddlebags and pull a spare tunic free and quickly struggle out of the sodden one, replacing it with the other. I almost wish I could leave the wet one on. It smells much better than the spare.

"We need men to bury the dead, men to travel along back to the main body of the River Trent and warn the other force of what's happened here. I'll travel to the holy site in the hope that it's not been burnt to the ground by the Raiders."

I'm peering that way as I speak, trying to make some approximation of the landscape in the west.

"I'll seek out Edmund," Hereman announces, and I'm pleased. There'll be no arguing from Edmund if he sees his brother.

"My men and I will bury the dead," Lord Osferth announces and that leaves me with the rest of my men to seek out the nunnery or monastery.

"Sæbald, go with Hereman," I instruct, hoping it'll be the shorter of the two distances because no matter how much he tries to hide it, he's wincing as he rides. Whatever injuries he sustained, are more severe than he's allowing, and no doubt compound his original wound.

"Lead on," I instruct Scef as soon as I'm mounted, and then give Haden a firm nudge with my knees and my booted feet to ensure he knows I mean him to cross the ford.

Haden refuses to move, and I sigh heavily, and then the damn bastard moves, and I almost lose my grip. Why will no man or beast obey, as they should?

Could this day get any longer?

Scef, with a dripping Rudolf at his side, directs us along the eastern bank of the river.

"This is really the River Trent," Scef announces, although no one has asked him. "That bit that goes to Repton is a loop, nothing else. It's this part that flows to Lichfield, and further on."

I grunt, interested despite myself. Quickly, the view before us clears, and I can see a trackway that leads both east and west. Scef doesn't even hesitate but turns his horse to the east, and a cloud of dust quickly envelopes him.

"Keep an eye on him," I instruct Pybba. The man nods and moves his horse closer to Rudolf and Scef, who still talk as though this is nothing but a jaunt in the sun.

My eyes are busy, trying to decipher whether others have come this way, and at speed, only it's impossible to tell. The trackway is baked hard. I imagine it would take far more than the hoof of a horse to make an impression now. Maybe even the huge warrior that it took so many of us to fell would have left no footprint.

There are fields filled with crops, slowly parching in the heat of the sun, but other than for my men and I, it's preternaturally calm, and that once more puts me on edge.

"Ware," I instruct my small force, not that they need it. None of the men rides unarmed. Even Pybba, with only one hand, has managed to hook the reins of Brimman around the stump, so that his seax is ready, should he need it.

And still Rudolf and Scef talk.

I'd tell them to hush, but the words seem to wash over me, the sound merely an accompaniment to my growing sense of dread.

I can't believe I'm the first to realise, but I'm already spurring Haden on, the smell of smoke tickling my senses, as the other men quickly follow suit.

In the distance, a thin trickle of smoke is almost obscured by a spattering of cloud cover, and I swallow heavily.

Whatever happened here, we're far too late.

In front of me, a small collection of what were once buildings takes shape. All of them are now smouldering ruins. I imagine the fire that still burns is all that's left. None of the buildings are whole, none of them.

I turn, gaze at Scef, unsurprised to find his mouth hanging slack in surprise, his hand outstretched as though to point out the monastery. Only it's no longer there.

"Bastards," I complain again, keen to see all that I can. I force Haden to ride closer to the scorched ruins than he might like, so that he argues with me, and I'm forced to slap his right shoulder to get him to obey me.

I notice the residual heat first, and only then see the blackened remains of those who were killed here.

"Damn fucking bastards," I all but explode. It's my priority to bury the dead, and although all signs point to this being the work of a few days ago, I can't be sure.

"We need to make it back to the others," I direct, even though Wulfred is already half out of his saddle, no doubt preparing for the grisly task ahead. His questioning look almost has me changing my mind.

"Surely, we've killed them all, or they've fled?" Wulfred argues. I'd like to agree.

"We can't be sure. We need to get back to the others. At least they've been burned. It's not as though the wildlife will disturb them if we leave them here." Wulfred accedes unhappily, and there's a murmur of surprise from Pybba, but everyone glances warily around.

The sense that all is not right is beginning to infect us. I'm far from surprised.

"Quickly," I instruct. Rudolf rushes to turn his horse aside, but Scef has less success.

"Get a move on," I growl, bringing Haden close enough to slap the other animal's rear end. The horse nearly rears, and a nicker of annoyance pours from his mouth, but then, he's following Rudolf, and I'm even closer.

"We canter," I command, already forcing Haden on. The day is finally coming to an end, and shadows are forming, which might fool the animals. I'd sooner be back with the full force before full dark falls.

Haden lumbers to speed far more slowly than usual. Perhaps he too is feeling the drain of our extended day. I don't encourage him more than I need to. Otherwise, he'll argue with me. I don't have the fucking time for his shenanigans.

The trackway thunders below the hooves of my nine men and me, and I'm aware that we look like frightened fools desperate to be gone from the place of slaughter. It doesn't sit well with me. Not when we're the victors.

Eoppa's words run through my mind. Have we killed the Raiders who did this, or are they still out there, somewhere, perhaps keeping a safe distance because they've seen what happened at Repton?

I've sent men to counter the ship that went east and left many at Repton to hold it for me, and to bury the dead. Perhaps, I should not have done so. Maybe, I should have sent more men to ensure the local areas were safe.

Frustrated with my thoughts, I force them away, trying to

concentrate on what I've accomplished that day, and on what will be resolved in the coming days.

It doesn't feel nearly enough, but I must abide by my decisions.

Fuck, being a king and not just an aggravation to all who would have preferred me to follow King Burgred's instructions, is far from as easy as I thought it would be.

And then, above the pounding of the hooves, I hear the sound I'd hoped not to hear, not now, on the cusp of the end of the day.

"Be aware," I bellow, head down. The ford is just ahead.

But we're being chased.

"Arm yourselves," I roar, the sound of jangling harness and the heavy beat of racing hooves seeming to reverberate through my entire body.

"Fuck," a swift glance risked over my shoulder, assures me that we're not being chased by Mercians, but by Raiders. No Mercian would ride so poorly. How they've even managed to make the animals move so fast is beyond me. I hope the fuckers don't whip them or I'll whip them.

"Fuck, fuck, fuck," the words keep echoing around my head. Only then we're at the ford, and already Lord Osferth, somehow alert to the danger, has his men rushing to form a shield wall, not protecting the crossing, but rather the beaten down path I wanted to take, back to the main river.

"Ride through," I bark, already reaching to untie my shield from my saddle, eager to jump from Haden's back as soon as I know someone guards our backs.

Narrowly, I avoid impacting one of Lord Osferth's men in my headlong dash but allow Haden a little further to come to a full stop. I have men following me. They need to reach the same place that I do or they'll be a crash even without the Raiders getting involved.

"*Skjolde*," echoes from behind me. I know only too well what that means.

"Hurry," I encourage my men, jumping clear from Haden. A flick of my hand ties his harness close to the saddle so that I need not worry about him tripping and falling if he becomes restless at the smell of yet more spilled blood.

All my aches and pains evaporate with every step I take back toward the shield wall.

The ford is no longer visible to me, not from my place on the higher ground, but the sound of the water fills my head, as I elbow my way through to the front of the line of warriors.

"How many?" I bellow. I didn't have time to count. Not in that brief glimpse.

"No more than thirty," is the reassuring response that comes from Lord Osferth. He's fighting to the right, I'm closer to the riverbank, and for a moment I consider my last altercation by a river. Could I do the same here?

I dismiss the thought. The ford is too shallow to drown warriors.

No, we'll have to fight them, or they'll make their way to Repton, or worse, further south into an unprotected Mercia.

Better they attack Repton than anywhere else.

"*Våben.*" The voice is filled with confidence, coming from somewhere to the rear of the Raiders who now face us. I consider that the man doesn't fight with his warriors, and just as quickly dismiss it. No man who refuses to share the same risks as his fighters would ever keep them. Not unless he paid them exceptionally well.

If these men had money, then why would they be attacking Mercia?

"Be ready," I bellow, hoping my voice isn't too out of breath, and that the rest of my warriors have had the time to steady themselves for yet another attack.

How many times must we fight this day? How many deaths must we witness? It feels as though there's no end.

Behind me, I hear the stamp of a hoof and know it to be Haden even without looking.

I grin, a wry thing that almost splits my tight face with its force, and then I grip my seax more loosely, slowly relaxing the strain that's forced my fingers to show white. I will never win if

I'm so anxious. I never have done in the past.

"Advance," it's Lord Osferth who gives the instruction, and I repeat it. We outnumber the Raiders, just. This won't be easy, but neither should it be impossible.

With steady steps, the linden wall moves forward, a single line, spread too thin, but without the numbers to reinforce it.

I expect to hear the enemy advancing, and the silence surprises me until I appreciate that it would be difficult to hear anything above the sound of just over fifty warriors on the move, all wearing iron, and all breathing heavily.

The rumble of noise drowns out even the sound of the river.

We've taken three steps, seven, twelve, and still encountered no resistance, but I refuse to peer around my shield. I'm not new to the games of battle.

And then it happens, from the far right, to the centre, and then to me, our shield impacts our adversary, and the shoving has begun.

The ground beneath my feet has been little disturbed by the passage of my horses and men. It's so damn dry, but the river close by has kept it from cracking, as outside Repton. I note the green shoots that could tangle my feet, but my concern is with my foes.

I can smell them. I can almost taste them, but more than anything, I want to kill them.

But not yet.

With my hand on my shield, my shoulder is already aching and screaming for some respite. I try and focus on anything but the agony sheeting its way across my back.

I've been bound and gagged, I've been a victorious warrior, killing my enemy and Raiders wherever I could, but now I must fight once more.

The foe behind the shield in front of my shield is strong. I can tell from just that first touch, but I'm sturdy as well. No matter my twinges, the needs of the defence override all of my complaints.

A blade attempts to wedge itself between the shields. I allow it, knowing that to batter it away, when it's ineffectual, will distract me from holding my protection tight.

The weapon catches my eyes, the flicker of its edges being highlighted by the fading light of the summer's day.

It's not a good weapon. It's too thick and too blunt to be genuinely useful. It would take a strong man, or a foolish warrior, to try and attack with such a blade.

It does half the job for me, without me even being involved. The warrior who wields such a blade will tire far more quickly than I will, and they've not spent the entire day fighting.

But, it is persistent. As I thrust all of my weight behind the linden wood, I watch the edge work its way both up and down. It even goes a little bit side-to-side, as the person who holds it must move position, perhaps also change hold on it, in an effort to seek me out.

So far, little has happened, other than the two sides meeting, and a few weapons seeking an entry behind the shield of the other. My senses prickle, and I consider that the Raiders are waiting for something.

Is this all a game for them? Do they think they'll receive support from Repton, or from another force that raided with them? Perhaps more than thirty warriors attacked the monastery.

I feel as though I'm being watched. And worse, I feel exposed.

It's not my natural feeling. Far from it.

"Engage," Lord Osferth's cry from my right assures me that I'm not alone with my worry.

"Engage," I yell, my seax already stabbing at the probing weapon, hitting it with such downward force on its side that the blade falls harmlessly near my feet.

"Fucker," but by now my seax is filling the gap, and my opponent, caught out, hasn't moved their hand. I feel the edge slice through flesh, and when I pull it back to me, it gleams with the ruby of blood. Not my first kill, but first blood. At least for this battle.

The shoving and heaving abruptly become more and more

frantic, and I strain to determine if there's a reason for it. Have the Raiders been reinforced? Have we?

But I can hear nothing. Grim-faced, I seek another target.

We've made no progress, either backwards, or forwards, and certainly, there are no dead to trip me as I labour. I need to change that.

But my foe has had the same thought.

"'Ware." The cry from Rudolf comes only just in time, as a colossal war axe appears above my shield. Whether wielded by a giant or not, it tries to take down my guard. I thrust my seax upwards, keen to either intercept it or find the hand that holds it.

Rudolf is there first.

He leaps upwards, his shield held in place by those to either side of him, ensuring their shields stay close together, and suddenly the rain is red.

I spit the foul taste from my lips, conscious that Rudolf grins with triumph.

"'Ware," I exclaim, not wanting him to fall victim to over-exuberance.

Immediately, with the war axe still falling through the air, to land harmlessly behind him, Rudolf is reclaiming his shield. I turn to meet his eyes. There's no fear there. Not at the moment. But then Rudolf has only ever tasted success.

I know it can't always be like that. I have the scars to prove it.

"Attack," I add my urging to the efforts, although my men don't need it.

The push and shove is real, sweat beading my forehead, mingling with the blood of the warrior with the axe, but still, the shield wall is doing nothing.

Surely, we must face more than thirty enemies? Either that or we're weak, and this shield wall will stand all night, only folding when exhaustion finally wins, as opposed to skill.

I won't have it.

But what can be done to change it?

The shield wall seems to shiver and then I move forward two steps, thinking the rest of it will do the same. But a quick glance toward where Lord Osferth fights assures me that's not the case. While my men and I move forward, he seems to move backwards. Do they mean to use my tactic on me and shunt us into the water? I shake my head.

I won't allow it.

"Hold together," I roar, hoping that the warriors realise the danger.

"Back," I order, and as one, we reverse those two steps.

"Bastards," Hereman rumbles from close by, and I agree, although I say nothing. I'm trying to determine how we get out of this, and how we make it a victory.

I don't like a stalemate. It sucks the strength of a man, almost as quickly as a bleeding wound.

"Any suggestions," I ask, but Hereman makes no response. I turn to him when the silence has stretched too far, and realise that his thoughts are elsewhere.

A snaking blade tries to find his feet, and he holds his ground until the edge comes too close for comfort, and only then does he stamp down. At the same time, I slide my seax between the confined space between our two shields, and once more, my blade drinks hungrily. A screech of outrage greets the action, but I immediately pull my seax back. The integrity of the shield wall is all that's important for now.

"We just need to attack them," Hereman huffs, his keen eyes meeting mine. "This can't go on. Drop the shields, take their lives."

His words so closely mirror mine, that I'm forced to reconsider my thoughts about Hereman. I always thought him reckless. Perhaps he has been, or maybe he considers the risks and then acts anyway.

"Spread the word, quietly," I feel forced to point out, and Hereman grunts, turning to Ordlaf who fights at his left.

To my right are Eoppa and then Rudolf.

"When I give the command, we're going to drop our shields, attack them face to face. Let Rudolf know, and tell him to share with Pybba, and so on. Do it quietly." Again, the caution. The

Raiders are no doubt listening, trying to determine what our next tactic will be. I need it to be a surprise. I need them to fall to their knees, exposing their backs and their necks, so that my seax can feast.

Only when I consider enough time has elapsed for everyone to know, do I give the command.

"Drop," I instruct, the word taken up by every single man in the shield wall. As one, we pull our guard aside, the clatter of wood on wood alerting me that not everyone completed the action smoothly. Damn fuckers should have thought about that first and decided who went to which side.

For the briefest of moments, I'm faced with a wall of near-black shields, all of them showing signs of wear, none of them entirely black. Not anymore.

I see helms, shields, and weapons, all trying to make an impact on our shield wall, only it's not there anymore.

A man falls, a screech on his lips because the very thing keeping him upright is no longer there. Hereberht steps forward with quick movements, and his seax is slicing open the back of the man's neck.

To my right, another shield falls, this one seems so slow that I'm sure the warrior will take note of it, and regain his feet, only he doesn't. Pybba takes the man through the back, making nothing of the leather that covers him. A squeak of protest dies on the man's lips.

And then they're all falling. Every single warrior has lost their balance, and the weight of the shields they hold drags them down. Few will have been balanced mostly on their back foot. No, most, if not all will have had all of their weight on their front leg and their shoulders.

I want to stand and watch the Raiders plummeting to the ground, but this is the chance to win, and we must take it.

"Attack," I yell, the cry taken up by every man to either side of me. I hear the rush of heavy feet over the hard surface.

The man who lies before me squirms and tries to recover, legs flailing, right hand clenched around a long sword, trying to snake through the grass. But I finish him, a neat scratch to the back of his neck, that suddenly opens up deeper and deeper, spilling maroon into the summer grasses.

To my right, Rudolf has also taken the life of the man he fought, his movements quick and economical. How much he's learned in the last few days.

But, as I suspected, not all of the enemy were in the shield wall.

I stand and face five mounted warriors, all of them watching with wide eyes from behind helms that show the sigil of a wolf. These are Jarl Halfdan's men.

I rush toward the lead rider. It seems that between me moving away from the shield wall, and coming into contact with him, only one word leaves his mouth. It comes in one continuous groan, and I can't decipher it.

On fleet feet, I eye him up. His horse is puffing, the exertion of the last gallop almost too much for it. Still, I'd sooner not kill him to reach his rider.

I lick my lips, throw my shield to the floor, and then run ever harder, and ever faster.

Just when it looks as though I'll arrive at his side without him even noticing, brown eyes flicker my way, brown beard and moustache making the maul of his mouth seem vast.

But it all takes too long. His hands might flicker for the seax or sword that he rides with on his weapons belt, but I'm already leaping through the air, weapon ready. If I don't slice him with my blade, then I'll unseat him with my weight.

My seax snakes out to my right, the grip reversed, ready to flick across his neck, or his chin, or even his forehead if my aim is poor. Only it isn't, and with satisfaction, my hand flashes and then the air is filled with crimson, and the man is falling, falling beneath the weight of my body.

I go with him, unable to stop my forward momentum. We land on the ground in a tangle of limbs and weapons, all air knocked from me. As I disentangle myself and stand, I at least have the knowledge that I'll breathe again.

My enemy will not.

His eyes show understanding, his body juddering on the floor, and I stab down with my seax.

I'm not a cruel man. He shouldn't suffer when his death is inevitable.

I've not come alone. Although I do turn to face one of the four remaining riders.

Hereman, Rudolf and Ælfgar have chosen their targets, and that leaves me with one warrior to kill. And he's already turning to aim his horse back the way he's just come.

"Bastard," I yell, reaching for the horse of my fallen foe. I won't get to the mounted man in time. There's no chance.

As my feet reach for the stirrups, the other horse is already showing me its back end. If I had a spear, I might just be able to take aim and kill the man, but I don't, and I realise that if I attempt to throw my seax, it'll merely fall harmlessly into the ground.

"Come on." I guide the horse I've mounted, alert to the fact the animal is attentive as it quickly obeys, stepping calmly on the cooling body of the man who only moments ago rode him.

With a firm clench of my knees and small encouragement from my feet, the horse is quick to respond, turning to follow the other.

I don't even have time to look around to ensure that every one of my men lives. I hope they do. Such an easy victory shouldn't have claimed any of their lives, or their names will never be added to Edmund's growing list of warriors to fete and sing about.

The animal has a comfortable pace, and in no time, it's stretching and reaching with every clench of its powerful hind legs. I'm gripping tightly and rising from my seat to ease the animal's path.

In front of me, the other warrior has the smallest of leads, as he turns to crash along and through the ford. Enough light remains in the day for me to be able to track him. No doubt the Raider hopes to make it back to Repton itself, perhaps abandon the horse and swim the wide Trent. I imagine, he thinks there'll be more warriors there to help him, no doubt from one of the many ships moored there this morning.

I grimace, as my animal more slips that walks through the ford, the water definitely deeper than when we went the other way. Then we're once more on dry land, and I hope the man I pursue begins to realise that there's no hope for him that way either.

The other horse is a patchwork of browns and whites, with a white scar slicing through the left side of its rump. A lucky wound, for it could have been much lower, and the animal would have been lame.

As the ground flies beneath my horse's gallop, I grit my teeth, urge the animal to go faster and faster, sure that it can soon catch up with the horse we follow. Only the Raider in front is slapping his mounts rump with the flat of his blade. With each blow, the animal seems to redouble its efforts to escape me. I'd kill the bastard just for those blows.

The warrior's desperation to return to Repton is so much greater than mine, because I know there's no hope there for him. In effect, he gallops away from me, only to face many more enemies.

I almost consider leaving him to find out the truth all alone. I know men are standing a guard on this side of the river, and that they won't hesitate to kill this Raider. But equally, I can't risk that the man turns tail and goes somewhere else. A lone Raider could still cause no end of heartache for the Mercians. He could kill a man, claim his wife and children and live out the rest of his life pretending to be someone else, threatening his new wife and children to keep his secret.

Or, he could ride all over the place, preying on the old and the sick, and make his way that way.

I'll not have it. So as much as I wish I could return to Haden, I don't. But keep on, encouraging my horse, although at a less frantic pace. There's no need to kill the beast to kill a man. The horse is of more worth to me alive than a Raider is. Only then the warrior surprises me.

I had thought him heading for Repton, over the rough ground beside the river, but instead, he reins his mount in and starts to dash toward the west. What does he know that I don't?

I follow. One Raider loose in Mercia is one Raider too many.

A bend in the river swiftly comes into view, and as I quickly try and take stock of where we are, I see the burning remains of the monastery on the far bank. The river here is too deep to attempt a crossing. I'm sure of it. So, what is the Raiders trying to do?

I squint into the deepening shadows. I feel as though I've lived three days in just this one, and then I see it.

Further along the road from the burning buildings, there's a stray rider, hovering almost out of sight. I'm not sure if it's a man or a woman, a child or an adult, but neither do I care.

A string of words pours from the mouth of the man I pursue. I'm sure they're Danish, but I don't quite understand them, the accent too thick to truly be decipherable, and every other word lost by the speed of his passage.

The person on the other horse startles at the cry, and then stills, as the man repeats the shouted words.

My forehead furrows. What the fuck is this?

I don't understand, but the man who shouts suddenly has his words cut short, as his horse misses a step, front legs collapsing beneath it. While the animal fights for balance, the rider is thrown clear. He lands with a terrible crunching sound on the ground, only just missing being upended into the much deeper river water.

I rein my horse in, pleased when he pulls up smartly, and in a tight, straight line. This horse is undoubtedly one of King Burgred's. These bastard Raiders have stolen all the previous king had, not just content with his crown and reputation, they've taken his good horses as well.

Despite the aching in my thighs and along my arms, I leap clear from the saddle, seax ready, and rush to the fallen rider. A wild cry from across the river causes me to miss a step, but even before I get close enough to truly see, I know my enemy is dead.

I look up, meeting the eyes of the Raider across the river. They've drawn ever closer to the riverbank, hope on their face that shimmers despite the gloom. But I know it's useless.

I walk to the body, turn it over, and then wince.

The warrior's eyes are filled with churned mud, a slither of blood at his nose and his mouth, but it's his legs that tell me all I need to know. Neither one is straight, both lie at odd angles and the harsh outline of the whitened bone gleams through.

I bow my head, just for a moment, stepping no closer, and not even bothering to hold my seax in a killing stroke. This man is dead.

A howl of despair fills the eerie quiet, but by the time I can look up, the rider has turned their mount, and the thud of the animal retreating chimes in time with my rapidly beating heart.

"You fucker," I bend close, keen to see who this man was, and now take the time to bury my seax deep inside his chest, where it flutters, alive, but not for much longer.

I turn aside and spit.

The man is clearly a Raider. The emblem of the wolf is depicted on his byrnie, and on a chain that lies around his neck.

This man, I'm almost confident, was perhaps Jarl Halfdan's son, or maybe a nephew. I shake my head. Such a waste, and yet it makes it one less for me to kill.

My attention moves across the riverbank, seeking out the horse and rider. But they're both gone, and that only leaves me with even more bloody questions.

CHAPTER 7

It's full dark when I return to the ford. Only the glow of flickering flames has allowed me to see my way, acting as a beacon that I couldn't miss, a star guiding me home. For a moment, I wonder why none of my men followed me, as my tired horse lags beneath me.

"Who's there?" It's Pybba's voice that fills the night air when I'm close enough for sound to carry, and I shudder, because it's filled with grief, and I fear for what's befallen my men in my absence.

"Coelwulf," I reply, my attention elsewhere, trying to determine if the ford has flooded again, or if the water is low enough for me to cross.

"Coelwulf?" the shock of the reply has me looking upwards, even though I can see no one. The fire is close enough to fill my eyes with afterglows that can't be dislodged no matter how many times I blink.

"Yes, Coelwulf. Why? Who the fuck did you think it was?" A slither of anger slices my words at the strange reception I'm receiving.

A light separates itself from the fire, and then two more, and I'm peering into the faces of Eoppa, Pybba and Rudolf who form a line on the opposite side of the ford. Their faces are white, or so they appear, even from the shadows cast up by the billowing flames and the steady breeze that's turned the water from its gentle flow.

"We thought you were fucking dead?" Lord Osferth has joined my men, and indeed, I feel as though all eyes look my way, despite the darkness.

It's Rudolf who skips his way across the ford, not seeming to mind if his boots get wet, and all but prods me with his fingers when he's close enough to do so. The flaming brand nearly singes my eyebrows, and my exhausted horse is spooked enough to sidestep away from him.

"It's fucking Lord Coelwulf," I don't much appreciate the incredulity in young Rudolf's voice.

"What's all this about?" I demand to know.

"We thought you were dead or taken. We didn't know where you were." It's Pybba who speaks, his voice already so much lighter.

"I chased after the surviving Raider. Surely you saw me go?" When no one answers my question, I realise that clearly, they didn't.

"Well, that explains why none of you bastards came after me?" I complain, allowing Rudolf to lead my horse with one hand while keeping the brand away from the animal's eyes.

The rush of the water fills my ears, and for a brief moment, I can't hear what anyone is saying, and neither can they hear me.

"Truly, did everyone think me dead?" I ask when I'm close enough to make conversation without shouting.

"Yes, they did. And a right scene there's been." Rudolf's voice is deluged with relief and aggravation combined, and I reach out to ruffle his hair, only to stop myself. He's a warrior now. Not a child. I must try, and fucking remember that.

"Well, I suggest you all pay a bit more attention in the future," I state, a spurt of anger making my words sound harsher than they should.

"I could have died, and none of you would have even known where to look for my body." I'm making my way toward the main group of warriors, and toward the heat of the fire. Along the way, I have to circumnavigate around new burial pits. The scent of damp earth makes me consider how close I might have come to being a denizen of one such place.

"My Lord," Eoppa stands before me, his eyes glinting dangerously in the light from the fire. He bows quickly and then reaches up to grip my forearm. He says nothing else but turns to walk away. Funny fucker. Always has been.

Lord Osferth greets me next. His eyes are round pools of white in the darkness.

"We truly thought you dead," he states, my presence belying his words, and yet it seems they need to be said all the same.

"Well, I'm assuredly not. Did we lose anyone?" I turn to Rudolf, who hangs his head, unhappy at being the one to tell me, and then Pybba speaks. I almost fear to hear what he has to say to me.

"Some wounds, Wulfred has been knocked unconscious, Ordlaf has a cut on his forearm. Nothing really, not when we thought our lord and king was dead."

I absorb that but make no apology. By rights, I should be fucking furious with them for losing sight of me. By rights, they should be fucking incensed with me. Maybe we can avoid all the crap and just accept that we're all wrong.

"And the Raiders?"

"All dead, or so we thought."

"All dead then," I agree. I offer no explanation of what happened between the Raider who tried to escape and me. I don't explain where I buried him, or what occurred between the man and the rider on the other side of the River Trent. I wish I knew whether it meant there were more fuckers in Mercia, or if it was just one additional Raider.

Rudolf passes me a beaker of water, and I drink thirstily, trying to assess what's been happening in my absence. Has Lord Osferth taken the lead or my men? I'm genuinely not sure because everyone seems to mingle, the single fire the only source of heat and light, and all of them flocked to it as though moths to a candle.

"What news of Edmund and Icel?"

I turn, hoping to see Hereman and Sæbald, but I can't pick them out in the gloom. Rudolf's shuffle of unease alerts me to what's happened.

"They've already gone to report my death?" I surmise, standing before I've truly had time to sit down, and wishing I could eat something to fill my aching belly.

"Right, we'll have to send someone to intercept them, or bring them back." I don't want to pick on my men. They're all tired, and I'm not alone in thinking that I don't wish to face Hereman's fury and delight combined.

Neither, I realise, do I wish to explain myself to Edmund and Icel. They'll be beyond furious.

"I'll go," Rudolf offers, still holding his brand, speaking into the silence.

"You can't go alone," I state, hoping that Pybba won't offer to go with him, relieved when he holds his tongue.

"I'll go, My Lord."

"My thanks, Ælfgar. If they've made their way to Edmund already, tell him that I'll see him with the sunrise. I must sleep, for now."

A bowl of something warm is placed into my hand, and weariness covers my body, as I spoon it hungrily into my throbbing belly.

Fuck, it's been a bastard long day, and I'm not more than a handful of miles from Repton. I still need to make it to Torksey.

And, I'll have to contend with Edmund and Icel.

I'm pleased that a deep and bloody wide river currently divides us.

"What the fuck were you playing at?" I glare across the expanse of the River Trent, grateful once more that it is so bloody wide and deep.

I feel as though I've barely slept, but Edmund is keen to argue with me, even though everyone can hear us. I want to berate him, but even that will have to be done in such a public way that it defeats the object. Even if he were beside me, and I could whisper to him to shut his flapping mouth, he would fucking refuse. The man is beyond angry.

The fact that Icel is silent at his side assures me that his thoughts are, for once, mostly the same as Edmund's.

With Hereman and Sæbald beside me on the riverbank, I feel hemmed in. It's as though I must account for an action that, in and of itself, was the correct one.

Bastards. Don't they know that I'm the fucking king?

"You're the fucking king," Edmund growls, aware that more and more of my men are coming to stand behind me. I almost smirk because our thoughts are perhaps not so distant from each other as I might have considered.

It seems that Edmund does know I'm the king. Perhaps he's just forgotten what that means. Or, maybe he never realised.

"You can't ride off unprotected. What will Mercia do if it loses two kings in as many months?" Edmund continues to roar. I'd like to stride away, mount Haden and resume my journey to Torksey, but I can't dismiss the fact that Edmund will probably just follow me, chastising me from the other side of the Trent. His voice is certainly loud enough that he'd be heard. Daft bastard.

"There are always more men keen to be a king," I mutter under my breath, too quietly for anyone to hear but myself. Yet Hereman stiffens, and I suspect he might just have caught the intent behind the words.

"What was that?" Edmund barks, his keen eyes clearly picking out my moving lips.

"Nothing," I retort. I feel like a fucking child.

"Tell me what you fucking said," Edmund snarls, his eyes seeming to expand ever wider. If we were stood together, this argument would have descended into fists and kicks by now. I almost wish it could. I'd set him on his fucking arse quick enough, and then he'd not have the breath to carry on as he currently does.

I'm the fucking king, not him.

I almost think that Hereman might just tell his brother what I muttered, but it seems even Hereman isn't fool enough.

I try a different tactic. "Thank you for your concern, Edmund. I'm safe and well, and there are more important things to be worrying about than the fact I rode off without protection. I am well, and the man I chased is dead. But Mercia is riven with more Raiders. They're not confined to Repton. You need to be aware of the danger."

Now, I think that Edmund's face couldn't have turned any redder, but it does, and his mouth opens and closes as though he wishes to speak but can't find the words.

Icel's hand on his shoulder is shrugged aside.

Icel glances at me, his face bland.

"My Lord King," he almost bows. "We are aware of the danger. I would respectfully request that you're always accompanied by at least two men. Even in battles."

The suggestion sounds so reasonable I'm nodding in agreement even before I consider what it means. Two men! Well, in the past I've always had Edmund and Icel, or Edmund and Hereman, or Edmund and Ælfgar. Well, really just Edmund and then whoever else there was. It's not a bad suggestion.

"Have you seen any Raiders?" I demand to know. Edmund still struggles to control himself, his eyes boggling from his face, as they flash dangerously between Icel and I. It seems Edmund doesn't appreciate this more reasoned conversation, echoing from one side of the Trent to the other. I'm surprised the damn ducks and fish don't stop their daily activities to listen. Everyone else certainly is.

Icel has himself more firmly under control, and the rest of my men are watching the exchange, some with a wry smirk on their faces, but most of them just look pleased to see that I live.

"Dead bodies. Many of them. A few tracks here and there. I believe some escaped. We haven't seen any remnants of actual Raider warbands though. Not as you seem to have done."

I grunt at the news. I wish I knew more about what had happened in Repton while the Raiders pretended to rule there.

My focus was on Kingsholm. And when the Raiders were at Torksey, I believed King Burgred when he said that there was a peace agreement in place and that the Raiders would stay in northern Mercia.

I didn't believe it, but neither did I factor in that the Raiders would be out looking for food, horses and probably, women. In my mind, they were confined at Torksey, just as I thought they were held at Repton. I should have thought more rather than just accept the words. Damn fuckers.

These Raider parties, wherever they might be, and however significant they might be, could have infiltrated almost any village and we'd be none the wiser.

I want the Raiders gone. I don't want them sitting down to meal after meal, enjoying Mercian food, or Mercian ale, and certainly not, Mercian women.

"Then we ride armed and prepared," I confirm, hoping the argument has been averted. I've almost forgotten about Edmund.

"Fucking hell Coelwulf, you're the bloody king." I note he doesn't call me 'lord' but decide not to comment.

"You're the one person who can't die here. I think you should go back to Repton, and wait for everyone else to track down the fucking Raiders. Go and wait with the ealdormen. You should be commanding from there, not bloody Ealdorman Ælhun." My eyes flash over Ealdorman Ælhun's men who accompany Edmund. It seems they're not insulted by the tone Edmund employs.

With my back half turned, as though to mount Haden once more, I'm forced to swivel once more to meet Edmund's face. It still flashes with red, and his hand hovers over his weapons belt as though he expects an enemy to appear from amongst the bloody river rushes. Damn fool. I hope a sodding duck doesn't appear. It'll be beheaded before Edmund even realises what it is.

"A king is no good to people sitting on his fucking arse," I growl. "King Burgred sat on his arse. He expected the warriors of Wessex to aid him. Then when King Alfred refused to send more warriors, he expected the fucking Raiders to keep to their oaths. A king must ride at the head of his warriors. And more importantly, I must ride with my warriors."

"Yes," I hold my hand up, keen to forestall the argument. "Yes, I am the king of Mercia now, a position I'm honoured to hold, and one fraught with danger. But firstly, I'm Lord Coelwulf of Kingsholm, and I've always fought against the Raiders, and I'm not about to sodding stop now."

I don't wait to see Edmund's response to my words. The argument has been going on for long enough. Too many eyes watch it. Too many ears listen. What if there are fucking Raiders just waiting in the woodland, or along the riverbank? What if they've heard of the unease that's rippling through my split force? It would be easy for them to take advantage of the rift, and that's not something I'll allow to happen.

We must speak with one voice, and attack with one set purpose.

"Mercia is bigger than one damn king," I complain to Haden. I jump and swing my leg over his side, ensuring my saddle is comfortable for another long day.

My body twinges and aches. My arms are over-strained from the multiple shield walls of yesterday. Yet, I can show no weakness before my warriors, and certainly not if the Raiders do covertly observe us.

Edmund should know that.

I instruct Haden to walk close to the river, my keen eyes raking in the sight of warriors on the opposite bank.

It takes a few moments, but quickly Edmund mounts up and then moves to ride at the front of the mass of men. His head continually flickers toward the open fields at my back. Edmund shows no interest in what obstacles there are before him, and what might be happening on his side of the river. He relies entirely on Jethson to set the pace and avoid any obstacles.

Damn fucker.

Icel is more alert. His gaze constantly roves forwards.

Pybba and Rudolf ride just behind me, Scef close to them. He's silent, other than when Pybba speaks to him about the landscape opening up before us. Pybba tries to draw the local knowledge from the scout, and I appreciate that I should be doing that, but right now, I just want to be alone with my thoughts.

Hereman has taken it upon himself to ride far in front, scouting the land as he goes. I'm sure he'll soon grow tired of that. Sæbald is to the side of me, his face bleached of all colour. I know that he's either wounded from yesterday, or struggling with his older wound, but he's too damn stubborn to say, and I'm not about to humiliate him by noticing.

I ride in silence, ears straining, keen to be the first to know if something isn't right. I've looked toward Repton, visible once more on the horizon, and seen the smoke billowing in the air. It's not as thick as yesterday and is a visible reminder of all that has been accomplished since our early morning attack on the place. Yet my men are sullen.

Lord Osferth has chosen to ride to the rear, with some of his most trusted men. The bodies of yesterday have all been buried. The Raiders have been placed in a mass grave. The Mercians have been individually interred. The work was all done when I lurched back into the makeshift camp last night.

Haden is firm footed beneath me, and I grow tired of the slow pace. I would sooner canter or gallop, not meander along as though there's no urgency to our tasks. But I'm also aware that we all need some time to rest.

I lost none of my men in the battle at Repton. The same can't be said for Lord Osferth and the warriors he leads for Bishop Deorlaf. Every so often, I hear a voice raised in sorrow, and I bow my head low each and every time. I have no problem with the men mourning. I'd think less of them if they just carried on regardless.

The weight of being king, despite what Edmund seems to think, threatens to bury me alive with the responsibilities I suddenly have.

The river meanders north and then south again, and I'm forced to bite back a desire to ride closer to the main trackway that doesn't seem to so closely mirror the twisting path of the river. I don't want another public argument with Edmund, and neither can I deny that the river seems to be where all the action has taken place so far. The Raiders have stayed close to the river. They must see it as where their strength lies.

"Down there," Icel's bellowing cry wakes me from my musings, and I turn to see what's worried him.

"A body, on the riverbank," he shouts. Rudolf rides closer to the river, keen to see it, but I'm there as well, already dismounting, and eager to see who is dead.

The river flows deeply here. The force of the water is evident in the sucking and gurgling noises that reach my ears even above the jangle of horse harness and the loud echo of each hoof step. In the height of summer, and with the land so arid and dry, the river seems to threaten to burst its banks.

Struggling down the thick undergrowth, and grasping riverweeds, I catch sight of the marbled flesh first.

I've seen enough dead bodies not to be surprised. Really, all I need do is check that they're dead. But something drives me to drag the body entirely clear of the water, where a leg dangles in the depths, rising and falling as though the person still lives and breathes. I don't want to be drinking dead Raider anytime soon.

Everyone seems to stop to watch me about my task, even Icel and Edmund on the other side of the Trent.

The body is sodden and heavy, and my arms scream at this new outrage, but I've started, and I'm not about to abandon my attempt now.

Nearer the top of the banking, Rudolf tries to lend his aid, and I'd laugh, but he's the only one keen to help. His hands grip and slip from the white arms.

"Don't be fucking sick," I mutter under my breath. He's just as much in full view of everyone as I am.

"It fucking stinks," Rudolf complains, lips pressed together, head down. The body is ripe. More so than the ones we encountered yesterday. The fact it wasn't fully submerged and the flies have already been busy about their work, no doubt accounts for it.

"Everyone does when they're dead."

"Fuck," Rudolf complains, slipping and sliding. He's seen many bodies before. But of course, most of them hadn't been abandoned half in and half out of a river. Only as we get to the top of the bank, do I realise the problem.

"A belly wound," I comment when the body flops, face-up, starkly white against the green of the grasses. Rudolf looks to where I point and promptly rushes away.

"Poor fucker," I'm talking about Rudolf, not the dead man.

The slipperiness of his insides is no longer inside the body, instead dangling almost to his knees. Rudolf isn't the only one to seek somewhere more private to void his first meal of the day.

"Fucking bollocks," Pybba complains, whooshing his hand in front of his nose, as though he can drive the pervading smell away.

"Someone dig a hole," I order, aware that no one wants to come close to the body. I'd like to wipe my slick hands, but I don't know where. Certainly, I don't want to use my trews.

The dead man still wears his weapons belt, but it's empty, the weapons either taken by the water or discarded when he made a run for it to reach one of the fleeing ships.

"Do you think he made it on board and was then thrown off?" Pybba's question has me turning upstream, as though I can find the answer there, as though a ship will appear with the laughing Raiders on board, keen to answer.

"No idea," I admit, shrugging my shoulders. I'm trying to decide why I felt the need to retrieve the body. Certainly, there was no real reason to handle something so cold and slippery.

Only then I notice something I haven't before.

"This man is fucking Mercian?" I ask the question, noticing the stitching on his tunic, unlike anything I've seen a Raider wear. It's something that I've seen the Mercians adorn their clothes with. The religious symbols are hard to miss. No Raider would think to allow crosses to be worked into his clothing.

Pybba leans over the side of Brimman, his position precarious with just the one hand.

"Be fucking careful," I growl, but he ignores me.

"I don't know him," Pybba confirms, but that doesn't surprise me. We wouldn't know many of the people who frequented King Burgred's court.

"Get Lord Osferth," I demand, and the ripple of my request fills the still air, as though the wind slicing through summer crops. I bend now, trying not to smell the body, carefully reaching out to run my hands over the embroidery close to the neck. The stitches have buckled under the water, and yet I can still determine what they are.

Was this man working with the Raiders? Have I found another fucking traitor like Ealdorman Wulfstan? The thought disgusts me. Bad enough to see Raiders outside Repton. Twice as bad to find yet more traitors.

Fuck, I wish I'd stayed close to Kingsholm.

Fuck, I wish I hadn't allowed Bishop Wærferth to convince me to claim the kingship of Mercia.

"What is it, My Lord King," Osferth's voice permeates my thoughts. I point at the stitching, and then down, onto the chest. A small broach is still just about holding onto the fabric, the depiction of a holy cross easy to decipher with the riverweeds pulled clear.

"Bloody bollocks." Lord Osferth's explosion of anger surprises me. Crouched down as I am, I find myself looking up, and up, and then further up, to find Osferth hanging over his horse's head, just as Pybba is doing.

"Who is it?"

"It's Ealdorman Wulfstan's son. I didn't realise he was missing."

"Did he fight for Mercia or for the Raiders?" I won't assume that he was a traitor just because his father was. If that were the case, people would have to believe that I was incompetent because my father was.

"For Mercia. He fought with Ealdorman Ælhun's men. He must have tried to follow them north." Lord Osferth can't seem to wrench his eyes away from the corpse, no matter how much he might like to.

"How many others were there who tried to get on the ships?" I muse. I've realised that because I was unable to forge a path to the side of the Trent, I'd assumed no others had.

Maybe some of the men we feared dead, are actually alive or were when the ships left Repton. I've not yet seen a sail along the Trent, and I'm aware that the Raiders are more than likely going to make it to Torksey long before I do. Especially with all the interruptions we've had so far.

A voice cuts through the air.

"Bury the fucker and be done with it." Edmund, as patient as ever.

"A Mercian," I holler over my shoulder, not even turning to meet his irate gaze. I know what it'll be without having to look.

"What the fuck's a Mercian doing here?" Edmund demands to know all the same, and I feel my eyes roll.

"What do you think we're trying to do here," I stand, brushing my hands down my tunic, and glaring at Edmund with incredulity.

He shrugs his massive shoulders at me.

"What?" Edmund asks, his voice filled with rage.

"Calm the fuck down," I command, realising that Edmund was never going to be good at leading the men from his side of the river. I should have kept him with me, and allowed Icel and Hereman to command the men over there.

Too late to change it now.

"Lord Osferth says it's Lord Wulfstan's son."

"Traitorous bastard."

"No, he fought for Mercia, not the Raiders. Don't taint the one with the other." I really wish every conversation I had wasn't overheard by so many.

"Then bury him and get going. I doubt the Raiders are busy exclaiming over every corpse they fling from their ships."

I hold my tongue. In fact, I bite it and taste blood. Edmund is right. Even if I wish he weren't.

Already I can hear the thunk of war axes ripping up the earth, and I'm pleased. The man deserves a decent burial, but it must also be done quickly.

With the aid of Hereman, returned to discover what's holding up the main force, I carry the slimy body to the side of the hole. It's been dug above where someone has decided the reach of the river stops, even when flooded. It'll be easy enough to find should anyone wish to claim it. As the black earth covers the marbled body, I swallow thickly.

I have no problem with killing Raiders.

It's the Mercian deaths that pain me each and every time.

"Ride on," I'm pleased to instruct when the body is covered, and I've risked a trip to the water to clean the gore from my hands. Hereman rushes to take the lead once more, and I concentrate on examining the riverbank to Edmund's side. If we happen upon another body, I want to know if they're Mercian or Raiders. But, I also know that I need to increase the pace.

I want to reach Torksey and fast. This meandering about under the warm sun might well be appreciated by my aching body, but my mind is considering what will happen if the Raiders manage to lock themselves inside Torksey. I have no idea of what defences they have there. None at all. I don't, in all honesty, know anything about Torksey. I don't even think it existed, not before last year.

I want to expel the enemy from Mercia. I want them to never consider Mercia as an easy target in the future.

"Fuck it," I mutter, Pybba the only one to hear me.

"It must be done," he offers, as though a party to my thoughts.

"Of course, it must be fucking done," I sigh with frustration.

"Then you better give the order," Pybba states. He has enough experience in war to know that speed must be our ally, not caution.

"Bastards," I complain, just to enjoy the fact I can agree with myself.

"We must ride faster," I lift my voice to give the directive, and a shudder seems to pass through everyone, even the horses.

Speed might save us.

Dawdling certainly won't.

CHAPTER 8

Hereman remains at the front of our party, but Rudolf and Scef join him, as I encourage Haden to more than his jaunty trot.

The horse I rode yesterday has been loaded with supplies, and now rides beside Wulfstan. I'm sure that Haden somehow knows I rode a different horse yesterday, and more than once. He's challenging to control and repeatedly, I'm forced to turn him tightly in a circle to get him to follow my commands. Even small dips in the landscape unsettle him. Damn horse. More contrary than bloody Edmund.

Wulfred is conscious once more, and his foul oaths pollute the air. I imagine his head pounds, but he's not actually complained and so I must assume he can cope with the faster pace. Ordlaf rides close to him, and he makes no reference to his injury either. My men are made of more than just blood and bone.

The sound of hooves fleeing over the hard earth fills my hearing, the clatter of iron a discordant counter to the steady beat. The broad river remains clear of more bodies, but I think there'll be more, sooner or later. How can there not be?

Overhead, the sun reaches its zenith and begins to tumble toward the western horizon, but for now, our course is entirely eastward.

There are no sails on the river, and the horizon remains clear of any fires that might point us in the direction of the enemy.

I find the waiting unbearable. I've never enjoyed hunting. The thrill is not in the chase, but in the killing, and the winning. And even, in burying the dead when it's all over.

We don't stop for food, but rather eat in the saddle, chewing almost impossible with the gait of the animals. Still, my rumbling belly demands to be filled. I know better than to ignore it.

We see few settlements, not so close to the river. It surprises me. I've always known a river site to be a good one, with the promise of fresh water and fish. Perhaps the Mercians here have grown wary and weary of the Raiders over the last half a century. Maybe a location so close to a known thoroughfare into the heart of Mercia is to be avoided at all costs.

Perhaps there were once villages here, but they've all gone, preferring a life somewhere else, where the threat of an early, and brutal death, is not quite so immediate. The ground remains relatively flat, until in the distance a lone mound appears, somewhat to the left of the river.

I direct Haden toward it. I want to see as much as I can before the sun sets on another day.

Rudolf, Scef and Hereman ride with me. I'm amused that they don't wait to be asked or told. I imagine we're all thinking the same thing.

"Let's see if we can track down the bastards," I encourage Haden when he comes to a sudden stop at the base of the mound.

"What?" I ask him, kneeing him for encouragement, but Haden isn't alone in being reticent.

"Fuck," I complain, allowing my damn horse to win for once, and striding up the mound. It's nowhere near as high as it needs to be. Still, on reaching the top, I immediately backtrack and hunker down, my hand extended outwards, flapping, to encourage the others to do the same.

There are men visible in the distance, and two ships as well. Perhaps Haden could somehow sense we weren't alone. Why I feel the urge to make excuses for his nature is beyond me. But I do. Each and every time.

I bob my head high, hoping to catch sight of Edmund or

Icel, but they're too far away, a little further behind us on the opposite side of the river where it seems to swell and triple in size. The bloody thing twists and turns, and sometimes one of the groups is in front, and sometimes we ride together. For now, we're in front, and Edmund's group are lagging behind, not visible. I imagine it boils Icel. I smirk.

"Go back and warn them," I instruct Rudolf, the most agile of us all, and he doesn't even argue. That surprises me, as I once more peek my head over the summit.

"There's two ships," Hereman confirms. I nod, although he doesn't see it.

"How many Raiders?" this is the more important question.

"Alive and moving around? Not as many as you might think."

I glance at Hereman, surprised by the comment. He's squinting, his green eyes tight against the bright sunlight of a late summer evening.

"Unless the fuckers are all sleeping."

In front of us, there's an expanse of flat ground. It leads down toward the riverside at such a slight angle it's almost impossible to determine the land dips at all.

"Are the ships able to move?" I'm hoping they're not, but I need to be sure.

"The one is half sunk, the other little better." Hereman squints again. "They're trying to salvage what they can from the one to repair the other."

He sinks down beside me, his shoulders low so that his head can't be seen by anyone from the other side.

"I believe they're ripe for killing."

I nod, my face twisting in thought as I consider how best to go about it. This, after all, is what I wanted to happen. I don't want anyone to escape from the justice of my Mercian seax. I make my way back to the majority of my men.

I turn to Scef.

"Do you know this place?"

He nods, his face white with worry, chewing his lip.

"They say it's an old burial mound, but if it is, it's ancient and no one has ever found a way in to prove the point, one way or another." The admission brings a smile to my face. I imagine this is one of those places that the young lads try and tempt their friends to enter, calling them cowards if they refuse. I've heard of many such sites, and equally, of many such antics. I might even have been a party to something similar when I was no older than Scef.

"And the land beyond here?"

"The river curves sharply to the north for a while, before turning east once more."

"Does the woodland run all the way?" I point, to where the woods have slowly grown in density, and creep closer and closer to the river, although it can't be seen from here. From the top of the barrow, I can see far more than from ground level.

"No, it's open ground. The woodlands are harvested not far from here. The new growths are small. There's nowhere to hide."

"Fuck," I complain. I'd have liked to take them by surprise, but that doesn't seem possible.

"Well, it'll just have to be a full-on assault," I grumble. Such a lack of true planning sits ill with me, and my mind is busy with possibilities. And then one strikes me.

"Is there a bridge close by?"

Scef's face slackens in thought.

"No, My Lord King. Not a bridge, but another river meets the Trent, about half a day's walk from here. If the rivers run low, it's possible to cross, with care." He speaks slowly, as though unsure and I wait, seeing if he might change his mind before I make the decision.

"I've been there, I know there is. I've used the crossing." Scef speaks as though to reassure himself.

"And on the southern bank? Are there trees that could mask our warriors?"

The plan forming in my mind is entirely dependent on his answer.

His mouth scrunches in thought, and I consider that I shouldn't be relying on his memory to plan my next attack.

What if he's wrong?

"The ground dips away, steeply. They need only travel until the river is out of sight, and then no one will be able to see them from this side of the river."

I grin at him. "So, you know what I'm considering then?"

The lad nods, his eyes suddenly alight with the idea. "But you're not to fight. My warriors will do the fighting."

"My Lord King," Scef tries to protest, but I shake my head. "No. You won't fight, and you won't argue with your king about that, either."

I stride away then, beckoning Lord Osferth to join me. I can see a problem with this, but I'm sure there must be a way to resolve it.

"Raiders," I confirm. "We can attack them. They're all wounded, and we probably outnumber them, from what Hereman can see. But, we need to get word to Edmund and the other force."

Lord Osferth glances from my face to the vast expanse of the river before us. We've not yet seen a possible way to cross, because if we had, I'm sure that Edmund would have taken advantage of it to come and bellow his rage into my face.

"Any of your men swim?" I ask, already assuming the answer will be no. I'm hunting for Rudolf, seeing if he's managed to find Edmund and Icel, but he's still missing from our group.

"We should have decided on some means of communication," I grumble, pacing to the side of the river with irritation. From here, the burial mound, if that's what it is, blocks the view upriver. The Raiders won't know that we're here, but it's possible that they might see Edmund's force if they stay close to the meandering riverbanks. Not that the enemy is going to believe them capable of attacking from all the way over there. Not without a ship. And not without the aid of a bridge or a ford.

Hereman approaches me.

"We need some ropes."

"For what?"

"To get someone across the river, safely."

"Safely?" I state. "I can't see it being safe, not at all." I glance at the wide river as I speak.

"Well, if you want to do what you want to do, it's the only option. Either that, or we'll have to ride back the way we've come so that you and Edmund can bellow at each other from the two sides."

"We could do that," I confirm, not looking forward to another shouted conversation. "Or someone could do as you suggest."

"Yes, but then Edmund will do the same and retrace their steps, and it's his force that you want to travel further than our own."

Hereman is correct. Even I can admit that.

"Tell me about the fucking ropes then?"

And he does.

"I don't like it," I confirm when he's finished. Hereman, as pragmatic as ever in the face of his schemes being questioned, shrugs.

"If it works, it hardly matters if you like it or not!" I pause, unsurprised by his belligerence, but speechless in the face of it.

"Fine, arrange it," I decide. Thinking about it for too long will only make me doubt my decisions and doubt doesn't sit well with me.

And so, I find myself that night, a good distance away from the barrow, close to the river, but I'm not the one chosen to cross it.

Opposite, Edmund and his men have somehow realised what's happening and called a halt to their forward march, relief on their faces at drawing level with us.

"Rudolf, you don't have to do this," I call to him. There have been arguments about who gets the task. I would have preferred one of the heavier men to do it, but not one of them has wanted to. Rudolf, with all the eagerness of a puppy, has agreed without truly considering what it is he must do.

"I'm doing it," resolve floods his voice, and I swallow my unease, determined only to ensure he lives.

"Then you know what to tell Edmund."

"I do, yes," Rudolf confirms, ensuring the rope around his

waist is tied tightly. It's made not from hemp, but rather from harnesses tied one to another. I'm sure as fuck it won't support Rudolf's weight if he's unfortunate enough to get swept into the river.

Neither is Hereman happy with what's about to happen.

"I said rope, not harness. And the other fuckers need to have one as well."

"We can't tell them to get one," I've heard Rudolf telling him.

"Well, they've got damn minds, why aren't they using them?"

To that, Rudolf has wisely stayed silent.

"Right, I'm going," the voice only wavers a little, as Rudolf, naked other than his trews, edges toward the dark, rushing water. There's daylight yet, but the river is cast in shadow. The tepid gurgles and surges have become a great sucking noise in the silence caused by the men at rest.

"Bastard," I mutter, already straining. Hereman has taken the position at the front of the queue of warriors holding the make shift rope. He's responsible for letting loose enough for Rudolf to make his perilous journey, and also releasing enough for others to take the tension.

I should have taken the position, but he's refused to allow me. Now I don't know where to stand for the best, but I know I need to see.

As Rudolf enters the water, a judder runs down his slim body, and he pauses. I know he wishes he hadn't offered. I wish it as well.

But, there's a scurry of movement on the other bank, and I hope it means that Edmund has understood his brother's intent.

But, the harness I hold suddenly runs loose, and I have to clench my hands tightly to take the pressure and stop it running away.

I peer into the water, wondering why Rudolf hasn't cried out, only to realise why.

He hasn't yet stepped too far into the current. It's merely the harness he takes with him spooling in the turbulent waters, reminding me of my task.

"Fuck," I complain, and I'm not alone. Hereman turns furious eyes along the row of men who are supposed to support him, and I'm not surprised.

"Stay alert," Hereman calls, his voice rough. I nod.

"I'm going," Rudolf's voice only just reaches my ears.

"Fucking bollocks," I mutter again. My throat feels too tight, and my breath too fast. I'd sooner face someone in battle, in fact, three someone's, weaponless, than endure this. It feels inherently wrong to rely on the harness for this task. The purpose of the leathers is to keep men and women on their horses, not to stop someone from drowning.

Rudolf sets his eyes on the opposite riverbank, and I begin to work my hands, one over another, as I pull tightly. In front, Hereman releases the rope in time with Rudolf's steps. Already, Rudolf's shoulders are being covered by the surging water, and it won't be long until he has to try and swim, rather than walk.

I know the river must be deep. How else would the Raiders have managed to get their *knarrs* and *langskips* down this route?

It's when Rudolf swims that we'll really need to be alert.

Sweat beads my forehead, and my hands feel slick. I should have worn my gloves, but as I turn to check, it seems I'm not the only one to have made a mistake. Far behind me, Lord Osferth can be heard muttering to himself.

"What's the problem?" I call to him, almost pleased to not be watching Rudolf's dubious advances.

"Nothing, My Lord King. I'm just going to tie the harness around the tree, for additional support."

It's a good idea, and in a matter of moments, I feel a thrumming on the harness, and I grip it tighter, only to feel much of the tension taken from the line. My back eases, and I take the opportunity to wipe first one hand and then the other on my trews.

Hereman's eyes are trained on Rudolf, but mine slip upwards, noting the activity on the other bank. I quickly realise that Edmund and Icel are also devising a rope or a selection of harnesses that can be thrown to Rudolf as well.

As for Rudolf, he's swimming now, but the current is strong, threatening to take him too far upstream, perhaps even into the view of the Raiders. I clamp my lips tightly shut so as not to shout a warning.

"Bloody thing," Ælfgar complains, through stiff lips from behind me.

Scef is watching keenly, close to Hereman, his mouth opening and closing, although I can't hear the words he's saying to himself.

"He'll be taken upstream?" The cry comes from behind me, and I want to glare at whoever makes the doom-laden statement, but I don't.

"Shut your fucking mouth, and do your part," Pybba's voice is filled with resolve. He can't help with the harness, not with only one hand, but he can participate, all the same, making sure no one speaks what everyone else is thinking.

Abruptly, Rudolf disappears beneath the surface of the water, and my eyes rake the scene before me. Time seems to stretch too long, and still, he doesn't reappear. More than halfway across the wide expanse of the river, he's too far away for one of us to rush to his aid. Yet, the harness remains taut.

"Come on, you little fucker," I mutter under my breath. Pybba and Scef are scouring the river, having both rushed closer, looking for Rudolf's head, but there's nothing.

"Look," I snap my head to see where Scef is pointing, but I don't see Rudolf, but I do focus on Icel, wading into the river.

He has a harness tied around him, and it seems to me that the river must be shallower on his side because it takes a long time for the fluid to cover his chest. And then it stops there, as he battles the current with his weight.

"There," again, my head snaps to see what Scef's found. Rudolf has resurfaced, and beats his arms against the water, lifting his head clear.

"Come on Icel," if my thoughts could make the larger man reach the smaller, then already the two would be clear of the water, but of course, I'm merely a man. I can't enact miracles such as that.

My eyes flicker between the two men, my hands tight on the harness as it bucks with the current. It seems as though the two will never meet. For every step closer that Icel makes, Rudolf seems to drift a little further.

"Reel it in," Pybba is quicker witted than all of us.

"Reel it in," he demands once more when none of us makes a move.

"Fucking do it," Pybba growls, the menace in his eyes enough to make other men scramble to carry out his commands as he peers at us from beside the river. The harness begins to slip through my hands once more, and I yank on it tightly, my arms complaining at this new injustice.

"Heave," Hereman takes up the call. "Heave."

Slowly, almost so slowly that I don't think it's even perceived, Rudolf begins to swing back toward Icel, under the control, not of the river current, but of his harness.

Icel flails forwards, his beard sodden, his eyes fixed on his prize. And then, between one blink and another, Icel is gone as well.

"Shit," I all but shriek. I can't lose two of my men on such a foolhardy expedition.

Rudolf continues to come closer to where we last saw Icel, and on the other bank, Edmund directs the rest of my men to keep a firm hold on Icel's harness. I pity them such a task. Icel must weigh at least four times as much as Rudolf, if not five.

And then Icel's head reappears as well, his arms beating powerfully against the water. He reaches for Rudolf and pulls him tightly to his side, before beginning the task of making his way to the other side of the river.

"Release, slowly," and the reins are again moving through my hands, the toggles and catches leaving deep welts in my hands.

We all watch, hardly believing it, as Icel and Rudolf are dragged onto the far riverbank. Rudolf's entire body is white, shining as brightly as the marbled dead we found only yesterday. The harness remains around his waist, and we still hold it, loosely, as it vibrates above the expanse of the water.

Goda sweeps a cloak around Rudolf's shoulders, still hobbling and showing his bruises, even in the gathering gloom.

"Is it still fastened?" Hereman calls back.

"Yes, around the tree," Lord Osferth calls. There's movement from across the river, as the harness is removed from Rudolf's waist, and secured, not around a tree trunk, but rather around a piece of stone.

Only when everyone is convinced that the makeshift rope is secured, do we let go, first one hand, and then slowly, both. The harness continues to vibrate, and then settles, swaying in time to the wind that ripples the deep water.

Icel dismisses the aid of anyone, I can tell, even from here, as he turns and makes his way to his horse, Samson, to pull the wet clothes from his body and replace them with dry ones from his saddle bags.

I sink to the ground.

"Fuck. That was a shit idea," I expel. I nearly lost two men. It would have been my fault if we had. And it would have been under idiotic circumstances.

"It worked," Pybba hears my criticism as he reaches down to offer me his hand to stand again. "It worked. That's all that matters. Don't tell Rudolf it was a shit idea. You risked his life and Icel's." I nod. It seems as though everyone has suddenly become much wiser than I have.

Perhaps they should lead this attack. Maybe they should be named as king.

"It'll be easier to get him back, now that the rope stretches all the way across the river."

"I hadn't considered that," I admit, peering at the other, hastily assembled camp. Rudolf is talking earnestly to Edmund, gesticulating as he does so. Whatever is being said, I can see full well that Edmund is incredulous at what he's being told. I'm almost pleased not to have to speak to him myself.

Only this morning, he was furious with me for riding alone. Now, I imagine, he's almost incoherent with his rage for an entirely different reason.

Only then Icel joins the group, and the conversation seems to become less animated.

"I wish I knew what they were saying," I mutter.

"I'm sure you can fucking imagine," Pybba offers wryly.

"Edmund will be refusing. Icel will be agreeing, and all the time Rudolf will be trying to convince Edmund that it's a good plan."

"Why will Edmund refuse? It is a good plan."

"He'll refuse because he doesn't like the force being split into two, but at least this way, he can see we're all well. With your plan, he won't even have that reassurance."

"Edmund is a warrior."

"Yes, but we are all he has. Even Hereman. Even though the two spend most of the time pretending to hate each other. It's always been the same."

"But he'll agree?" I'm curious as to what Pybba will say.

"He will. Eventually. But if it all goes wrong, he'll blame you even more."

"Well, perhaps I should keep a sodding river between us in the future. It certainly makes it easier to tolerate Edmund."

Pybba almost smirks at my statement, but then he grips my arm as I turn to walk away. I need to eat. These last few days seems to have stretched into weeks, I can hardly remember what I did this morning, and I have no idea when I last ate.

"The task you set yourself is not an easy one," Pybba says, his bright eyes meeting mine. "It never was, but now it's even more complex."

"What point are you trying to make?" I can hear the defensiveness in my voice, but Pybba merely grunts.

"No point. Just an assurance that we all know that it isn't easy."

I feel my cheek tug upwards, uncertain how to respond to Pybba's words.

"We'll save Mercia," I state, as though that was Pybba's point all along.

"We will, My Lord King. We will. But, we need to do it together. And we need to accept that we can't be heroes all the time. We'll fuck it up along the way. Probably more times than we care to admit."

"I," I open my mouth to speak but find my mind blank of all words. Apart from two.

"Thank you," I state, laying my hand over his, and squeezing it tightly. My strength makes him wince, but then, his grip on my arm is far from a gentle caress.

Rudolf doesn't return that night, the colour bleaching from the sky as he argues with Edmund, making it impossible to take the risk. There are no fires to drive the dark back, and instead, I set a heavy guard, determined to take my rest by the tree trunk to ensure the harness stays in place.

I lie, staring at the sky, the expanse of night vast before me, the number of stars impossible to count, the moon a slither of itself. It makes me feel small and inconsequential. It's as though each star is a Raider, and it's impossible to remove them all when there's only me to counter them.

I sleep poorly, the wind rising and causing the harness to thrum noisily. Still, I don't release it or offer the position to someone else.

I'm surviving on little sleep, and even less food, but I've had worse in the past.

As soon as there's the hint of daylight on the eastern horizon, I rise from my uncomfortable position.

"Let's get him back," I mutter, as I shake shoulders, and bring the warriors I need to manage the harness, fully awake.

"Are we ready?" Hereman cries.

"Yes, yep, alrighty," echoes from the men surrounding me, and I almost smile. It's a gloomy day that'll steal the good cheer from my warriors. It hasn't arrived yet.

"Right, take the strain."

My hands, in their gloves this time, take a firm hold on the rope. They're sore from yesterday, but at least it's cold enough that I'm not sweating.

On the other side of the river, Edmund and Icel have the rest of my men in position as well. The harness, tied around the great lump of shimmering black rock, is in the hands of my warriors. Rudolf has a collection of make-shift ropes tied around his waist, but as he lowers himself into the water, I see that this time, everything will be different.

Our original harness stays in place, although it is lowered so that Rudolf can grip it, and pull himself across.

"Pity we didn't do that last time," Hereman complains, his hands free from holding the reins as he watches Rudolf's faltering steps into the river. Whereas Icel barely had to swim to reach Rudolf yesterday, Rudolf all but disappears beneath the water in only a few steps.

I grit my teeth, refusing to allow the worries in my head to gain any prominence. If I don't think, it can't fucking happen, or so I reassure myself.

But, only when Rudolf is back on dry land, do I truly relax.

Rudolf discards his rope from the opposite bank and jauntily steps to my side. He's shivering, water running from his hair, and down his legs.

"They'll do as request," he announces, Pybba on hand to offer his cloak for Rudolf to wrap around himself.

I peer at Rudolf, the hint of a smirk on my lips.

"That's it. They'll just do it?" I ask, curious even though I've got what I want.

"Yep, not a problem. They'll be on their way now." Rudolf points, his white hand appearing from beneath the cloak. I look and see that indeed, the men on the opposite bank are mounting up and moving on.

I wave my hand in acknowledgement, and Icel returns the gesture, with a final glance to ensure all is well.

"What took you so fucking long then?" I chide and only now does Rudolf relax his erect stance, flopping to the floor with a squelch of water and wet skin.

"Fucking bollocks," Rudolf explodes, all the joy gone from his face. "Edmund's such a grumpy old fart. He refused, time and time again. Threatened to come over here and give you a piece of his mind. Called you every fucking name under the sun, and some I've never even heard or thought of, and," and Rudolf's forehead wrinkles, allowing the water trapped there to sparkle under the strengthening sun, "some that I'm sure are absolutely impossible."

I chuckle darkly, turning to ensure that Edmund is no longer witnessing the conversation. He's gone. Thankfully.

"He's a shit," I agree. "You did a good job if you managed to convince him. More than I can usually do."

"Wasn't me. Icel agreed with the scheme. Edmund still wanted to argue, but he seemed to give in as soon as he realised Icel had no further complaints and was happy to comply."

"To be expected," Pybba offers. He's become as inquisitive as Rudolf, and I stifle a chuckle at his blatant curiosity and his listening in on what should be a private conversation.

"Then we just need to wait," I state, turning to survey the makeshift camp. Not everyone has woken. There was no need for everyone to aid in Rudolf's recovery, and as much as I'd like to allow everyone to sleep on, I don't want to be caught like this. Not when I have a plan brewing.

"Come on, you fuckers," I announce. "Time to rise and shine. We need to choose our position, and we need to make sure the Raiders don't fucking realise what's about to happen."

There are grunts and groans aplenty. Even I feel some sympathy for those struggling to stand because their arses and backs ache so much. But fuck it, no one ever let me lie abed when there were battles to plan, and Raiders to kill.

CHAPTER 9

Once more, the sun is rising, as I palm my seax and prepare my weapons belt.

We've hidden the horses in the woodlands to the west, just before the thick growths begin to become more ragged. Now I wait for the right moment to attack the Raiders.

From the viewpoint yesterday, I was able to see that only small repairs had been made on the one ship. To me, it appeared that men and women were too exhausted to work, slumped in sleep wherever they felt safe enough to risk it.

Good. It'll make it easier for us to attack if no one can escape on the river.

The Raiders have not even lit a fire, and certainly, I've seen no one out scavenging for food.

"Let's hope it's not a ploy," Hereman complains beside me. We're waiting, just to the bottom of the mound, for the time that I think will be most opportune to attack.

I'm not sure how the fuck I'm supposed to know, but no one else has any suggestions, and after all, I *am* king, as I keep complaining to myself.

"Fucking hell, Hereman," I state angrily. "The time for such comments was yesterday before we set all this in place."

Hereman turns to gaze at me, shrugging his shoulders.

"Well, I'm just saying. It is possible." His words are slow and not at all defensive.

"Fuck, it is. I just assumed they were all knackered and

couldn't go on. Do you think they expected us to follow them?"

Again, a shrug of shoulders greets my words. I turn aside, focusing on the grass at my feet and not the sudden worry that almost makes me reverse my decision.

I'm a man of action. All this needing to think before I act is not good for me.

"Fuck it. We outnumber them or nearly do. Even if it's a ploy, we just need to kill 'em, like last time."

Hereman flexes his back, moves his neck from side to side, and I hear the audible pop and wince.

"Getting fucking old," he complains. I hold my tongue. I know we're the same damn age. His dry chuckle assures me that his intention was to wound.

Along the line of men, I can see that everyone stands ready. I wouldn't usually advocate attacking downhill, but I want the element of both surprise and fear.

"Right, here we go," I call, the words forwarded from one to another.

My right leg takes the first step, and for a moment, I consider what I would do if no one followed me.

Fuck it, I decide, I'd just go anyway.

I'd rather die alone than with the grudging support of people who don't believe in my vision.

The left leg follows suit, and I'm aware that I'm not alone. Good.

The way is steep, making me wonder why, if this mound isn't natural, the people who constructed it would have made it so damn difficult for themselves.

As I near the top, I bend low, indicating with my hands that everyone should do the same. I was only here a short time ago, but I need to check again, all the same.

I poke my head upwards, eyes trained on where the Raiders were earlier.

They've not moved. Well, I don't think they have. Only then a flash of colour distracts me, and I realise that the one ship has been repaired, despite my belief that no one was working on it.

"Shit," I complain to myself, squinting into the bright daylight.

I'd hoped to catch sight of Edmund and Icel, with the rest of the men, coming from the north. Instead, I can't see them, and it looks as though the one ship is about to resume its journey towards Torksey.

"Bastards," I mutter, sliding back down from the peak and considering what I need to instruct differently, if anything.

"No," I speak aloud, and Hereman looks at me with concern.

"The ship, they've repaired it," I explain.

"Well, we'll just kill the others, and try and get to them as well." His easy acceptance of the change firms my resolve.

"Right, we go then, but make sure everyone knows to kill those not on the ship first. We don't want to be caught out by the dead seeming to walk amongst us."

Hereman nods, turning to deliver the words along the line, while Pybba does the same to the other side of me.

Rudolf is with him, entirely recovered from his trip across the river, and keen to make another kill.

I suddenly miss the wide-eyed youth he was, only a handful of weeks ago.

How times have changed him, and how much he's grown.

"Attack," I roar, and as usual, I'm the first to leap upwards, take the steps that have me cresting the barrow, and pouring down the other side.

I've heard men and women speak of mountains that shake and spew forth hot rocks in a flow of molten red. I hope that's how we appear now.

I keep my eyes focused on where I'm stepping, the ground threatening to swallow my knees and leave me rolling, not running toward the Raiders.

As my focus is on my feet, my thoughts bizarrely considering how well they've healed, I'm not sure when the Raiders realise they're under attack.

A wail of outrage reaches my ears as I step on the reasonably flat ground once more, and it makes a grin touch my tight cheeks.

The fuckers.

We race, side-by-side, reaching for weapons, and shields, carried so far on our backs so that we can immediately begin our attack.

I don't want to encounter a shield wall.

I don't much like killing the weak and the wounded, but I appreciate that all I'm really doing is finishing the task begun at Repton.

These men and women should have been dead two days ago. Every breath they've taken since then has been stolen from someone else who should have enjoyed it.

The ground is littered with all sort of discarded items, trip hazards one and all, and I'm forced to keep one eye on where I'm going, and one on the ground.

And then I'm amongst the survivors from Repton.

The first man I encounter stands proudly, a seax in his hand, but his face is bleached of all colour, his beard a thin and straggly thing, and the smell of corruption rolls from him.

This man is already dead. His body just hasn't realised yet.

I slice across his neck, and he makes no effort to deflect my blow, instead gripping his seax.

"Fuck," I complain, as I fell him, cruelly knocking the seax from his hand.

"You'll die without the promise of your Valhalla," I spit. Already moving to the next Raider.

Hereman has scythed through three men and a woman, whereas Pybba and Rudolf work together.

A hand scrabbles on the well-trodden ground before me, and I quickly rush to the man and stab him through his chest.

"'Ware of the ones who look dead," I bellow. A cruel trick to play, but these men and women seem desperate, even now, to protect those they fought with.

In front of me, a motley selection of no more than six warriors stand shoulder to shoulder. These men look as though they might once have been formidable. Now tunics hang half-shredded, and byrnies have been discarded or show where wounds have already been inflicted.

Hereman joins me, Pybba and Rudolf as well.

Together we rush to meet the feeble defence, the men staggering backwards when they realise how fierce our resolve is. One dies with a seax through his heart, another with a crack of my elbow that sees him fall to the ground, his head connecting with a poorly placed piece of stone.

He's dead the moment it happens.

I don't take that kill.

That kill was merely fate.

Now everyone is running toward the ship. I can see where it bobs in the water, the current already trying to take it upstream, despite the cries of those who aren't yet on board.

There's no sign of Edmund and the rest of the men, but I'm convinced they'll arrive, and soon.

"Take the ship," I order. We can fight on the deck, provided we can get on it.

Another hasty collection of twenty warriors stands to protect those trying to escape. These warriors all carry wounds, and one of them is propped up by little more than a gnarled piece of wood, his leg missing below the knee point.

I wince. A nasty wound. But an injury it would have been possible to recover from. If only he'd been the victor and not the loser.

My warriors have quickly fallen back into line, the screams of those left for dead in their wake, flooding the air with a menacing silence.

Frightened eyes look our way, the brightly coloured sail already billowing in the gathering wind.

"Get the fucking ship," I repeat, all but dancing into one of the men on the improvised shield wall. He carries a hastily found piece of wood, no doubt from the broken vessel, as a shield wall, and it's a heavy thing, glinting blackly beneath the summer sky.

My shield rams into it, but the man holds it firmly, winning my respect.

My seax aims for his exposed ear, the wood held length-wise and not width-wise, and he moves his head, keen to resist the edge of my weapon. Only then do I realise he has no weapon but the improvised shield.

"Daft bastard," I roar into his face, but I can't help but admire him, as my seax finds its mark, eventually, cleaving the ear off in one swift movement. Blood fills my vision, and I taste the life-blood of another, the fluid seeming to fall so slowly, that the man watches his ear tumble through the air with a strange disinterest.

And then I stab, through where his ear should have been, my blade forced against the bones of the skull, trying to resist me until I drop my shield and use my other hand to hammer it home.

"Fuck," I complain, stepping back quickly, as more and more blood burbles from his mouth. The shield lands on the floor, only just missing my feet, as I reach for my seax.

"Sorry," I mutter. A terrible way to die. It takes too long, and I see understanding even as hands reach up to try and stem the flow of blood.

"Sorry," I offer again, and this time I succeed in retrieving my seax, the man's mouth open in a soundless cry of pain.

"Fucker," I complain, kicking him to the floor for good measure, trying to close his eyes with the action. I don't need to see those resentful grey eyes in my dreams.

The twenty men have all been felled, some more quickly than others, and now comes the more difficult part.

There's no natural anchorage here. The ship has been accessed by a couple of planks of wood, running from the riverbank. Those on board have kicked them free.

Still, some of the wounded try and find a handhold to pull themselves on board, and I think we'll have to do the same. Only Rudolf has other ideas.

"My Lord," his young voice, so different to the others on the field of slaughter, permeates my haze, and I turn to gaze at him.

"Bloody bollocks," I roar, trying to find the words to stop him but realising that it's the best idea of all.

"That stupid bastard has no idea of danger," Pybba barks beside me, as we both rush toward the ruin of the other ship.

"No, and he has quick thinking as well."

"It'll kill him more quickly than a bloody blade," Pybba shouts, and I agree with him.

The other ship has somehow, either through chance or good luck, been washed up just a little further upstream than the one that now floats. The fleeing vessel needs to cross paths with the wreck before it can get into the deeper part of the current. Rudolf is standing on the end that juts out into the river, just waiting for an opportunity to jump aboard.

"He seems to love the fucking water," I shout to Pybba.

"Well he bloody didn't yesterday," the older man offers.

I know what we're both thinking. Rudolf is seemingly careless of his life, or, we're both too old, and concerned with ensuring that he lives.

Neither is a sound mind-set to have. Not at the moment.

The wood of the wreck creaks as I rush on-board, a swill of water threatening to cover my boot as I step onto the hull, before reaching with my foot for the first rowing bench. Beside me, Pybba is doing the same. Together, we skip our way to Rudolf, arms extended to stay balanced as more and more of my warriors follow the action, Hereman foremost of all.

Lord Osferth and his men are busy trying to prevent anyone else from boarding the complete ship. A splash assures me that they're successful.

And then I'm beside Rudolf, who, eyes narrowed, tries to judge the approach of the other craft.

The men and women on board, far more men than women, seem blind to the new threat, and no one stands to protect the front of the ship. It seems they believe that as soon as they're in the current, they'll be safe.

I beg to differ.

Closer it comes, closer and closer, and only then do I peer down, realise just how far up we are. It'll be a long way to the deck, and an even longer way to the water, gurgling hungrily. It's black and uninviting, and I wish I could at least see a fish swimming along in there. But I can't.

"Fuck," I mutter as the wood of the ship shifts precariously beneath my feet. I'm half-turning, to complain to whoever has upset the delicate balance when I catch sight of Rudolf. His arms and legs whirl madly, flying through the air, his eyes full with either delight or fear. It's impossible to know.

He lands, somehow, on-board the other ship, arms outstretched, his legs cushioning the move, as he bends deeply.

"Bloody bollocks. Follow him," and Hereman and I are obeying my words.

The sky flashes before me, the sun too bright, the blue haze of a cloudless day disorientating, until I'm falling, far too quickly, and far too out of control. I'm not about to make an entrance in the same way as Rudolf. I'll be lucky if I'm not on my fucking arse.

And then my feet impact the wood of the other ship, and I'm standing. Only Hereman is not, and he rolls toward me, dangerously out of control.

"Bollocks," I complain, leaping aside so that his flailing arms don't knock me over. Then I rush back to him, to try and aid him when he can contain himself, because our presence hasn't gone unnoticed.

Wild eyes look my way, men and a few women, who no doubt thought they'd escaped suddenly faced with an enemy once more.

Rage flashes in disbelieving eyes, and then Hereman has found his feet. The three of us advance, standing as close together as we dare, weapons ready.

Rudolf wears his weapons belt, and it bristles with lethal-looking edges, although he chooses to take hold of an axe and a seax. Hereman has fewer weapons, but the reach is longer on them as he too hefts a seax, but pairs it with a sword. I have my trusty seax, and whatever else I choose to grab from my weapons belt. None of us has shields. But in the confined space of the ship, that might actually be an advantage.

The ship is crammed full of people. Some, I realise, are hunkered down almost below the rowing benches. Others sit on them, and yet more try to squeeze on.

Few of them look eager or able to continue the fight, breathing heavily and struggling to stay upright. But there are nearly eight of them who advance toward Hereman, Rudolf and I.

I don't have time to check behind to ensure others are following us. A sudden splash and cut off cry, assures me that others are trying, but perhaps not succeeding. I hope Pybba doesn't attempt the transition.

"Stay alert," I growl, already deciding on my first target. In another life, he was no doubt a warrior of high renown, but now his clothing is ragged, and his face is pale beneath the ruddy beard and moustache that covers it.

I can't see the wound he carries, but it's there, all the same, evident in the way his seax arm hangs too low, and in the tightness around his lips.

This man had hoped to make it to Torksey and there recover his strength. That's not going to be happening. Not now.

Yet, the ship, as it floats its way into the current, is far from a steady place to launch an assault from. The thud of more bodies landing behind me reassures that there are more than three of us, and yet the odds are still stacked against us.

"Fuckers," I bite.

"*Skiderik*," the Dane offers, and a grimace of relief touches my lips. This man means to fight and die as a warrior.

I make the first move, determining that his left side is the weakest as his weapon is held so loosely in his right. It doesn't appear a natural placement, and so it proves.

My weapon stabs toward his left, the movement quick and concise. I don't make a mark on him, but in an effort to protect himself, he overbalances, the lurch of the ship helping me. His arms whirl to either side, desperate to stay upright. As he falls backwards, crashing into another warrior coming to reinforce the small line of men able to stand, I dance forward, a flick of the blade. His neck is streaming, and he knows that he's about to breathe his last.

To my left, Hereman has taken his first kill, the warrior lying curled around his deadly wound, blocking what little space there is.

Rudolf has yet to make his mark, but I don't think it's because of a lack of skill on his part.

"Hurry the fuck up, Rudolf," I breathe. With deft movements, his opponent, an older man, perhaps my age, mistimes his next jab and Rudolf skewers him below the shoulder.

It's not always a deadly blow, but the man must already be wounded because he tumbles to the wooden deck as well.

The water and streaming blood are mingling, the red a mockery of warm wine.

Ælfgar and Wulfred have joined Hereman, Rudolf and I. Ælfgar growls, his weapon poised, while Wulfred limps, just a little.

"Bastard thing," Wulfred complains.

"A bad fall?" I ask. His silence assures me that's all it is.

"Let's finish this, quickly," I instruct my men. There are five of us, against probably fifty. But while everyone in the ship is looking at us, the remaining warriors are continuing to attack the boat. Lord Osferth has led fifteen of his men on from the other side, and although the ship is moving, I don't think it's entirely free from the bottom of the river.

We have time yet to take their lives.

I crack my neck from side to side, lick my lips, and propel myself forward.

The men and women fall so quickly now that I hardly detect any physical features. My eyes train only on whatever weapons they have to hand, and I make a quick determination as to how to knock it clear or counter it. Each and every time, a body slides from the blade of my seax. So many fall that the hull of the ship becomes as dangerous as the ground of a battle site, and I'm forced to give more and more thought to where I stand than to the killing blows I delve out.

And then I'm facing only Lord Osferth's men, and I turn, the haze of battle dissipating, to look at the carnage we've enacted on those who thought to retreat from the assault at Repton.

I'm panting, my face streaked with sweat and blood combined, but there's only one thought on my mind.

"Where the fuck is Edmund?"

CHAPTER 10

There's no answer from anyone, but a lot of heads swivel, as though we can summon him and the rest of my men just by staring at the place where we thought they'd appear. Pybba is making his way back from the second ship, his movements attesting to his disappointment that he couldn't do more to help.

"Fuck," I complain, trying to forge a path back to dry land, avoid the reaching hands of the dead and dying.

I might have been cruel while I fought, but now that we're the victor, I reach and stab or slice any who still live, their air bubbling through frozen mouths, and I'm not alone in doing so.

The river is not awash with blood, because little of it has escaped from the ship, but it's a pitiful scene all the same.

When I jump to the ground, I mistime my steps and inadvertently land on a static foot.

"Fuck," I offer again, struggling to stay upright. I'm festooned in blood and don't want to add more to my already overloaded clothes.

I look as though I've walked through bleeding rain.

Lord Osferth rushes to help me, but I force myself upright.

I'm not going to kill dozens of men and women only to fall jumping from a damn ship.

"Is that all of them?" I ask. I've not had eyes on everything that's been happening.

"Yes, it is. The men are checking, all the same."

I gaze around me. The barrow stands starkly green and covered in some sort of summer weed that's flowered leaving bright white patches all over it. In contrast, the grassy area before me has been heavily trampled and now sprouts only the dead. The white is there, but it's not the healthy glow of new growth. Far from it.

"Fuck," I exclaim, it's almost as though it's all I can say.

"Hereman." He comes to me quickly, his eyes scanning the horizon. He knows what I'm going to say, even before I open my mouth.

"I'll make my way up the mound, and retrieve the horses, and in the meantime, seek out any sign of Edmund and Icel. Give me five men. I won't need more."

"Choose," I offer, "and include some of Lord Osferth's amongst those five. Their horses might not take kindly to strangers handling them."

"And what shall I tell Haden?" A smirk of amusement on his strained face assures me that while Hereman is as worried as I am about Edmund, he believes all are safe.

"Tell him to fucking do as he's told, or he'll just be left behind."

Hereman's laughter is so loud I almost think thunder echoes through the air.

"I'll try, My Lord King," and he bows and lopes away.

"Stop calling me that," I call after him, but he merely shrugs his shoulders once more.

"Bastard." I determine on having the last word.

Then I turn and seek out Lord Osferth.

"This was nasty but needed to be done. We'll bury them, if we can. It might be better to just set the ship on fire."

The men not going with Hereman are already beginning to move around the bodies, I see Pybba and Rudolf smirking about something, but the burial mound draws my eyes.

"We can put them close to that," I point. There's no time to inter the dead inside the mound, but graves close to it will do the job. I'm sure of it."

"But there's so many of them," Lord Osferth states flatly, no doubt keen to be heading north again. Just as at Repton, it appears as though the dead outnumber us.

"Yes. But I don't want to come back to this when the eyeballs have all been eaten, and the maggots are forming. The stink will be disgusting. No, we'll do what we can. Just having them all in one place will make the task easier."

I think Lord Osferth will argue with me, but instead, he smartly turns away, already calling men to his side. I watch him go, deep in thought. I'm thirsty, but my water is with Haden, and I don't fancy trying the contaminated river water.

"Bollocks," I sigh, beckoning Ælfgar to my side.

"Come on, let's get this done."

It takes too long, and yet as I slink to my arse, much, much later, there's still no sign of Edmund and the others, and the slither of worry begins to grow.

If we came upon this many Raiders, how many might they have found? Somewhere, out of sight, my warriors may be facing a hard battle, and the fact that I'm not there to aid them sits uneasily with me.

The dead are buried, and they've been well and truly pillaged of any wealth they might have had. Rudolf and Pybba are collecting strange coins and delighting in the shimmer of their golden surfaces.

The sound of thundering hooves reaches my ears, and I'm standing, almost before I've fully sat down.

"It's Hereman," Lord Ordlaf cries from his post on guard duty.

"Good." I'm curious to know what he's seen. I'm also keen to discover if Haden has behaved and brought me my water or if he's been left behind.

Hereman's face is far from cheerful as he rides toward me, Haden in toe, fighting his harness.

"Behave, you daft bugger," I call and immediately my horse looks up and meets my eyes. We share a look. What it means, I don't know, but Haden's already calmer and trots to me without further complaint.

I pat his black and white nose, as I reach for my water bottle, waiting to see if Hereman will speak.

Hereman's lips are held tight, his moustache almost obscuring it entirely. When he does speak, I'm perversely amused to consider where the sound comes from.

"Nothing," he says. "I say nothing. Something must have waylaid them."

"Aye," I confirm, trying to banish my brief well of worry and concern. "We'll find the others tomorrow," I confirm, hoping Edmund won't argue with me.

"It might be too late," Hereman comments as he dismounts from his horse.

"It won't be. They're not stupid."

"Well," Hereman arches an eyebrow at me, and I reach out and slap his powerful shoulder.

"You take that up with Edmund, when we find him, which we will."

"Of course, My Lord King." Before I can say anything else, Hereman is leading his horse away, and Haden is nosing at my sleeve.

"Hungry, are you?" I ask him, trying not to think about the fact that Hereman insists on calling me his lord king. I might be. He doesn't have to keep fucking reminding me about it! He can just call me Coelwulf, as always. Rudolf might not get away with such but Hereman would. Does he not realise that?

I feed my horse, and I mingle with my men, ensuring all are well, relieved when no one has more than a cut or bleeding nose, and then do the same amongst Lord Osferth's warriors. At some point, I realise, I'll have to start calling them my men. But not yet. Not fucking yet.

The following morning, I rise sluggishly from my sleep. We've camped away from the barrow and the ship, which still carries its grizzly cargo. I didn't want to burn it during the night. It would have worked as a beacon to anyone else riding through the countryside. But now I need to ensure it burns, and flames well.

Sæbald meets me at the side of the ship, his face wrinkled at the foul stench that's already developed thanks to the warm summer's day and barmy night.

"Poor fuckers," he complains. Sæbald and some of the others have pulled the dry grasses from the ground that the horses chose to ignore. Now we pack the front of the ship with them. They'll make it burn before the flames catch on the clothes and the fat bursts from the bloating bodies.

"Stupid fuckers," I argue. "They should have stayed in bloody Denmark."

"They should, yes." Sæbald winces, his wound still paining him. I peer at him when he's not aware of my scrutiny, but he seems well other than for the occasional wince.

Just bruising then, or so I hope. I'm always surprised by how long it takes to heal bruises. I almost think broken bones are quicker. Certainly, shallow cuts are.

When all is ready, I step forward with my flaming brand. I thrust it into the mass of dried grasses and discarded clothing that's been bundled together to ensure the ship burns well.

The water sucks and flows around the two wrecked ships. If I weren't so keen to burn the bodies instead of moving them, I might well have had them manoeuvred into position so that they blocked the river.

Men stand quietly as the ripple of the flames begins to creep over the dead. The yellow is hard to see, under the bright daylight, but a haze of heat quickly develops in the air, accompanied by the stench of burning flesh.

I cough away the smell and then turn.

"Right," I command, striding to where Haden is waiting for me, being kept calm by Rudolf. "We need to ride quickly today, but warily. Who knows how many more ships we might come across?" I make no mention of Edmund, Icel and the rest of my men. There's no need to. We're all thinking the same thing.

As I ride away from yet another slaughter-field, I hear the wood groaning and buckling, and the hungry reach of the advancing flames.

Ash and bones.

That's all that'll be left of the dead.

In front, Wulfstan and Wulfred take responsibility for scouting. Behind, Lord Osferth's men guard our rear, as we gallop along the path of the river.

In no time at all, the burning ruin is left behind us, and I don't even turn to look back. What concerns me is what's happening in front of us.

My eyes are keen, and I keep close to the river, hopeful of finding some sign of Edmund and Icel. But of course, I instructed them to ride away from the river. Still, the lack of any activity either on the far bank or mine begins to add to my unease. The river takes great delight in sending us first one way and then the next, as though it's never heard of a straight fucking line.

I do spot ever-growing numbers of bodies floating in the river, or discarded along the riverbank.

"Bastards," I complain, having called a halt and dragged the first body clear of the river rushes to ensure he's a Raider, not a Mercian.

There's a stab wound in the man's chest, potentially recoverable from, but since then it seems his allies have decided to end his life. A jagged cut marks his throat, and as I turn the body, a fish flops through the cut, and I turn aside and gag.

"Bloody bollocks," Rudolf comments, his voice tight with disgust, whether at the fish or the wound I'm not sure.

A broken-down stone wall close to the river, allows me to leave the body covered, if not buried beneath the earth.

The second body, floating in the centre of the river, is beyond the reach of any of us. And then there are more and more. All of them face down.

"What the fuck?" I'm not alone in being concerned. These people, I must assume, are all Raiders. Why I consider, would they have been allowed to escape, only to be killed later? Unless of course, all of them have died from their wounds. But I don't think that's the case, not if the body we did pull from the water is anything to go by.

"It seems they had no need for the wounded," Lord Osferth has been riding amongst his men, but now brings his horse close to Haden. Haden huffs but stays firmly under my command. Cantankerous brute.

"Indeed. Or, they hoped to pollute the water and kill us that way."

"Or they encountered the other men?"

I've considered the possibility, but unless Edmund and Icel have found themselves a ship and sailed against the Raiders, I can't determine why there would be so many bodies in the river.

"They lacked time to bury them, I suppose," I consider, but I know it's not the truth.

My unease continues to grow with each and every body found in the river.

I'm a man of action, not of deep thought. If this is meant as a warning, then I take it as one. If it's anything else, I'm not sure what is being conveyed.

Abruptly, the river opens up before us. I can see where Edmund and the rest of my men should have crossed over to the northern bank, at a spot just below where the rush of another river joins the Trent.

There's nothing to show that my men did cross. There's nothing to show that they didn't.

There is, however, another abandoned ship, snarled up in the shallow water.

"Fuck," I encourage Haden and then slide from the saddle, keen to get a closer look.

This ship, like the one we encountered yesterday, has been wrecked, no doubt, because of lower water level. It's unexpected where two such vast rivers join together. They probably didn't see it coming, or perhaps they did and could do nothing to halt its progress.

A handful of bodies greet me from inside the ship, but I can tell that many more have escaped.

"Chance then," I consider the bodies I've already seen. Not a warning, but just the aftermath of the death of yet another ship.

"They've continued on foot," I nod grimly at Lord Osferth's comment. This isn't what I wanted to hear.

"But which side of the river? And where are Edmund and the rest of the men?"

There are just too many questions, and I have no answer for any of them.

"Fuck, my feet are wet," I growl, only now aware of the water seeping inside my boots.

Frustrated, I stamp clear of the shallower water, leading Haden. Hereman, Pybba and Rudolf are exploring the ground, Wulfstan and Wulfred far in front and doing the same. My eyes though, keep sweeping the far bank. Is it possible that all this happened yesterday? Could Edmund and Icel have attacked the ship and brought about the deaths of these Raiders? And if they did, why are they not here, now, to tell me about it?

I bite my lip, frustrated at how little I know and how much I must try and follow the reasoning of others.

"A host certainly went this way north," Wulfstan rides close to me to offer his conclusions.

"Are there any more dead?" I ask.

"Not yet. The ones who could walk would have been the healthier ones."

"We need to check over there," I conclude, not dismissing Wulfstan's words, but realising that the same must be determined for the southern bank as the northern.

We've seen no Mercians, other than those who were dead, and the landscape feels deserted and bare. It would be too easy for the Raiders to walk through the kingdom unhindered.

"Sæbald, Ælfgar and Ordlaf, check the southern bank. Look out for any signs of Raiders. I need to know which way they went. And see if you can find sodding Edmund as well."

Edmund's continued absence is plaguing me.

Does he expect me to somehow know what he's been doing? If he does, then I've failed because I have no idea.

Leading Haden, I stride some way along the river, eyes on the ground, keen to decipher what I can. I hear the noise of the horses crossing the ford, and also the sound of Lord Osferth instructing his men to set the ship alight. I have no problem with that. We've wasted too much time burying the dead as it is, and the smoke from the other burning ship is still just about visible further downstream.

Sæbald, Ælfgar and Ordlaf mirror my actions, only on the other side of the river. I'm surprised by how quickly the water grows deep again, and also starts to increase in width as the rivers finally join. Before too long, I can see my warriors but not hear their conversation.

The riverbank shows signs of others passing by, the odd piece of discarded fabric or a glittering piece of some discarded weapon or jewel. Still, there's nothing as obvious as an abandoned ship filled with bodies.

Haden bumps my shoulder, and I stand, gaze into the distance. I wish I knew what was happening there. Truly I do. I'm also curious as to how we're supposed to cross this new river. Scef hasn't mentioned it, and I realise I'm once more relying on his to help me.

"Right, we'll go back," I agree, my eyes seeking out Sæbald and Ælfgar. Ordlaf is lost to my sight, but the men show no concern. I holler to them, but it seems my battle voice is lost over the expanse of the rushing river. I hear the plop of a fish dancing above the water, but nothing else. Well, at least someone is listening to me.

I'll just have to hope that the others realise I'm turning back and that they should do the same.

The low water quickly comes into sight. The ship is burning, not brightly, but rather smoky, and vast swathes of black reach into the sky. I sigh. I would sooner the wood had been less damp, but it was a damn boat, in the river, what did I expect to happen?

I half hope that Edmund will see it and come to see what's happening, but equally, I realise he's more likely to stay away. Rushing toward a blazing building is a sure way to finding an enemy, not an ally.

As I get closer, a figure appears from beside me, and although my hand reaches for my seax, the move isn't completed because it's Rudolf who shadows me.

"No one else available?" I ask him with a querulous note in my voice.

"Nope, none of the other fuckers wanted to arse around having another fight. They're all knackered." The tone is as light as I've always come to expect it, but it masks something else. I don't ask him what. I know what it is. I've carried it for many years.

A sudden commotion reaching my ears does have me reaching for my seax, Rudolf as well.

"What the fuck is it now?"

From the other side of the river, Sæbald, Ordlaf and Ælfgar have erupted from behind a mass of trees overhanging the river, and they rush toward the ford. I leap onto Haden's back, keen to meet them and find out what's happening.

"'Ware," I bellow to the men standing around, watching the ship burn, and immediately the cry is repeated amongst them all. By the time I arrive back at the burning boat, everyone is armed, as we wait for the three men to appear.

They're all shouting, but I can't hear the words, not with the roar of the fire and the rush of the river.

Frustrated, I knee Haden forward, to go to them, only there's a hand on my harness, and I know of only one person Haden would allow to get so close to him.

"Rudolf, let the fuck go," I growl.

"Sorry, can't do that. You don't rush into danger when others are rushing from it. I believe you taught me that."

I try and encourage Haden away, even consider digging my heels in his flanks, but then I don't because I can already see the problem.

"Shield wall," I bellow, yanking on Haden's reins so that he turns quickly, and steps back onto dry land.

Already, Lord Osferth's men are reaching for shields, and

standing shoulder to shoulder.

Their horses have been left untied, to tug at the worn grass beneath their hooves. As quickly as I can, I do the same to Haden, sliding from his back, and slapping him to have him move away. Dever follows Haden, and then we're just waiting.

Sæbald is barrelling toward me, too fast to be able to stop. Eoppa is too slow to react, standing at my right, and so I push him, hard. He overbalances, somehow managing to fall backwards, and not forwards into the rushing path of Ælfgar who follows hard on Sæbald's heels.

"Where's Ordlaf?" I roar.

I can't see him, but then there's a burning ship blocking the way.

"Here, My Lord King," Ordlaf answers me himself from somewhere far down the line of waiting Mercians.

"Good," I mutter to myself, keen to face whoever threatens my men.

As fast as the three rode, I expect the Raiders to appear just as quickly. But they don't. Indeed, I'm all but thinking the three were fools when the Raiders finally appear.

There are more of them than I'd like to see, perhaps as many as forty. They all walk, each mirroring the movements of the others. I realise that these men are part of a jarl's favoured warband. The warriors know how to fight, and also, how to survive in a hostile land.

I'll kill them all, for sure as shit, they've done that to my missing men.

At least half of the men have shields, and quickly, I watch them realise the force they face is far greater than they imagined. As though trained in the action, all those with a shield stand in front of someone who doesn't. It means their shield wall is half as wide as ours but twice as deep.

I swallow heavily, trying to think of a quick way out of this fight.

But I don't see that there is one, not unless the river somehow aids us.

As though reading my thoughts, I glance down, noticing as I do that the low water level has actually fallen even further.

"No help from there then," I complain.

"Wait for them," I order. I want our opponents to make the first move. The burning ship will be part of our defence, or so I hope, but it'll mean that our shield wall will contract and then expand again, provided the Raiders choose this crossing as the battleground.

My feet are drenched, my boots slick over the stony bottom. They've recovered from what befell me in Repton, but it's not because I've been kind to them.

I would almost wish the Raiders gone, but there's a battle to be fought, and men who need killing.

"My Lord Coelwulf," I don't expect to be hailed by one of the warriors facing me. Luckily, Hereman's quick thinking aids me.

"What of it?" he snarls from his position further along the row of shields, to the left of me.

"I would speak with you. You can still accept the four jarls as lords of Mercia. They would forgive this insurrection. Eventually."

Laughter greets those words and not just mine.

I'm incredulous that the Raiders still believe they hold Mercia.

"Jarl Halfdan would rather an ally, than an enemy, as I told the other Mercians." The man coughs, a swirl of toxic black smoke blowing into his face as though to drown out his words.

"Jarl Halfdan can have his death, not an alliance." This time it's Pybba who replies, and I see the confusion in the Raider's body language. This clearly is not a ploy they've ever encountered before.

But the man doesn't open his mouth to speak again, merging back into the mass of shields. It'll be a battle then.

I've not missed the words the man spoke. Does he mean Edmund? Has Edmund made an alliance with Jarl Halfdan. Or did Edmund and Icel attack this force as well? I wish I could ask, but I can't. I won't show weakness.

My seax is barely clean of the blood I shed yesterday. Now I'll have to use it again.

When this altercation is won, I'll need to sharpen my blade. And more importantly, for me, get my boots dry again. Somehow.

Yet the Raiders don't immediately strike. If I didn't know better, I might have thought they were considering whether to attack or not. But, they have no choice now they've made themselves so visible. They can either meet death here or running through the fields, hacked down by blades from above them.

I know what option I'd choose.

And then they're moving forward, the trickle of water covering their boots, and making its way slowly up their legs.

"Be ready," I warn, bending my knees so that I'm prepared for this new confrontation.

"Shields," I order, and we all stand, guard raised, waiting for the Raiders to reach us. I'm not going to them. I'm not going to make it easy. They can fucking come to us.

My breathing is even, my hand tight on my shield, the other loose on my seax.

And yet time draws out.

"Fuck this," I eventually announce, dropping my defence to see what the Raiders are doing.

They're still there, but they've faltered, as though waiting for someone to direct them.

I look along the row, trying to determine if they do have a leader. But it's impossible to decipher. They all look the same. No one wears a uniquely elaborate helm or carries a fine blade.

Admittedly, I don't either, and I give the order to my men. Still, I would expect there to be some way to determine the real leader of the Raiders. They've never struck me as particularly good at guile and subterfuge.

A gust of wind sends the flames from the burning ship spiralling into the summer sky, and I grimace. I'm not going to stand here all day. I've got more important things to do.

"Where are my other men?" I bellow, at least determined to

have an answer to that. But silence greets my question. I wish Wærwulf were here. He speaks the best Danish and could ask the question in their tongue.

And then, from behind, I hear the sound of hooves moving through the water, and watch as the Raiders part to allow a warrior on horseback through.

But it's not the warrior, with his elaborate helm, that seems to sprout the wings of a raven from either side that concerns me, but rather the horse he rides.

I swallow heavily. I'd know that chestnut stallion anywhere.

My heart freezes, but my body is already moving of its own volition. I didn't want to lose the advantage, but now I need to kill all of these men. Each and every one of them, and I'll do it alone if I have to.

My seax high, my shield in front of me, I dash forward, careful of the slippery riverbed but determined to make a kill.

The first of my opponents is far from ready, his guard lowered as he looks at the mounted warrior. I slice his nose clear from his face before his eyes are even on me. I follow the blow with a stabbing motion straight into his open mouth, hammering the handle of the blade so that it digs deep, and quickly. He crumbles, his shield dropping from a lifeless hand and into the gurgling water.

"Bastard," I offer, slicing my blade before me, grip reversed in an instant, so that I can stab the man behind him. This warrior has no shield but fumbles for a seax in his weapons belt. I carve his throat while his hand still flounders. He falls at my feet, and I turn. I want the mounted warrior as my next kill. I want to kill him with my bare hands, ensuring I'm the man to demand retribution for killing my oldest friend.

But, the rest of my men have joined me. Eoppa is hacking away at two men directly to my right, the enemy defensive line disintegrating more quickly than a piece of vellum under water. I pause, time my involvement perfectly. As the second man raises his arm to attack Eoppa's back, I lunge forward, pierce him below the shoulder, forcing the seax ever deeper, keen to ensure he's dead.

"Finish him," I growl at Eoppa, as the man stumbles heavily, and the other warrior pauses for just a moment too long to watch his probable friend's death throes. Eoppa takes the opportunity to attack his exposed right arm.

The mounted warrior has hardly moved, even though the smoke from the blazing ship is almost so thick it's impossible to take a deep breath.

I stride through the water, noting as I do that it's turning to the tan of sandstone, and also starting to ride higher. It could become even more of a problem than it already is.

But I want that mounted warrior, and I want that fucking horse back in my hands.

Pybba abruptly barges into me. I hold out my arms, ensuring his balance has returned to him before stepping around him and adding another to my list of kills. The man, his face blackened by bruising, leers at Pybba, no doubt thinking him an easy target. I'd allow Pybba to finish the man, but I can't lose another of my warriors, not when it seems so many are lost to me already.

"My thanks," Pybba huffs.

"Kill all the fuckers," I growl, and immediately, he's chosen his next target and moved back amongst the pockets of fighting.

Why the mounted man remains is beyond me. Surely, he should have realised by now that there's no chance of success, but still, he lingers, despite the animal's obvious distress.

"Bastard." My seax slices the face of yet another enemy. The grey eyes of the man turn from triumph to horror at the move. I bend, hook my arms around Wulfred, floundering in the water, a bloody gash on his right hand, and again, ensure he can stand and fight before I move on.

Ahead, I can hear Hereman's roar.

"Fuck." I knew Hereman would go for the enemy, and it should be his kill, but equally, the mounted warrior needs to be mine as well.

Rudolf dashes passed me, in a flurry of too-long arms, and too many elbows, but I don't follow his progress. Instead, I finally have full sight of the mounted Raider.

He fights Hereman, the other man clearly picking him as his target from the very beginning.

Jethson, Edmund's horse, is unhappy with his strange rider. That much is clear to see. The animal bucks and tries to dislodge the man. I could just stand and watch Hereman and Jethson kill the warrior with his elaborate helm. But I need to be the one to open his veins and watch him bleed to death before me.

With as little thought as Rudolf attempting such a feat, I lean backwards, tense all of my muscles, and then release myself. I aim directly at my opponent, my seax supple in my hand as my feet leave the riverbed.

And then I'm flying through the air, and as the air is expelled from my lungs, my arms wrap around my foe, and my legs straddle Edmund's horse.

"There's no fucking way to escape now," I exhale, my seax already at the man's neck as Jethson shuffles forward and backwards, upset with the additional weight.

"Fuck," the word bursts from my mouth, and I'm turning to face an irate and equally horrified, Hereman, his blade digging into my leg, just above my ankle. He didn't know what I was going to do. All the same, he's the first man in a long time to actually get his blade beyond my guard.

I wince, but my seax stays steady, as Hereman's jaw drops and he immediately pulls his weapon back. Neither of us misses the flash of red that shimmers along the wet edge.

"Bastard," but my concern is with the other man.

"Where the fuck, are my men?" I exhale into his ear, only he's trying to evade my embrace almost with no thought for his safety.

"Damn," I complain, my leg pulsing with pain. I know my seax is close to his neck, but I can't see beyond the bulk of his body. His stench is overwhelming, and abruptly, Jethson has had enough.

With nothing to hold on to but my enemy, we're both falling through the air. The flicker of the continuing battle crosses my vision before I'm unceremoniously dumped into the water, the air gone from my lungs.

"Shit," it's Hereman who recovers the quickest, slapping the heaving sides of Jethson and encouraging him out of the way, as he seems to stand to assess the success of his action, sides heaving.

"Fuck, fuck, fuck." Only then do I realise what so distresses Hereman.

"Shit," my seax has all but severed the man's head while we were falling, and I've not even noticed. Blood pulses all over me, and I struggle to stand and fling the body away from me. I watch, furious, as the water covers the body, hair flowing freely from beneath the intricate helm.

I'll get no answer to my question, not now.

Only then do I become aware of the well of silence around me.

I turn, meeting the eyes of Pybba, Osferth and Rudolf. No one is fighting. There's no one left to fight, and everyone watches me.

"Fuck it," I protest, all but banging my fists on my bloodied chest. I strike out, left foot first, to make it back to the far side of the riverbank, keen to abandon the body, only to stumble, my leg seemingly stuck on a piece of stone.

Hereman is there, nearly managing to catch me before I splash once more into the water. I gasp, the unexpected mouthful of water, unwelcome, as I gasp for air, my leg pulsing.

Strong arms under my shoulders bring me back to the surface, and then more hands are rummaging around me, and I'm being pulled from the water and toward where Haden waits for me.

The silence unnerves me, as does the throbbing that seems to come in waves and waves.

"I'm alright," I complain, horrified by the reediness of my voice.

I pass Jethson, head tossing, hooves busy as he lingers in the shallows, unwilling to go any closer to the burning ship.

"We'll carry you," Hereman instructs, no argument in his voice. I want to argue and demand to be allowed to make my way there. But I find my energy flagging.

How fucking deep did Hereman cut me, all be it unintentionally?

It seems as though the river crossing is much, much longer than I remember when I could walk that way myself. I'm relieved when I'm hefted onto dry land, soft grasses beneath me.

"Here, let me look." Hereman, drenched and dripping with just as much blood as I am, moves quickly to hike my trews and gaze at the wound. I see a mass of tangled flesh and a river of flowing blood.

"Bloody bollocks," Pybba exclaims. I can tell I'm being shadowed by my men so that Lord Osferth and his own can't see my wound.

"Cover it," I complain, but Hereman is shaking his head, unhappiness evident in the slump of his shoulders. He stands quickly, reaching for his knife, not his seax, but Pybba moves to block him.

"I'll do it," I hear him mutter. My head is roaring with the sound of my rapidly beating heart, and I can feel my breath coming too quickly.

"Drink this," Rudolf tries to thrust a drinking bottle into my hand, and when I don't take it, holds it to my lips.

The drink isn't water, and it burns on the way down, the bitterness seeming to drive back my pain and steady my heart all at the same time.

"Fuck," I complain. My leg still pulses, but the blood flow is reducing thanks to a tight piece of cloth just below my knee.

"Bastard thing," I lean forward, almost touching it. Then Pybba is before me, his face grim, and the heat from his blade rippling the air.

"Do it," I direct, immediately aware that this is the quickest way to permanently stop the bleeding, even if it leaves me with an ugly scar.

"Do it," I demand through gritted teeth. Then my head is arched backwards, my eyes taken by the view of two swallows flying high overhead, as I try not to buck against the searing heat held against my skin.

I wish I'd swallowed more of the vile drink. I wish I knew where Edmund was. But more, I wish Hereman hadn't tried to slice my foot from my leg. In those few moments, I consider how I'll take my revenge as the smell of sizzling flesh reaches my nostrils, and all I want to do is gag.

But then, the pain is gone. It's replaced by a thrumming from my leg all the way up the left side of my body.

"Fucking bastards," I expel, facing all of my warriors once more.

I meet Hereman's worried eyes but say nothing further. No one need know. Better to have them think an enemy did this to me than Hereman.

He nods once and then turns away, his unhappiness evident in his slouched shoulders, and desire to be away from us all.

"My Lord King?" Lord Osferth's voice is high as he finally casts his eyes over me.

"Ah, you are well?" he asks, and I nod, even though I feel as though I'm on fire.

"Help me up," I instruct Rudolf and Pybba. I test the weight of my body on my left leg and realise I'll have to limp for a few days or wince with every step. Probably both.

"A glancing blow," I offer, my lips stretching far too tightly for it to be called a smile.

"The Raiders?" I ask, keen to have the attention away from me.

"All dead, My Lord King."

"My other warriors?" Lord Osferth shakes his head, as behind him, I see a flurry of sparks from the fire fly into the air.

"No sign of them," he confirms, regret in his voice.

"Fuck. But at least the Raiders are all dead."

Lord Osferth looks as though he wants to say more, but I turn to move away, slower than usual. I feel sick to my stomach and want nothing more than a few moments to recollect myself.

"We'll add the bodies to those that already burn."

"Good, we don't want the river polluted further," I confirm, grateful when Rudolf hands me a waterskin filled with cold water. I swallow it hungrily. I might not want to eat anytime soon, and certainly not anything that smells as bad as my flesh, but I need water, and probably dry clothes.

I totter as I tip my head back, unbalancing myself all over again, grateful for a strong arm on my back.

"We ride on?" Lord Osferth asks. I focus on the warriors busily bringing the dead to the funeral pyre. The bodies haven't been stripped, but I can see enough to know that the men are well and truly dead.

"Yes, we ride on," I confirm, although my thoughts are consumed with what's befallen my men. "We need to make it to Torksey, no matter what."

"Tell me," and I turn to find Scef watching me with wide-eyes. "Are there more fords or bridges along the way?"

He bobs his head.

"Yes, My Lord King. There's another ford at Littleborough and a long bridge at Hethbeth."

"Then there's ample opportunity to make it to the other side of the river if need be. Hopefully, we'll find our missing men then."

Lord Osferth bows his head to move away, but I realise I don't know everything about this latest attack.

"Are there any more wounded?"

I detect the slight dip in his shoulders and reach out to grip his arm, trying not to overbalance.

"Tell me," I demand to know. Shadowed eyes greet mine, the sun abruptly disappearing behind a solitary cloud and making me shiver.

"Three men dead, and four badly wounded."

"Bastards," I commiserate. "We'll bury them. There's time."

But Lord Osferth is shaking his head, as though to deny it.

"The men would sooner wait, return them to families."

I nod. I applaud the sentiment, as misguided as it is.

"Loved ones will not want the mottled and stinking remains of their dead. Have them buried, carefully. You'll have to carry the news back to them and bear the brunt of their anger, but at this time of year, we can't leave bodies. We wouldn't do it to the

Raiders, and we're sure as fuck not going to do it for our own men."

Lord Osferth squares his shoulders, although his face remains despondent, as the cloud moves away and suddenly we're both blinking in the brightness.

"You make a good point," Osferth agrees, only now turning to walk away, and beckon more men to his side.

I remain peering at the burning wreck.

"And what of my men? Do we all still live?" I ask Pybba. I wouldn't expect Rudolf to be able to answer such a question if it were negative.

"Sæbald has a new cut to the face, Hereman has a wicked-looking eye and Eoppa has hurt his ankle, slipping in the water."

"And the horses?"

"All fine."

"Sæbald," I call him to my side, wincing at the evil-looking slice.

"Lucky, you kept your eye," I conclude.

"I am yes. Very lucky. Damn fucker."

"Did you see any sight of Edmund and the others?" I'm trying to think of a reason why Edmund would have lost his horse, and yet still live. I'm struggling to find an answer that satisfies me and which doesn't involve his death.

"No, nothing. Only those men who came after us. But the road is far to the south of the river. They might be down there. We didn't want to go that far to check."

I grunt. I agree with his decision.

"Have that cut seen to," I order him. Rudolf has brought Haden to me, and I pull my spare tunic from the saddlebags. It's not any cleaner, but it is drier. Then, I struggle into his saddle after rubbing his long nose in greeting. He whiffles my hand and then seems to accept my half-apology for sending him away so peremptorily earlier.

"You'll be my legs, for now," I tell him, settling in the saddle and trying not to wince as I strain my left leg. Damn thing. My wrists are still reddened from my 'captivity,' but I've not worn an injury other than that for some years. And now I have two. I need to be more careful in the future.

The thought unsettles me. Before, no one would have overly grieved for me if I'd met my death fighting for Mercia. Now, it seems as though the weight of responsibility has highlighted frailties I didn't know I possessed.

I pull both of my boots from my feet, marvelling at the whiteness of them, and hook them onto the saddle to dry.

Only then do I encourage Haden into the stream, keen to take stock of what's happened, and also, to cross the River Trent one more time. I want to peer into the far distance in the hope that I might see Edmund, Icel and the rest of the men.

"Careful," Pybba's comment almost has me rounding on him for treating me like a child. Only the change in sound coming from the river snags my attention, and I realise why the caution was uttered.

"Bollocks," the level of water has risen dramatically, and if I don't want to get wet again, which I don't, or risk Haden, which I don't, then I need to stay where I am.

"Shit, fuck, arse," I mutter to myself, hoping no one else hears, alert to the snort that comes from Pybba's nose.

"It's always the way," he consoles. "Always."

My shoulders sag, and I turn Haden aside. Enough has been lost and too much has been risked that day. I will have to hope that Scef was right when he spoke of a bridge and another ford further downstream.

I fucking hope Edmund is waiting there for me.

Or he's going to feel my wrath, and I don't think he's going to like that.

CHAPTER 11

Hereman rides with me when we turn our horses once more to follow the path of the river to where Scef leads us to yet another crossing.

The long curve of the banking takes us out of sight of the Trent, but I don't believe it matters. Wherever Edmund and the rest of the men are, it's not anywhere close.

I think it's better to have Hereman where I can keep a close eye on him.

I might be concerned by my two injuries, but he's both wounded his leader, and potentially lost his brother. He entrusts Jethson to no one but himself, and the horse is unruly beside his own.

I would sooner Jethson was nowhere near Haden. The two don't like each other and never have. But I'm not about to argue with him.

I've flung my cloak around my shoulders, keen to drive away the chill that's determined to take a hold on me.

I know I should have dried myself by the fire, but I want to press on. There's daylight yet, despite the battle at the river, and I'm keen to find the crossing and then the bridge that Scef remembered. But first, there's the matter of yet another obstacle where a further river pours into the Trent.

Lord Osferth's men are sullen behind us whereas Pybba, Rudolf and Scef lead. Eoppa and Ordlaf scout, but not too far in the distance. I can't afford to lose more men.

I've warred with myself about the reasons for my journey north, and yet I can't, no matter how much I might want to, convince myself that my task isn't urgent and in need of completion.

I could send men back for reinforcements from Repton. But the countryside has proved to be unruly so far. I won't risk more lives. Not until I know more.

"We'll clear the scum from Mercia," I inform Hereman. His brooding silence oppresses even me, as we turn our horses to cross the river, the animals able to walk, for all the water swirls almost to their belly. I'm not one for conversation, just ask Rudolf, but Hereman's bleakness is starting to get to me.

"Aye, or we'll die trying to," it's not so much of a complaint, as an admission of what needs to be done.

"At least we'll get a part in Edmund's song, should we die." Only, I realise after the words are spoken that we might not.

"Fuck, sorry," I mutter, but whether Hereman heard either of my comments, I get no reply.

The river continues to be a constant chime to the pounding of the horses' hooves over the hard-packed earth as we return to the bank of the Trent. We see no people. No one tends to the crops that grow, raggedly in the fields. I'm not surprised. I can't imagine anyone wanting to risk a life over food. Not when they should have some closer to home.

Rudolf, closer to the river than I am, leaps from his horse and rushes down the slope, and my hand reaches for my seax, my eyes wide, and my posture tense.

When he scrambles back up, a wicker fish trap in his hand, with four large specimens flapping inside, I sigh with relief.

"We'll eat well tonight," Rudolf crows, slipping the fish free before bashing them with the handle on his seax. Then he scrambles back down the banks and returns the fish trap. I watch him, wishing I could be concerned with my stomach rather than with my worries.

I knew being a king would bring me little enjoyment. I didn't appreciate it would drive all of it from me.

We set out again, but even I'm aware that the daylight is fading and that we won't be able to carry on indefinitely. The full moon is some days away, the night will be dark, and I don't want to take unnecessary risks.

"Rudolf," he rides to my side, eagerness etched into every part of his body, a grin on his face because of the fish he's found. I don't know whether he realises that Edmund might be dead, or whether he just refuses to consider it.

"Ask Scef to find somewhere for us to camp tonight. Higher ground, if it's possible."

Without agreeing, Rudolf rides his horse back to the two others, and I can see them speaking. Scef looks around him, no doubt considering what he knows, and then seems to reach a decision.

Rudolf changes the direction of his mount slightly, and then we're heading inland once more.

The land rises steeply, and I confess, I'd not realised. With the horizon ablaze with reds and oranges, Scef leads his horse up a slope that looked like nothing. I'm amazed to discover it offers a view over the Trent and the landscape both behind and in front of us.

"A good choice," I call, taking my time to put my boots back on as I dismount while the men make themselves busy organising the camp for the night. The leather is clammy but no longer sopping.

"We need a fire," I confirm when expectant eyes look my way. I won't sleep without something warm in my belly, and Rudolf has fish, for some of us. And he's not alone. I saw other men doing the same as we made our way along the river.

There's a ridge of trees that will offer dried wood to burn. We've set enough funeral pyres on our journey. It's not as though our movements can still be a secret from any keen to know if they're being followed or not.

I land heavily on the ground, gripping tightly to Haden's saddle for support.

"Fuck," I gasp through tight lips. I could have done without such a stupid injury, but it is what it is.

Grabbing my saddlebags, I release Haden from his reins, and with a gentle slap, he makes his way toward the other horses. Hereman is there, seeing to his mount and his brother's and I know my horse will be no extra burden for the man, even if Haden and Jethson need to be kept apart. Hereman wants to be alone, if kept busy.

I know how he feels. I limp to the rapidly growing fire and slump down on the hard earth.

"Bloody bollocks," I complain, my leg wound pulling tightly. Only then I feel Pybba's eyes on me, a toothy grin on his face.

"Oh, fuck off," I mutter, and he laughs, the sound full-bodied and joyful.

"Sick bastard," I aim at him, but he just continues to laugh as Rudolf, disturbed from skewering the fish, looks from one of us to the other. A flicker of unease covers his face, but then he does the only sensible thing available to him and decides to ignore us both.

That makes me smirk, and then I'm guzzling down my water bottle and hunkering into my cloak. There's a sharp breeze blowing along the hill, rustling my clothes and setting my hair loose. But it has its perks because the fire catches quickly and in no time at all, the flames are turning almost blue, and Rudolf is closing one eye as he tries to decide when the fish are cooked.

"He's fine," Hereman slumps into our circle speaking of Haden, and more and more of my men join us.

We make a sorry sight. Exhaustion seems to weigh us down, as does the lack of a good night's rest and the knowledge that there's still so much to do. None of us mentions our missing comrades, but I know that they're not far from our thoughts.

I feel sullen and damn old, but every time I consider allowing myself to wallow, I feel Pybba's eyes on me.

Damn, he's a mean old bastard to throw my hard stance back in my face.

Lord Osferth and his men have built two other fires, and as the night turns dark and then even darker, the three points of light are welcome.

Yes, they advertise our presence, but three fires seen from a distance could be interpreted as just a handful of men, maybe even just a trading party.

I eat my portion of fish, sharing with Rudolf and Pybba, and offer what supplies I have of hard cheese and smoked meat.

It's a meal of two halves, the one hot and delicious, the other chewy and labourious. But it stills my rumbling belly.

Hereberht agrees to take the first watch, Wulfred the second, and I insist on the third, no matter what anyone else says. I know the danger will come in the early morning when the sky is still dark with only the faintest slither of light and when man and beast waver between wakefulness and deep sleep.

Lord Osferth has two each of his men accompany mine, and then, when fatigue threatens to send me to sleep sitting, I roll in my cloak, facing the fire, and close my eyes.

The sounds of the night rush in quickly, from the rustle of the wind-blown grass, to the shifting of the insects and small animals that share my bed for the night. Not forgetting the unease of the flames, wavering fitfully in the stiffening breeze. It smells like rain might greet us in the morning.

I clear my thoughts, knowing sleep to be more critical than silent arguments with myself.

Tomorrow everything will be new.

Tomorrow, I hope to find Edmund.

Tomorrow will come too soon.

I'm woken by rain falling on my face. Hard rain.

"Bloody bollocks," I sit up, my body arguing with the movement. The fire has long since gone out, and I can hear the mumbling of others as they too are disturbed in their sleep and pull cloaks and hoods higher, but it's still black as night.

I lumber to my feet, peering around for Wulfred.

"Here, Lord Coelwulf," his voice reaches me from a point close to where the horses are moving around, a darker patch in the black of night, and I hobble my way to him, teeth gritted against the agony of my pulsing wound, the falling rain blurring my vision.

"Any problems?" I ask, fumbling with my hood because it keeps blowing free of my head.

"Nothing. No movement. An unusually fucking quiet part of the night." His voice thrums with unspoken worry, and I catch a glimpse of blue lips.

"Go, sleep. I'll be fine until daylight."

"My thanks," and Wulfred is gone without further argument. The second watch is always the worst. I'm still not able to get my hood to stay in place, and my hair is plastering itself to my head, water running uncomfortably down my back. Am I to spend all sodding day wet?

"Fuck." I try and wriggle myself into a more comfortable position, but it's impossible. Instead of sitting for my watch, I make my way to Haden. It's easy to see him in the darkness because the inquisitive animal is the only one standing amongst the collection of horses resting, their limbs as exhausted as those of my warriors. The white streak on his nose is so bright it's as though a flame burns there. It appears that he knows I need him.

"You should be asleep," I chastise him, rubbing my hand along his nose in greeting, but I'm grateful not to be the only one awake.

I consider the best way that he could protect me from the thundering summer rain. Eventually, I realise I'll have to stand beneath his head if I don't want to get wet. Not that it'll make him a comfortable ride come the daylight. A wet horse is up there with a wet dog. To be avoided if at all possible.

And I'll probably have a cricked neck as well. But the fact that I might not be drenched makes it far more appealing.

"You keep watch," I order him when I've finally ensured he understands what I want him to do, and we've stopped sidestepping each other as though we dance. "I'll do the same," I offer, reaching up to rub my hand the length of his long nose in solidarity.

Warm horse breath greets my request, filled with the heady scent of fresh grass. Whether Haden understands my words, I really don't know. Still, his strength and companionship make the dreary part of the night pass far more quickly than I might have hoped.

I'm vigilant and also resting, all at the same time. Every time I almost close my eyes in sleep, my leg twinges, or Haden huffs noisily in my ear. Between the two of them, they ensure no one attacks the camp.

As dawn begins to break, far away, and beneath a thunderous grey sky, I appreciate that the rain is far from done with us. Another sodden day in the saddle beckons, and I'm not alone in my complaints.

"Too fucking hot to ride, face aflame, and now this, sodding typical." Ælfgar's querulous voice reaches me first, and I stifle a smirk. I feel the same as him, but I'm not about to tell him.

"Shut your fucking mouth," Eoppa retorts. "It's not like it's only raining on you, is it?"

But it's Scef's words that make me reassess my complaints.

"The river will be high today, or if not today, then tomorrow," he opines, coming to ensure his borrowed horse is well. Rudolf greets him. The two seem to have boundless energy and enthusiasm for our predicament.

"The Trent floods as soon as a woman cries," Scef says, his voice rich with condescension and the certainty that past experience gives him. "They'll be no getting across the fords anytime soon, and even the bridges might be underwater. It depends on how long the rain lasts. But," and he pauses, and when the silence goes on for longer than I'd anticipated, I peek out from beneath Haden and watch him.

The youth is standing, hand on his mount, peering slowly around him, one eye closed, as though he assesses the potential rainfall still to come.

"I would say at least today, and possibly tomorrow as well. This isn't a little summer storm, but rather a great downpour. The farmers both look for these and resent them. They refill all the troughs and ensure the plants are well-tended. Provided the growths are at the right height, all will be well."

Before Scef can realise I'm observing him, I duck back beneath Haden, my face already awash with fresh rain. I shiver, but not from the cold. I shiver again. I'm not one for portents, I never have been, but the thought of the wide Trent running unchecked worries me.

Maybe, I consider, this sudden squall will upset the Raiders more than those chasing them. I can only hope.

It's Pybba who realises my place of near concealment and comes to me, a quizzical look in his eye, his severed stump open to the rain.

"Damn, this itches," Pybba offers, handing me a bowl of nearly cold pottage. I eat it hungrily. My belly still aches with the need for good food. This certainly isn't it.

Pybba stands silently beside me, a clear sign that he means to speak to me. The cloak of his hood is pulled around his face, and his eyes are the only bright spots on his darkened face. The rain seems to fall even heavier, and I shift, a wince on my lips.

"How's the leg?" he asks, as though he's waiting for that opening.

"Tight. Sore. A pain in the fucking arse," I offer, a wry smile on my lips.

"What are you going to do with Hereman?" My eyes narrow. Does Pybba know? He offers nothing further, or not that I can see.

"About what?" I decide that pretending not to understand the question is my best response.

"Edmund."

"I can do nothing until we find Edmund."

"And the other matter?" Now I see the pink of his tongue running over his lips, as he lifts his stump to peer at it in more detail.

I notice the savage red of the burn is fading to a less prominent pink, but I fear it will always be a messy wound. My leg will probably be the same.

"It wasn't his fault. I don't hold him responsible, and he knows it."

"He might know it, but it plagues him all the same."

"I can't do anything about that," I retort, stung by the words. "I can't take back the wound. I wish it hadn't happened as well. It fucking aches like a bastard."

"Well," and Pybba snatches the nearly empty wooden bowl from me. "It's just a little scratch," and he's walking away from me, and I feel my mouth open in shock.

It seems that no matter what I might think, I do need to do something about Hereman. Bloody Pybba. Sticking his nose in where it shouldn't be.

It seems to take too long to mount up and be ready, everyone having to take special care with clothes, weapons and provisions under the onslaught of rain.

I detect little in the way of individual conversations, as I feed Haden his oats and lead him to a puddle that's formed overnight and now brims with water. He drinks thirstily, but the thrum of falling rain is loud, overriding even my breathing and my heartbeat.

"A fucking miserable day to ride," I offer to the sky, expecting no one to reply.

"A day to make advances while everyone else hunkers down to wait it out," Lord Osferth speaks from beside me, and I almost jump in shock.

"Well, we can't stay up here and cower, so we may as well," I confirm, filling my voice with far more enthusiasm than I feel, unsure what intent lies behind those words. I'd been hoping that the heavy clouds would lift and allow me to find the Raiders and their ships on the Trent, but it seems impossible now.

"No, we can't," Osferth states, and I turn to gaze at him.

Osferth is younger than I, by at least ten years, if I had to guess. When I first met him, he was bloodied from battle but calm, even in the face of so much death and destruction. At some point in the last few days, such calmness has left him, and now he seems uneasy. There's a constant tick above his left eyebrow, and where others might have lines on their foreheads, he seems to carry furrows, as though gauged from the earth with a hoe.

His eyes are hooded as well, and I think from more than just the cut below his eye that's taking time to heal. I consider that he carries a wound that no one knows about. But before I can ask the question, he's turned his horse, perhaps on purpose, and made his way back toward the crest of the hill. I watch him go, head on one side.

Such endeavours as these affect men in different ways. Perhaps Lord Osferth can't cope with the constant stresses of not knowing where the next battle is coming from. Or maybe he fears that we won't be successful.

Or maybe it's just pissing with rain, and he'd sooner be in a great hall somewhere being brought ale or mead by the servants. I know I would rather be there, but I've never been one to consider what I could be doing. All that matters is what I am doing.

"Right," I roar. "Time to go." And with Haden a willing accomplice, I begin to pick my way down the slope. My eyes peer through the gloom caused by both the rain falling as though the sky simply can't hold it anymore, and the heat of the summer-baked land causing the water to evaporate once more.

It's as though we move through a strange otherworld. Demons and ghosts from the old stories perhaps populate it, and it's pregnant with the probability that our enemy knows where we are and might well attack us.

The ground is slick, and I'm forced to hold onto Haden tightly to prevent falling. My wound twinges with each and every step, a counterpart to my heartbeat and panting. I'm pleased when the ground is flat enough that I can risk mounting up without worrying that Haden might slip and injure himself on the steaming grass.

Bad enough that I carry a limp. I wouldn't want him to do the same.

"Scef," I beckon for him to join me, and he comes, with Rudolf as his constant shadow, but I allow it with only a slight lifting of my eyebrows. Rudolf grins at me, as though aware he's being too keen.

"Tell me of the River Trent," I ask Scef. I know the rivers close to Gloucester and Worcester. I might not like being on a ship, but I'm aware of the cantankerous nature of the Severn and its tributaries. I feel I've overlooked something by not taking more interest in the Trent.

Scef looks at me in surprise.

"What do you want to know?"

"Anything that might aid me, or hinder the Raiders. This rain, will it affect the level of the water?"

For someone so keen to give his opinions to Rudolf earlier, Scef seems strangely reticent now. I have to assume it's because he's wary of me, and not for any other reason. I admit I've not always spoken kindly to him.

"My Lord King," Scef swallows heavily as he pauses, and I have my confirmation. "The Trent is liable to rise, significantly in the next few days. Rain such as this, if it persists, and I think it will, might cause the river to burst its banks in places where the land lies almost level with it. But, it's not the winter. I don't believe there will be a great deal of flooding. But it all depends on how much longer it rains, and where it's raining."

"Where it's raining?" I ask, seizing on the word.

"Yes, My Lord King. The Trent takes in water from a vast area. If it's raining like this all along its banks, then it'll be bad. If it's just here, it won't be such a problem. I can't say. We'll have to wait."

"And the fords and the bridges?"

"The fords will be passable, with more care than usual, if the current is strong. The bridges should be okay, as long as the higher waters don't wash too much rubbish along. It's not unheard of for a tree trunk or three to take out the supporting beams."

"My thanks," I turn back, trying to find the banks of the Trent through the grey mist. But it's impossible. There could be a thousand warriors out there waiting to attack me, and I wouldn't know until one of them held a blade to my throat.

"My Lord King," the voice is uncertain, and I turn in surprise.

"Speak freely, Scef. You should know that."

A thin smile pulls at the youth's lips, and yet he doesn't look anymore reassured.

"The bridge that'll still be passable is at least a day's ride from here."

"Then it might take us a day," I concede. The news isn't what I wanted to hear, but neither can I blame him. It's not as though Scef's summoned the rain and made the journey to Torksey yet more challenging.

"My Lord King," with his head bowed, Scef turns his horse aside, but I nod to indicate I want Rudolf to remain where he is.

"Tell me, how are you?" I ask him. While we ride together, I've seen little of him and certainly, not enough to know how he fares.

"Damp," Rudolf smirks, pulling his hood over his head once more. His cheeks are chapped from the rain, and combined with the bruises it makes him look terrible, although he still smiles, his teeth gleaming white in the gloom.

"Us youngsters don't mind a bit of rain," Rudolf grins, already encouraging Dever away from me before I can react.

"Cheeky fucker," I call after him. I'm merely greeted with a chuckle that echoes strangely in the damp chill. It cheers me, despite the illusion of my age. And his youth.

I can only hope that he lives as long as I do to be ridiculed by young lads who think age is a bad thing.

The hard-packed ground close to the river seems to have splintered into many hundreds of small rivers, all pouring down toward the main river itself. The surface of the river, as far as I can tell, is being churned to a muddy brown, and it's impossible to see the opposite bank.

We could be being trailed by Edmund, Icel and the others, or hunted by the Raiders, and I'd have no idea. I've not even set any scouts. They wouldn't be able to find me, to tell me an attack was imminent, even if they saw the Raiders in time.

Muffled sounds of horses and riders fill my ears, just visible above the roll of the rain.

"I thought it was the fucking summer," Hereman's words pull me back to the here and now, and I realise I've almost been sleeping in my saddle. I only hope no one's noticed.

"If we're lucky, maybe we'll get a thunderstorm to go with it." I offer. I'm surprised that Hereman has sought me out, and even more that he's opened his mouth to speak to me.

"How is it?" he asks, and I know he speaks of my leg.

"Healing," is all I offer. I'm not going to tell him how much it pains me, how much it itches or even how much I wish it had never happened. There's no point in making the current situation any worse.

A harrumph greets my words, and I expect that to be the end of our conversation. Only it isn't.

"I've never much liked my brother," Hereman begins, and it takes more of my resolve than I think it will not to make some sarcastic remark in reply.

"But he's always been there, my brother. He's always looked out for me and ensured I had all I needed."

I think Hereman refers to his childhood. Hereman is a good five years younger than Edmund, maybe more. That would have made Edmund a man when Hereman wasn't. I wish I remembered more of that time, but I was not interested in my brother and his warriors. I had my own concerns that felt pressing but have since proved to be precisely the opposite.

"Brothers do that for each other," I offer. I'm floundering. I'm not sure what Hereman wants from me, and certainly, I'm ill-equipped to give it.

"You and your brother weren't close?" Hereman states. I consider how best to answer.

"Brothers can have a care for each other without living in each other's pockets. Coenwulf had his eyes on a different prize. He was my father's heir and heir to the kingdom of the Hwicce. He was to be an ealdorman one day. I wasn't to have that honour."

"But did you like your brother?" Hereman pauses. I would

sooner not be having this conversation at all, and certainly not when so many can hear my replies.

"He was my brother," I turn to meet Hereman's eyes. "I never thought liking him or not liking him was an option. He was just there, and should always have been there."

"Was he kind to you?"

"Not particularly, but neither was he un-kind. He was just there, as was I to him."

Hereman looks down at the hands on his reins, and I watch a fat drop of water slide its way down his nose, and only slowly release its hold on the surface and fall, to merge with the others on his gloves.

I feel as though I should be offering platitudes and assurances that Edmund still lives, but I've never been one to offer what should be said, only ever what I can say. There's a whole world of difference in those sentiments.

"You probably knew my brother better than I did," I concede, unsure why as soon as the words leave my mouth. "You were his man, and you rode by his side."

"Only for a matter of months," Hereman states flatly, raising his chin and peering into the gloom rather than meeting my eyes. "Edmund forced him to give me the place. Otherwise, I wouldn't have been a warrior."

"Then your brother must have believed in you."

"Maybe. Or maybe he just did it because he felt guilty and didn't want to be worrying about me."

"Does it matter what reason he did it for?" I want to sigh at Hereman's circular way of thinking. It seems that nothing I offer will make him happy. Perhaps I should just have provided an assurance that Edmund was fine.

"No, I suppose not," Hereman concedes. "But I'd like to think he did it because I showed potential and not because he could. Your brother would have done anything for Edmund."

"Coenwulf relied on Edmund a great deal. Edmund relied on Coenwulf as well. He didn't think too highly of me when I had to assume the leadership of Coenwulf's warriors."

And now Hereman laughs. I turn, shocked by the wide beam on his face.

"No, Edmund didn't think you'd last a day, let alone a decade. He thought you'd run from every fight and never even make a kill."

This isn't news to me, but I find it strangely unsettling to think that more people realised this than just Edmund and I.

"He thought you'd piss your trews and shit yourself when you faced an enemy."

"Then," I state, no trace of humour on my face. "I'm fucking glad I did neither of those things."

In fact, but I hold this to myself, it's Edmund that's more likely to piss his trews and shit himself. Hereman subsides to silence but still rides at my side. I wish he'd go away, but I don't demand that he does. He can stay, as long as he keeps his fucking mouth shut.

I don't want to think of the days following my brother's death when he succumbed to a Raider-given wound that festered despite my Aunt's ministrations. Even now, we don't talk of it, but it goes unsaid that the weapon that infected my brother's chest was fouled with Raider shit. There can be no other explanation for why such a simple wound killed him.

I was almost too late to speak with Coenwulf, as he lay dying at Kingsholm, Edmund pacing, my Aunt aggravated by the constant movement. In some ways, I would wish I'd been later still, but I'd arrived in time to hear the words that changed my life forever.

"They're yours now, brother. Treat them well, and remember their first loyalty has always been to me, not you."

With that, my brother had taken his last breath, and I'd been left bent by his side, unsure what to do, but knowing I didn't want the responsibility of a warband when I'd only ever been a member of one.

"My Lord King." Lord Osferth forces me from my musings. At some point, Hereman has wandered from my side, and the rain has, if possible, intensified. I'm sodden and cold, even my hands threatening to shiver inside their gloves. If I'm forced to undress when we make camp, I'll have to peel myself from my clothes, rather than pull them.

"Lord Osferth," the words stick and so I cough and try again. "Osferth. A terrible day," I begin, but he's not here to make small talk.

"I smell smoke," the words are ominous and immediately, I'm aware that the gloom, although I thought it impossible, has thickened.

"Scef?"

"He knows of no settlement nearby, although he confesses, he's not entirely sure where we are."

"'Ware," I call to my men. I don't want to draw my seax from its scabbard in such poor weather, but neither can I ride unarmed. The single word echoes unevenly in the dampness.

"He does suggest that we could shelter in the woodlands, over there," Osferth juts his chin in the direction he means, and I can just about decipher a darker patch in the gloom.

"Lead on." I don't give it more than a moment's thought. We could be riding into any sort of ambush and it would be impossible to know. I'd sooner wait out the storm.

Haden willingly turns aside from the river when I give him the instruction. It seems I'm not the only one who's miserable.

But I stay alert, desperate to make out what the strange shapes and sounds are that I can both nearly see, and almost hear, but it's a fruitless endeavour. I'm pleased to bend my head low and allow Haden to take us under the rich canopy of tree branches overhead.

Immediately, my ability to see increases, and the ground, somehow remaining dry, offers a refuge for my sodden horse and me.

"Stay alert," I instruct, the words circulated from one to another, but I'm sure they don't really need to hear them, it's just that I need to say them.

The sound of the rain lessens with each step inside the tightly packed woodland, as I slide from Haden's back and then stand, lifting my head and shoulders from the slump I've used during the day's ride.

"Come here, lad. I'll take that from you."

A handy tree branch offers me somewhere to place the sodden saddle and saddlebags, and then I pull a blanket, with the hint of damp, but not the weight of water, and run it over Haden's tall black and white body.

I'm aware that others are doing the same, and I approve, although my seax is back in its scabbard, ready to be brandished should I need it.

Only when Haden is settled, do I begin the task of warming myself.

"Bastard thing," the oath pours from my mouth as the world turns dark and my tunic remains tangled in my arms, head and hair.

My lower body is chaffed white, but my upper body is caught.

"I'll help you," Rudolf calls. His hands struggle as much as mine do to pull the fabric free, but eventually, it's off me, and I can see once more.

"My thanks," I offer. He hands me the soaking garment gingerly, as though he doesn't really want to feel the cloying wet.

"Did you wash in the rain?" Rudolf demands to know as I take it from him. I swear it weighs heavier than my seax.

"No wonder I felt cold," I offer, reaching for my tunic of yesterday that's dried in the confines of my saddlebags. It's not a pleasant aroma.

"Scef says this woodland follows the Trent, but from quite a distance. With the weather like this, we could ride beyond the Raiders or the rest of the men, and not even know."

"So best to stay here then?" I muse. I can't see beyond the end of the trees. It is almost as though night has replaced day. "Did we at least find the source of the smoke?"

"No, but the men are starting small fires. We need them to get warm again."

With my drier tunic on and my cloak discarded, I already feel better. Still, I appreciate that not everyone will have spare clothes with them.

"We'll stay, for now. Maybe if the weather clears we can carry on."

"Scef says that won't happen. Not today, and maybe not tomorrow. He doesn't think the rain will stop anytime soon."

"Fuck," I complain, twisting my lips in thought. This is not going the way I imagined it would. Far from it, in fact.

"Tell everyone to stay alert, and not to go wandering off for a piss. Stay close and stay ready."

Rudolf moves off to mingle amongst the men, and I watch him weave, duck and slither around the hive of activity. Hereman has unsettled me by talking about the past, a place I decided not to frequent after my brother's death. Now, it's as though it stalks me, even through the gloomy mist. It's more debilitating than the worry that Edmund might be dead, and the Raiders seeking me out.

The dead should be dead, their voices lost to me, but Coenwulf lingers, even now.

I consider what he'd think of me being proclaimed King of Mercia. He wouldn't fucking believe it, that's for sure, but would he approve? I swear I don't know. Would his approval mean anything to me?

It's impossible to know, and I thrust the invidious thoughts aside.

Sæbald has had the most success with a fire. I slither my way to stoop beside the warming tendrils just beginning to make themselves felt in the confined space. My wound pulse with every movement as I attempt to not grimace with every step.

"A good job," I commend him, and he grins and then winces, no doubt his injuries making themselves felt as well.

"Ordlaf says he'd beat me, but the daft sod is still trying to build the perfect fire pit." Sæbald nods his head in the direction of another small gathering, and I suppress a smirk as Ordlaf, his voice high with a protest, tries to move people out of his way. His hands are black with dirt.

Not that Sæbald has ignored the need to contain the fire.

After all, it might be sodding raining, but there's no need to risk Mercia's precious trees.

From my new vantage, almost on a level with my feet, it's actually easier to peer through the tightly packed tree trunks, to ensure all of the men are well. I'm not alone in seeking the warmth of a fire, and I'm convinced that our activities for the day have come to an end.

The delay frustrates me, but even I can see that it's better to dally than ride unheeding into a Raider army. I'd sooner keep all of my men alive, and Lord Osferth's as well than lose them just because I'm impatient.

It seems I am an older man, just as Rudolf taunted me.

Fucking bastard.

CHAPTER 12

I wake from a deep sleep, disorientated, my wound throbbing dully, but something even more tedious finally rousing me.

My hand goes to the back of my neck, and the slither of wetness there, and I use what little light remains from the fire to assure me that it's not blood.

"Fuck." Somehow, I've managed to turn in my sleep so that persistent raindrops fall onto my neck. Either, I've found the only fucking gap in the entire woodland or, more likely, they slowly drip from one leaf to another until landing on me. These splashes could have fallen days ago and only now strive for the ground.

I twist out of the way, determined to seek sleep once more, only I can hear men talking, and I realise that the constant pound of beating rain has stopped.

I lie still, all the same, trying not to draw attention to myself, keen to know who speaks and what it's about and more importantly if I should be worried about.

The conversation is evidently far from newly started.

"Bishop Wærferth. It was his suggestion, the ealdormen all followed it."

"But why him, that's what I don't understand." I don't recognise the voices, although it's evident they speak about me, or so I think.

"His grandfather was King Coelwulf."

"Who the fuck was King Coelwulf?"

"King of Mercia. Decades ago."

"So why does that mean he gets to be king now?"

Silence falls between the two men, and I smirk, because the conversation is nothing to worry about, and I can almost perceive the one man thinking of his response.

"Ask Bishop Wærferth," the man who seems to know what's happening answers. His voice is filled with frustration that he has no ready answer. Going on my vast experiences with Rudolf, I can't see that that man has made the right choice.

Surely, they understand why I've been chosen as king. But then, maybe they don't. Even I find it strange. Certainly, I didn't think, when my brother died, that it meant I would one day be named as king of Mercia. I became an ealdorman, but I expected that, just not a kingdom.

"Did you hear something?" My senses are alert as well because I thought I heard a carefully placed foot somewhere close to the treeline. Is it possible that the Raiders were so close to us that they've been able to find us now that the rain has stopped?

My hand reaches for my seax, my movements slow and careful. At the same time, I try to breathe as quietly as possible and focus my attention on where I heard the first footfall.

Only there's nothing, and long moments go by. Even the two I've been listening to have fallen silent. All the same, I think I must have been imagining things.

Only then I hear not one but two footfalls, and they're closer than the first.

I kick the body next to me, Sæbald, gritting my teeth because even that movement seems to reignite the throbbing pain in my left leg.

White-eyes glare at me in the gloom, but I shake my head, hoping he'll know enough to listen.

Again, I hear more footsteps, although the deep covering on the woodland floor muffles much of the sound.

Sæbald's arm reaches above him, and he grips the foot of whoever else joined our party last night. The man has his back to me, but I take it to be Wulfstan. I can tell he's awake because the stillness that emanates from him is too studied, and of course, his deep snoring has come to a thankful end.

More and more of the camp seems to be coming alert, soft sounds attesting to warriors ready to attack as soon as we know where the assault comes from.

I wish I could see more.

And then one of the Raiders makes a mistake, and the snap of a twig seems to resound through the trees, more loudly than a bell summoning the religious to their church services.

Now I appreciate that not one of the men sleeps. Not one. But all of us hold our nerve and pretend as though we do. I spare a thought for Ælfgar. He had the task of watching throughout this part of the night. I hope he's not dead. I'll kill anyone who takes the life of another of my men. I'll not have it. Not when I'm supposed to be the fucking victor.

Shapes flicker through the gloaming, and more and more, I can determine how many there are and where they're going. Why, I consider, they came at us from such an angle is beyond me. Especially as they continue to creep around us. Why didn't they circle behind us if that was their intention? I don't approve of their tactics.

I'll not fall prey to Raiders who think so little of their enemy that they can carry out such a fucking half-arsed attack. I'll not have it.

I feel a tremble of movement from Sæbald, and I hiss, aware the sound is too loud and probably heard by everyone. Yet the sound of feet moving around us doesn't stop.

"Wait," I breathe the word, hoping that everyone who needs to hear it, does so.

I'm holding on for the opportune moment. It's not yet upon us, but it will be, soon. I feel my body tensing, my leg wound demanding to be remembered.

"Fucking bastard," I speak under my breath to the damn pain. I swear it irks me more than Pybba's wound ever did him. The flesh is knitting together, reuniting the two severed sides one to another, but I wish it would hurry up.

And then there's another loud snap of a breaking twig, and the voices of others trying to shush the Raider. I feel rather than see that someone is nearby.

My heart thunders in my chest. I need them near enough, but not too close. I need Lord Osferth to wait until it feels as though it's too late.

Laboured breathing reaches my ears, even over the symphony of my heartbeat.

"For Mercia." I erupt from my place of sleep, seax extended, turning to meet the Raider who stands close enough to touch. His face is almost a blank mask apart from where I can see the slither of his tongue poking through his lips.

"Die you bastard," and my seax is at his throat and he has no time to respond, none at all. And he's falling to the floor, and I turn to find my next target.

The entire campsite is a welter of noise and activity. I don't know how many Raiders there are. As a handful of dried mulch is thrown into the embers of the fire closest to me, a flicker of light erupts. It throws our campsite into a momentary haze of red, as though we're drenched in blood already.

I see then that at least twenty Raiders are intermingled amongst my warriors and those of Lord Osferth's.

"Fuckers," I scream. The next man to fall does so with his hand on his seax and an expression of surprise on his face.

These men were too cocky and too sure of themselves.

I know the sort. But there will be others who are more challenging to kill, with more considerable skills and a superior understanding of their talents.

I peer into the vastness of the woodland, just daring someone else to erupt from the depths, but it's hushed, and I rush to aid Sæbald who faces two opponents. As I reach the fire, I kick yet another selection of the dry woodland bed onto it, and a flicker of scarlet illuminates the scene of the attack.

My warriors all face at least one enemy, and only Sæbald meets two. Pybba and Rudolf work as one, with Scef cowering behind the darkness of a tree trunk, no doubt sent there by

Pybba.

Lord Osferth and his men are up and fighting as well.

What surprises me is how silently my warriors work.

Above the din of iron on iron, it's the Raiders who shout one to another, their voices showing their fear at being discovered.

The warrior I face is a compact man. His head is entirely shadowed so that it appears as though something otherworldly has command of the war axe he twirls with considerable skill. I can see why Sæbald struggled as much as he did.

Without my shield, I have to rely on my seax to stop the blade of the war axe.

Hand fumbling on my weapons belt, I reach for and grip my war axe in my left hand. I need something to counter the flurry of blows that land with practised ease against my blade.

"Bastard," I complain, pleased when yet another sets the flames from the fire dancing high. Without the slither of light, I would have taken a hit to my shoulder. But instead, I counter it with my seax, and then left-handed or not, I aim a low blow at the man's belly.

He jumps clear of my reach, the light aiding him just as much as it did me, but my seax is suddenly free from its task of preventing his weapon hitting me. I thrust it forward, keen to stab and slice.

My opponent, panting, still moves quickly, only then I have a piece of luck.

The woodland is densely packed. My foe finds himself backed against one of the many massive tree trunks. His ability to swing his axe is restricted, and no one can come to his assistance.

"Who are you?" I ask. I want to know who I kill. I want to have it sung about in the decades to come.

I don't expect an answer, unsure if the man understands my words or not.

"I fight for Jarl Olaf of Norway," a new name for me, but perhaps not to others.

"And you'll die for him," I smirk, only the man ducks below my war axe's reach, and he's beneath my arm and then behind me, our positions reversed.

"And who are you?" he asks, the lilt of his accent punctuating the words, as he follows each one with an attack aimed at getting beyond my defences.

"Ealdorman Coelwulf," I exhale, frantically trying to think of a way out of my predicament.

The man's laughter surprises me.

"I've heard of you. You'll be a good kill to add to my already extensive list."

"And are you Jarl Olaf of Norway?" I ask another shower of sparks illuminating the finely worked metal-linked coat the man wears. A Thor's hammer hangs heavily around his neck.

"It's not your concern." A gust of hot air makes me wrinkle my nose, as my opponent rushes closer, his war axe busy, trying to force me to protect the wrong side of my body, while he goes for the other.

The trick is too commonplace for me to fall for, and with two weapons, I don't need to choose where to plant myself.

I take the strikes, the force of the man's strength seeming to sap mine as time and time again, he lands a clout on either my seax or war axe.

"No, but if you wish your name to be sung about with mine, then I would know it. I have a list of kills as well. I could add you to it. If it was worth my while."

The warrior hesitates at my words. I rush into his momentarily still embrace, twirling my seax as I do so that I can reach behind him, the intent to stab him in the back.

Only he recovers quickly, and instead of embracing him, I stumble on a hidden tree root and tumble to my knees. A slither of pain roars up my left leg from the cut there, and I duck, hearing the whoosh of air being displaced by the reaching axe.

"Shit," I turn, still on the floor, and hold my seax upwards, warding off yet another blow as I untangle my legs and move to stand upright.

More sparks fill the air, and I'm aware that the fight is over for many, but not yet for me.

My opponent must see the same, for once again, he's distracted, and this time, I'm quicker to take advantage.

I stand, fling my war axe over my head to shield my body as I do so, and at knee height, I use my other hand to thrust my seax into the man's groin. I sight the spot carefully, and then thrust all of my weight behind the action.

The man above me pauses, confused, his war axe to the side of his body, his eyes drawn to mine from the deep cowl of the woodland darkness.

"Care to tell me now?" I ask, and the man opens his mouth as though to speak, only a torrent of blood is flowing down my hand, the rush making me thrust backwards or risk wearing all of the man's fluid, and I think he's left it too long.

"Olaf," the word stretches as his breath shortens and I nod, satisfied that this is the man who led the assault. It seems only right that I should be the one to kill him. A pity it took so long.

A whoosh of shimmering rain erupts into the air. It doesn't come from one fire, but rather the few that the men have been sheltering close to after being drenched the day before. I force myself to my feet, as my opponent thuds forward, and while his face impacts the soft ground, I turn to examine the camp.

I'm not alone. White-eyes greet me from the depths of the murky recesses, but no one fights on. We have won. Once more.

"Is everyone here?" I bellow into the sudden silence, my voice carrying forcefully, making Sæbald, who stands closest to me, wince.

I arch an eyebrow at Sæbald, taking in his bleached face and the slither of blood that drips from his shaved chin.

"You might want to grow a beard now," I offer him, thinking the man won't like to have a scar in such a prominent position.

"Chance would be a fine thing," Sæbald argues, wiping the blood clear and examining it where it mingles on his fingers.

There's a body slowly weeping into the ground behind him.

"A good kill?" I ask, still waiting to check that everyone else is there. The wait seems to be extended beyond my patience.

"Does everyone live?" I call when the reply is too slow to reach me. It worries me. Such a silence after a battle is always one for concern.

"My Lord King," it's Lord Osferth who calls me to his side, and I stride through the maze of trees to where I can see him standing close to one of the fires. It gutters, and a foul stench erupts from it.

"A casualty?" I ask, and he nods, the action coming to me more through the grating of his beard over his byrnie than because I watch him.

"Who is it?" I ask. I wish I knew the names of every man who fights for me, I genuinely do.

"Seaxwulf," Lord Osferth's voice is hollow and echoing, and I realise I've missed something. I look around me, hoping for someone to answer my unspoken question. When nothing is forthcoming, I bend and pull the smoking body from the fire. A gasp from Osferth warns me not to turn the body. There's no need to see the ruin the embers have caused. None at all.

And then some realisation prickles at the back of my memory, something I didn't even know I knew.

"Your son?" I ask, and Osferth nods once more, the sound answering for him once more, not the action.

I don't know what to offer into the expectant silence. I've had no son. But I know what it is to grieve a brother and a father. Is it similar? I wish I knew.

I swallow heavily, the weight of regret threatening to undo my exuberance at thwarting yet another underhand attack on my men and me.

Osferth's men seem as ill-prepared, as I am to comfort their leader.

"We'll bury him, with all the honours a warrior deserves." By that, I mean with all of his equipment, even his sword. We'll consign it to the ground so that it might never again slake its thirst for blood and death.

Still, Osferth says nothing, and I'm torn between going about my usual after-battle business and remaining by his side. I gaze into the near distance, wishing someone would come to my aid.

But of course, they don't. Instead, every other man is abruptly busy, bending to tend to the battle dead, to take whatever wealth they had.

"Where did they come from?" I ask of no one, and then remember my concern for Wulfred.

"Wulfred, where are you?" I call, only then thinking of Lord Osferth's night guards.

It's Rudolf who provides the answers, dashing to my side with an uncertain expression on his face when he looks at Osferth.

"Wulfred is wounded, by the tree line. A wound to his leg, high up, he can't stand. Osferth's men are dead."

I nod, the news not unexpected.

"There are horses beyond the trees. Not our horses."

"Go with Pybba and Scef to tend to Wulfred. Make it so that he can ride if you can."

Rudolf scampers away to do my bidding, but I've not solved the problem of Osferth.

I stand, hands opening and closing, my seax back on my weapons belt even though it's not clean. I want to be doing something to dispel the energy crackling along my limbs, but I can't. I'm the king, and Osferth deserves something more than to have his son's death so casually accepted.

"You three," I call Osferth's men to me, and they come, one limping, one wincing and one looking as though he's taken a blow directly to his nose, as blood mars his mouth and chin.

"My Lord King?" the man with the broken nose speaks, although his words are muffled.

"Help me to carry young Seaxwulf clear from the woodlands. I would have him buried in the light of day."

"My Lord King?" There's confusion in the words, and I know they wait for Osferth to give his agreement. Only he doesn't.

The furrows on Osferth's forehead have all fallen away, and the tick on his left eyebrow is finally still, as is all of him. Osferth hasn't so much as moved since discovering his son's body. If I didn't know better, I'd doubt that he still lived.

"Come, assist me," I put more force into my words, bending to take hold of Seaxwulf's left arm. I don't want to carry him alone. It seems wrong to sling him over my shoulder and drag him from this place, but I will if the men don't aid me.

Only a decision is made between the three. Between us, we carefully turn Seaxwulf, as I ensure his blistered face is covered by part of his cloak, and then we carry him through the trees. I think Osferth will remain behind, and I'm surprised when his footsteps join our own.

Stepping from the shelter of the woodland feels as though I walk from night into day. In the distance, the sun is glinting in a watery sky, the pale grey of the day before seemingly gone, although a cold wind blows and I shiver before stepping clear of the trees.

I need to decide on a suitable place for the burial, and Lord Osferth is giving me no hints. Neither are the three other men who all puff at the additional strain after the fierceness of the attack.

I look for Scef, but he's distracted by Wulfred, and so I decide based on the patch of sunlight that illuminates the earth just clear of the woodlands.

"Here," I instruct. "Here. The sun will warm him first each and every day."

Seaxwulf is more dropped than gently laid on the floor by the others, and I begin to suspect that Seaxwulf was perhaps not much liked. I've not witnessed the men being so disrespectful to Lord Osferth so far. But of course, a son doesn't become the father just because he sprouts from the belly of the woman the father bedded. I wish I could remember Seaxwulf, but I can't. Not at all.

"We'll dig a grave," I state, brokering no argument. "And then we'll find stones to mark it."

More and more of Osferth's men slither from the treeline, but none of them come to offer their aid. I grit my teeth, sink my seax into the soil, and then tug backwards, hoping the ground will open easily despite the deep layer of leaves. When it doesn't, I switch to my war axe, and this time the tightly-packed earth moves enough that we can all place our hands inside to tug free the strangled grasses that have interwoven in the thin soil.

The work is accomplished quickly, and I turn to Lord Osferth to try and gauge his reaction, but his face is expressionless, his body limp. I clear my throat noisily, and when no response is forthcoming, I nod to the others. Between us, we lay Seaxwulf in the grave, on his back, his clothing intact, his sword in one hand, his seax close to the other.

Just as I'm about to order the soil placed over the young man's body, a strangled cry erupts from Osferth. He dashes forward, flinging himself over his son's body. He cradles the mass of singed hair that still covers the blistered face, as though he were a babe and not a man who's grown to become a warrior, and lost his life fighting for his kingdom.

I sigh heavily, the weight of Osferth's grieving almost forcing me to the floor beside him.

All men think they'll live forever, even men who fight with blade and shield.

I turn aside. I don't need to witness this. Instead, I lay a hand on the shoulder of two of the men who've helped me this far. I hope to convey my sorrow in that act, and also my belief that Osferth will find no solace with me close by.

After all, he might lay the blame at my feet. Grief-stricken men and women often assign blame incorrectly. It wouldn't be the first time, and certainly, I wouldn't fault Osferth if that proved to be the case here.

I strike out to intercept Pybba and Rudolf, where they assist Wulfred. They're trying to get him mounted, and I can already tell that it's not easy to accomplish.

"Poor fucker," Pybba's words, and his jutted chin, alert me that he means Lord Osferth and I grunt, trying to block the keening from my ears.

"What about you, Wulfred?" my warrior is pale and trembles slightly. His tongue, when it pokes through his dry lips, is the only hint of colour on his face. Even his brown beard and moustache seem to have faded to grey.

"I'll be fucking alright, you bastard," Wulfred gargles, and I'm pleased to see that his injury hasn't stayed his foul tongue.

"Good to hear it. What happened?"

"The damn shits came out of nowhere. I heard nothing but the slither of a blade cutting a fucking neck, and then they were before me. Bastards. I fought them off, tried to shout for aid, but one of the fuckers threw a stone at my mouth, all but choked me, and then they fucked off and left me bleeding to shitting death."

I grin, despite the diatribe. Wulfred should be at Kingsholm, not here. But he is at my side, and I'm grateful to him.

"Will you heal?" I ask him, although the question is directed at Pybba.

"Of course, I'll fucking heal and kill the bastards that did this to me."

"That might be too late," I state, eyebrow arched. Has he not realised the fighting is over?

"Well, I'll kill the next Raider bastard I see then and wear his fucking balls like a chain around my neck." The image is so incongruous that I find myself chuckling, no matter the sorrow I felt only moments before.

"I'll hold you to that," I state, grinning still, while Wulfred spits and mutters to himself as he's finally mounted. Rudolf rushes to ensure the wound is correctly covered.

"Here, try this." I pull some of Eowa's moss from around my weapons belt. I've been hiding it as much in plain sight as possible. I carry weapons to kill, and moss and herbs to heal. "The lad in the woodlands close to Warwick used it for our wounded there. It should help."

Pybba takes the moss with a sceptical look that almost makes me laugh once more. Of us all here, he should know best the power of plants to heal our wounds.

"I have no honey," I explain, and he nods, sucking his teeth as he surveys Wulfred. I can see from the staining on his trews that the wound is high, perhaps the fucker who did this to Wulfred tried to take him in the groin as I did to Jarl Olaf. Maybe Wulfred is damn lucky to be alive.

"There, now, keep an eye on it," Pybba states, slapping Wulfred's dirty white stallion on the back as he moves to retrieve Brimman. I turn, my eyes grazing the scene of Seaxwulf's death rites, hoping that it's all over and done with. But it isn't.

"Will it rain again?" Scef remains close to Wulfred, no doubt in case the man falls.

"Later, not now." When Scef offers no further information, I sigh and head back toward where Haden will be waiting for me.

The smell of iron and rust fills the air, which yesterday was so enticing because of its clean scent. The Raiders have defiled this place with their weapons, and now I'll need to bury them as well. I hope their stench doesn't linger for long.

Eoppa and Hereberht have remained under the trees, seeking out the dead Raiders, and dragging them to a spot close to the tree line. I agree with them that I don't want them buried under the trees.

They have a pile of treasure steadily growing on a discarded cloak. I smirk to see Rudolf casting a calculating look at it all, and then turning away, perhaps with disgust.

But before I find Haden, I come upon the man I killed last. His body steams in the warming air, and the scent of corruption fills my nostrils. Rudolf has beaten me to it, and his nimble fingers are quick to release the catches on the weapons belt, cloak and the arm rings that snake, silver and twisting, along his right arm.

"Daft bastard," I comment, seeing all his wealth in the growing light. "If he'd moved more quietly than an ox, he might have killed us all."

"Rich fucker," Rudolf confirms. I'd berate him for taking the proceeds of my kill, but I know Rudolf far better than that. Sometimes we both forget that our positions have changed so much in the last few weeks.

"Stupid fucker," I counter, bending to tug on the man's arm and take him to where Hereberht and Eoppa are furrowing a burial for them. The body slides easily over the disturbed ground, and Rudolf stays at my side.

"Lord Osferth's making a fucking scene," Rudolf complains, although he does pitch his voice softly.

"What was Seaxwulf like?" I ask, still unable to remember him.

"No idea. I would swear I've never laid eyes on him before today."

I turn then, stopping so abruptly that Rudolf doesn't realise I've even ceased walking.

"That's strange. I thought the same, but I just assumed it was because I've been busy leading the way to Torksey."

"Nope," Rudolf has finally stopped and turns to peer at me. "Nope. You're not wrong. The others agree as well."

"I see," I concede, looking down at Jarl Olaf in an entirely different way, and considering Lord Osferth's mourning in a wholly new way as well.

"I fucking see," I expel, pleased to fling the body into the hole beside the others.

"I fucking see," I mutter again, while Rudolf wisely holds his tongue and Hereberht and Eoppa eye me with surprise.

It's not difficult to see what's happened here.

"Bastard," and I don't mean the fucking Raiders.

CHAPTER 13

I say nothing to Lord Osferth of what I suspect, eager to be gone from this place of death and revelations.

The horses are as keen to leave as I am, but the riverbank has become impassable. We can't even ride within sight of it because the torrents of rain still flow from the higher land that surrounds it.

My mood is dark, my wound aggravating and no one comes close to me, as though I ward them off just with my sullen countenance and hunched shoulders.

Scef gives no further accounting of when it might rain again, and as the sun continues its arc in the watery blue sky, I begin to feel that the threatened rain mocks me. It'll come, I'm sure of it, but only when it's most inconvenient.

Pybba, Rudolf and Scef lead the way, but in a change from previous days, I send Sæbald and Ælfgar to the rear of our decreasing numbers.

Lord Osferth lost two guards and also another man in the attack. And his son. But I don't count his son amongst the number of men lost to me. It seems he should be counted amongst Jarl Olaf's tally.

I wish I'd not insisted on such a fitting burial for the youth. He should have been flung in the grave with the fucking Norwegians, of that I'm sure.

It might not be raining, but the sound of running water is all around me, making me lick my lips, thirst creeping its way into my consciousness.

This journey to Torksey should be over with by now, the other half of my men and Ealdorman Ælhun's men reunited in victory. But it's not, and although the belief remains strong, it's a belief in myself, not in the vision of a restored Mercia that Bishop Wærferth foisted on me.

I ride armed, my shield covering my right leg, even though it's uncomfortable, and my seax, only roughly cleared of Jarl Olaf's blood, loose in my hand. Haden, as always, seems to know my mind. His gait is steady and quick, his canter constant and assured. I wish everyone could be as reliable as he's chosen to be, for once.

I refuse to stop, despite the complaints that reach my ears, and the sly looks that only Rudolf dare send my way. I want to be at the bridge. I want to find my other men, and I want to set such a speed that the Raiders, with their feeble horse handling skills, will find it impossible to match.

Jarl Olaf's horses have been added to my stock, riding unburdened, but claimed by another. I won't have them as a long string, tied one to another, but rather where they might prove useful should one of the mounted animals falter or tire quickly from Haden's speed.

I eat in the saddle, pulling some dried meat from my saddlebags. I chew it slowly and only then chase it down with the contents of my water bottle. My belly churns with each bite, and the taste of betrayal sours the food. I only persist because I need my strength. I would be foolish to relinquish it in the face of betrayal.

After all, Jarl Olaf and his warriors are dead. Now I need to hunt down the others. If I must, I'll lay a siege at Torksey and hold there until the Raiders have nothing to eat but the rats and field mice that they happen upon in whatever dusty field they've laid their camp.

When the rain returns, as the long summer evening begins to bleed away to the west, I stoop inside my cloak. I'm determined to reach a spot in the distance, that I've seen Scef pointing out to

Rudolf and Pybba.

I hope it'll be easier to guard than the woods of the night before. Only I'm caught by surprise when the scent of smoke filters into my thoughts. I turn and stare into the growing gloom, only then appreciating that we've found the bridge that spans the elongated Trent. There's a small settlement to either side of it, the smell of wood smoke strong in the air.

"What is this place called?" I shout, hastening to Scef's side, roused, finally from my grumpiness of the day.

"Swarkeston," Scef replies promptly, his voice thrilling with the delight of sharing his knowledge.

"The bridge is long," I exclaim, and he chuckles.

"It is, My Lord King. The Trent has been known to reach from one end to the other, and so the bridge was built to be long enough to ensure no matter the flooding, the opposite side could still be accessed."

I confess I'm astonished by the engineering skills on display.

With what light remains, and the aid of a burning brand on each end of the long wooden bridge, I can see the stone pilings jutting clear of the water, by some distance. The wooden walkway gleams with the sheen of excellent wood felled from Mercian trees, perhaps even the woodlands that guarded us against the rain last night. Even now, I can see the pride with which the men and women who make this place their home hold the settlement, just from the immaculately tidy and cleared trackway.

I've never been so far north on the eastern side of Mercia. I had no idea that such could exist. It makes the bridge the Gwent Welshmen are rebuilding for me in Gloucester appear insubstantial, even though the Severn is a contrary beast, difficult to tame.

My mouth hangs open, and Scef continues to grin at me, as though he built the bridge and it's his to revel in.

"But we should be wary," I announce, suddenly aware that this would be an excellent settlement for the Raiders to have taken command over.

"Perhaps, but the men and women who live here have long been vigilant," Scef announces. "They have almost as many weapons as you, My Lord King."

"All the same," I meet the eyes of Pybba, and with only the slightest huff of annoyance, he rides forward, Rudolf at his side, although I hang onto Scef's bridle.

"Just a little caution," I advise, hoping all the same that Scef is correct. Although it would surprise me. How could near enough three thousand warriors go both up, and then down the river, without coming into contact with these people?

"My Lord King," Pybba's voice is almost impossible to decipher as he emerges from the first shelter he's entered, Rudolf remaining alert outside. I sigh. The fact he called me king alerts me that not everything is as it should be.

"Stay here," I caution everyone else, encouraging Haden forward. His steps are heavy and reverberate loudly on the hard surface of the trackway. It's not quite as firm as one of the ancient roadways, but it's a reasonable effort.

"What?" I ask when I'm close enough not to have to shout.

"Bodies," Pybba says, but there's something in his voice that has me wrinkling my forehead and jumping down from Haden's back, forgetting as I do, my wound.

"Bastard thing," I complain, trying not to hop about with the pain of jarring it all over again.

"Daft fucker," Pybba's words reach my ears, but I determine to ignore them.

I turn then, and gaze over the bridge, toward the other settlement, just as quiet as this one, and yet, is it?

I bend low and dip my head into the sturdy building. It's not big, but it's well made. The stench of iron and salt greets me at the doorway, and my eyes open in surprise at the sight.

I expected to find many dead Mercians. But that's not the case. Yet, there are bodies splayed inside the small hut. I don't know how they got there, but I hope I meet the men and women capable of such ferocity.

Staring eyes greet me, a hint of Jarl Olaf in them. I shrug my shoulders.

"You should have stayed at bastard home," I spit, and then I'm outside once more, a tight grin on my face.

"Shall we?" I beckon Scef to me, as I mount Haden once more.

"Do you know these people?" I indicate the twin settlements with my sweeping arm. Scef nods, his good humour fading away with concern. "I think you'll need to speak for me. As you say, these men and women are fierce, as those bastard Raiders discovered." I jut my chin toward the building, and comprehension flees over Scef's face, and the beam is back on his face.

"Come on then," Scef urges his mount to step foot onto the long wooden bridge. It echoes loudly in the gloaming.

I turn my head to the rest of my force, my eyes skimming over Lord Osferth for I don't wish to have to look at the man with my new understanding of his son's death. "Stay here, be alert." I caution, and then I follow Scef, Haden, for once, not doing the dance of a thousand hooves before deigning to walk over the bridge. Pybba and Rudolf come with me. Perhaps I should have chosen someone else, but I need Scef to remain calm, and he trusts Rudolf, and Rudolf goes nowhere without Pybba these days. There was never really a choice for me to make.

The water rushes beneath the wooden planks. The deluge of the day before has turned the water into much more than a sluggish stream. I wouldn't think anyone would stand a chance of traversing at the place we met the Raiders yesterday. I imagine the water would be almost to shoulder height, and far too dangerous to attempt any crossing.

I peer over the side of the bridge, shuddering a little at the expanse of space down below.

"Must the ships who use this waterway lower their sails?" I call the question to Scef.

"No, My Lord King, although some prefer to. It's high enough for all to pass."

I purse my lips, considering the knowledge. The Raiders have clearly sailed beneath this bridge, not that it's a complaint. There would have been no means to stop them, not unless there had been enough spears and arrows to rain down on them, and I don't know anyone who has three thousand of either.

By the time we reach the middle of the bridge, I'm aware that we're being watched.

"Scef, call out your greeting and your name, let them know we're not the enemy."

Scef shrugs in the darkness, and I replay my words. Perhaps we are one of their enemies, I don't know.

Scef still hasn't spoken, and the air rushes from his mouth as I speak again.

"Call out your greeting and your name, and let them know who I am. It'll be for them to decide if I'm an enemy or not."

"Hail Swarkeston," Scef's voice booms over the expanse of the bridge that remains, and I sense some movement from the darkness.

"It is Scef, son of Scef from Repton. I'm escorting the Lord King to drive the Raiders from our river."

"Tell them how many we number," I add.

"There are four of us on the bridge, and near enough fifty more men behind us."

Scef rides with his hands to either side of him, his intent to show he's unarmed clear for me to see although anyone further away would struggle to decipher the movement. My hand hovers close to my seax. The stillness from the lower settlement warns me that all might not be as it appears.

The dead Raiders assured me that Swarkeston had defended itself well. But perhaps the Raiders have made this southern end of the settlement their home, and have stashed the bodies of the Mercians somewhere else. Maybe this is all a trick.

"Hail Scef, son of Scef" the voice that replies is even louder than Scef's, no doubt used to shouting from one end of the long bridge to the other.

"Be welcome," it continues. I listen carefully, trying to detect the hint of an accent in it, but there's nothing. The man sounds Mercian to me.

"Do you recognise the voice?" I ask Scef quietly. His response is not the reassurance I might have hoped.

"Maybe."

"Then be alert." I hope that Rudolf and Pybba hear my words as well. I'm unsure how far the sound will travel over the rushing water. Certainly, I don't want the enemy, if they are enemy, to know that we suspect anything.

I keep my eyes forward, trying to determine the edges in the darkness, but it's impossible. And the flaming brand waiting for us at the other end of the bridge merely makes the shadows darker and causes spots to dance before my eyes.

It seems to take a long time to cross the wooden bridge, and I truly appreciate the skill that's gone into building and maintaining it. I might think Haden, my sword and shield, my most valuable possessions, but any man or women involved in constructing and maintaining the bridge is much, much richer.

Finally, Haden steps onto more solid ground, the echoing steps of Pybba and Rudolf's horses resounding for a few heartbeats more. Then the four of us are in a line, shoulder to shoulder, our animals, for once, behaving as though they too sense the unease.

A figure emerges from beside the flaming brand, obscuring their face so that I can't see whether it's a man or a woman. A long silence falls.

"Scef?" the voice is that of a man.

"Hail Æthelnoth," Scef replies, and I relax, just a little, my fingers aching from being held so tightly for the length of the bridge.

The figure emerges swiftly from the gloom and walks to greet Scef, although he hasn't dismounted.

"What you doing on a fine horse like that?" Æthelnoth asks, clearly having not quite believed that Scef is with the new Mercian king.

"Ah, well, this is King Coelwulf, the new King of Mercia. I'm guiding him to Torksey."

"New king? Aye?" I can see the man more clearly now, and

imagine he looks at me with the same interest that I do him.

"Well met," I offer, dismounting and walking to offer him my arm in friendship. "We haven't met before. But my men and I are hunting the Raiders. I travel on the northern bank of the Trent, and I have other allies on the southern side. Have you had much trouble since the Battle of Repton?"

My grip is firm, but not the firmest and yet I detect a slight wince on the bearded face of the other man. I release my grip just a little. It's too easy to forget my strength when I meet men and women who aren't warrior trained.

"Some, we gave them a good kicking when they tried to come ashore. Damn bastards. Killed old Ecgbert and his wife. Nasty pieces of shit." I'm unsure whether Æthelnoth means Ecgbert and his wife or the Raiders. I hold my tongue and wait, releasing my grip entirely and pretending not to see the relief that touches his cheeks.

The figure is similar in height to me, but nowhere near as broad. He's certainly no warrior.

"You killed all those Raiders?" I enrich my voice with respect and just a hint of surprise.

"Well, I only took one or two, it was Ceolnoth who did most of the damage."

Only now does another figure emerge from the shadows. The new arrival has the build of a warrior, and the scars, flashing white and puckered in the flames, to show that he has been a man to deal death.

"Well met," I extend my hand to him, but he shies away, and I look to Æthelnoth.

"He don't really like meeting new people," Æthelnoth explains.

"Then, you have my thanks for protecting your people, and I'm sorry about Ecgbert and his wife." I would prefer to know everyone's name, but they're not being offered to me, and I don't want to press the point, even if I am the king.

"We're not sure what to do with the dead," Æthelnoth muses.

"When did the battle take place?"

"Two nights ago. Evil bastards tried to steal our food. We showed 'em what's what, didn't we Ceolnoth?" Ceolnoth might not like meeting new people, but his broad beam explains why he's tolerated in the settlement.

"Burn them," I offer simply. "It might be a waste of a good building, but better than having to bury them. Here," and I fiddle with my moneybag almost discarded on Haden's saddle and pull out a handful of coins. "Burn them and use this to buy new wood." I have no idea if it's enough.

Æthelnoth nods his head slowly, as though considering whether he'll do what I suggest or not, and then takes the coins all the same.

More and more people have appeared from the darkness, and I try and meet as many curious and defiant eyes as possible. These people embody Mercia. They might never have come into contact with me before today, but I approve of them all. They share my fighting spirit.

"And have you seen any Mercians?" I finally ask the question that's brought me over the long bridge even though my reception wasn't assured.

"No one, other than you, My Lord," Æthelnoth wavers over the title, as though unsure whether I truly am the king.

"The bishops have given me their support, and their men, as have the ealdormen."

"What, even Ealdorman Wulfstan?"

I pause before answering. I don't know what these people thought of the man.

"Ealdorman Wulfstan is dead. He was a traitor working with the Raiders."

A gleam steals over Æthelnoth's face at the news, visible even in the dancing flames from the brand.

"Did you kill him, personally?" The words surprise me, and yet I can understand the need to know.

"Yes, I did. I won't have traitors serving Mercia." My voice thrums with the truth of my assertion.

"Then, I might rightly call you my king as well," Æthelnoth

states flatly, clearly all the acclaim I'm going to receive from this solid individual. "That bastard allowed the Raiders access when they took Repton. He had his men hold us aside so that we couldn't attack them from the bridge with stones and flames, as we normally would. They even took the arrows from young Æthelflæd and Eadhild and smashed them into pieces. Poor girls. There'll be no game now until they get replacements, whenever that might be."

As though conjuring them from the vapours of the surging river, two women appear before me. They're not girls at all, and the look on their faces assures me that Æthelnoth's words are tolerated rather than accepted.

"I'll replace the arrows and send more if you require more." I can't see that these people go hungry, not with the river as a constant source of food, but their position is a powerful one. I would do well to reward them.

"There are six of us who can shoot," I don't know whether Æthelflæd or Eadhild responds, but one of them does, her voice gravelly and considering. "Enough for ten bows would be helpful to train the next generation with."

I incline my head to the pair of them.

"I have some I can leave with you now."

"Then you have our thanks, My Lord King. We'll use them to ensure the river stays clear of the filthy scum and their beast-breasted ships."

"Mercia is grateful to you for your care."

This seems to satisfy, and the women merge back into the dimness as I stifle a yawn.

All the same, Æthelnoth sees it. "You're welcome to sleep within our hall this night. We're sheltering on the southern bank, for now. The northern one is free, as are the stables."

"We'll do that, with thanks. But tell me. Did you plan on making the bridge impassable, is that why you're all here?"

"No, My Lord King. Your arrival was anticipated, and we came this way, unsure if you were ally or enemy. It's a proven tactic of ours. It's hard for an enemy to surprise us when there's only so many who can attack width-ways along the bridge."

"I approve of such a ploy," I offer. "I'm expecting some of my men to ride this way soon. If you see them will you inform them that I was here and that I'm heading for Torksey, as previously agreed."

"Of course, My Lord King. And if we see any Raiders, we'll do our best to add them to the stinking pile of bodies we already have."

"Yes, do that," I agree and then pause.

"Shall we light the fire tonight for you? We have some experience of burning the dead."

Æthelnoth pauses, and I wonder why he speaks for everyone. He's not the sort of person I imagine leading others in a crisis, but perhaps they appreciate his patient nature.

"Yes, if you would, My Lord King. The wind is favourable and will blow the stink upriver, terrifying those who might yet linger."

I mount Haden then and turn him back across the bridge. If anything, his hooves sound louder now. The water is so forceful that a cloud of condensation obscures the view before me. In the time I've been gone, the Raiders could have attacked my men, and I'm cautious once more. My fingers whiten around the handle on my seax, my thumb rubbing over the end of the well-handled leather.

"Hail," I bellow when I can once more see the glint of the brand.

"Hail your fucking self," Wulfred retorts, forcing a bark of laughter from my mouth.

"Well, at least I know it's really your own true charming bastard self," I exclaim, Haden, picking up his pace as we near the harder ground.

"Aye, My Lord King, not like there's another chap such as I in all of Mercia."

"No one else as foul-tempered and evil-mouthed as you, that's for sure."

His grinning face greets me.

"We can shelter in the great hall tonight. And we get to burn the dead bastards." A rousing cheer greets my words from amongst my men, if not Lord Osferth's.

"And what of the bleedin' others?" Wulfred asks.

"No sign of them," I sigh on the admission, once more dismounting from Haden and leading him away to find some shelter for the night.

Only then, I pause.

"Rudolf and Pybba, take the arrows I promised back across for me. I'd sooner they had them." My instructions acknowledged I focus on Wulfred's muttering.

"They'll be at Torksey," Wulfred announces, his voice carrying to me even though he stands watching the bridge to make sure no one erupts from along its length. "They'll have fucking sped off and beaten you to it. Edmund and Icel will have done it to win acclaim from you." Wulfred sounds assured and yet I can't help but think of Edmund's horse, now amongst my own.

If that's what's happened then why the fuck has Edmund cast aside his favoured, and ill-tempered stallion and allowed it to fall into Raider hands?

I can't help but think Wulfred's view of past events is far too rosy.

CHAPTER 14

The fire, when it's lit beneath the building containing all the bodies, glows sullen and then flares bright blue as it ripples its way along the hair and fat of the dead.

I stand down-wind, and yet the stench envelops me all the same, and I curve my lips, trying to breathe through my nose and not my mouth.

I don't want to taste the fucking dead.

Fatigue sucks at my limbs, along with an unusual sensation for me, that of worry.

Sæbald joins me.

"Will Gyrth be healed by now?" his voice is soft, as though he doesn't want others to realise his concern.

"Hopefully. And Bishop Wærferth will have sent him back to Kingsholm."

The following silence assures me that Sæbald has more to say to me, but that he's just taking his time, considering what to say.

"Lord Osferth knew his son was close. He chose not to tell you."

I turn, startled from my reverie.

"What?"

"Two of the men sought me out. We've struck up a friendship, of sorts. They didn't want to be seen speaking to you."

"And you believe them?" I demand to know.

"Scurfa and Æthelwilf have nothing to gain from telling me lies."

"Well, how do they know that?

"Scurfa came upon the two guards before one of them was dead. He said that Osferth had told him to let his son inside the perimeter."

"Fuck."

"I know, My Lord King, apologies."

"Don't call me that," I retort, knowing my rage has been stoked and with it a desire to be difficult. "Call me My Lord if you must, but not the other. And I prefer Coelwulf."

Sæbald nods, as though he expects my reply, and says nothing further.

"Fuck, fuck, fuck," the words tumble from me, as I stride to Wulfred.

"My Lord," he doesn't get to finish his sentence.

"Call me fucking Coelwulf or nothing at all," I snap, and he grins.

"Aye alright then. What you want, fucking Coelwulf." His words might amuse on any other day, but I just ignore them and the grin slides from his face.

"It seems we have a traitor in our midst. Be wary of Lord Osferth's men and who he sets on guard duty. I want to know if you suspect anything, anything."

Wulfred's relaxed pose stiffens at my words, and I can almost hear him wishing he hadn't opted for the task.

"You'll be fine," I find myself reassuring him. Wulfred is not without skill. He just rarely chooses to use it.

I make my way amongst all of my men then, seeking them with my eyes and whispering of betrayal in their ears. That is until I come to Hereman.

He's found himself a wine jug from somewhere, as he peers moodily into the fire. I settle beside him, on the well-walked path that leads straight to the wooden bridge, folding my legs beneath me.

"Bastard," of course, I forget about my wound, and it tugs tightly, and I bite my lip when the word doesn't alleviate the pain.

"What?" Hereman's tone is sullen and heady with wine.

"You need to put that bastard thing down," I indicate his wine. "There are traitors amongst us."

When Hereman makes no move to do my bidding but rather slugs more deeply, I reach out, to knock the jug from his puckered mouth.

"Tell me something I don't fucking know," he complains, swivelling his body to move the jug far from my reach.

"Here, try some," he passes me his wine, and I'm about to refuse when I catch a whiff of it.

"A ruse?"

"Of course," Hereman slurs.

"When did you know?"

"How did you not know?" is his understated response, and I growl, angered by all this.

"They're not your men. They're not your warriors. I think you keep forgetting." His words are sobering, and I acknowledge the truth of them without further rancour.

"But we need them to defeat the enemy."

"Do we? We've been doing okay so far. How many did we kill inside Repton? More than enough to send the other shits fleeing for the north."

"Where the fuck is Edmund?" the words are out of my mouth before I can stop them, and Hereman's breathing all but stills.

"He'll be playing this game, and better than you are," he offers. His words are softer than the crackle of flame, that now roars blue and superheated, the clothes of the fallen fuelling the rampaging fire.

"Then I wish I knew what his 'game' was. I don't want to spend all my time second-guessing myself." I struggle to my feet as I speak, trying not to tip into the fire.

"We'll learn the truth in Torksey. Provided we make it there alive." And then Hereman grabs my arm and pulls me closer.

"I'll stay awake tonight. You must sleep and re-gather your wits. You're not as astute in your thinking as you should be."

I think it a complaint from Hereman, but his eyes reflect

understanding as well as burnt umber from the fire, and I expel my angry reply.

"My thanks, old friend." I turn and move through the men still watching the inferno. They allow themselves to be warmed by the spectacle of limbs cracking and splitting, as the sturdy wooden trunks of the building slowly begin to buckle and then blacken.

Eyes watch me as I move away, and under the gazes, I struggle to think of where I should seek my bed until Rudolf appears from nowhere, his eyes white rims in the dark night.

"This way," and he guides me not to the great hall, from where I can hear loud voices and even louder snores, but rather to a small building, the scent of hay and dung rife in the air.

Haden stands to attention, his back rigid until he sees me. Pybba is there as well, as are more of my men and all of the horses that we would need to make a quick getaway.

"We thought it best," Rudolf announces, and I realise once more that my men are doing my thinking for me. It's not the way it should be. My focus should be on keeping the eleven of us safe. Instead, it's grown to encompass all of Mercia. In particular, the men I've been separated from or left behind at Kingsholm or Worcester.

Perhaps it is too much for one man to consider.

"My thanks," I offer, moving through them and settling beside Haden as he decides to relax for the night, and makes himself a bed on the floor, taking up more room than I'm sure he should. With my head leaning against the comforting warmth of my beast, I allow myself to drift to sleep. It pulls me under, taking me between one breath and the next, and the oblivion it offers is more than welcome.

"Coelwulf."

"What?" I feel as though my mouth is stuffed with hay, and turning over, I realise it is.

I spit it clear and turn to meet Wulfred's red-rimmed eyes.

"Fuck? Is it day already?"

But he's shaking his head, a finger to his lips, and I swear I can see, in the guttering shapes from the funeral pyre, his tongue spewing foul words at me for speaking aloud. Next, his hand reaches for his ear, and I realise that I must listen.

Haden is more alert than I am, beside me, and I strain to hear while fighting for clarity of thought. My head is foggier than the river mists, and I almost struggle to remember where I am and why I share a bed with my horse.

Only then it all comes crashing back to me, and I'm silent, almost fearful of breathing.

White-eyes seek out mine, and I appreciate that most of us are inside the stables. By that, I mean most of my warriors. I don't have a clue where Lord Osferth is.

I listen for creeping footsteps. Only the sound I'm supposed to be hearing is louder than that and louder even than the rain that has resumed its relentless drone since I closed my eyes.

It seems that Scef was right to warn there would be more rain, perhaps it just took longer than he thought. The river level will inevitably rise even higher. I reconsider the height of the bridge and realise the decision to make it so high and long was a sound one.

And then I hear the noise.

The hammering of the rain on the roof almost entirely drowns out the rhythmic beat of oars in and out of the water. Yet once heard I can't convince myself that it's anything other than what it is.

Many hands quest for weapons, and Wulfred finally opens his mouth to vent his anger.

"Fucking cock sucking dogs," almost polite for him.

"From the north?" I whisper, convinced that while silence is needed, we're far enough away from the river that our conversation can't be overheard.

"Aye, from the stinking north," Wulfred breathes, only to hold his finger to his lips once more. Even I've heard the scuff of a footfall from outside.

"With Osferth?" I ask, almost refusing to believe it a

possibility.

"So, it seems."

"Fucking bastard." Wulfred grins at me in the gloom, his teeth flashing whitely. Damn, the man has straight fucking teeth.

"Eoppa remains on watch duty, so as not to arouse suspicion. He pretends to doze, but he has his weapons ready."

"Hereberht has his eyes on the stable as well."

I quickly count the pairs of eyes gazing at me, aware that not everyone is there.

"Hereman?"

"He went across the bridge some time ago."

"Fuck." I can't seem to think of anything else to say.

"We need to get outside. We don't want to be trapped in here." I agree with Wulfred's sentiment, but equally, we need to be able to do something to counter the threat. There are few enough of us. If Lord Osferth has turned his warriors against us, we'll be severely outnumbered, and that's before whoever is in the ships is counted.

"Mount up," I command, aware it's an unusual decision to make. But no one comments. They move quickly to their horses, flinging saddles as quietly as possible onto the beasts, and shushing them softly when they make too much noise.

Rudolf rushes to help Pybba and Scef is the quickest of all, even though he's never ridden a horse as fine as the one he does now.

The sound of the approaching boat or boats seems to grow more and more menacing, and I give a swift thought to how the people who live here have survived for so long, perhaps fearing such a noise each and every night.

I don't like it. Not at all.

"They're coming," Hereberht's hiss, from somewhere beyond the building, is filled with loathing. Eoppa has seen to his animal as well. Hereberht will be mounted as soon as he's reunited with his horse. As to Hereman, I take his horse, the animal pliant beneath my hands. If only the master was the same. Unless. But no. I dismiss that thought.

Edmund's horse I leave alone, even though the animal seems to want to fight. Without someone to ride Jethson, I don't know what he'll do. Better to leave him behind.

"Now," I order. Somehow the stable door is wide open. The flicker of a moon-filled sky shows me all I need to know as I emerge with as much speed as it's been possible for Haden to build up in such a confined space.

There's only one ship on the shimmering river, making its way to the submerged quayside, lit now with a slither of flame. The weapons inside the craft bristle sharply, as though the points of teeth. I know that I've been betrayed once more.

"Damn the fuckers," I exclaim, meeting the eyes of Hereberht from behind my shield, seax in hand. He's been waiting to the other side of the stable door, no doubt ensuring no bastard sealed it tight preventing our escape.

There's a thick band of men obstructing the path to the bridge, visible because of the slight incline the stables rests on. They block the possibility of a quick escape to the lower side of Swarkeston that the inhabitants took when they faced attack.

I can see, on those shields which flash with the motif of an eagle, that the enemy are Mercians and it enrages me even though I accept it as somehow my due.

These men don't know me. Lord Osferth doesn't know me.

I've been keeping my portion of Mercia safe. They perhaps think that they've been doing the same here. Only I've arrived and changed all that.

Damn the fuckers.

In a clatter of hooves and a rush of air, my warriors are beside me, even Scef, although I wish he weren't. As I briefly cast a look from one of my men to another, Pybba to my right, Rudolf his shadow, with Wulfred to my left, I feel a stab of pride.

These are my loyal warriors. These are my men, and their intention to save Mercia from the Raiders is the purest it could be. We've made no accords with the enemy, other than the Gwent Welshmen and they've been Mercia's enemy for so long, they feel as though they're allies.

"Charge," I give the command they must all have been expecting, my voice loud in the damp air, and Haden bunches beneath me, and lets fly with a burst of speed. Somehow, he tempers his long stride to match those of the smaller horses, and it's with a clash of screaming horses and fleeing hooves, that we round on Lord Osferth and his men.

I keenly watch the body language of the warriors. When we begin our attack, they stand tall and proud, displaying their shields, their spears, sword or seax ready in the other hand. But when the horses show no sign of slowing, I see we've broken them without a single cut being made.

Haden scatters two men with his speed, and I feel the thud of their bodies being knocked aside, only my eyes are on the ship and her deadly cargo.

The Mercians are not the real enemy, no matter their treason. They'll be easy to kill because I know they fight only because their leader orders them too. Oath-sworn men must stay true to their oaths, even when they hate them.

But the fucking Raiders. Well, they might be more challenging to beat.

Along the bridge, I suddenly see a flicker of flames, joined by a whoosh of fleeing air, and I know that the arrows are being put to good use. I appreciate then that Hereman hasn't scampered away, pissing his trews, fear souring his belly. No, Hereman has once more understood far more than I have.

But the ship has made landfall, and the clatter of heavy footsteps is clearly audible even above the roaring of the river, the screaming of dying men and the deadly rain of flaming arrows.

As soon as I feel my men have joined me, I lick my lips, taste the iron of my sweat and grin.

"For Mercia," I bellow and we ride as one. If we were seen from the side, I swear people would think there was only one of us. But no, united with Eoppa, there are ten of us against these fucking Raiders.

Haden steps with an unfailing ability to the quayside,

bringing the other riders with him.

I position my shield over my left leg, keen to protect my mount and myself.

These Raiders won't stand and fall without fighting for their lives.

They're persistent fuckers.

The leading warriors are two huge men, spears glinting in the moonlight, baldheads showing they eschew the protection of a helm, and I grin. They're big, and they're powerful, but even men such as these have weaknesses.

"I'll take the man to the right," Pybba calls to me, his voice rich with the satisfaction of facing an enemy he can beat.

"I'll take the left," I confirm and then I'm once more crashing Haden into a wall of human flesh. Only, his forward momentum abruptly stops just before meeting my opponent. Instead of crashing into him, I pull back on the reins and Haden understands my demands immediately.

Holding tightly to his neck, my seax back on my weapons belt, Haden thrusts first one front hoof and then another into the man's head.

The first strike misses. The second does not. And Haden, skilled at such a manoeuvre, holds his position for just long enough. The man, despite his weapon and his size, and his evident skill, tumbles to the floor. A deep crack sends the stench of iron spiralling into the air.

Beside me, Pybba has taken his man as well, but by thrusting him aside.

The two lie steaming, some of their allies faltering as they erupt from the depths of the ship, no doubt considering whether they wish to die here or not.

But behind them, another man snarls at them, his words unintelligible, but whatever he says, the men leap from the beached craft, and begin to advance on us.

We might not have the advantage of the narrow bridge to help us, but the wooden planks of the quay are just as limiting. Especially where the water surges over some of the planks, turning them slick.

Without much light, it's impossible to see where the quayside begins and ends, and I hold my position, as more and more flaming arrows descend from the heights.

Cries of outrage reach my ears, and more than one man is forced to stop and extinguish the ripple of flames that takes root on his shoulder or cloak.

And then one of the arrows flies true, and a man dies with a flaming projectile penetrating his throat from the side.

A small cry of delight reaches my ears, and I smirk. Such skill. I'm impressed.

"*Skjolde*," the Danish voice cries once more, and I know what they have planned.

"Back," I screech at Pybba, and he turns Brimman quickly and makes his way to dry land. I follow more slowly, Haden keen to demonstrate his skills at walking backwards.

"Shields," I repeat the Danish cry. The Mercians who professed no loyalty to Lord Osferth are forming a defensive line in front of my mounted men, as I palm my seax back into my hand.

There are more Raiders than there are loyal Mercians. But not by many. With the aid of Hereman and the archers on the bridge, I'm convinced there are enough of us to end this quickly and efficiently.

"King Coelwulf," the voice is unknown to me, emerging from behind the small line of shields held in place on the quayside. The fire arrows have stopped, hopefully not because they've run out, and I see shields covering that angle as well as the front and rear-facing one. Only the side that opens to the river from the north remains clear.

"Who wants to fucking know," Wulfred bellows from his restored place at my left.

"I'm Jarl Hroald. The Danish jarls have sent me to take King Coelwulf to answer for his crimes. I don't want the rest of you." He speaks the words easily as he steps in front of the three shields held tightly together at the front of his offensive. A man who's bothered to learn how to speak with the people he means to subjugate is lethal and far-sighted.

"I'm going nowhere," Pybba calls, and I see how much this simple trick confuses Jarl Hroald by the way his head tilts from side to side. I can't see his eyes, not beneath his elaborate helm, but I can see that he's a warrior, and clearly one with a gift for languages.

"The Jarls want it known that the war will only continue until King Coelwulf answers for his crimes at Repton and along the Trent."

"Then there'll be war." This comes from Hereman. From his place on the bridge, his voice emerges from the mist as though it belongs to a creature from the otherworld.

Again, Jarl Hroald's head turns, surprised to find his answer coming from anywhere but in front of him.

"Where is Lord Osferth?" I don't think the man deserves an answer, but he gets one, and I almost smile as Osferth's severed head is rolled from behind the Mercian shield wall to land, with a wet splash, just in front of Hroald.

Jarl Hroald falls silent, perhaps assessing this task he's been set. Maybe he'll lead his men away and leave it at that. I hope he doesn't. My blood is high, my body strung for war, as pliant as the strings of the archers.

I see the expelled air before Hroald, not as a cloud, but rather in the settling of his shoulders. He turns then, slithering back between the shields held before his men, and I think that the battle will start now.

But it doesn't.

And then I hear a low whistle, and the sound of yet more oars over the rushing water reaches my ears.

Now it seems we are indeed outnumbered.

Or perhaps not.

The rumble of running feet over the bridge has clearly been going on for some time, and I've simply not been aware. It's the return of the fire arrows that snags my attention first.

"*Skjolde*," the request for shields come from the second ship, and it makes for a strange scene, visible in the embers from the destroyed building and the brief sparks of flame that fly across the water.

I focus instead on Jarl Hroald. His ally is dead, and the force he faces is not quite as docile as he might have hoped.

And his surprise second ship? Well, it's descended into chaos, snatches of flame having lodged and taken root, most noticeably in the tightly furled sail.

"For Mercia," I call once more, and Osferth's loyal Mercians begin to advance on the quayside, and I slip from Haden, keen to join them.

"Pybba, Rudolf, Eoppa, Wulfred and Scef, stay mounted. The rest of you are with me."

I don't wait to see what the men think of this new division. Already warriors are jogging to join the slither of the shield wall from the bridge. I realise that Swarkeston must be far more extensive than I had at first thought.

"I'm behind you," I encourage the Mercians, the ground beneath our feet slick from the heavy rainfall of the last few days, the river creeping ever higher with the fresh onslaught that still falls. We all tread carefully, keen not to land on our arses.

Sæbald stands at my side, and I flick a glance over him, reassured when his eyebrows arch as though to defy any thoughts I might have held about his fitness to fight.

And then the shield walls crash together, as the Mercians rush the last few steps, keen to prevent the Raiders from getting any firmer footing. Behind me, I hear heavy breathing and turn to catch sight of Ceolnoth and Æthelnoth, Hereman as well.

The fire arrows continue to fall from the bridge, bedevilling the second ship, which seems to turn on itself in tighter and tighter circles, as though a whirlpool has formed. Mercia's great river is determined to dislodge the warriors and have them drown in her depths.

The warrior before me stumbles and falls, and I reach down, grab him and shoulder him aside, hoping Hereman or one of the others will see him safely to the rear of the fighting.

"Fuckers," I mutter, my seax ready to take as many lives as possible.

But the confined space is tight, and I struggle to even raise my seax for a blow. Neither do I wish to push the shield carriers so far that my men risk being sucked into the rapidly flowing river. It's the Raiders that I want to drown, not my warriors.

I take a moment, try and reassess the options. All the while I'm forcing all of my weight against the shield. I don't want to give the Raiders even a toehold on Mercian land. Neither do I want a protracted standoff. The night is yet dark, and it's our ally, not an enemy. If the Raiders see how few we number, it might just embolden them.

My eyes flick toward the cries rising from the river. I catch sight of the second ship, fully aflame, men leaping from her side, despite the fact they wear their battle gear. I doubt any of them will have the strength to swim ashore, but I'll have the riverbank scoured when this is done with, all the same.

A sharp poke close to my leg has me looking down, the reach of a spear clear to see.

"'Ware," I roar. It seems the Raiders have devised a means of attacking us without it being obvious.

I hear the swish of an axe through the air, close to my ear, and then I realise the spear tip is no longer there but instead hacked to the floor.

"And the others," Æthelnoth is encouraging Ceolnoth to work his way along the backs of my men to do the same to the other reaching blades.

"Filthy fuckers," the words are not Wulfred's, although I think they are. Instead, it's Sæbald who mumbles the mantra beneath his breath.

"Devious shits," I agree, and still I've not conceived of a way to stop the attack.

And neither do I have to.

The rumble of advancing hooves suddenly fills the air, and I'm thrust aside by Sæbald just as Wulfred flings his mount through the hastily opened gap in the shield wall.

I swear my mouth drops open in shock, as Wulfred, spear stabbing downwards, forces his horse to clatter its way onto the wooden quayside. He doesn't even turn, and then Rudolf is following him before the Raiders can close the gap caused by four of their men being trampled by the great beasts. Rudolf's actions give me an idea. With a hand on Sæbald's arm, we're following Rudolf through the warriors, slashing as we go. When we're not hacking, we use our shields for tumbling the Raiders into the water.

Any other day, the river water would hardly have reached so high up the banks, but now it does. Those thrust aside scramble to the surface, weapons discarded but their leather byrnies dragging them down, and those with metal-linked coats stand no chance because everywhere is wet and slippery, the rain adding yet more peril.

I hear the strangled cries of men gargling the black water, as I continue to lay into any enemy unfortunate enough to face me.

White-eyes greet mine, and despite the fact these men have weapons and clearly great skill, they falter, with no choice but to face me or risk death in the never-sated river.

The sound of bodies falling into water fills the air, quickly followed by frantic splashing, only to be cut off abruptly, or quickly run feeble with exhaustion and the realisation that they will meet their deaths. The rain of flaming arrows continues, some not even still aflame as they hit the enemy in arms, hands or chests, the rain dousing some but making them no less lethal.

Somehow, Wulfred and Rudolf manage to turn their horses before they reach the river itself. As they rush back through the mass of seething men, the damage they inflict more than doubles.

But that leaves Sæbald and I marooned on the wrong side of the force that remains.

I realise it quickly, seeking another way out, wondering whether Wulfred and Rudolf will return again. Only Jarl Hroald is suddenly in front of me, a dirty great cut billowing blood on his face, where his cheek guards have been hacked away.

"You make it to," only his words are cut off, and I never know what he's going to say as an arrow screeches passed my ear, embedding itself in his exposed throat.

The sizzle of flesh makes my nose wrinkle, as he staggers and tumbles, oh so slowly, into the waiting reaches of the eager river behind him.

I'm breathing heavily, aware we've succeeded through far more luck than skill, but succeeded we have.

The Raiders who made it ashore are either dead on the quayside or drowned beneath the gentling waves of the Trent. That leaves only a few men who yet cling to the flaming second ship.

I peer at them, starkly illuminated in the yellow flames of the fire, and I sigh.

"Fucking fools," I don't like to see such a waste, even if they are my enemy.

"You would have thought the daft fuckers could swim," Wulfred expels, his horse leaning forward to lick my ear.

"Get away with you, you daft shit," Wulfred tugs the animal's head away. I reach up, hand all bloodied, and run my fingers along the elegant nose of the sandy coloured horse. Cuthbert has always liked me more than his rider.

"You're as fucking crazy as your rider," I praise Cuthbert, and the animal seems to accept that as his due. Cuthbert, what a name for a horse. Monks are called Cuthbert, not bloody horses.

I turn to gaze at my warriors, noting who limps and who doesn't, my eyes seeking each and every man to ensure they still live. Only then turning to the bridge.

"I see why Ealdorman Wulfstan took your arrows?" I bellow, a snatch of laughter my only response.

My leg wound is making itself felt again, now that the battle-joy has started to fade, I meet the eyes of the residents of Swarkeston.

"Remind me never to make you an enemy," I grip Æthelnoth's forearm, and he grins, for all it is Ceolnoth at his side who shimmers with blood's dew.

"Right," I call to my other mounted warriors, Pybba, Eoppa and Scef. "Check the river bank until the light fades. We don't want any of them scrambling back on dry land."

"What of those in the second ship?" Æthelnoth asks his bearded chin indicating the men who yet live.

"Are there any arrows left?"

"A few, a waste, though."

"Then we'll just watch them until the river takes them," I shrug. They're no risk to us. Not now.

"Maybe a few arrows then," he capitulates. "I'd like some damn sleep."

The cries of the forsaken men are loud.

"My thanks for coming to assist me," I feel the need to say before he turns aside.

"Well, you're the king. I could hardly say bloody no when your man came to me."

"All the same, you have my thanks." Æthelnoth grunts, about to leave, taking Ceolnoth with him, only he pauses.

"Burn the dead, My Lord King. It'll save me the bother." And then he's gone, and as I watch the drowning men in the growing daylight, I hear the whistle of more arrows, just five of them, each aimed directly at a floundering man. Then there's nothing but silence, and the lap of water, and the odd crackle of flame.

It's almost as though the attack never happened.

CHAPTER 15

"How far is to it Torksey?"

I direct the question to Scef.

It's almost midday, and we've not long been mounted and on the way.

The battle of last night is laced with flickering images, and hazy memories, almost as though it truly didn't happen. Only the freshly burning funeral pyre slowly bleaching blackness into the clear sky attests that my night was not filled with the much-needed sleep I should have been getting.

"Another two days at this speed," is Scef's eventual answer, his eyes half-lidded as though he replays the journey in his mind.

It's not what I want to hear.

Scef's silence assures me that he understands that only too well.

Hereman, reunited with his steady horse, and his brother's unsteady horse, rides as close to the river as the burst bank allows. He's scouring for the dead and dying, and already, his spear glints redly. I've tried to thank him for his actions of last night, but in his eyes, it's clear that he thinks I doubted him.

I don't have the words to convince him otherwise.

I won't pretend that I didn't.

Rudolf and Wulfred are still riding high on the acclaim they've received for their daft if successful tactics. I don't want to chastise them. Will warning them now make them less inclined to be so impulsive? I fucking doubt it!

Pybba is more thoughtful. He and Sæbald have been mingling with the remnants of Osferth's Mercians. There are more of them than I would have expected.

My force is no longer as impressive as when we left Repton, but there are many more dead Raiders than there are Mercians. And for now, my men are complete. Well, half of them.

I still comb the opposite side of the river for signs of Edmund and Icel, a flicker of iron in the sunlight, or a gleaming horse's hide. After the attack of last night, and the lingering rain, summer has returned to the landscape. The stench of damp is ripe, but I don't see any of those signs.

I doubt it will take long for the river to return to its typical habitat, slinking back along the sodden landscape.

While I'm impatient to arrive at Torksey, I'm also torn by the knowledge that if there is only my small force, it won't be enough to drive the Raiders from Torksey. Not when they so patently know that's my intention.

Should I return to Repton? Should I summon more warriors to my side, call out the fyrd, as is my right as king of Mercia?

"I can't see there'll be any of them left alive when we make it to Torksey," Rudolf's high voice, and extravagant boast has me rolling my eyes, a smile tugging on my tight cheeks.

"There speaks a man with all the experience of decades of fighting the Raiders."

I might have let the words go unanswered. Pybba, seemingly unhappy with Rudolf and his charge into the river, isn't prepared to allow it to slip by unremarked.

Rudolf turns to face Pybba, his eyes dancing. Never one to be cowed.

"What, you think there are still a thousand Raiders?"

"I think there are more likely two thousand Raiders," Pybba retorts. Tired heads have lifted themselves upwards at the words, and I'm aware that this argument has become incredibly loud and public, and I'd sooner it wasn't.

"Two thousand? But there were three thousand who went to Repton. King Coelwulf killed over three hundred of them before he even made it to Repton. We killed nearly three hundred at Repton, and that was just at first count?"

"So that leaves two thousand four hundred." Pybba seems determined to win his argument just with pure logic. I suppress a wry smirk.

"How many were on those two ships?" Rudolf looks around as though someone else will answer the question for him. When they don't, he continues. "At least a hundred. And how many did the men and women of Swarkeston kill? At least another fifty."

"So, two thousand and two hundred fifty remain."

"And all those others? The men who attacked the woodland, the warriors who came upon us just outside Repton?"

"And they number a thousand do they?" Pybba jibes, but whereas when the argument began, it was ill-tempered, Pybba's voice has softened. It seems he's now keen to ensure that everyone understands the odds we face. He would rather the truth than allow the men to arrive with puffed up chests thinking the enemy almost annihilated, the task all but completed bar the final altercation.

"And who's to say there aren't reinforcements at Torksey?"

"And who's to say Edmund and Icel haven't enjoyed the same slaughter?"

Speaking Edmund's name aloud earns Rudolf a scowl from Hereman. It surprises me because I thought he'd been too caught up in his own thoughts to be paying attention to the raging debate.

"So, if Edmund and Icel have killed as many warriors as we have, that will mean, what two thousand warriors? Maybe some of the women and children survived as well, I don't know. So, two thousand and a few against our depleted force?"

Pybba raises his one hand to encompass the mass of men who follow me, although we're spread thin and snake upwards with the slope of the river. There's little order today, and while I should probably enforce it, I don't think that any of them need reminding to remain vigilant. They know we're being hunted just as surely as we're hunting.

From amongst Lord Osferth's men, Edwin has emerged as the one to keep order amongst the twenty or so who remain. Not that we escaped injuries last night. There are more bruises and cuts, but overwhelmingly there are burn marks. Before Lord Osferth staged his rebellion against me, he had the throats slit of some of those he must have known would never stand with him in betraying Mercia.

That's the reason for our delay. We had graves to dig, and bodies to entomb amongst the sticky mud. Those eleven men will be more deeply mourned than Osferth and his band of traitors. They were thrown into the burning building with their newfound allies. They didn't deserve anything more.

Rudolf's forehead furrows in thought, as he runs back through Pybba's numbers. I can see his mouth opening and closing as though he wants to deny the reasoning, but simply can't.

"Coelwulf." Hereman's deep voice shatters the lighter atmosphere. I turn to glare at him, almost wishing he'd kept his thoughts to himself, as he rides close to the river.

"A ship," he explains, as though understanding the intent behind the look.

"Another one?"

"It's abandoned," Hereman announces, but I'm already forcing Haden closer, keen to have a good look at what he's found. My hand hovers near my seax, just in case, and I rely on Haden's sure footing over the muddy ground close to the rippling, surging water.

The ship does indeed appear abandoned, wedged against a bulwark of a long-toppled tree that bobs in the wave-ridden water. Its hull gleams with the sheen of honey, but I can see the rowing benches clearly, and all but the front of the ship is entirely exposed to the warming sun and steady breeze.

"Strange," I offer, not sure what else I can make of it. "Be aware," I lift my head to call, not sure if it means the occupants have come ashore, or if the ship has been abandoned for some other reason.

"Perhaps it slipped its moorings," Hereman offers softly, as we ride ever closer to it. My shoulders ache with my tense body, my leg wound a distant ache. My hands are ready for an attack, and my knees are keen to turn Haden aside if it proves necessary.

"What, and just came to a stop here?" I know I'm incredulous. It looks far too premeditated to me.

"Perhaps, Coelwulf. The river has been stirred up since the storm."

I grumble to myself, not wanting to speak any more until I know the truth of the seemingly innocuous find. I've an idea starting to form in my mind. Perhaps not the best I've ever had, but if the ship has truly been deserted, then I don't see why I shouldn't claim it as mine.

Hereman and I come to a stop opposite the ship. It's empty, and there are no footprints in the slowly drying mud to show that anyone escaped alive from it.

I pause, considering my options.

It's a ship, complete with sail, although tightly furled in the hull, and oars, although stored beside the sail down the centre. No one is doing anything with it, and only the carved dragon's ship head, buried in the dead tree, alludes to the fact it's a Raider ship.

"Is it water-tight?" I demand to know, watching as one of the Mercians under Edwin makes their way to the side, and then steps inside cautiously. The ship barely moves as it accepts the additional weight.

"It seems so," the voice calls, the bruised nose alerting me that this man helped bury Seaxwulf, walking the length and breadth of the craft, peering under the rowing benches and inside the sail, as though someone might be hiding there. Then, a smirk on his bruised face, a red cut glowing in the bright daylight, he jumps from side to side, once more testing it. I almost can't look for fear the man will fall through the hull if it proves to be weak.

"It's a good ship," he calls, being helped back to the riverbank by Scef, who's gone to peer more closely at the ship.

"It has no maker's mark," Scef stands to attest. "It's not a

Mercian craft. I assure you." I didn't need that declaration. The ship head was enough for me to know it wasn't Mercian.

"Well," decision made I speak. "It is now. We'll claim it and take it with us along the river. How many men will it take to row?"

The ship is not the longest I've ever seen, and there are benches for only ten rowers on either side. But I don't think it needs twenty men to direct upstream, not when the river is so flooded. But, I know little about boats, and so I wait for someone else to speak.

"Six," Edwin announces, and the original man nods vigorously in agreement.

"No more than six."

"And do we have six men who might prefer to row rather than ride?"

I think no one will agree for a heartbeat, but then a few men begin to nod, Scef amongst them. Rowing might not be easier than riding, but maybe it will be.

"Then I suggest we move the ship alongside the land force. I can't see a reason not to keep the ship. It'll make it easier to cross the Trent, should we have the need."

No one argues with me, and I find I miss Edmund's sour derision. Six men dismount, and tossing aside the heavy byrnies, take only light weapons with them into the wooden craft, leaving their horses in the care of someone else.

"What are you thinking?" Pybba asks me when we're riding once more, the sound of men calling one to another trailing us. That, and the splash of oars dipping in and out of the water.

I have no good answer for him, but I dredge one up from deep inside.

"They take all our belongings. I may as well take theirs when the opportunity presents itself."

"But why?" Pybba persists.

I grin.

"I don't fucking know, but it's a bloody ship, and we're on the fucking river bank. Why not?"

"Because it'll slow us down, and I thought you were in a rush."

I concede that by staying silent, and Pybba sighs to himself, moving his mount aside, and returning to the river, seemingly keen to watch the men and their pitiful attempt to row.

I have no answer. But, why the fuck shouldn't I have it?

The men who control the ship are not the most skilled. That becomes clear almost immediately, as they bump along the riverbank unable to force themselves into deeper water.

I consider abandoning the ship there and then, but my idea is growing even with each screech of outrage. Having men able to control the vessel correctly is imperative to the plan.

Unsurprisingly, it's Scef who seems to gather the men together and forces them to move at the same time, ensuring the course of the ship stays true. Once that happens, everything seems to run more smoothly.

I muse as I ride, considering my plans.

Pybba, sighing softly to himself every now and then once the ship can keep pace with us, holds his tongue, for which I'm grateful.

"Scef," I call to the youth. My voice carries easily to where he and the rest of the men are allowing the current to guide them, taking a break from the labour of rowing as sweat gleams on their foreheads.

"My Lord King?" he calls back.

"Have you ever been to Torksey?"

"No, but I know of others who've made the journey." He keeps his eyes on the river, seemingly content to hold the conversation in so open a manner.

"While it was under Raider occupation?"

"Sadly, yes."

"What did they tell you about it?"

Now he turns, eyes narrowing, his lips pursed in thought. His beard and moustache flash auburn in the bright sunlight, and I'm surprised by how controlled they seem. No man is clean-shaven anymore, apart from Sæbald, and even he has a small fuzz beginning to develop, although it leaves his healing wound exposed. It's simply too much effort to warm water for shaving, and no one wants to do it with cold water and risk looking as though they've fought a hundred Raiders single-handedly.

"It's big." Scef announces, unease in his voice. I think he'll say nothing else but then his chest heaves in acceptance, and he speaks once more.

"It's along the eastern bank, not the western one. There's no means of crossing the river, other than with ships, which numbered at least fifty, if not more. Frithestan has never been good with numbers," Scef complains as an explanation. "If there are more than he can count on fingers and toes, it's not likely to be a correct reckoning."

"Have they built defences?"

"Yes, My Lord King. Their camp stretches along many fields, and all along the river. But they rely on the natural shape of the land for protection along the river. In all honesty, Frithestan thought it more like an island than a true part of Mercia."

"And what did Frithestan trade with them?" A brief flicker of fear crosses Scef's face, as he tries to avoid my gaze, but I shake my head.

"I just need to know what they have. They've been there a while now. Have they purchased seasoned wood to build halls, or fortifications, iron to make weapons, or merely animals for slaughtering?"

"Frithestan traded in livestock."

"Traded?"

"Yes, My Lord King. He paid with his life for transacting with the Raiders. He grew too sure of himself, maybe overcharged them a little. They didn't take kindly to it."

I bow my head at the words, and Scef turns aside. I don't know who Frithestan was to him, but it doesn't matter. We should all grieve for those lost to the Raiders. That includes those who tried to make a little coin from the bastards.

"So, we're on the wrong side of the river," Pybba complains into the growing silence.

"For now, yes." I concur. "But they have ships, so I'm sure that they'll come to find us if they want a fight."

But I'm not thinking about the Raiders seeking us out, I'm thinking about how we can fool them, as we did at Repton.

It seems the jarls are still keen to stop me from becoming king of Mercia, even if I have been voted king by the western bishops and ealdormen. It appears that they think it's possible to bring about my death through stealth and deviousness. I think I might just have to try a similar trick.

When I call a stop to the day's activities, the men from the ship, stagger up the steep bank, keen to have the aid of welcoming hands from some of their fellow warriors. Scef makes sure that the boat is secured against the gradually lowering river levels, two ropes tied around two different tree stumps. I stand and stare at the ship.

"What is it you mean to do?" Pybba, so silent throughout the day of riding, is beside me, stripping a piece of long grass with his hand and his teeth.

"I don't quite know yet."

"But you plan something?"

I turn to meet his eyes. They hold neither fury nor acceptance.

"I always plan something." I offer, trying for a smile.

"Sometimes it even works," Pybba states flatly, turning his back on me and walking back toward the fire that Rudolf's tending. I muse on his words but accept it's not a criticism.

"Scef, did you say there was another ford?" I ask him, warming my hands before the fire for all it's been a hot day.

"Yes, but to the north of Torksey. There's another bridge before we reach Torksey," he confirms.

This has me thinking, and I eat without really tasting the hard cheese and bit of fish that Rudolf and some of the other men have managed to catch while we travelled. I drink clear water, from a beck that runs into the main body of the Trent. I squint into the fire, trying to see the future and determine what I should do to make the best use of the men and resources at my command.

We mount a good watch that night, not prepared to endure another attack when the sun leaves the sky. But everything remains quiet, and that's almost more worrying than another attack.

What are the Raiders planning for me next? And more importantly, what am I planning for them? In this toing and froing between us, I must never underestimate them. Equally, they must keep underestimating me.

We reach the bridge at Newark by midday the following day, and I confess, I'm a little disappointed. It's nowhere near as impressive as the long, sweeping bridge at Swarkeston, and the greeting we receive leaves much to be desired.

While my eyes are peering at the bridge, assessing its stability and suitability, Scef is introducing himself to the men who guard the bridge from this side of the river. He works to assure them of who we are.

I'm not surprised to be greeted by suspicious eyes. Even Scef doesn't know these men, and so we could be anyone, claiming to be anything. I think that's how the Raiders have so far been so successful.

Yet, here Scurfa and Æthelwilf come to our aid, Sæbald as surprised as I am. We watch in shock as the two muscle their way to the front of our straggling line of riders and riderless horses, the ship, for now, out of sight.

"Hail Newark," Scurfa and Æthelwilf call out greetings to the two dour-faced men, standing with weapons raised. They seem only a little put out by the arrival of so many warriors before them. I admire their tenacity.

On the far side of the bridge, the Foss Way runs close to the settlement, a gateway into the heart of Mercia from the Humber River. But this side seems almost abandoned, and we've been following the line of the river, without the aid of any sort of trackway.

"Scurfa?" the question is incredulous and followed by a bellow of "Æthelwilf." The two men are off their horses and embracing the others, smiles beaming from all faces, and I detect that the two men are called Denewulf and Ealhferth. However, I don't know which is which because the voices are all bellowing at the same time.

"What are you doing here?"

"King Coelwulf is tracking down the Raider scum."

Now I feel the scrutiny of those four eyes. I know I'm being judged. I can't imagine I appear overly kingly in my days' old tunic that's been wet and dry so many times I'm sure it's shrunk and stinks more of the river than the river itself.

"What happened to King Burgred?" Again, suspicion, and it perversely pleases me.

"Damn fucker made an alliance with the Raider bastards. Took himself off to that holy place they all rant about." I know this is a test.

"And the Raiders?" I bring Haden forward then, sitting as proudly on my horse as I can muster, hoping that he behaves himself. For once.

"The four jarls of Repton should have travelled this way in the last few days. They're fleeing for their lives, and I mean to kill them all."

Now the four eyes sweep behind me, while I gaze at the bridge and the substantial settlement on the far side of the Trent. I know what they're thinking.

"You and who else? There's only about forty of you."

"There are more of us journeying on the far bank," Scurfa speaks for me, and I almost smirk to hear the pride in his voice. He doesn't even know Edmund, Icel and the rest of the men and yet he almost has more faith in them than I do.

"And we have a ship?" Now all eyes turn to the ship, powered by Scef, wallowing slowly toward us. I'm pleased that the men have finally worked out how to row as one. Otherwise, I might not have appreciated Scurfa's endorsement of it.

"One bloody ship? The Raiders have at least fifty."

"So, you've seen them then?" This is what I want to know, and my voice has chilled. I don't know these men, and I don't know what deal they might have done with the Raiders.

"We've seen some of them." The voice is suddenly guarded.

"Some of them?"

"Yes, some of them. Not as many as normal."

"No, not as many as normal." The one echoes the other, and I consider why they've been sent to guard this side of their bridge. Are they fierce warriors because they certainly don't look like it? One of them even holds his shield upside down and doesn't even realise.

The bridge behind them might not gleam with the health of the one at Swarkeston, but it is still well maintained and would allow easy access for riders and carts. But it doesn't act as a gateway between twin settlements as it did at Swarkeston. Indeed, the first houses are some distance away. So, a bridge, and an important one, but not the primary focus of the village. That must be the road behind it.

"And you let them pass?"

"Didn't have much choice a few months ago. Ealdorman Wulfstan brought his men here and ensured that we knew the Raiders were our allies. We didn't want to do it."

I wave my hand, as though to dismiss the sudden worry.

I can't blame everyone for letting the Raiders through. I can blame Ealdorman Wulfstan, but of course, he's dead.

"And when they've been coming this way in the last few days. What did you do?"

Now the two men look at each other, their unease evident. Haden shuffles forward, bends his head and nips at a stray piece of green grass growing just within reach. Damn beast.

"We sent them on their way," the taller of the two men finally admits, standing straighter. "They came under cover of darkness, and we let them go, pleased to see the back of them."

"Probably very wise," I try to endorse their actions. Not everyone can kill the Raiders. Some just want to survive, whatever it takes.

"Do you trade with them at Torksey?"

Now the smaller man shakes his head vehemently.

"No. We've always refused. No matter what they offered."

"And have you seen any Mercians in recent days."

The two men look at each other once more. I almost tire of their strange behaviour, but I need to know the answer to my question.

"No, My Lord King. Just the ships."

It's not what I want to hear. Not at all, but I was expecting it.

"If you see any mounted Mercians tell them their king wants them at Torksey. Tell them to stay on whichever side of the river they've travelled along until now."

I see the backs of heads as the two bend their heads but I'm already moving Haden away. I don't want to cross to the other side. Not here. Neither can I split my force. Not any further. As the two men said, there are not more than forty of us, and in all honesty, I don't think they can count that well. There are thirty-two of us, not forty.

"How many ships did you see?" I ask, just because I need to do a rough estimate.

"Seven went to Torksey, and three came from Torksey."

I absorb the news. Three ships. Two of them burn, and one of them now belongs to me. Where the men have gone, I don't know. I hope they're dead, either thanks to the river or thanks to my other warriors. I don't mind which.

The two men still look at me, as though expecting me to berate them. I don't feel the need to.

"Inform the rest of your neighbours that Mercia has a new king. Ensure they know my name is King Coelwulf and that Ealdorman Wulfstan is dead, at my hand. And tell them that you need to mount a bigger watch, at least until I return this way."

I leave the slight criticism hanging in the air, but both men nod. I consider what they'll report of our meeting, what they'll say about me. There's nothing in them that shows they respect me as their king, but then, they've not seen the slaughter I've left in my wake.

"How far is it to Torksey?" I ask of them then.

"Half a day at speed, a bit longer if you walk," the taller of the men says. He peers upriver, as I do, as though we can see Torksey, although it's impossible at such a distance. I really wish I knew if he were Denewulf or Ealhferth but Scurfa and Æthelwilf have made no introductions, although they stand close, listening carefully, pride on their faces.

"You'll need to move aside from the river," the smaller confirms, having decided to be helpful. "The river doubles back on itself. There's no need for you to do the same."

"My thanks. I need to know that."

"The ship will make quick work of it," he goes on to admit. "The river is easy to navigate."

I pull Haden away from his grasses and aim his head the way I wish to go.

There's still no sign of my missing men, and that continues to worry me, but we're getting close to Torksey.

One way or another, I'll soon know the truth.

CHAPTER 16

We benefit from a cloudy sky and an obscured moon. The oars, manned by sixteen of my men and some of Edwin's loyal Mercians, seem to glide through the water, and our practice has come in handy.

The mass of fires that attempts to drive back the darkness adds a smoky haze to what can and can't be seen. But what can be seen is telling enough.

The number of fires, impossible to count from our place on the river, attests to a vast collection of Raiders encamped at Torksey.

Or does it.

I'm not the only one tasked with counting the dark and silent ships we pull ourselves beyond. Only ten ships managed to escape from Repton, and along the way we've captured one, and burnt another two. That should mean that there are only seven ships at most. But there aren't.

It seems that the Raiders didn't wholly abandon Torksey when they took Repton, or if they did, they've been reinforced by new arrivals from the North.

I consider whether they work together or whether the new arrivals might not resent the return of the failures.

"Twelve," Scef whispers softly, just audible beneath the stirrings of the river. I agree with him and hold my tongue. We must remain hidden. We ride in the Raider ship, with our weapons hidden beneath the rowing benches, but really, I don't want to arouse any suspicion. I don't want to have to explain why we try and row clear of the settlement without thinking to stop.

The river here stretches wide, much wider than at Repton, and I hope its width will protect us.

I need to see, and I need to know before I decide on the suitability of my idea.

As Scef told me, his second-hand knowledge proving to be correct, the Raiders rely on the steep cliffside to protect themselves, where it juts clear of the Trent.

The rise is lit with a sporadic collection of flaming brands. The distance between them proves to be different for each individual brand, as though some have perhaps not been lit. Or, maybe some have already guttered burning themselves out.

And there are guards, but it seems not many.

"The quayside," again, Scef whispers the warning. If possible, the men and I fall even more silent, not even daring to move the oars for fear the enemy might detect us.

I count quickly. No more than five men stand beside what must serve as the quayside and main entrance into the settlement. This part is on a tiny piece of lower-lying land. They have a smoking fire before them, but in what little I can see, they don't even hold their weapons but discard them in an untidy heap beside the fire.

They're too confident in the placement of their camp, and loud voices strain across the wide river, shocking us with laughter and good cheer.

"Fuckers," I think, although I keep the words inside my head, not wanting to risk even the smallest whisper. The ship continues to glide through the water, unheard above the laughing and joking.

This is not how my men keep watch.

And still, the high cliffside continues, as we pass by the men, and continue to glide in the darkness, only rowing every so often, when the ship threatens to lead us onto the riverbank.

My heart thunders loudly in my chest, but my breathing is

even and calm. Just as with Repton, I need to know what I face.

Twelve ships are nothing in comparison to the many that were at Repton. Yet, it attests to considerably more men than I currently command. What, I think can one ship do against so many?

The number of burning brands noticeably diminishes long before the steep embankment comes to an abrupt stop, and here I peer into the gloom, needing to see.

"There's no ditch, inland," Scef offers, his eyes much better than mine.

I nod, and then softly grunt because Scef can't see my action in the dark.

"Keep going, as I said," I caution softly. We can't turn here, not so close to the settlement. If we are to return back downriver, we need to come at it just as silently.

Now we row, Scef keeping a soft beat so that we all move together and don't send the ship squirrelling along the river, first left and then right.

Littleborough is somewhere ahead, a ford that will ground the ship if we're not careful and alert, but I don't think we need to go so far. We have the bridge at Newark and the ford at Littleborough. And the Raiders are at Torksey.

Have the people who live here been forced to work for the Raiders or risk death, or will they join me in attacking the enemy? Such thoughts occupy my mind until Scef's hiss cuts through the air.

Ahead, a few flickering flames appear, and Scef turns to gaze at me.

"Turn the ship," I confirm, knowing that in this we're entirely in the debt of the men who have some ship-skills. I can use my strength to row, but to navigate, no, that's down to Scef.

The young man leaps to the rudder, forcing his weight on to the stubborn piece of wood, as the ship slowly begins to veer toward the far shore. I wince, the sound of oars in the water seeming to be far too loud, and yet I detect no movement along the riverbanks. No one hunts for us, not north of Torksey.

"Back," Scef's voice reaches my ears, and I do as commanded, not even considering it strange to take the youth's instructions until the ship has been turned and oared back to the far shore.

Once more, we make our way passed the Raider settlement at Torksey, oars held as steady as possible to maintain the ship's course. Once more, I count the number of boats, and so does Scef and others as well. I'm considering what I'll do and how I'll do it. I have my idea, but I can't say it's any less risky than the approach taken at Repton.

But, we succeeded at Repton. We will succeed here.

I put aside my fear that at Repton, we numbered many more, and had even more ready to support us when the heart of their camp had been destroyed.

Such thoughts should have plagued me days ago, when we first left Repton, or when we realised that Edmund and the rest of the men were missing.

Now I must do what I can, and with what I have.

The night is dark once more, almost as though it wishes to aid our endeavours.

I've left Scef, along with Edwin and three of his men who he believes will be able to do what I instructed them. I hope they can. There's a great deal depending on their success.

At the last moment, as the sun was leaking from the sky, I'd had a change of heart and beckoned Pybba to me.

His heavy sigh had assured me that he knew my intentions before I opened my mouth.

"I fight better than half of this lot," he mumbled softly. There was acceptance in his words, maybe even a soft breath of relief as Rudolf nodded along as well, although why he was listening in, as always, I was unsure.

And then the force had separated. Now, as I direct everyone to silence, and to wait, I almost wish I'd not taken this decision.

It's even more dangerous than the tactic used at Repton. Am I leading men to their deaths?

Only then a flicker of light flares in the western sky, the sign

I've been waiting for, and I have no choice. Not anymore. Not if I mean to ensure those men, on the riverbank opposite Torksey, live to see the sunrise.

The night is too dark for me to see the faces of the men who still ride with me. Hereman, Sæbald, Ordlaf, Ælfgar, Wulfstan, Hereberht, Rudolf and Wulfred, as well as the remaining Mercians who fought for Lord Osferth but are now led by Edwin. But I know they're with me. I also appreciate that they expect my attack to be a success. I wish I shared their confidence.

"Wait," I caution. I feel that some are already keen to encourage the horses on. To breach the pitiful defences on the landward side of Torksey. To kill the fuckers who tried to claim Mercia for themselves.

But we need to wait.

For now, the four drunken Raiders who guard the primary entranceway on the landward side haven't even seen the flames, reaching into the sky. Certainly, no one has been roused from their bed.

"Wait," I growl again, reaching out to grab the harness on Wulfred's horse.

"Bastard brute," Wulfred complains, and I appreciate that it's Cuthbert that's keen to begin the slaughter, not the rider. Named for a monk but blood-thirsty. I like the beast even more.

We wait, to the north of the only landward gate, but still able to see the small flickering fire that the watch men must be allowed in order to see. There's no ditch running around the extent of the long, long camp, although only half of it is now occupied. The arrogance of the fuckers infuriates me. When did Mercia become so weak that her enemy could take root beside her river systems? Not even bothering with wooden spikes and a high wall and a low ditch to keep the Mercians at bay?

Certainly, that's not what happened to the Raiders at Repton. At Repton, much time and effort went into the construction of the fort for the jarls and their especial followers. Of course, they left the majority of their warriors to fend for themselves.

Underfoot, Haden shifts, and the pungent aroma of standing

water reaches my nostrils. I appreciate that we've been lucky in coming here. Scef was most adamant that much of the area was usually waterlogged. Still, the rain of a few nights ago has barely touched the surface that the long and hot summer months have desiccated.

Come the middle of winter, or during the early summer rain, this camp might just have been a position of great strength. But not now. And, I hope, they've not even realised, and won't, until we're riding through the centre of it, our horses kicking any who tries and stop us. In our wake, we'll leave nothing but the dead and dying.

And this time, there'll be no chance of escaping along the Trent, not if the reaching flames of the distant fire have done their work.

Yet, the camp doesn't stir, and even I begin to feel the impatience I feel coming in waves from the rest of my warriors.

"How much longer?" Rudolf hisses the words, but I don't respond. I have no idea, and the question hangs unanswered, and no others follow it.

How much longer, indeed?

We need to attack when it's still dark. Otherwise, the Raiders will realise the paltry size of my force, and we need it to be as black as possible. It feels as though it's taking far too long.

I can hear the guard men laughing amongst themselves. I can even hear the clink of metal pieces on a wooden board and know they must play the game of strategy they call *tafl* to pass the time. Perhaps they wager coins or night duty, or maybe they just play because they can. I don't know, but I do know these men aren't worth whatever they're being paid.

The fire on the horizon seems to blaze, the scent of burning reaching even my nose, and I'm aware there's a reasonable distance between where I stand and where the river lies.

Haden notices it as well, walking forward and backwards as though unsure what to do, and not seeming to trust my decision to stay still for yet longer.

I reach down and lay my hand as far along his face as I can, hoping to calm him. The jangle of his reins as he turns his head feels overly loud in the still night. And yet finally, I hear something else.

I grin. Perhaps my plan will work after all.

"What can you see?" I direct this at Rudolf, trusting his young eyes better than mine.

"They're moving away." His whispered voice is high with excitement. This is what we've been waiting for.

"All of them?" I want to be sure before I give my instruction to rush through the abandoned gateway.

"I think so," but his voice has slowed, his head canted to one side as he tries to determine if they've all rushed to the source of the fire.

Not that they're alone. I can hear an upsurge of shouting and frustration, all sleep-addled, and I know that more and more of those inside the camp will be making their way to the riverbank. They've been thinking themselves safe from attack.

"Well, even if one or two remain, we should be able to crush them," I confirm, but still I hold back. I want to allow time for the gate wardens to be gone from their posts. I need them to be so far away that they won't realise they're under attack from entirely the opposite direction.

The sound from inside the camp continues to intensify. Even from my place of concealment, I can see the leaping flames that Pybba and Scef have kindled amongst the ships and boats. The ships wallow in the Severn or are drawn up beneath the steep cliffside for repairs. I'm surprised by how high the flames leap and I consider that the grasses we found must have been incredibly dry, even after the deluge of a few days ago.

The ground has been parched for weeks. The summer heat has sucked the moisture from the plants and any stray pools that have formed alongside the Trent.

"Now," and with that, I aim Haden towards where the gate wardens stood before they realised fires were ravaging the ships.

Haden's gait is smooth beneath me, his bunching muscles stretching and contracting as his hooves fly over the baked earth that the Raiders relied on to remain as bog and marsh.

I ride low, my hand on my seax, my shield held over my left knee, ready for the first kill.

The sound of my heartbeat is steady, a counterpart to the thrum of Haden's hooves. My warriors, and those of the Mercians, are with me, and I feel a grin touching my tight face.

The journey to Torksey from Repton has been long, tedious and fraught with disaster and treasonous activities. Now, I'll finish the battle I began there. I'll eject the Raiders from Mercia, and I'll finally be free of them.

And then I can turn my attention to ruling Mercia. The thought is more terrifying than the enemy I face and yet also more satisfying.

"Ah," one of the gate wardens has remained, and his wide white-eyes appear from the blackness of the night, his face showing his fear. Between one heartbeat and the next, he's turning, keen to run from beneath Haden's hooves, but Haden has other ideas. The gargled shriek of a terrified man is cut off as I hold myself steady and allow my mount to make the kill for me.

I've not been able to see much inside the camp, not without giving away my presence because of its slight elevation in comparison to the rest of the land. My eyes flash quickly, trying to take it all in. At the same time, I'm checking no one else is going to dash out from beneath the leaning-wooden structure that must serve as a sort of barracks for those on watch duty.

I slow Haden, reach down and pluck a piece of flaming wood from one of the two small fires burning close by and fling it at the browning thatch that covers the building. Immediately, fresh flames spread, leaping from dry thatch to drier thatch. By the time I turn aside, the entire building is aflame, and all of my warriors are inside the settlement.

"Kill them all," I roar, just to reiterate my decision that we should take no prisoners. I have no need for them, none at all.

I turn Haden, aiming him down what seems to be a set walkway. On either side, embers burn in fire pits and flung open canvases reveal that people have dashed from their beds to combat the fire.

The horizon close to the Trent seems to burn brighter than daylight, a haze of glowing red.

In front of me, a figure emerges from their home, bleary-eyed and stumbling. I encourage Haden to the side of the man or woman. Before they know I'm there, I've gripped my war axe, not my seax, and as the blade impacts the skull, knocking them staggering to the floor, blood sheets high into the air, and I feel it land on my lips, as I ride on.

A better kill.

"Spread out," I instruct, aware that the battle joy is threatening to engulf me and make me insensible to the needs of the rest of my warriors.

Rudolf stays close to me, as I've commanded him to do, Sæbald as well.

Hereman, his bright shield manifest in the flames of the guardhouse, and the fire on the river, leads Hereberht and Wulfred. They beat a path through the canvasses as though the tents are not really there. I watch as more and more flames sprout along the temporary structures.

We'll burn them. Or we'll slice them and have them bleed to death. Either way, they'll be dead, and Mercia might well be re-established at last.

Wulfstan, Ordlaf and Ælfgar have formed their own small group with Eoppa leading them.

As for the Mercians, they've similarly split into smaller groups of three or four. Between us, we reach almost from one end of the settlement to the other, our focus on making it to the river, and more importantly, killing all we come upon.

The sound of a horse's distress fills the air, but I can't look because it seems that my attempt at making an entrance under cover of the ravaging fire hasn't quite worked.

A horse rushes toward me, its eyes reflecting the fire and showing fear, someone mounted, although it seems to me that they have neither harness nor saddle to keep them in place.

I grimace. This could be an easy kill or a difficult one. Anyone mad enough to ride in such a manner might well be consumed only with vengeance.

"Steady," I command Haden, and then at the last possible moment, I release his bunched muscles. He flees forward not at all concerned by rushing headlong at another horse.

I meet the other rider in a welter of crashing hooves. Haden rears, his front hooves beating against the other horse. The pitying cry of a wounded beast fills my ears, and I reach to command Haden and bring him back under control with the power of my knees and boots. I want to kill the warrior, not the damn horse.

But Haden can smell the blood in the air, and it seems to send him wild and beyond obeying my instructions.

"Fucking do as your told," I roar at him, only for the air to fill with the crunch of fracturing bones. I look down, unsurprised to find eyes staring at me from a broken face. A thunder of hooves and the horse is careering toward the unguarded gateway. I watch the flicker of white as it makes a bid for freedom.

Haden skips beneath me, as though determined to get a final stamp on the dead opponent, and then he responds to my instructions once more.

"Come on," I urge him forward. The heat of the burning canvases is a scorch against my cheeks, and all around I see little but reaching flames.

They're damn hungry today.

In front of me, the trackway opens up. I turn Haden, confused for the time it takes me to realise that this is clearly some predetermined place where men and women came together to eat and drink. There are long wooden tables, devoid of all items, and a vast stone fire circle, empty now.

I turn, keen to assess the progress that's being made.

"Fuck," I knee Haden back the way we've come.

Rudolf battles against a warrior who stands, weapons flashing wetly. Rudolf remains mounted on Dever, turning him time and time again, to avoid the cutting slashes.

Before long, both Rudolf and his horse will be too dizzy to

fight on.

I ride, seax in hand, and reach down to slash across the enemy's back. He wears little but a tunic, and I feel blood well beneath my touch, but it's glancing, and the man barely seems to realise he faces another opponent.

Unheeding of the shelters around us, I turn Haden firmly. I'm glad he responds to my instructions even though he tramples through a collapsing tent, the fabric, perhaps bleached by the heat of the sun, floating to the floor as though a shroud.

"Come on," I encourage, and this time, our attack is slower and better aimed. The blade cuts deeper, almost becoming impaled in the body of Rudolf's enemy.

I catch a glimpse of Rudolf's face, his eyes fixed only on his opponent, his weapon of choice, a war axe, ready in his hand. As the man buckles under the force of my blow, staggering forward with his weight unbalanced, Rudolf holds his weapon low. He then lifts it quickly, obliterating the man's jaw and sending him tumbling backwards, collapsing to the ground as soon as Haden has ridden beyond him.

"My thanks," Rudolf puffs, but really he would have been fine on his own, it's just that I'm keen to get this over and done with as quickly as possible.

Sæbald appears, chest heaving, his horse wearing a coat of shimmering red.

"Fuckers," he complains, his face white and I hope he's not aggravated his old injury.

"Come on," I command, already kneeing Haden to continue my onward attack toward the river.

Our advance, while perceived by some, is still mainly going unnoticed and unchecked but I know that at some point soon, the battle will become even fiercer. Surprise must be our ally.

A crack of falling timber reaches my ears, audible even over the rush of Haden's hooves. My eyes reach skywards to watch a succession of masts begin to fall, the sails, unfurled for a reason I've yet to discover, shredding under the onslaught of the flames.

Even with my poor eyesight, I see the blue fabric with the

wolf's head, and I nod, pleased that Jarl Halfdan has lost such a potent symbol of his power.

Halfdan, brother to fucking Ivarr. Both of them leading wave after wave of Raiders against the Mercians, as well as the men and women of Wessex and East Anglia.

How I thrill to know I might kill him before the sun rises.

The collective gasp of horror and outrage overawes all else. Still, no one looks my way, and I can see, only ten or so canvasses away, where the inhabitants of Torksey have massed to watch the destruction of their ships.

"Nearly there," I urge, hanging low over Haden's head so that he can use his great speed to get me closer and closer to the enemy.

Hooves thunder behind me, and I know I'm not alone.

My men will ride with me through fire to protect Mercia.

We might be entirely outnumbered, but we have our horses to add to our number. For now.

I use my war axe from my high position. Confused faces look my way in the strange half-light of ravenous flames that seem to chase me as much as they do my enemy.

None are expecting a mounted warrior. None. I take lives with calculated ease, almost as though I scythe the grain in the fields. Only I won't be making any sort of edible pottage with the heads that tumble.

It all seems too easy, and I try to contain my delight at how quickly I'm accomplishing my audacious plan. I don't want to get carried away. Somewhere in this settlement, there will be warriors able to mount a sturdy response. No doubt, they battle to save their ships.

This, after all, is the flaw in the plan. I want to kill the jarls and their loyal retainers. But of course, they'll be the ones who sleep closest to the centre of the sprawling collection of canvas and shabby looking timber structures.

But suddenly, there are too many people before me to carve a path through them all. My axe is busy, but people have finally woken from their lethargy. Finally, it seems, the Raiders realise this attack is not just on their ships, but also from the east.

"'Ware," I thunder, flinging the words back over my shoulder in the hope that everyone will hear them. I lick my lips, taste salt and iron and consider my next move.

I don't want to risk Haden amongst the tightly packed throng in front of me. Eyes turn my way, focusing on the mounted warriors as opposed to the burning of the ships, and the chance of escaping from Mercia. They can swim for all I fucking care. They can let the river take them, hopefully to its bottom, and then onwards, out toward the massive Humber and then into the sea.

But I can't deny that being mounted gives me a massive advantage against so many. I stay high, keep my war axe in hand, and take careful aim at those who are too slow to rush from my advance. Those who escape from me must still find a path that doesn't lead them beneath the hooves of another horse.

"*Skiderik.*" The words reach my ears from the left, and I stab down, eager to make a strike on the stringy looking warrior, with his eating knife flashing in his hand. He wears nothing but his trews, and I can see his tightly corded chest, the veins prominent on his neck and arms, even in the glow from the twin fires.

Perhaps, on another day, he would have been a worthy opponent.

But not today.

"Same to you, you bastard," I lean down and spit into his face, my war axe following closely on the end of my words so that he's closed his eyes to ward off the flying spittle. My axe cleaves through his nose, with half of its normal force, but lethal for all that.

But this man marks the beginning of men and women who have made it their life's work to deal out death.

Another man takes the place of the first, this one almost tall enough to see over Haden's shoulders. He carries not an eating knife, but rather a war axe, no doubt chosen in the chaos of the raging fire as more useful to prevent the fire from spreading amongst the camp, a weapon to dig tracks to try and thwart the advance of the flames.

That went well, I consider, eyes high beneath the shelter of my helm.

"You fucker," the words are slow and considering, and I grin. If this is all the Raider has learned of my language, then I'm pleased.

"Shitting arsehole," I spit, as his war axe tries to land a blow on the exposed area of my thigh between my shield, and the fall of my metalled byrnie. I turn Haden, quickly, using my knees and boots. He swiftly flicks his hooves forward, and the man skips back, only just avoiding landing on the body of my first attacker.

The enemy leers at me in the reddened flare of the fire, the smell of smoke almost stifling in the still summer air, and I return the favour.

"What now?" I taunt him, but rather than lashing out, he seems to consider what to do next, and while my eyes are focused on him, I know others are thinking of joining the attack.

"Fuck," I hack down at a reaching hand trying to grab one of my weapons, and use it against me. I turn Haden once more, causing him to dance both left and right, his hooves unheeding of any who might be in his way.

Rudolf and Sæbald are behind me, alert to the danger, and their mounts quickly cover Haden's rear end, while I focus on the Raider.

A slash of something long and white marks his clean-shaven face and I think it lucky he recovered from that wound. He's not going to be crawling away from this altercation.

Only I feel as though my men and I are being squeezed.

As I feared, this is where the Raiders have congregated. While the crash of more and more falling timbers fills my ears, the Raiders are beginning to turn away. Hands reaching for whatever weapons can be found to counter the attack.

I suck my lower lip, and make a decision. I turn Haden to the left, his forelegs kicking, his rear legs sending broken body parts high. He forces people to duck away to prevent wearing the body fluids of their fallen allies.

I reach out, as far as I can, derisive with my war axe and the Raider responds, his war axe seeming to whirl through the air at ever greater speed, as it tries to land a blow on Haden's shoulder. Only it's my war axe that meets his, and while he tries to wrench it free, I release the reins and stab down with my seax.

The blow lacks force, in my left hand and not my right, but it still digs deep into the neck of my enemy.

He rears upwards, his war axe almost forgotten about, as he reaches to pull me from Haden's saddle.

I grab hold of the reins again, hand sticky, seax clutched there as well, lean away from his strength, lifting my war axe so that his own drops to the ground.

And then he's gone, and I look down, searching for him, and then a slow grin spreads across my face.

"Well, that went fucking well," I offer, but the man is on the floor his right foot severed by his falling axe, and I'm free to force a path through those in front of me once more. Behind me, I hear my dying enemy, and I know that his blood will flood from the wound, hot and unstoppable, consumed by the parched ground beneath us.

From Haden's back, I have a good view of everything in front of me. It seems that some effort is being made to douse the flames leaping and writhing from one ship to another.

A man, wearing the gleaming metal of a linked coat, stands on something that juts him above the crowd. I take it to be a wooden barrel or a tree stump. He bellows indistinguishable words, and men and women seem to leap to do as he commands, rushing from the river itself to the ships.

But, for each flame that seems to dwindle to an ember, another area begins to burn.

"Fucking bastards." But for once, the words are filled with my respect as I think of the archers and their flaming arrows on the far side of the river. So far, it seems no one has stopped to consider why the flames won't die down.

There's a clear path around me, Rudolf and Sæbald keeping a

watch to either side to ensure no one attempts an opportunistic attack on Haden or me.

"Him," I point to the Raider. I hope it's Jarl Halfdan, I genuinely do. The arrogant shit from Repton, who spoke as though he were a king, even though he wasn't, needs to have his life ended. If not for him and his brother, Mercia wouldn't have endured the years of hardship that it has.

"We take him and then we own everyone here." I've not truly been looking, but as I go back through my fleeting memories of the attack, I'm sure that I've seen no other emblems of the lesser jarls. Is it possible that only Jarl Halfdan holds here, refusing to believe that Mercia is no longer his? Have Jarls Anwend, Guthrum and Oscetel done the wise thing and gone hunting elsewhere? I hope so. It would make the number we face far less.

I encourage Haden on, not bringing him to a stop, even when we encounter more people rushing to the river. They don't rush to help their allies douse the ships, but rather in an attempt to escape the attack coming from the rear.

Screams reach my ears, and Haden adds his own. Haden is his own force, and people scatter or tumble beneath him. I poke my seax at those who think to prevent me, and then I hasten him to a gallop, an open piece of land emerging between Jarl Halfdan and me.

My eyes are trained only on the man, and someone has finally decided to alert him. Hard eyes look my way, determination in the way he hefts the sword offered to him.

I meet his look with a grin. Does he know who faces him? I've no idea. Certainly, he'd already run from the slaughter at Repton before I was reunited with Haden. Yet, there's something in the way he tests the sword that makes me think he does appreciate that his opponent is formidable.

I stay mounted, although I don't know if I'll engage Halfdan from such a height.

I don't want to risk Haden any further than I already have. Halfdan seems to be the sort of man who would think nothing of severing my beloved mount's throat. I won't allow that. Haden has been with me longer than Edmund.

"Jarl Halfdan," my voice rings with derision, the sounds of the attack taking place all around me, seeming to fade away so that he can hear me easily, and equally, I can hear him.

"Lord Coelwulf." He doesn't call me king, and that infuriates.

"King Coelwulf." Rudolf's young voice is filled with menace behind me. Halfdan's eyes flicker to my young squire, who's become a warrior thanks to his attack on Mercia.

"King?" Halfdan chuckles darkly, the sound causing me to bite down on the rage that floods my body. I'll not let him better me with such a tactic.

"King," I incline my head.

"Do you come to make a peace accord with me as that fucking weakling did?"

"Do I look as though I come in peace?" I don't even raise my hand to indicate the chaos all around me, but Jarl Halfdan's eyes still flicker from my face and look, all the same.

"You've sent flames so high into the air, that all of my allies will come to my aid. You'll be dead before the sun rises, and it won't fucking matter what your bloody intentions were."

I don't allow myself to chuckle and luxuriate in the words that fall like stones from a cliffside, loud but ineffectual.

"I would welcome your allies joining the fray. Better to have you all dead than just one of you."

A shadow touches Halfdan's cheeks, as though unsure why his bluff has failed to incite any fear in me. He forgets that I'm the king of Mercia and that doesn't make me as craven as Burgred.

"You could still join us?" Halfdan offers, changing tact, his tone beguiling. Yet his smile has drained away by the end of the sentence, almost as though he knows I'll never accept such a suggestion.

My silence is all the answer he's going to get. Still, he looks behind me, and a tendril of unease ricochets down my back, but I know Rudolf and Sæbald will be protecting me. They'll offer a warning, if and when it's needed.

Yet Halfdan persists in looking behind, and I sigh heavily.

What does he see? Does it terrify him or merely embolden him? I don't think I care to delay any longer.

Casually, I swing my left leg over Haden's broad back, sliding to the ground, and landing as squarely as I can so as not to excite the wound that's finally healing. I reach for my seax and come around Haden's head to untie the shield that waits for me, the painting of the double-eagle head calling to me and demanding that I shed blood to feed it.

With both in my hands, I pause, take a breath and then meet Halfdan's eyes once more.

I remember, in the hall at Repton, that Jarl Halfdan came before me without weapons, armed only with the shimmering wolf etched onto his tunic. I thought it wanted to hunt, but I was wrong that day. Will I be wrong today?

Halfdan wears no helm, and once more, the thick white scar that lines his face is starkly visible. I would advise the fucker not to use flames to backlight him. It makes the old injury appear far more visible than he might realise. It twists his face, and not into the wolf that he might fancy it does.

But he does have a weapon, and I see it glinting in the dancing flames.

I doubt it's doused with blood like my seax, or my byrnie. I fairly reek of the stuff.

I spit, trying to drive the taste of all those I've sent on their way to whichever god they hope will welcome them after death.

Halfdan seems to quiver, and then his eyes focus on me.

I see a smile trying to force its way over his face, but it never quite makes it.

"Where are your allies, or should I say former allies? Have they left you? Have you been too fucking arrogant to realise you've lost?"

Now it's Halfdan who doesn't answer me.

"I've killed them all, you know," I continue, as though discussing pigs for the winter months, and not his sworn men. "Whoever you sent after me is either mouldering in the ground or feeding the fishes. Or my particular favourite, being blown all over Mercia. Never to return home and never to feel the weight of a weapon in their hand again."

Pure fury sweeps over Jarl Halfdan's face. I was prepared for such games. Halfdan was not.

With no more thought, I lunge toward him, to where his sword hangs too limp in his hand, almost as though he doesn't realise it's there at all.

Yet, the blow I try and force against his exposed left side is easily parried, almost languidly. I spin, seax high, shield ready to bat aside any half-hearted attempt he might make while I swivel.

His sword is in front of me, just slithering beyond my nose as I step back, seax prepared to batter it aside, only it's not needed. I begin to appreciate that Halfdan might still retain the skills that have made so many warriors pledge their service to him.

I grin, canting my head from one side to the other. Halfdan might just be a man worthy of my skills, not like all the others I've faced before.

Again, his sword moves almost quicker than sight allows for, but my shield is already high, deflecting the blow, and sweat is starting to bead down the other man's face. The night was not warm, not until the fires caught sharp hold, and smoke began to flood across the exposed landscape. Now it's hard to breathe, and the air feels claustrophobically hot, as though I've stepped into the Hell the holy men are so fucking obsessed with.

Not that it concerns me.

Now we come at each other, having assessed the skills of the other, and accepting that we're equals in talent, if not in weaponry.

My seax, being shorter than his sword, attempts to get in close, to rip across his belly, or to dig deep into the enticing space beneath his arms. His sword tries to gouge my face, perhaps even my neck.

We move, swirling one into another and then back again.

My blade, needing less room to work in than his sword, claims first blood, even if it's little more than a scratch. His hand, which had been reaching to grab and hold me in place, falters. He caresses his belly, the grimace on his face at the wetness encouraging me. I follow up with a firm thrust of my shield rammed into his elbow, forcing him to stagger backwards.

Only now do I realise that our actions are being observed by more than just Sæbald and Rudolf. But only because I hear the bellowing of Pybba from across the river, and glance upwards. How he's forced his voice to expand and fill such a vast space is beyond me, but I hear him all the same.

I also hear the continuing clatter and blood-gore of the battle on this side of the river.

A bright blooming inferno almost takes my gaze from Halfdan. Only the following crash of splashing water assures me that whoever burned has exchanged a fiery death for one of more peaceful drowning.

And then Halfdan has his blade reaching for my chin. I continue my steps closer to him, encouraging him to think me unaware of his plans. Then, when his blade has almost bitten deep, I turn, showing him my back, allowing the byrnie to absorb the cutting edge. I thrust my head backwards, connecting my helm with his forehead. I'd have liked to sever his nose, but I'm too damn tall. Instead, I take him in the forehead.

While Halfdan staggers, stunned from the force of my helm on his exposed face, I stab backwards with my seax, hoping to find the soft part of his belly and hammer home my weapon home.

I feel my seax scrape and then bite deep, but before I can truly make the blow count, Halfdan is suddenly no longer behind me, and it takes all of my skill to stay standing.

"Fuck."

I spin, seeking him, and find him no more than five steps away, holding his belly and panting.

"Fucker," I advance on him, seax poised to finish the attack, my shield ready to hammer him in the face once more, perhaps even get his nose this time.

Only it seems that Halfdan has other ideas. Or rather three of his warriors do.

I don't see where they come from or even appreciate that they're there until my ears detect the hurried footfall of others and the sound of iron on iron reverberates through the air.

I keep my gaze on Halfdan only for another warrior to step between us, forcing me to pull up short.

"*Skiderik*," the new man hisses, and although I dodge, from one side to another, I think he's a bastard as well to get in the way of my attack on Jarl Halfdan.

This man, similar in height and girth to me, comes accoutred for battle. His byrnie is thick and well made, and the emblem that flashes from it is clear to see. The wolf. This man has come to save his jarl, and I feel my lips curling in a smile.

"Too fucking craven to fight your own battles?" I holler, my comment directed at Halfdan although I'm eyeing up my new opponent.

He doesn't have a shield but rather a long-handled war-axe, the edge glistening in the fiery dawn, and also a shorter blade, wider than I'm used to seeing. I throw my shield aside as well. I'll meet him as an equal.

"Fucker," I offer him, rushing forward to deliver the first blow. I don't have time to spend all night waiting for him to do something.

My speed surprises the other man, even his helm seemingly etched with the sigil of the wolf, as I aim a blow at his neck with my seax. His wide-blade easily deflects it, but while he's doing that, my war-axe whirls, and I feel it impact his right shoulder without any counter moves. It might be a weaker blow, and it might not have drawn blood, but it's shown me something about the way my new enemy fights.

He follows up my attack, saliva dripping from his open mouth to land in his bushy beard, with one of his, aimed at my seax arm. The impact on my elbow is hard, but I clench my hand tightly around the handle to prevent myself from dropping the weapon I rely on.

His rumble of annoyance as I counter with a low blow to his

right leg, the trews ripping, and offering a short slash, assures me that I need to do more to anger the man.

Behind him, Jarl Halfdan looks on, his eyes watching every move his champion makes, and I wonder that he doesn't make a rush for freedom, although where he'd go, I'm unsure.

The gasping of both Rudolf and Sæbald is loud in my ears, and I have to hope that they're acquitting themselves well against their opponents because I can't look to ensure they are.

I howl with frustration. This has been going on for too long, and Halfdan should be dead, at my feet, not watching me with the hints of amusement playing around his face, a hand stemming the blow from his belly.

He should be fighting me, not his lackey.

"Coelwulf," this cry catches my hearing just as I'm hammering home another blow with my war axe on my opponent's byrnie. The axe digs deep into the padded material. I feel it rip as I yank it back, breathing no less heavily than Rudolf and Sæbald.

I recognise the voice, but my enemy, war axe over his shoulder, is gearing up for another attack, and I stay focused on him.

Before he can strike his long-forecast move, I rush inside his reach. I stab upwards with my seax to impale him in the soft flesh beneath his shoulder, exposed to me while he makes his attack.

Immediately, I hear the thunk of his weapon hitting the floor, and then I'm close enough to smell the ale on his breath, the fetid scent of sleep mingled with it. I twirl my seax, bringing it to his neck, and with his eyes on me, I slice deep and true, allowing the immediate eruption of red to cover my gloved hand.

I watch him as his body stills, catching up with the reality of what's happening to him, and then his body slumps, as though there's nothing to hold him up anymore. He follows his war axe to the floor.

"Bastard," I kick the body, and glance up, keen to continue my offensive against Halfdan, only he's not there anymore.

"What?" I'm heaving much needed air into my body, as I slowly turn to survey the settlement.

Rudolf and Sæbald are both watching me, festooned as I am in the bloody harvest of this night. But it's Hereman who's called for my attention, and I pick him out and then turn to where he points.

"Shitting bollocks," I complain, wiping my bloodied blade on my trews, leaving a dark stain in its wake.

Out on the river, somehow missed by Pybba and Scef, there's one ship, and only one ship emerging from the smoky depths. The Raiders are rushing toward it, those who still live anyway, and amongst them is Jarl Halfdan, I can tell by the light that reflects from his byrnie.

I watch him, knowing I can't prevent his boarding because of the distance between us, as he half-limps his way to the ship.

Whoever is in command of the vessel, is skilled even with the ten men on the oars. They've managed to bring it close enough to the steep cliff-edge without getting it lodged on any of the burning wrecks. And now he hovers there, taunting the retreating figures to jump on board if they mean to live, even Halfdan.

As my breath heaves, I watch Halfdan pause, as though unsure if he'll survive the fall, only then he sets one leg behind him, and rears forward, flinging his arms wide, his legs scissoring in the air.

The person next to him makes a mistake of moving at the same time and trying to reach the relative safety of the boat when there's really not the room.

I wince, watching as Halfdan realises the danger and shoulders aside the other flailing body. As a loud thud reaches my ears, signifying that Jarl Halfdan has made it, another, wetter sound also rings out.

"Poor fucker," I've run to the edge of the raised ground. I can see where the other person is all but impaled around one of the oar holes, feet in the water, head in the ship, all but lifeless. A thrust from one of those lucky enough to escape sees the motionless body tumbling into the water, whether dead or merely stunned, he'll be dead soon enough.

And then my eyes find Jarl Halfdan. He's standing on the wooden deck of his ship. His stance is proud for all he's lost many of his warriors and followers under the blades and hooves of so few Mercians. And for all, he once more retreats rather than engaging in battle.

"Fuck, fuck, fuck," I complain, a swift glance assuring me that there's no more resistance in Torksey. The dirty smoke of so many fires has obscured much of it. I hear only the cries of the dying above the crackle of the advancing flames.

At least we won't have to bury them.

"Coelwulf," my name reaches me as though an echo from down a long, dark tunnel.

Pybba is before me, beckoning me onto the ship we took upriver only yesterday.

I turn, glance once more behind and reach a decision, helped by the knowledge that the Mercians are already taking command of Torksey.

"Men," I bellow, hoping they hear me above the roar of the flames.

"On the ship," I wave my arm and hear my cry taken up by others, and then Rudolf is streaming toward me, Sæbald as well, and I rush to Æthelwilf.

"Hold this place, and keep my horses safe," I tell him, bent double and hands on my knees because the air is too thick to satisfy my body's demands. "I'll take the rest of my men. Set guards. Kill the dying. I'll be back. Soon."

As though expecting the instruction Æthelwilf nods, and then a grim smile spreads over his blackened face, and I consider that he's been rolling in the embers of one of the fires.

"A great victory," his voice is rich with satisfaction, and I return his grin.

"And it will be even greater when Jarl Halfdan is dead."

A gleam in his eyes assures me that Æthelwilf feels the same, and I rush back toward the ship. I realise that my men are on board, or at least most of them are. I know someone is missing, but I can't determine who it is, not in the poor light. I run, as I saw Jarl Halfdan do only moments ago, and then I land, heavily in the hull of the ship, as it wobbles beneath the impact. Those on the oars, under Scef's instructions, are pulling us back into the main flow of the river, away from the smouldering wrecks.

I stand, licking my dry lips and wishing that I had something to drink that wasn't the fouled water of the Trent. My eyes rush over the heads of my men, assessing them and trying to decide who's missing.

"Where's Hereberht?" I demand to know, seeking out Eoppa amongst the crew of men slumped wherever they can find space.

Eoppa's pain-riddled eyes meet mine, and I know he's gone.

"Fuck," I complain, the lump in my throat almost too hard to swallow around. I stride to Eoppa, lay my hand on his shoulder, trying to convey my sorrow at Hereberht's loss.

"A fine warrior."

"Yes," Eoppa's voice feels small and feeble, and I lift his chin with my hand, noting the blood that shimmers there. "He was a fine warrior," I confirm. "He died protecting Mercia."

"No," and Eoppa is angry now, shaking my hand loose from his chin. "He died protecting me from a woman with a fucking cauldron for a weapon."

I nod, absorbing that information.

"Then don't fucking let that death be a waste. Accept it for what it was, and battle on, every kill done so in his name!"

I think Eoppa will hit me then, but instead, he sits straighter, despite the wince that crosses his face and nods.

"I'll kill the fucking lot of them, and offer them all in Hereberht's memory," Eoppa announces. His words are met with a ragged cheer, and I stride away from him, sure my work is done, even if I feel lesser because I've led yet another man to his death.

"We'll catch them at Littleborough," I announce when I can trust my voice again. "We'll catch them, and we'll finish the slaughter."

Ahead, I can hear the splashing of oars, and I peer into the river haze, but it's impossible to see if the enemy are closer than I think.

"You did well," I offer to the men who are rowing and who set the enemy ships ablaze. "I could see the flames from the far side of the camp."

Pybba grunts, his attention on Rudolf and the blood that oozes from a shoulder wound, but Edwin does look pleased.

"It was easy," Scef is also keener for the praise. "The long grasses are so dry that we barely needed a flame to set them alight."

I grin at him, trying to appreciate his delight even though my heart is heavy.

Hereberht is gone, and that only serves to remind me of my missing men. Somehow, I've managed to push aside the fact that I've not see Edmund, Icel and the rest of them for days, and neither have I even caught sight of them. It sits uneasily with me.

I need this victory. I didn't need it to cost me the lives of so many of my men.

My thoughts turn to Kingsholm, and those who still owe me their oaths and yet who've not fought for me in the last few days. There are youths there, similar to Rudolf, and also older men. Men who might have thought their fighting days were over but who I might just need to recall. It doesn't sit well with me, but they knew what they were getting into. Or at least, I fucking hope they did.

CHAPTER 17

The flames that continue to burn inside Torksey light the sky as though it's dawn, and it shocks me when darkness and a thick layer of smoke quickly cover us.

"We could fucking row right passed them and not realise," I grumble, but Scef shakes his head.

"I'd hear them," he assures me, and I subside, keen to clean my blades, and think of completing my battle against Jarl Halfdan.

It's as though Sæbald reads my thoughts. His voice reaches me from further along the ship.

"He favours his right side," Sæbald offers, only then turning to meet my eyes. "You can take him if you attack on the left. He seems to lack strength there."

"My thanks," I offer, aware that no one else is really speaking and that all have heard the words.

"How many?" I ask them because I'm not sure how big the force is that we must face.

"No more than thirty," Pybba provides the answer, his tone brooding, as every man in that ship looks around, keen to count and assess the odds.

"We'll be outnumbered then," I confirm. I've not even considered how we're going to overpower the enemy, but I have an idea forming.

"Will their ship go over the ford?"

Scef scrunches his face tight in thought.

"Was it a *knarr* or a *langskip*?" Scef asks Pybba.

"Fuck knows. It wallowed deeper than this."

"Then a *knarr*," Scef confirms. "And then no, it'll not be possible to row it over the ford at Littleborough. They'll have to get out and carry it."

"Then we need to be there to stop them doing that," I encourage, striding to relieve one of the Mercian rowers whose pace has faltered. Sweat glistens on his forehead, and he's almost too keen to give up the place, but I know it to be hard work.

"Speed the count," I instruct Scef, feeling the strain in my arms from the very first stroke.

Scef's voice calls more urgently, and I breathe deeply, allow my mind to focus only on what must be done.

The sounds of Torksey are quickly left behind, each stroke bringing me closer and closer to the man I need to kill. Yet, in the darkness, even the moon obscured by a heavy bank of clouds, I can't tell where we are, even though we travelled the same way the night before.

I want to demand to know where the fuck we are, but I hold my tongue, my shoulders an agony. Will I even be able to continue my attack when we catch up to Jarl Halfdan? I growl at the thought.

"It's ahead," Scef's voice reaches me, through my angry thoughts, and I gaze upstream, keen to see everything.

Amongst the gloom, I'm convinced I can pick out the odd shapes of men moving, perhaps even the ship, backlit by a few lights coming from the settlement of Littleborough.

"Row," I roar, the sound startling even myself.

The ship Halfdan is in might be a *knarr*, but this is more flat-bottomed, perfect for navigating the Trent and its fords. I hope we can catch them up while they labour with their deeper hulled ship.

A flicker of flame appears in the distance, drawing my eye.

"What the fuck is that?" I ask, but it's Rudolf, rushing to the front of the ship that answers.

"There's another bastard ship out there."

"Fuck," I roar. I don't want to be denied again, not when we're so close.

"Quicker," I howl and from somewhere all of us find more power and more strength, and I think the ship must be all but flying over the water.

And then I hear the grate of the wood over shallower depths, and it falters, a judder thrumming along the length, knocking all of us.

"Shit," Scef's frantic voice is all I need to hear to know the ford is lower than we might have thought given the recent rain.

"Everyone out," I command. "Weapons ready." I'm already reaching for my seax and war axe. My shield is still lying, abandoned, inside Torksey.

"Stay upright. Don't let the current take you," I instruct, the words thundering through my chest. "We've lost Hereberht this night. His death was glorious, on a battlefield, facing our foe. We'll not let the water take us."

The light in front of us has grown, and two fires burn either side of the ford, their flames doing little to combat the darkness, but enough that I can just about make out where we are, and where Jarl Halfdan must be.

"Stay upright," is my final instruction. Then I'm jumping from the ship, landing in knee-high water, the movement aggravating my wound. I stay standing, somehow, and then I'm wading to where I can hear others trying to move as quickly as possible through the waters.

"Rudolf, Sæbald, Hereman," I call the three of them to me, and they join me quickly. The water seems to swell around my knees, and I know the remainder of my warriors are also with me, as Edwin and his men move to join us.

"Scef, stay with the ship," I order him. He's not a warrior. He can take the ship and retreat, should he need to.

Whatever he says in reply, I miss because my legs are moving through the swirling water and the noise is so loud I can hardly believe it. I won't be sneaking up on anybody. Not here.

"Bastard," Hereman's voice follows a sudden splashing sound, and I grimace, as I hear him dipping low into the water.

Whatever he's lost might be gone forever.

"Fucker," is his next word, and I think he's probably managed to retrieve it. Lucky git. If I dropped my seax in the swirling current, I know I'd never find it again.

"Surely it should be fucking morning by now," I growl, frustrated by the blackness of the night. If I could only see where I was going, I know that Jarl Halfdan would already be dead.

But my wishes are as nothing against the force of the moon and the sun.

"Careful," I offer the warning to Rudolf, as he labours next to me. The ford is wider than I would have thought and littered with wooden pilings driven deep into the riverbed, between the flagstones that Scef told me made the crossing passable.

"Fuck," Rudolf rears up, changing tact, only for Ordlaf to crash into him.

"Look where you're going, you daft fucker." The comment brings a chuckle to my lips, and I would turn and roll my eyes at Ordlaf but how the fuck would he see me?

And then, above all the noise we're making, I hear the sound I want to, the heavy breathing of someone labouring in front of me.

"We're nearly on them," I shout the caution, unheeding of whether my enemy knows or not. The movements in front of me double in effort, and I grimace. Fear will make some fall.

And then it seems that my words have brought the action to fruition.

A hand on my leg and I'm stabbing down, barely stopping my forward momentum as the gargling shrieks of someone drowning resound in my ears.

"'Ware," I bawl for the sake of my men.

The body releases from beneath my seax seemingly picked up by the current, and then it's gone from me. But it's not the only one.

I hear the rustle of water as Rudolf skewers his own drowning warrior, the sound seeming to skim through the air, like a stone thrown in calm waters. One after another, my men must stab down, and then, a warrior stands in front of me.

I can sense them, rather than see them and my seax whistles before me, slicing across the forearm of the person who thought to take me unawares.

"*Skiderik*," rumbles from the throat.

"Enemy," erupts from me at the same time. I realise I face not one man, but rather a wall of them, all trying to block the path forward.

I swing with my war axe, keen to fell the man as soon as possible. The wet sound that leaches into the night air assures me that the swing is excellent, as I stab forward with my seax, driving all my strength behind the blow.

The man falls, a gurgle on his breath, the water covering him, as I stride beyond him.

In the light from the single brand on the waiting ship, I've seen my target, and I thirst for his blood.

Jarl Halfdan, his glittering tunic betraying him once more, is close to the ship. I can hear creaking wood, and perhaps even the sound of the sail being hefted, although how it will aid them when there's no wind, I don't know.

I wish I had a fire arrow to set the thing ablaze, but of course, I've left Scef behind and no doubt, those of Edwin's men skilled enough to try such a feat now war with seax and not arrows. My mind flashes back to the women at Swarkeston. What I would give for one of them here, and now.

And then, as though my thoughts have made the action possible, a haze of fire seems to erupt in front of me. I look away, blinded by such fierce brightness after so long in the smoky gloom, and in that moment, I know that Halfdan slips away, for when I can see again, he's gone.

"Bastard," I roar it at the sky. I need his death. I need his blood on my blade.

"'Ware," the cry comes from Pybba, and suddenly there's something else out there in the water with us.

Spraying water covers me, and I stand, seax raised, keen to face the new threat. Where has Jarl Halfdan found mounted warriors from at such short notice? Did he have a scouting party away from Torksey itself, or is this just happenstance? How would they even know where to find him?

It sounds as though fifty or more horses have entered the ford, their hooves loud on the flagstone flooring, the threat that they bring, forcing me to stop my headlong rush to intercept Halfdan. I must protect my men. I can't allow others to die. Not when we've almost accomplished what must be done.

The spark of blazing flames makes it challenging to see who comes amongst us now. It lightens the area in front, but behind everything is shadows and tricks on the eyes, and my heart is beating, thudding loudly against my chest as though it's a hoof on the flagstones.

"To me," the words catch in my parched throat, the sound barely travelling further than my ears.

"To me," I raise my voice louder. When no one responds, the thud of the horses' hooves, making it impossible to hear anything when combined with the thrum of the river, I roar the word, "Mercia."

I don't expect the response, not at all. It almost buckles my knees there and then. It almost adds me to the number of bodies that my men and I have already sent tumbling down the river, no doubt to get entangled in river weeds or against rocks and boulders jutting up from the riverbed.

"Coelwulf?" And I swear, I could be weeping, if I weren't so damn fucking pissed off.

And then, a warrior erupts in the water beneath me. He swathes me in water. It's as though a sodden cloud has just dumped its rain on me in between one breath and the next.

CHAPTER 18

"Will you shut the fuck up?"

Even the roar of warriors squaring off to face him can't drown out Edmund in full flow. He's astride a horse that tosses and dips its head, clearly unhappy being in the water while war is waged all around him.

Suddenly, between one blink and the next, the grey light of dawn has lessened the murkiness, and I can see so much fucking more than before. That includes both Edmund and the man who thinks to take my life by travelling beneath the level of the murky water and then erupting in front of me, weapon raised, ready to strike. Only Edmund's unexpected arrival and the breaking of daylight have undone his plan.

Edmund continues to howl, his voice somehow rising above the fiercest of bloody battles, the roar of iron on wood, the screams of those who fight for the right to breathe another day.

"*A man of the Hwicce,*
He gulped mead at midnight feasts.
Slew Raiders, night and day.
Brave Athelstan, long will his valour endure."

"I've heard that one before," I snarl at Edmund. My double-eagle headed blade is in my hand. Blood shimmers along its edge in the glowing light as though the silver sheen has been festooned in ruby dew throughout the long night.

I'm quickly assessing how best to take the life of my freshest opponent. Water pools down the man's blue face, his teeth flashing against the growl of his lips. His eyes try to pierce me with the power behind his gaze. It's as though the sun pours through him only to condense into one single beam of light.

"*Beornberht, son of the Magonsæte.*
A proud man, a wise man, a strong man.
He fought and pierced with spears.
Above the blood, he slew with swords."

"And that one," I bellow, still reeling from this stunning turn of events. My seax is raised to ward off the reasoned blows from the man who thinks to kill me by stealth. I can see how much he desires my death in the careful placement of his reaching blade. It only makes it more imperative that I'm the one to deal death.

I thought Edmund dead, but he evidently isn't. Where the fuck has he been?

"*A man fought for Mercia.*
Against Raiders and foes.
Shield flashing red,
Brave Oslac, slew Raiders each seven-day."

"Will you shut the fuck up?" I'm all but screaming. Edmund is never one to be silent when the words of battle are in his mind. But those words distract me, as does his suddenly arrival.

I war against one of Halfdan's warrior, while Jarl Halfdan attempts to make his escape. I can glimpse, over the shoulder of my enemy, the ship that holds Halfdan. I can see it begin to track upriver, my enemy on board. I can't allow Jarl Halfdan to escape. This man is an inconvenience, but a bloody good warrior all the same.

Edmund is not helping me, even if he thinks to excite my warriors and me to greater endeavours.

"*Sturdy and strong, it would be wrong not to praise them.*
Amid blood-red blades, in black sockets.
The war-hounds fought fiercely, tight formation.
Of the war band of Coelwulf, I would think it a burden
To leave any in the shape of man alive."

The words elicit thunderous acclaim from my men who fight beside me, their positions realised more through sound than sight. Edmund knows how to stir the blood of even the most exhausted man. And we are drained. This battle has waged all night.

I growl once more, using my seax to finally make a killing stroke against my opponent. I watch with satisfaction as the man slips back below the surface he tried to use against me, only to pivot into another opponent.

This warrior, beard filled with blood and spittle, dripping translucent water from the river, leers at me. I wish to dismiss his well-aimed strikes with contempt, as they ricochet against my fast-moving blade, but I know it'll be my downfall. The wealth of scars on his exposed cheeks and lower arms, rippling with life as the water continues to slither from his body, testify to his skill. The fact he still stands, after all the battles I fought since Repton, shows that he's either a lucky fucker or a warrior of immense skill.

But, again, I focus on Edmund's roared words. This part is new to me. He must have composed it in the last few days, while we've been apart, and I thought him dead.

Damn the fucker.

What do the words mean? Every other verse he's ever composed has been for a bloody good reason. Why would this one by any different?

I wish I could just ask him, but I can't. Not here, and not now. My breath heaves through my body, great gulps filling my chest, as my foe tries to trick me with a weapon in each hand. I'm unsure where his real strength lies, is it his war axe, or his sword? Is it in both? I've faced such men before. They're fuckers to kill.

"*Bitter in battle, with blades set for war.*
Attacking in an army, cruel in battle.
They slew with swords, without much sound.
Icel, pillar of battle, took pleasure in giving death."

But those words freeze me. My enemy lands a blow with his sword on my lower right arm, my grip instinctively failing on my seax. Although the blade is useless against my war gear, the weight and shock are immense.

I don't know these words. I've never heard them before. But more horrifying, they speak of Icel's death. Edmund has never given words in his scop's song unless a man was dead. I want to turn, face him, demands answers to his fucking song.

"What?" I roar, trying to catch my seax before it plummets into the icy depths, while at the same time avoiding the reach of my enemy. My opponent tries to dance forward, take a slice from my arm again, but the water is too deep. Instead, he flounders, his balance deserting him, giving me the respite that I need.

With my weapon under control and raised menacingly to my right, my own teeth bared in a growl of fury, I slash the flailing man's left arm. The sudden well of blood stirs my warrior's heart. Another fucker, just waiting for me to find the right way to kill him.

The man howls, momentarily shocked into rearing back from my reach. I finally pivot, and see Edmund in all his battle glory. He's dressed for war in his leather byrnie, with his shield, and his helm, although it seems somehow different to me. But I don't have the time to determine what it is.

My eyes flash downwards. The horse, the horse I recognise too well. Icel's mount.

"What the fuck?"

Edmund's bellowing voice, his staccato of words, lends a rhythm to every warrior's movements that I admire. Yet I wish he'd meet my gaze. He's said nothing since bellowing my name in surprise and then beginning his recitation, as though he's the lord here and not me, overseeing everything from the back of that horse.

"Icel?" I call, disbelief colouring my voice and making it too small. "Icel is gone?" I force the words through my tight lips.

I need an answer. I need to know what's happened while my men have been divided.

I can't imagine fighting without Icel. I peer into the distance, beyond the straggling warriors engaged in battle in the shallow depths, wishing for more light to see by, desperate to catch sight of Icel's too familiar stance.

My seax is busy, even though I don't actually face my resurgent foe. When I don't see Icel where he should be, I focus only on Edmund. Fucking Edmund and his bastard words.

"Icel?" I demand once more, for while Edmund has finally become taciturn, his actions are far from still. He moves to batter aside the enemy who attempts to slice his mount's legs. The man is small and wiry and somehow manages to withstand the rushing water to remain upright.

"Icel?" I screech, hoping against hope that Edmund will answer me before I have to threaten him for a response.

His silence tells me too much, and also far too little.

The fact that none of my other abruptly returned men, answer, makes my blood run with more than just the icy cold of the damn river.

"Fucker," I scream. Only then, with the Raiders dismissed from my thoughts with a cut to his water-wrinkled neck, turning his chest pink, the water as well, can I take the place of the opponent that Edmund's just slain.

Edmund's low sword strike, from the back of Samson, finds the artery high on the leg. Now blood rushes from the body, pooling faster than the river current, surrounding him in the fading warmth of his life. The man finally stumbles, his eyes already rolling in his head. He knows he's dead. His body just hasn't caught up yet.

Edmund pants, his chest rising and falling, his green eye busy around the scene, checking the state of the attack, until it settles on me. The contempt I see chills me, as does the realisation of his wound. I've been bellowing for news of Icel, to know why he's now a part of Edmund's song, but perhaps I should have been asking more immediate questions.

"Your eye?" I probe, my gaze rushing over the other figures that fight from their mounts, desperate to know if others are missing. It's impossible to tell as broad backs greet my eyes. I can't tell who is Beornstan, or Eahric, Goda, Ingwald, Oda, or Osbert or Eadberht, although I do pick out Wærwulf in his purloined equipment that once belonged to Jarl Sigurd.

Neither can I see enough to recognise all of the horses encouraged into the fast-flowing water.

And it seems I shouldn't make that assumption anyway.

Edmund's finally quiet lips twist in anger, his bloodied sword poised, seemingly ready to attack me. His silence continues, as does his defiant stare.

My gaze darts to the empty socket where his eye once mocked me.

"Icel?" I breathe the word, and the flicker of agony in Edmund's green eye tells me all I need to know.

"You fucking bastard," I rage, three quick steps bringing me within killing distance of him, my seax ready for the strike, even though the water tries to push me away from him.

He doesn't even flinch, the over-confident fuck.

"I gave you one fucking job. To keep my men safe."

His lips warp one more, a slight tick of unease on his unshaven chin. Then he grins, the movement so quick I almost miss it.

With his own rumble of fury, Edmund encourages Icel's horse on in the frigid water. His iridescent sword is outstretched, his intent clear to see, his gaze never baulking, Samson unable to ignore the command to rush toward me.

I always knew he'd be the one to turn fucking traitor.

I brace myself, prepared to hobble that horse if I must, to cut Edmund from his place on that saddle, where he doesn't deserve to be.

Icel was loyal, always loyal, it seems that Edmund has not been. I can't fucking believe it, but all the same, I'll deal with the consequences of such betrayal.

I grit my teeth, keep my eyes wide-open despite the spray flying up from Samson's hooves, my seax outstretched. Only then Edmund is beyond me, his sword busy in the glowing light as yet another enemy erupts from beneath the water close to where I'd been standing a moment ago. I look one-way and then another, unsure what the fuck is happening.

Jarl Halfdan's departing ship is still visible on the other side of the ford. I feel his eyes on me, as though he too, has taken advantage of the light to reveal himself to me. I grimace widely, hoping that my teeth flash blackly with the blood of all those I've killed. His men, not mine.

Rudolf battles a man twice as big as him. I'm spurred to action as Rudolf tumbles backwards into the water. Only a mounted warrior rushes to Rudolf's assistance, scything the head of the blond enemy from his shoulders with a roar of defiance. The sound of the head hitting the water seems to last far longer than it should, and Rudolf is looking up, a grin on his face as the warrior turns the horse and faces me.

Wærwulf. I think he'll come to me, only he guides his mount with just his knees, and rushes further along the ford. The thunk of hooves on the flagstones is muted by the water, another enemy claiming his attention.

I stagger to Rudolf, holding him upright as water streams from him, and I feel his body shaking, or at least, I hope it's him who's trembling.

He looks at me and his eyes no longer light with the joys of youth, a question on his lips.

"I don't fucking know," I answer before he can ask, and he falls silent, the two of us holding each other up as we watch and watch, and I try to make sense of everything that's happening.

I can't deny that it's my mounted warriors who now battle against the Raiders, men no doubt keen to make a name for themselves and be the one to bring Jarl Halfdan my head. Yet I'm confused by Edmund's greeting to me, and by his words.

My eyes flicker over the men stabbing and hacking with their weapons. I can't believe there are so many enemies beneath the shallow water. Where are they coming from? How can they hold their breath for as long as they are?

Rudolf's body tenses, as though about to strike out once more, but I hold him close.

All is chaos. I can't be sure that the mounted warriors won't injure one of us.

"To me," I call, my voice thinner than I'd like it to be.

"To me," I bellow this time and feel gazes flicker to me before feet rush toward me. Hereman is shadowing his brother, his strides strong and purposeful and I know he's beyond hearing anything I say. But Ælfgar and Sæbald immediately begin the journey to my side from their close positions.

Further out, the rest of the men don't seem to hear me.

The river runs with spilt blood, gleaming as though priceless gems in the burgeoning sunlight, but for once, there's calmness around me. I use it to recover my breath, trying not to think of the cold water reaching up my legs. My boots are sodden, my leg wound complaining at the dampness, and other small injuries are beginning to throb.

I glance at Sæbald. His face is compressed in a grimace, and blood slides down his nose to hang, as though transfixed, in the air, only to fall with no sound into the streaming water.

Ælfgar holds his left arm tightly, and again, I see a shade of blood, but he merely grunts away the pain, hefting his blade once more.

And then I hear a thundering splash, and heart-pounding, hand on my seax, I wait for the next attack.

Only the sound isn't close, for all it feels like it.

"What the fuck?" I demand to know, but Rudolf is pointing toward Jarl Halfdan's ship, and I follow his gaze.

A spear juts just below the waterline, sticking proudly through the wood, as Halfdan dashes backwards from the prow of the ship.

A whistle through the air and another spear follows the first, and although I want to see where it lands, I also want to know who threw it.

I scan my men, turning my head from side to side, and finally settle on Hereman. I should have realised. He already hefts a third spear, although the second hasn't yet landed. As he releases it, I hear the unmistakable sound of a spear finding its target. When my eyes return to the ship, all I can see is yet another spear, standing proud from behind the prow.

"That's one down," Rudolf informs me, clearly more interested in whether the weapon finds a target than in who throws it. And before the Raiders on the ship can react, another spear lands. This time, I watch it skewer someone through the back, and they hang, motionless, the projectile fixing them in place.

"Fucking bollocks," I breathe amazed by Hereman's skill.

Chaos has erupted on the ship, everyone rushing to the far end as Hereman finds yet another spear and releases it. I watch, almost not believing what I'm seeing as the craft lurches forward, the end closest to me clearing the water.

Now I can hear the shouts of panicked men and women. Wide-eyed with shock, I observe the ship as it appears to teeter. For a heart-stopping moment, it seems to return to the water, only for the proud mast to over-top the craft. The previous screaming subsides into garbling screeches as mouths fill with water.

"Bastards," but I approve, and suddenly I know what needs to be done.

"Upriver," I bellow, my blood running hot. My desire to take Jarl Halfdan's life has redoubled where before I felt only dismay that he'd managed to evade me.

Only, as I stagger through the water, do I realise my mistake. I have no horse to charge up the riverbank, and I need one.

Frantically, I glance around, hoping that one might just appear, but Edmund has seen what needs to happen now, and he turns his mount quickly.

"To the ship," he bellows and men who I thought resented his leadership, spur to do his bidding, covering me in a deluge of water.

I hit dry land, and begin to run, trying to force as much strength and speed as possible into my legs. The rest of my men won't outdo me, even if they are mounted.

"My Lord King," a voice from nowhere, and I turn, hand on my seax, prepared to slash whoever has managed to get so close to me. When I look back, I see bright blue eyes above a tunic that's torn and splattered with blood, and more importantly, the reins of a horse in the injured man's hand.

"Take him," the blond man pants, and I hop and then jump, and I'm in the saddle, following my men, my blood hot.

I still have no idea where Icel is. But I do know that whatever is happening, I need to be there to take advantage of Jarl Halfdan's misfortune in choosing the wrong people to guard him. He needed warriors, not men and women frightened enough that they've brought about their own deaths.

The riverbank stays flat, and I see that this area must also be liable to flooding. More of my men join me.

"Coelwulf," Rudolf's high voice close to my ear has me turning to see five of my warriors mounted on borrowed horses, and streaming away at my side. I spare a thought for those we've left behind.

In the river, the sounds of panic and chaos fuel my hot blood, as does the clash of iron. Edmund and his men have found the enemy, but tendrils of mist cling to the river, and I have only the sound to guide me.

The horse beneath me has a smooth gait, and yet it really is too small to take my weight. I ride as high as I can, trying to relieve the pressure of having me on its back.

And then, with sunlight illuminating my view, as though a higher power shows me where my enemy is, the mist clears. I can see Jarl Halfdan and his fleeing men and women. I cast my eyes over Edmund, his horse abandoned, as he hacks at those lucky enough to struggle ashore, and not drown under the weight of their battle gear.

The riverbank has sprouted a new burst of colour, gleaming red, and the sparkle of damp iron. In the river itself, the ship, I see now it's a *langskip*, is entirely upside down. Or at least half of it is.

The keel flashes wetly, the detritus of the water clinging to it with as much tenacity as Jarl Halfdan.

Laughter burbles from my mouth at the sight of him.

Bedraggled and bleeding from a head wound, Halfdan grips tightly to an upturned oar hole, one arm through it, and another over it. At the same time, the river takes the ship further and further downstream.

He looks up, perhaps sensing my gaze, and I quirk an eyebrow, wishing Hereman were here with a spear or one of the Mercian archers. But I have nothing other than my seax and my war axe, and the urge to kill.

A blue-white hand grips hold of Halfdan's back. He releases his top arm, to batter at the survivor. I see a flicker of blond hair, plastered against a blue face. Then Halfdan punches the nose, more blood mingling in the water, and the survivor disappears beneath the surface.

"A fucking fine leader he makes," Rudolf calls, his voice ripe with the injustice of what he's just seen.

My eyes flicker away from Halfdan, noting the movement from the other side of the river, amazed when another mounted warrior dashes down to the riverbank and hacks at the man's back. I don't recognise the warrior, but I can appreciate his skill.

Rudolf, Sæbald and Ælfgar hurry to help Edmund and the rest of my warriors, but my gaze returns to Halfdan. He's hanging on desperately, his eyes peering into the distance, and a tendril of unease makes my spine quiver.

What does he know? What does he hope for?

And then, from a shadow where the river is still in darkness, I see what keeps him in the full flow of the river, clinging to an upturned ship that must truly sink soon.

The new boat is small, three men to each side, and it moves faster than the river fish, seeming to glide over the surface. I can clearly see, on the shields heaped at its centre that these men belong to Jarl Halfdan.

"Fuck," I explode, the distance between the rescue ship and Halfdan narrowing with every moment of indecision. "How many fucking ships does he have?" I ask no one because I'm alone, my warriors busy with their blades on the banks of the river.

Jarl Halfdan has lifted one of his arms, and waves frantically to the ship. For a moment, everything seems to slow. It's as though the oarsmen don't even see Halfdan, his voice failing to carry over the din of renewed battle. I witness the men considering whether they should just turn around rather than face my men and the rest of the Mercians.

I watch the argument erupt between them, teeth gritted, hoping they won't see Halfdan because they're too focused on what they should do. But from somewhere, one of the men turns and looks once more, and he must see his lord because he points excitedly, and the ship begins to move forward once more.

The river is so broad that Jarl Halfdan is entirely out of my range. I could risk throwing my seax, but no doubt, it would merely tumble through the air and then disappear beneath the shallow waves. I'm not going to risk my blade on an endeavour doomed to failure.

While my men butcher all those who thought to escape, I watch, helpless, as the smaller ship pulls up alongside Halfdan. He transfers his tight grip from the sinking half-ship to the smaller one. Then he forces his men to pull him inside. The craft threatens to tip as well, and only stays balanced because three of the men rush to the far end. In contrast, three others aid a sopping wet Halfdan inside the boat.

Quickly, they turn the craft, aiming back along the wide expanse of the Trent.

I expect Jarl Halfdan to stand tall and defiant in that small craft, but he doesn't, disappearing from my view. I harbour the hope that perhaps he'll perish all the same, from his wound, and from being submerged in the cold water for so long.

I harbour the dream, but I know I won't get my wish.

All the same, I encourage my horse to follow the broad path of the Trent, my eyes never straying far from the six men who work to take her to the Humber.

Eventually, I'm aware that I'm not alone. Still, no one speaks or offers any words, as my foe makes his escape. He might be alone, having left his thousand warriors behind in Mercia, all dead, but the fucking bastard still lives, and that means my war is far from over.

"Bastard," Edmund's voice is loud in my ears. I finally bring my mount to a halt, aware that to continue, as exhausted as I am, risks injuring myself.

I turn to Edmund, unsure if he means me, or Jarl Halfdan. I examine his mutilated face, trying not to linger over his missing eye, but it's impossible.

Only then Edmund's lip turns up in a mocking half-smile.

"Fucking bastard," he reiterates, and only then do I get the answer I've been asking for since Edmund materialised beside me. "He took Icel's life, and I must now take his."

CHAPTER 19

We ride in silence. Everyone is exhausted, even those who haven't been fighting all night and I don't want to ask any questions because I don't want to hear the answers. Answers will make everything too real, too painful.

My aim is to return to Torksey, retrieve the Mercians and then make a slow return to Repton.

Yet, there are bodies everywhere. They seem to litter the riverbank, slowly turning whiter than marble, as though the sun bleaches them.

The horses are as exhausted as we are, and progress is slow until we find the first of the bodies.

I stumble from the back of my borrowed horse, heartsick and aching all over. My clothes have dried on my back, and now they're hard to move within, and I'd sooner discard them altogether, but I need to be alert. There might be more warriors yet, hiding in hedges and field ditches and I'll not lose another man. Not after Icel. I refuse to even consider it.

Angled on the steep riverbank, the weeds and river plants well beaten down around it, I roll the first body. Staring eyes suddenly look upwards, black river mud smeared over half of the face, pooling into the flaccid lips.

"Fuck." The man is an enemy, and yet he's not really a man at all.

Ahead, I can see more and more bodies, and so I grip this one's hand and begin to tow him to the next outcropping of the dead.

In my wake, I leave a trail of dislodged plants and mud, a smear of brown that no doubt includes a vast quantity of red as well.

Beneath my gloves, I can only just feel the coolness of the body. It's the stillness that disturbs me more.

I glance up toward my warriors. Rudolf is the only one who rides upright, the rest all slouch, the sorrow of losing two more of our small number a massive blow when we're the victors. Or at least, we are the victors for now.

Fucking Jarl Halfdan. Wherever the fucker goes next, he'd be most unwise to step foot on Mercian land again. If I could have done, I'd have chased him all the way back to the land of his birth.

What galls the most is that Halfdan has inherited his brother's reputation and that of his father's. Men and women will flock to him, no matter his failures in the last few days.

Jarl Halfdan will fill their heads with tails of battle glory, and they'll believe it, despite the revelations to the contrary. Halfdan has lost his allies, and a vast number of his warriors, and yet he'll fight on. I know it, even if the truth is unpalatable.

Around the bend of the river, the next bodies linger. There are more of them here, maybe ten or eleven, and Rudolf jumps to assist me, as does Hereman.

Hereman's eyes are filled with the confusion I refuse to give voice.

Edmund hasn't spoken to him. Edmund hasn't spoken to anyone. Not yet. While I'm aware of a murmur from some of the others, Goda and Wærwulf the most vocal, I've not spoken to any of them. I've greeted them with my eyes, and tight smiles, but no words have been exchanged, and I fear the rift might become too vast to ever speak, and yet I can't. Not yet.

"Up there," I command. The three of us tug the unresponsive bodies above the line of the water and onto land that might just avoid the worst of the river in flood. I don't want to bury the bodies, only to have them torn free from the graves during a violent winter storm.

The ground is hard, unyielding, and yet it feels good to sweat and strain over something so honest. I need not think as my war axe pounds the surface, clumps of grasses flying loose, I need do nothing but time the blows with my heartbeat.

When the bodies have been tumbled into the ground, their valuables taken by the nimble, if grimy, fingers of Rudolf, I sigh heavily, returning the mud to the field, and looking up at Edmund.

I can't put this off any longer.

"What happened?" I ask. There's no anger in my voice. There's no blame. There's nothing but sorrow, and the need to understand.

Edmund's one eye greets my two good ones, and I refuse to be drawn into the ragged tissue where he once judged me with fine green eyes.

"We were attacked by Jarl Halfdan and his men." I grit my teeth tightly.

A huff of annoyed air fills the space between us, and my eyes fasten on Wærwulf, the disgusted expression on his face as he encourages his horse to a higher speed. He doesn't want to hear this. I'm unsure why.

Edmund swallows heavily, his chest heaving, as though trying to contain all of his emotions, but failing.

"It was my fault," Edmund finally acknowledges, the strain on his face testifying to just how hard it is for him to make the admission, as he tries to find strength to make the admission.

"It's all my fault that Icel is dead."

I expect someone, anyone, to gainsay Edmund's shocking announcement. When no one does, the reality of the words begins to permeate deep into my being.

Edmund, more than a brother to me for all these years, has done something so unutterably wrong that it's deprived me of Icel.

I reach for my horse, spring into the saddle, and resume my journey downstream.

I don't want to hear after all.

All that matters is that Icel, the great bastion of Mercia's long wars against Wessex, is gone, and I don't want to own that. Not yet.

CAST OF CHARACTERS

Coelwulf – King of Mercia – rides Haden
Edmund – rides Jethson
Pybba – loses his hand in battle – rides Brimman
Eadberht – member of Coelwulf's war band
Rudolf – Coelwulf's squire – rides Dever
Sæbald – member of Coelwulf's war band
Ordheah – member of Coelwulf's war band
Lyfing - member of Coelwulf's war band
Ingwald - member of Coelwulf's war band
Icel - member of Coelwulf's war band – rides Samson
Hereman - member of Coelwulf's war band
Hereberht - member of Coelwulf's war band
Gyrth - member of Coelwulf's war band
Goda - member of Coelwulf's war band
Eoppa - member of Coelwulf's war band
Oda - member of Coelwulf's war band
Wulfred - member of Coelwulf's war band – rides Cuthbert
Ordlaf - member of Coelwulf's war band
Wærwulf - member of Coelwulf's war band
Eadulf - member of Coelwulf's war band
Eahric - member of Coelwulf's war band
Beornstan - member of Coelwulf's war band
Wulfstan - member of Coelwulf's war band
Ælfgar - member of Coelwulf's war band
Osbert – member of Coelwulf's war band

Bishop Wærferth of Worcester
Bishop Deorlaf of Hereford

Bishop Eadberht of Lichfield
Ealdorman Beorhtnoth
Ealdorman Ælhun
Ealdorman Alhferht
Ealdorman Æthelwold – his father Ealdorman Æthelwulf dies at the Battle of Berkshire in AD871
Ealdorman Wulfstan – dies during The Last King

Vikings

Ivarr – dies in AD870
Halfdan – brother of Ivarr, may take his place after his death
Guthrum - one of the three leaders at Repton with Halfdan
Oscetel - one of the three leaders at Repton with Halfdan
Anwend – one of the three leaders at Repton with Halfdan
    Anwend Anwendsson – his fictional son
Sigurd (fictional)

The royal family of Mercia

King Burgred of Mercia
    m. Lady Æthelswith in AD853 (the sister of King Alfred) they had no children
Beornwald – a fictional nephew for King Burgred
King Wiglaf – ninth century ruler of Mercia
King Wigstan- ninth century ruler of Mercia

Misc

Cadell ap Merfyn – fictional brother of Rhodri Mawr
Eowa - forest dweller from near Warwick (from The Last King)
Oswald - Ealdorman Ælhun's warrior
Coenwulf – Coelwulf's dead brother
Wiglaf and Berhtwulf – the names of Coelwulf's aunt's dogs
Lord Osferth – oath-sworn warrior fighting in the name of

Bishop Deorlaf, his sigil is a single eagle
   Seaxwulf – Osferth's son
Edwin – warrior fighting in the name of Bishop Deorlaf
Æthelwulf and Scurfa – Osferth's warriors
Scef – Coelwulf's scout from Repton
Frithestan – Scef"s informant about Torksey
Jarl Hroald – Raider
Ceolnoth and Æthelnoth – men of Swarkeston
   Egbert and his wife – killed by the Raiders at Swarkeston
   Æthelflæd and Eadhild – the bow women of Swarkeston
Heahstan – leads Bishop Eadberht of Lichfield's man
Kyred – leads Bishop Wærferth's men
Wærstan – the blacksmith's son
Denewulf and Eahlferth – inhabitants of Newark

Viking Ships

These were called *langskips* (warships –which were longer, narrower and shallower and powered by oars), *knarr* (merchant ships – powered by a sail and partially enclosed), and a *karve* (a smaller type of longship which could navigate in shallow water).

Places Mentioned

Gloucester, on the River Severn, in western Mercia.
Worcester, on the River Severn, in western Mercia.
Lichfield, an ancient diocese of Mercia. Now in Staffordshire.
Tamworth, an ancient capital of Mercia. Now in Staffordshire.
Repton, an ancient capital of Mercia. St Wystan's was a royal mausoleum.
Newark, a crossing place on the River Trent.
Swarkeston, the site of a bridge on the River Trent.
Gwent, one of the Welsh kingdoms at this period.
Torksey, in the ancient kingdom of Lindsey, which became part of Mercia in the north
River Severn, in the west of England
River Derwent, joins the Trent close to Derby

River Trent, runs through Staffordshire, and joins the Humber (it is tidal north of Gainsborough, which is close to Torksey)

Kingsholm, close to Gloucester

The Foss Way, ancient roadway running from Lincoln to Exeter

HISTORICAL NOTES

This story is entirely fictional, probably.

I've said at the end of The Last King that King Coelwulf is Mercia's forgotten king. More of his story will be told, some of it with greater historical basis, but until then, the image of Mercia I'm portraying is different to the standard narratives of the period. I firmly believe that the 'truth' is far from known, and that it must fall somewhere between the current interpretation, and that which I'm offering instead.

An abandoned river channel at Repton is described on an old map as 'Old Trent Water', records show that this was once the main navigable route, with the river having switched to a more northerly course in the 18th century (Wikipedia). Having grown up close to the River Trent, I'm amazed by how little I actually know about it, and on occasion, have entirely ignored it in previous re-imaginings of the early English period. I do know that it has a healthy fish population – barbell, bream, carp, chub, dace and pike!

The bridge at Swarkeston did exist, as did that at Newark and the ford at Littleborough, which was an old Roman fording point. I've ignored a crossing at Burton upon Trent, close to Repton, because I wanted to include the scene with Coelwulf and his horse crossing the Trent at Repton. I was somewhat annoyed to discover that the Derwent joins the Trent but managed to just about include it. Ferries are mentioned in Domesday Book. As to the 'barrow' this has been a very literal translation of the place

Barrow Upon Trent, first mentioned in Domesday Book. As far as I can tell, there is no actual barrow there.

For information on the archaeological findings at Repton please see the following article which is free to access; 'The Viking Great Army in England: new dates from the Repton charnel' by Jarmen, Biddle, Higham, and Bronk-Ramsey. It is believed that the charnel at Repton contains the bones of 264 people.

For information on the archaeological findings at Torksey please see https://www.archaeology.co.uk/articles/viking-torksey-inside-the-great-armys-winter-camp.htm. The site chosen at Torksey seems to have formed a natural oval that was on higher ground overlooking the Trent's floodplain. At a high point, there does seem to have been a near-vertical cliff that plunged down to the river. It is possible that there was a market on the foreshore north of Torksey, which may have added to its attractiveness for the Raiders.

I always try and find 'characters' that lived during the period I write about. For the names of the ealdormen and the bishops, I've made use of the surviving charter evidence as found in the Online Sawyer, a wonderful archive of all things Anglo-Saxon and which I spend a great deal of time studying.

Bishop Wærferth, Eadberht, Deorlaf, Ealdorman Beorthnoth, Ælhun, Alhferht and Æthelwold do all witness the charters that Coelwulf is credited with having had produced in the following years.

I've made use of a map from Anglo-Saxon.net, which also appears in Edward the Elder ed. Higham and Hill to determine what was what in England at this time. It depicts the ancient roadways of the Foss Way, Watling Street, Ermine Street and Icknield Way, and also gives some hints as to hills and forests, if not always rivers. I'm also lucky enough to have a 'mapman' for a father who has antique maps of every county in England stretching back to the seventeenth century. These are invaluable for gaining an idea of what everywhere looked like in the recent past. And sometimes, he finds an old map that gives an idea of what previous generations thought the early English period looked like as well. The map at the beginning of this book has been cobbled together using many different sources and has involved a lot of agonising. I hope it helps readers understand 'where' places might have been.

I've chosen to use the term Raiders as opposed to Viking, because the northern people went 'Viking' they weren't Vikings.

The song that Edmund sings is a mash-up of a translation of the Gododdin poem as shown at faculty.arts.ubc.ca and my own imagination.

I am hoping that the Danish words I've included for shields (*skjolde*), advance (*rykke*), attack (*angreb*), weapons (*våben*) and bastard (*skiderik*) are correct. Please someone tell me if they are not!

My understanding of horses comes from teenager number 2, who spends a huge amount of time caring for a big beastie called Hayden. He's a lovely horse, and he 'stars' as Coelwulf's horse Haden, a name that proved to be far more ancient than I realised. I've also tried to incorporate more of the horses' names that teenager 2 is currently caring for during this terrible outbreak. Unfortunately, I had already written the scene with Cuthbert the horse and had to keep it because it made me smile!

The adventures of Coelwulf and his men will continue in book 3 which is available to pre-order now.

MEET THE AUTHOR

I'm an author of fantasy (viking age/dragon themed) and historical fiction (Early English, Vikings and the British Isles as a whole before the Norman Conquest), born in the old Mercian kingdom at some point since AD1066. I write A LOT. You've been warned! Find me at mjporterauthor.com and @coloursofunison on twitter. I have a newsletter, which can be joined via my website.

Books by M J Porter (in series reading order)

<u>Gods and Kings Series (seventh century Britain)</u>
Pagan Warrior
Pagan King
Warrior King

The Eagle of Mercia Chronicles
Son of Mercia
Wolf of Mercia
Warrior of Mercia

<u>The Ninth Century</u>
The Last King
The Last Warrior
The Last Horse
The Last Enemy
The Last Sword

The Last Shield
The Last Seven

The Tenth Century
The Lady of Mercia's Daughter
A Conspiracy of Kings (the sequel to The Lady of Mercia's Daughter)
Kingmaker
The King's Daughter

Chronicles of the English (Tenth Century Britain)
Brunanburh
Of Kings and Half-Kings
The Second English King

The Mercian Brexit (can be read as a prequel to The First Queen of England) (The Tenth Century)

The First Queen of England (The story of Lady Elfrida) (Tenth Century England)
The First Queen of England Part 2
The First Queen of England Part 3

The King's Mother (The continuing story of Lady Elfrida)
The Queen Dowager
Once A Queen

The Earls of Mercia (Tenth-Eleventh Century)
The Earl Of Mercia's Father
The Danish King's Enemy
Swein: The Danish King (side story)
Northman Part 1
Northman Part 2
Cnut: The Conqueror (full length side story)
Wulfstan: An Anglo-Saxon Thegn (side story)
The King's Earl
The Earl of Mercia
The English Earl

The Earl's King
Viking King
The English King

Fantasy

<u>The Dragon of Unison</u>
Hidden Dragon
Dragon Gone
Dragon Alone
Dragon Ally
Dragon Lost
Dragon Bond

<u>As JE Porter</u>
The Innkeeper

20th Century Mysteries

<u>The Erdington Mysteries</u>

The Custard Corpses - a delicious 1940s mystery

The Automobile Assassination

Cragside, a 1930s murder mystery

ACKNOWLEDGEMENT

I am once more indebted to my beta readers, EP, ST, CH and CS for their insightful and helpful comments, and for the ability to spot those really silly mistakes that I manage to miss.

Again, thanks to my children AP and MP for helping me in their respective areas of speciality, namely English Language/IT problems and questions about horses.

Thanks also to MapMan Michael - I think he must have in his possession maps of every English county going back to the very earliest John Speed. They are amazingly helpful when trying to 'plot' the physical historical background. And thank you to EP for help with the map. Oh, the map! What a bloody labour of love that was.

And a shout out as well for all my readers. You make it possible for me to write about the things I love. Thank you, thank you, thank you.

Printed in Great Britain
by Amazon

24627804R00163